"Last night was a mistake,"

Madeline said bluntly. "And it won't happen again. I'm not going to risk the integrity of this case by getting involved with my partner. Any involvement of a more personal nature is out of the question."

Involvement? Cruz repeated in a silent, savage echo. *Personal?* He wanted to reach out and shake her. But one look at her set face was enough to tell him that all his efforts would be in vain.

"All right," he agreed after a time. "If you want to believe that this case is the only thing that sent you running from my bed this morning, I'm not going to argue with you anymore."

"How kind." Her voice dripped ice.

"But—" he pinned her with a look "—when this case is over, what excuse will you use then, Maddy? What other reason will you find for us to stay away from each other?"

Dear Reader,

This month marks the advent of something very special in Intimate Moments. We call it "Intimate Moments Extra," and books bearing this flash will be coming your way on an occasional basis in the future. These are books we think are a bit different from our usual, a bit longer or grittier perhaps. And our lead-off "extra" title is one terrific read. It's called *Into Thin Air*, and it's written by Karen Leabo, making her debut in the line. It's a tough look at a tough subject, but it's also a top-notch romance. Read it and you'll see what I mean.

The rest of the month's books are also terrific. We're bringing you Doreen Owens Malek's newest, *Marriage in Name Only*, as well as Laurey Bright's *A Perfect Marriage*, a very realistic look at how a marriage can go wrong before finally going very, very right. Then there's Kylie Brant's *An Irresistible Man*, a sequel to her first-ever book, *McLain's Law*, as well as Barbara Faith's sensuous and suspenseful *Moonlight Lady*. Finally, welcome Kay David to the line with *Desperate*. Some of you may have seen her earlier titles, written elsewhere as Cay David.

Six wonderful authors and six wonderful books. I hope you enjoy them all.

Yours,

Leslie Wainger
Senior Editor and Editorial Coordinator

Please address questions and book requests to:
Silhouette Reader Service
U.S.: 3010 Walden Ave., P.O. Box 1325, Buffalo, NY 14269
Canadian: P.O. Box 609, Fort Erie, Ont. L2A 5X3

AN IRRESISTIBLE MAN

KYLIE BRANT

Silhouette

INTIMATE ™ MOMENTS®

Published by Silhouette Books

America's Publisher of Contemporary Romance

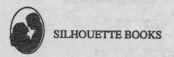

SILHOUETTE BOOKS

ISBN 0-373-07622-3

AN IRRESISTIBLE MAN

KYLIE BRANT

married her high school sweetheart sixteen years ago, and they are now raising their five children in Iowa. She has enjoyed writing since grade school, when she used to pen stories to amuse her younger sister.

Always an avid reader, Kylie became interested in writing again a few years ago. After her twins turned four, she finally managed to steal enough time alone to get started.

When she isn't busy with her job teaching learning-disabled students, she's reading, working at the computer or attending her sons' sporting events.

For Jared, Jason, Jordan, Justin and Alison,
who fill my life with laughter and love.

Chapter 1

The sound of men at play on the cracked asphalt of the basketball court reached Madeline's ears as she got out of the car. Slamming the door, she paused, surveying the scene they made. The court was a jumble of men, most stripped to the waist. A halfdozen others stood on the sidelines shouting words that could not pass for encouragement. None of them glanced her way and she felt a moment of uncustomary hesitation. There was something about the sight of all those masculine bodies gleaming with sweat in the late spring sunlight, the noise of their exertions and the jeers of their audience that almost made her reluctant to intrude on their male domain. She ruthlessly squashed that sentiment, raised her chin and walked toward the court.

She winced at the sound of human flesh colliding and a moment later a body hurtled into the chain links separating her from the court. She jumped back reflexively, but the young man just grasped the fence and jumped to his feet nimbly, sending her an appraising look. Seeing her chance, she called, "Is Cruz Martinez around?"

The man trotted back to the court. "Hey, Cruz," he called in a plaintive croon, "babe's looking for you." The word quickly spread across the court.

"Babe patrol, man."

"Go for it, guy!"

"Stud master!"

Madeline damned her fair complexion, which she could feel heating from the shouts of the men. She drew herself up even straighter and crossed her arms. The body language was unmistakable. It elicited further observations from the court.

"Uh-oh, BWA."

"BWA, son, watch out!"

Cruz Martinez grinned and bounced the basketball to the man next to him. As he jogged slowly toward the fence, he couldn't help agreeing with those final shouted assessments. BWA, Babe With an Attitude, was a chauvinistically accurate description of the woman waiting for him. For an attitude she did exude. From the top of her auburn head, flashing with streaks of gold in the sunlight, down her rigidly held body, to her shapely feet in narrow-toed shoes, this woman was uptight with a capital *U.* Cruz's gaze took a slow, thorough reverse journey up those slender legs, lingering on the gentle curves encased in her fitted skirt, appreciatively inspected the swell of bosom beneath her loose sweater and wandering back up to her pointed chin, full lips, straight nose and high cheekbones. He mentally lamented the fact that her eyes were hidden by large-framed sunglasses. Reaching the fence, he grasped it with both hands and flashed her the lopsided grin that never failed to melt the hearts of the strongest women. "You looking for me, ma'am?"

Madeline hadn't missed his blatant perusal, and that, accompanied by his cocky grin and suggestive drawl made her voice sharp when she fairly snapped, "Cruz Martinez?"

"Yes, ma'am," he agreed solemnly, but his eyes glinted with amusement. "At your service."

Madeline reached into her purse and pulled out her shield, flipping it open and holding it out to him. "Detective Sergeant Madeline Casey."

Cruz reached through the fence with one hand, more for the opportunity to touch her than to study the shield she was holding out. He brought it closer, taking his time looking at it. He made sure their hands met when he handed it back. "Very nice. Shiny. You been polishing that?"

Madeline ignored his bantering, just as she ignored the flicker of awareness she'd felt when he'd pressed the shield back into her palm. From the looks of him, he knew too well the effect he had on women, and his technique was probably well rehearsed. She fixed him with her own studied gaze, noting the well-muscled legs encased in fleece shorts. He was shod in tennis shoes, but unlike most of the other men, he wasn't bare chested. Instead he wore a ragged sweatshirt with the sleeves ripped out. With the sweatband around his forehead keeping his straight dark hair out of his face, and with an earring in one ear, he looked like a modern-day pirate. One would never guess that he was a detective sergeant of the Philadelphia Police Department.

She pulled her eyes from his forearms roped with muscles, secure in the knowledge that he was unable to see the direction of her gaze behind the tinted glasses. "Captain Ritter requested that I ask you to come in to discuss a case you're working on."

His smile never faded, but she thought she noted a flicker of wariness in his dark eyes. "And what case might that be?"

"I'm not at liberty to say." Her voice sounded prim, even to her own ears.

"You're not at liberty to say," he echoed soberly.

Though there was no hint of it on his handsome, bronzed face, she was certain he was laughing at her. He cocked his head. "You must have been busy if you've been tracking me down. On my days off I don't follow a planned schedule."

Madeline shrugged carelessly, although it had taken her better than three hours to trace him here. It had been her own decision to find Martinez herself. She'd wanted to pick their first meeting, to arrange to see the man, instead of the detective. It gave her some small advantage, and she'd orchestrated it with her usual meticulous precision. "When shall I tell Captain Ritter to expect you?"

Cruz took his time answering, enjoying watching her. She looked completely composed, every inch the tough lady cop. His eyes dropped to give her another thorough once-over. Although her face remained devoid of expression, her annoyance showed in the sudden clenching of her slender fingers around the strap of her purse. The corners of his mouth quirked. Detective Sergeant Madeline Casey wasn't as emotionless as she would have him believe.

"Yeah, sure," he finally replied, looking up at her again. "I'll go home and change first. Tell him I'll be there in about an hour and a half."

Madeline nodded and turned away, walking swiftly back to her car. She was no longer certain that she had gained an advantage in that encounter.

* * *

It was closer to two hours before Cruz showed up at the Southwest District headquarters, where he was stationed. He was ushered immediately into Captain Ritter's office. He hesitated in the doorway in surprise. Already seated across the desk from the captain was Madeline Casey. Cruz crossed the threshold and shut the door behind him.

Striding to the desk, he exchanged a handshake with the other man. "Captain." Captain Don Ritter had a long, narrow face with sagging jowls and deep-set eyes. He'd always reminded Cruz of a gloomy basset hound, but there was nothing wrong with the man's mind. He was capable of doing several things at once, all of them thoroughly.

"Detective Martinez." Captain Ritter motioned for him to take a seat next to Madeline. "Sorry to summon you in like this on your day off."

"No problem."

"I believe you met Detective Casey earlier."

Cruz's attention was once again diverted to the woman in the room, and his teeth flashed. "Detective Sergeant Madeline Casey," he said solemnly. "How nice to see you. Again."

"Detective." She nodded shortly. His dark hair was combed back and he'd replaced his earlier clothes with a pair of battered jeans, white shirt and cowboy boots. The jeans were obviously a favorite, well-worn and supple. The shirt was by no means new, but the stark contrast between it and his dark good looks was hard to ignore. The boots were the only incongruous aspect in the picture he made. In contrast to the worn clothes, they gleamed with polish. He looked only slightly more formally dressed than he had this morning, and no less dangerous.

Cruz slouched into the chair next to Madeline, keeping her in his sight. Her hair lacked the highlights it had glinted with in the sunlight, the fluorescent lights overhead turning it a pure dark red. She had it pulled back and wrapped in some sort of knot at her nape—a twist, he thought his sisters called it. He wondered how long it was and whether he'd ever see it hanging loose. The moment she turned her head to look at him, he caught his breath. Her eyes, which had been hidden by her sunglasses earlier, were a pure grass green, and tilted at the edges, like a cat's. She was one hell of a good-looking woman, although not pretty in the insipid tradition preferred by fashion these days. Her mouth was a little too wide, the lips a bit too full to be conventional. She reminded him vaguely of that red-haired movie actress who was all the rage now.

"Detective Casey will be joining us here at the Southwest District," the captain told Cruz. "She's being transferred in."

Silently wondering how that information was supposed to affect him, Cruz quizzed, "What district are you transferring from?"

"The Northeast," she said. She stared at him steadily. "Know anybody there?"

He thought for a moment, then shook his head. "I don't think so."

The room was silent for a moment, then Captain Ritter cleared his throat. "Well, I don't want to tie you up the rest of the day, Detective Martinez, so I'll get right to the point. I wanted to talk to you about that string of drive-by shootings you've been working on."

Cruz nodded. "I think some were the work of rival gangs establishing turf, and others were probably retaliatory shootings. Of course, I don't have much yet. The cases just recently got dropped in my lap."

"I had a meeting with the police commissioner yesterday," Ritter informed them. "The department has reason to believe that there's a large-scale supplier who's putting automatic assault weapons in the hands of these kids. There have been several other cases recently in which similar guns have been involved. Homicides, robberies, that attempted bank holdup at the First National?" His tone questioned whether Cruz had heard of it. The younger man inclined his head, indicating he had. "We've seen more assault weapons used in crimes in the last few months than in the entire previous year."

Cruz nodded. Drive-by shootings were becoming alarmingly commonplace, but it had been the selection of guns that made these even more dangerous. AK-47s had been the weapon of choice in all the crimes the captain had mentioned, and that was an ominous similarity. Cruz had never much believed in coincidence, and he had to agree with Ritter. Someone was selling these guns on the street, at prices too low for the gangs to resist.

"What I want, Detective," Captain Ritter continued, resting his elbows on his desk and leaning forward, "is for you to drop everything else and concentrate your investigation on the supplier of these weapons. I want him found and stopped as soon as possible. If you're right about these drive-by shootings being gang related, that means the weapons are already in the hands of kids. I hate to think of how widespread the distribution already is. I want you to give this your full attention. I've already had your other cases reassigned."

Cruz's face reflected his surprise at the captain's last statement. This investigation had to be important to warrant clearing his caseload. It was customary for a detective to work on several cases at the same time, and only rarely had he been ordered to drop everything to concentrate on one matter, as the captain was requesting. But he hated being relieved of cases after he'd already become involved in them. "It sounds like the drive-bys might be related in some way to the distributor," he said slowly. "I'd be glad to continue that investigation while working on the supply angle."

Ritter shook his head. "That won't be necessary. I want all your time available to wrap up this investigation as soon as possible." He hesitated, and then continued. "I was telling Detective Casey earlier that you're one of the best detectives in the district." He paused, but Cruz didn't respond to the compliment. "That's why I'm assigning you as her partner, for the duration of this case."

Like hell, Cruz wanted to say, but swallowed the words. Diplomacy was a gift and, with the captain, a necessity. He remained bonelessly molded to his chair, and when he spoke his tone was mild. "I usually work alone," he observed.

"I'm aware of that."

"I prefer it that way." Cruz felt compelled to continue. He turned his head to include Madeline. "No offense to my would-be partner."

"Will-be partner," Ritter corrected him. "That's the way it's going to be, Detective, at least on this case. You two can start tomorrow."

His tone brooked no argument, and Cruz subsided. With one last long look at Madeline, he rose and left the room.

She started to follow him, but Ritter stopped her. "Shut the door, Sergeant. I have something else I want to discuss with you."

Madeline obeyed, and returned to her seat. The look on the captain's face would have been a glower had it appeared on another's countenance. It only made his features appear more hangdog. However, there was nothing comical in the suppressed steel in his voice. "I know you didn't choose this assignment, Detective Casey, but I feel compelled to share with you my distaste for it." He gave her another fierce look, daring her to respond, but she remained silent. "I met with your captain at Internal Affairs yesterday, and I have to tell you, this whole mess bothers me. A lot. I don't like Internal Affairs doing undercover work in my district, conducting investigations on my men. I especially don't like it when one of my best detectives is under suspicion.''

''I understand, sir.''

His brows met over his nose at her even response. He rose to pace around the desk. ''Martinez is a great detective. Uncanny instincts. He's got the best record for closed cases in the district. He's also on the fast track for lieutenant. One breath of scandal could freeze his career for good.''

''I assure you, Captain, one thing Internal Affairs trains us in is discretion.''

The man snorted. ''You'll have to excuse me if I don't buy that. I've been around longer than you have, Detective, and I've seen a lot more. I don't believe for one second that Cruz Martinez is involved in the supply of illegal weapons, or that you'll find one shred of evidence to prove otherwise. But I am warning you, Casey—'' he pointed a finger at her ''—not to botch this case. Because if even a hint gets out that Martinez is under suspicion, I'll hold you personally responsible. Do I make myself clear?''

She returned his stare calmly. ''Perfectly.''

He frowned for a few more moments, but when she said nothing else, he waved her away. ''You can go. I understand your captain at Internal Affairs wants to see you this afternoon.''

With his warning still ringing in her ears, Madeline rose and left the room.

As unpleasant as the final scene with Ritter had been, Madeline would rather have relived it than met with Captain Brewer. Although the meeting was set for three o'clock sharp, she cooled her heels outside his office for almost half an hour before he was ready for her. Chronic tardiness was only one of Brewer's less endearing traits. Even worse was his tendency to brief her on a case by presenting her with the file, then proceeding to lecture her on its contents. She'd never been able to figure out whether he did it to all his officers, or if he did it specifically to annoy her. She suspected the latter.

Once she'd been ushered into his office he had her report on every detail of her meeting with Martinez and Ritter that day. Twice.

''So you found him playing basketball, eh?'' Brewer repeated for the third time. ''How'd he look to you?''

Madeline's face was blank. "Look?" Her powers of observation and her memory were legendary in the department, but she had a feeling that this man's appearance would not have escaped even the dullest-witted woman. There was definitely something about Cruz Martinez that left a lasting impression.

"You know," Brewer said impatiently. "How did he seem?"

She was quiet for a moment, wondering what the man was getting at. Finally she said, "He seemed . . . sweaty, sir."

Brewer glanced sharply at her, but Madeline's face was expressionless. "Very funny, Detective Casey. But what's he like? How did you read him?"

Madeline knew it would do no good to point out how difficult it was to form an accurate assessment of somebody after being in his presence twenty minutes. And she would rather have her tongue cut out than share some of the impressions she *had* formed of the man. She took her time before answering. "He seemed confident. Self-assured. I didn't detect any nervousness about being asked to come in and speak to Ritter." She shrugged. "If you're asking me what kind of cop he is, I don't have the answer to that yet. Although his captain seems to hold him in high regard."

Brewer merely grunted at this. "And you're sure he doesn't have any contacts in the Northeast District who he can call to check up on you?"

Her tone was bored. "It appears the information in his file was correct on that score. And he said he didn't."

"Good, then, good."

If Cruz talked to someone in the Northeast District, the investigation would be in jeopardy. He'd find out that Madeline had been placed there at one time, but had transferred out five years ago. And then he would wonder what she'd been doing in the time since.

"You say you've never met him before today?"

Madeline gritted her teeth. The man could get a job as a human echo. He seemed compelled to repeat everything she said. "No, sir, I haven't.

"Neither have I," mused the captain, "but I've certainly heard of him." He eyed her shrewdly. "Surely you've heard of him, Casey."

Madeline shook her head.

"Supposed to be a great detective," the man informed her. "One of the best. His captain's not the only one who thinks so. But I would have figured that you would have at least heard the rumors about him."

Her lips thinned. "I'm not much for listening to rumors, Captain." Actually, that was a huge understatement. Having been the subject of ugly speculation herself, she detested anything that resembled gossip. But she knew that wouldn't stop Brewer from repeating his, and he did so, with obvious relish.

"He's earned himself some interesting nicknames. Latin Lover. Pretty Boy." The captain smirked. "I understand he's quite a babe hound. His reputed success with women is famous throughout the department."

Madeline schooled her features into an impassive mask. "What does that have to do with this case?"

"Nothing," the man said with deceptive mildness. "Just thought you'd be interested. It wasn't included in that file you read on him, was it?"

Although her spine remained straight, her gaze unswerving, Madeline could feel her control slip a notch or two. The man was really incredibly irritating. "No, sir."

"I assume you've already memorized the file's contents?"

She nodded shortly, bored with his little games.

Brewer picked up a flat piece of granite that he used as a paperweight from his desk top. Leaning back in his chair, he began tossing it from hand to hand. "And?"

Feeling somewhat like a trained circus seal, she quickly recited what she'd learned. "A couple of weeks ago an informant told one of our men that a cop was involved in these arms sales. A cop who was also involved in one of the investigations having to do with their use. By finding out what was being investigated, and who was assigned, you came up with a list of five detectives, any one of whom might be the cop the snitch was talking about. Each of the five is being paired with an undercover detective from Internal Affairs. I'm to find out how Martinez lives, if he seems to have an extra source of income and who his associates are." She stopped here, her face showing none of the distaste she felt for the case. Hers was an inherently private nature, and everything in her shrank from the obvious prying that would have to be done here, especially to another cop. She had a question of her own to ask. "How reliable is the snitch?"

"He's proven reliable in the past, but we won't be using him again. Three days after he gave us that information he was found in a Dumpster, full of bullet holes."

"Then how do you know he wasn't wrong, or feeding you a line?"

This time it was the captain's turn to shrug. "We don't. But this could be potentially damaging enough to the department that we have to check it out. The brass will be breathing down my neck if we don't find something soon."

"If Martinez is as great a detective as we hear," she observed, "he would surely be smart enough to hide any money he had gotten illegally."

Brewer looked impatient. "Maybe, maybe not. You just do your job. If you uncover something in the course of the case that points to Martinez's involvement, turn it over to us and we'll have him removed from the assignment, pending a thorough investigation. You of all people should know how it works, Casey."

Her lips tightened at the gibe. Yes, she knew how it worked. He could have been referring to her five years' experience working for Internal Affairs, but she doubted it. The captain had a knack for returning to unpleasant memories, like touching a bruise over and over. She would have liked to make a scathing retort, but she swallowed it. Her voice was even when she asked, "Is there any other information you have on Martinez that I should know about?"

The granite piece made a slap against the man's palm as he tossed it back and forth. "Not much. I have heard that he grew up in the Hispanic section, over in the East Division. That's part of his local-boy-makes-good mystique."

"He wouldn't be the first person to grow up motivated to succeed."

The captain stopped his game of catch and stared hard at her. "He wouldn't be the first to grow up to want more, either. A lot more. I'm not making judgments about whether he's a dirty cop. That's your job. You find out and report to me. If he's clean, fine. If not, we'll nail him. At the same time you'll find the dirt bag arming every two-bit punk in the city. Just watch yourself, Casey. From what I've heard, Martinez is one smooth operator, on and off the streets." The rock flew in an arc again, and he caught it with his other hand.

She ignored his smirk, as well as his suggestive words. Not trusting herself to say anything more, she rose and turned toward the door.

"Oh, and Casey, I'll expect complete written reports from you weekly."

She gritted her teeth. Paperwork was the bane of any detective's job, and she hated it with passionate intensity. She left the room, wishing darkly that the piece of granite would slip and knock Brewer on the head.

Hard.

Cruz stretched his long legs out in the recliner, sipping the beer Michele Easton McLain had just handed him. Michele sat on the couch next to her husband, Connor.

"To what do we owe the honor?" inquired Connor lazily, referring to his best friend's unexpected appearance.

"Connor, don't be rude," Michele admonished him. "Cruz is welcome here anytime."

"That's right, pal," Cruz echoed. "Anytime." He winked at him. "And don't you forget it."

"Well, not *anytime,*" Connor corrected him, a glint of amusement in his pale green eyes. "Michele still insists on getting me to bed pretty early, you know." He heaved a mock sigh, ignoring his wife's indignant look. "Marriage! What can I say, I have to do what I can to keep her happy...." His words were muffled by the pillow his wife swatted him with.

Cruz laughed along with them. "Yeah, I can see what a strain it's putting on you. I was just telling Michele how weak you were looking. If you need any help in that area, just give me a call. I'm always ready to help out, buddy."

"Forget it," Connor shot back. "I'm sure your services are in great demand elsewhere."

"Well, since you're out of circulation, *amigo,* there are lots of devastated women out there, and they are so lonely. I do what I can."

From long practice Michele ignored their bantering. "Are you still dating Jill, Cruz?" she inquired. "You haven't brought anyone around since we all got together to celebrate your promotion."

"I still see her occasionally," he answered. "But I've been pretty busy lately."

"The department has been keeping his nose to the grindstone," Connor informed his wife. Addressing Cruz, he added, "I heard you picked up those cases on the drive-by shootings."

His friend grimaced. "They *were* my cases. Not anymore, as of today."

"Why, what happened?"

"I was summoned to the captain's office today." His brows lowered again just thinking about that interview. "He more or less ordered me to drop the case and concentrate on the supplier of the guns. He's reassigned my caseload, so I guess I don't have any choice. But what I want to know is, why me?"

"Must be your 'atta boy' file," Connor said, only half joking. Cruz's personnel folder was impressively filled with commendations, and Connor knew firsthand what a good cop the man was. They'd been rookies together, then partners. Their friendship had grown until they were as close as brothers. Later they had chosen different paths in the department, Cruz gravitating toward undercover work and Connor working his way up the officer ranks. But when Cruz had returned to plainclothes duty a couple of years ago, they had ended up in the same district. Whenever Connor was given a particularly sticky case to supervise, he always requested that Cruz be part of the investigation. He was among the few men on earth whom Connor trusted implicitly.

Cruz interrupted his thoughts, responding to his remark. "Yeah, he started on that bull, talked about my record, but I still wonder..." He shook his head. "Heck, you know me, I guess I just can't stand to have investigations yanked when I'm just getting into them. Plus," he added morosely, "he assigned me a partner."

Connor smiled in commiseration. "Bad luck, friend. I know you like to work solo." He picked up Michele's hand, threading their fingers together. Turning to her, he said in an aside, "I'm sure his new partner won't be as handsome as his first one."

Cruz slouched deeper into his chair. "Has your ugly mug beat hands down," he contradicted mildly. "And he's a she."

"Your new partner is a woman?" Michele asked interestedly.

"Ritter obviously doesn't know as much about you as he claims to," Connor gibed, "or he would have heard that no woman is safe from you."

"Go to hell," Cruz invited him good-naturedly. "Can I help it if I'm friendly?" His two friends laughed. The phone rang then, and Michele went to the kitchen to answer it.

"Who is she?" Connor asked. "Maybe I know her."

"I doubt it. Beautiful redheads were never your type. Her name is Madeline Casey."

"Casey?" Connor thought a moment, then shook his head. "Haven't heard of her. How experienced a detective is she?"

Cruz shrugged. "That's just it, I don't know. She's transferring in, and I'm stuck with her, unless Ritter changes his mind."

"Ritter?" Connor echoed. "Change his mind?" He shook his head. "Give up that hope. Sounds like you and Casey are joined at the hip, at least for the time being."

Michele rejoined them and said to Connor, "That was your mother. She wants us to come to dinner on Sunday. Your sister is going to be home."

"Sherry?" His interest was captured. "We haven't seen her since our wedding."

As his friends' conversation turned for a moment to family, Cruz tuned out. Joined at the hip. That wouldn't have been his choice of words, though it brought something anatomically close to mind. Madeline Casey was too head-turning to escape attention. Amid the male atmosphere of the basketball game, her cool, composed beauty had stood out in vivid contrast. She had presented a dispassionate pose throughout the day, but when he'd looked closer he'd been able to see hints of the woman beneath. Though her face had remained impassive throughout the meeting with Ritter, there had been a slight twist to her mouth when the man had mentioned Cruz's record with the department. Of course, he acknowledged silently, he wouldn't have noticed that small hint of emotion if his attention hadn't strayed, again and again, to those shapely lips.

He stared unseeingly at the empty beer can in his hand. He wouldn't be happy about having any partner assigned to him, but the fact that this one was a woman didn't have anything to do with his bias. He didn't doubt his ability to concentrate on the case at hand, regardless of whom he worked with. He'd been accused in the past of having a one-track mind, and that was probably true, when it came to his work. Every case was like a jigsaw puzzle with just a jumble of pieces at the beginning, each clue, each piece of information to be joined to reconstruct the whole picture. His analytical mind enjoyed the challenge, his determination was the drive that solved most of his investigations. He'd also been at it long enough that he trusted his own instincts, and didn't relish having to explain them to a partner. He hadn't worked with one for any length of time since Connor.

His mouth kicked up at one corner. But if he was going to be saddled with one, he thought wickedly, it sure didn't hurt that she was so easy on the eyes.

His gaze moved to the couple on the couch across from him. When their heads moved closer together, Cruz felt an uncustomary stab of envy. He was damn happy for Connor's good fortune in meeting Michele. It was a miracle that the other man had finally found a woman he trusted. And the way they'd met had seemed predestined. Michele worked as a child psychologist, but it was not in her professional capacity that she had come to district headquarters to speak to Connor a year ago. They'd been investigating a rash of kidnappings in the area and Michele had information to give them, information revealed to her through her clairvoyant senses. Connor had fought believing her, and in her psychic powers. But in the end it was Michele who had helped solve the case and save Connor's life.

He didn't begrudge his friend his wife, and Connor damn sure deserved some happiness. Cruz didn't suffer from loneliness often. But occasionally with Connor and Michele, or watching his own parents who'd been married almost forty years, he experienced an indefinable yearning for...something. Something more.

He shook off the unfamiliar melancholy impatiently. His life was perfect just the way it was. He knew a lot of people, and his leisure time was as social as he wanted it. He'd never met a woman yet who couldn't be forgotten easily when he became involved in a case. Most of the women of his acquaintance didn't seem to mind waiting around until he had time for them again. And those who did mind weren't missed.

Connor spoke then, interrupting his thoughts. "C'mon, Cruz, settle our argument. Michele still thinks of those little family discussions we get into at my parents as fights. Explain to her the dynamics of sibling conversation."

"You'll never understand," Cruz told Michele patiently, "being an only child yourself. But there's no such thing as arguing among brothers and sisters. It's all the art of negotiation and compromise, and merely improves our communication abilities." His eyes twinkled. "Surely you've read that in those child psychology texts of yours."

"What I have read," Michele replied dryly, "tells me that you two are full of it. You both just enjoy getting things stirred up and then sitting back to watch the fireworks."

The men laughed. "I think she's got your number," Cruz told Connor, "although she's completely wrong about me."

"Yeah, right," Connor retorted good-naturedly. "Can I get you another beer?"

Cruz shook his head and rose. "I think I'll be heading home. I've got a new partner to break in tomorrow, remember?" He said goodbye to Michele and then Connor walked out to the porch with him.

"Don't get too chummy with Madeline Casey," Connor advised him. "Sounds like this could turn into a high-profile case. You don't need any distractions."

"Your concern is touching, but I can take care of myself," Cruz responded. "Especially," he added in a drawl, "where women are concerned."

"Do not," stressed Connor, staring hard at him, "start thinking of her as a woman. That would be your first mistake."

"Sorry, buddy." Cruz slapped him on the shoulder and headed for the car. "But it would be impossible to think of her as anything else."

Chapter 2

Madeline hurriedly scraped her long wet tresses back from her face with a wide-tooth comb. She winced as she hit a snarl, and rapidly braided the mass, pinning it up off her neck. She walked quickly out of the bathroom and into the kitchen, checking the clock to see if she had time for coffee. She grimaced when she saw the hour. A phone call from her father had upset her daily routine, and now she had just barely enough time to get to work. She didn't like to hurry, not in anything. And she detested being late. She picked up the blazer that matched her navy slacks and slipped it on over her white blouse. Scooping up her purse, she found her keys and headed out the door.

As she drove toward the Southwest District headquarters she reflected upon that phone call. Her father had called to summon her—there was no other word for it, she thought darkly—to his home for dinner. She looked forward to their monthly dinners with the same anticipation she reserved for root canals, and had valiantly attempted to come up with a legitimate excuse to cry off, to no avail. People didn't say no to city councilman Geoffrey Casey often. He didn't allow it.

After thirty years of practice, the man could make her feel guilty with a single word, or with one meaning-filled moment of silence. Even knowing she was being manipulated didn't make it possible for her to turn those feelings off. It was easier to give in to the inevitable and try to prepare herself for the ordeal of spending an evening with him and get it over with.

Or that's what she'd told herself. But after hanging up the phone she'd mentally berated herself for failing to stand up to him. Not for the first time she wished that she, like her older brother, had moved far away from Philadelphia. Not that Kevin had moved, exactly; fled would be a better word. If being Geoffrey Casey's daughter was unpleasant, being his son was intolerable.

Madeline pushed aside thoughts of her family as she parked the car and strode toward the building that housed the Southwest District headquarters. She had left Martinez a message yesterday that she would meet him there. After inquiring about his whereabouts at the front desk, she made her way through the maze of desks and cabinets, and found him propped against the edge of his desk, talking to several other officers. One of the men noticed her first, and stopped in midsentence.

"Well, hello," the officer greeted her in a drawl, his gaze sweeping her figure appreciatively. "Can I help you?"

Some women might enjoy having four men watch them approach with avid interest. Madeline wasn't one of them. She ignored the look, and the suggestion in the man's voice. "No," she responded flatly. She turned to look at Cruz. "Are you ready to go to work?"

"Sure," he answered, a slight smile on his face. He noticed the other men's curiosity and made introductions. "Madeline, meet Officers Brent, Nolan and Detective Ryan." He indicated each man in turn. "Guys, this is Detective Sergeant Madeline Casey. She's new to the district." He allowed that to sink in before adding, "She's also my new partner."

"Yeah, right, partner in what, Martinez?" jeered Brent, the man who had greeted her. "This will be department business, won't it, kids?"

Before Cruz could frame a reply Madeline did it for him. "I'm sure the department would greatly appreciate it if you men would attend to your jobs and let us do ours." Her voice was even, but her no-nonsense manner had the three men backing off slowly.

"Yeah, sure," muttered Nolan. He lifted a hand. "Talk to you later, Cruz." He and Ryan sauntered off, and Brent trailed behind them.

Cruz cocked an eyebrow, his gaze slipping from her to the departing men, then back to Madeline. "That's quite a gift. Did you have to take a special course to learn how to impress people like that?''

Madeline pulled up an extra chair to sit it next to his desk. "I wasn't trying to impress them," she finally answered. "I was trying to get rid of them."

As she seated herself, Cruz walked around to his own chair. "Well, you certainly managed that," he murmured. He wondered if she was aware that giving men the cold shoulder like that would pique their interest, not dampen it. From the looks of the woman, she didn't much care. The corner of his mouth lifted. This was getting more and more interesting. He sat down and picked up two file folders and handed them to her. "I copied everything I had so far on the drive-by shootings. Then I found what I could on the rash of other crimes lately involving AK-47s. Take some time and go through these."

Madeline frowned slightly as she took the files from him. "I thought the drive-by shootings were being reassigned to someone else since we're working on the supply angle."

"They are. But we're going to have to start somewhere. Our best chance of finding the supplier is through one of his customers."

That made sense, so Madeline subsided and began reading through the first file. Cruz left for a short time and came back with two steaming cups of coffee and placed one of them in front of her. She reached out to take it, not looking up from her reading.

The files were thick and it took her more than an hour to go through them. When she finally finished, she rubbed the back of her neck, which ached from being bent over in her reading. She looked at Cruz, who was leaning back in his chair. His booted feet were crossed atop the desk, alarmingly close to his still half-full cup of coffee, and he was flipping through the pages of a report.

He glanced up, catching her gaze. "So, what do you think?" he asked.

"I think the sooner we nail the guy selling these guns, the sooner the streets will become a little bit safer," she responded. At least for a while. Until the next crook came along, looking to get rich and not being too concerned about how he did it. She couldn't help but be sickened by the reports of the bodies, mostly teens and young men, who had been shot by persons unknown. Persons wielding some of the most deadly weaponry available on this continent.

She looked at the man next to her. He was frowning slightly at the report in his hand. Was it possible that he was mixed up in these arms deals? And if he was, how would he handle having a totally unwanted partner assigned to him? Would he try to lead the investigation astray, destroy evidence or file false reports? Any of these means would be a way to deflect guilt from himself, but all would be harder to do with a partner working with him. Madeline hated the thought of having to examine every word, every action of his, looking for possible signs of incrimination. But that was exactly what she would have to do if she was to complete the job Brewer had assigned her.

She wondered, for what seemed like the hundredth time, why she had been picked for this case. She detested duplicity in any form. After the fiasco that had brought scrutiny to her own private life, she'd vowed to remain painfully honest in her dealings with others. Madeline wished she could believe that it was only her capabilities as a police detective that had affected Brewer's decision in pairing her with Martinez. But she knew the captain too well not to doubt his motives. If he'd thought that her role in the investigation would make her uncomfortable, that alone would have accounted for his decision.

She sighed silently. She should have known. Life had been going along a little too smoothly lately. Others might disagree, arguing that "boring" was a more accurate description of her life. But Madeline had had enough excitement while she'd known Dennis Belding to last her a lifetime. She would take uneventful any day.

She surveyed the file in front of her with a slight frown. She had a feeling that her partnership with Cruz Martinez was not, by any stretch of the imagination, going to be uneventful.

"So, you've already questioned the victim's family in each of the drive-bys," Madeline said, nodding at the files. "And you found that all the victims belonged to some kind of gang."

Cruz nodded. "Each of them was wearing gang colors when they were shot. But when the families gave me the names of their sons' friends to talk to, I hit a brick wall. All of those friends are fellow gang members, and they don't like talking to cops. I haven't gotten anywhere interviewing them."

"Counting the one earlier this week, that's seven incidents involving three different gangs," she noted. "Sounds like we should be expecting another shooting any day."

He eased lower in his chair and smiled a little. The lady was sharp, he'd give her that. Of course, it was just a guess, but he'd already arrived at a similar conclusion. The gangs had kept busy trading bullets with each other, but this was the first time that a member of the Lords had been shot. It didn't require a major leap of logic to guess that it was only a matter of time before the Lords retaliated.

Cruz tossed a picture across the top of the file folder in front of her. "Have you seen one of these before?"

"It's an AK-47 automatic assault weapon," she murmured, picking up the picture and examining it cursorily.

"Right. And until recently, these babies would have been hard to get." He leaned back in his chair, crossing his arms behind his head. "So, Detective Casey, let me pick your brain. What angle do you think we should pursue first?"

Madeline ignored the way the casual pose accentuated his well-defined torso. She answered his question surely. "I'd like to talk to the perp they collared trying to hold up the bank with one of these. Which district is he being held in?"

"The South," Cruz answered, "but we're not likely to get anything out of him. I heard he isn't talking."

"That's a little unusual. He was caught in the act, right?" At his nod, she continued, "They've got witnesses, the weapon and fingerprints. By now he should be copping a plea."

Cruz shrugged. "Maybe he will. But the one thing he isn't doing is telling anyone where he got the gun."

"I'd still like to talk to him," she answered. At Cruz's silence, she raised an eyebrow. "Well, wouldn't you?"

He was silent so long that she almost repeated her question. Finally he responded. "Okay. I'll set it up."

He turned to the phone on his desk and began dialing. Madeline studied him silently as he spoke into the receiver. She wondered at his unwillingness to follow through on her suggestion. Was he afraid the perp might identify him as being involved in the supply? Or was it simpler than that? Perhaps he just didn't believe it would lead anywhere.

When he hung up the phone and looked at her, his face was expressionless. "It's all set. Let's go." Madeline followed him out of the squad room, wondering if she'd imagined his reluctance.

She slid into the front seat of the unmarked car, and Cruz got behind the wheel. He turned on the ignition and said, "We'll trade off driving, if that's all right with you. Tomorrow will be your turn."

His offer took her by surprise, but since she really preferred to do her own driving, she readily agreed. "All right."

He expertly turned the car into the traffic. "How long have you been with the department?"

So he was a talker. That shouldn't have surprised her. He had a free and easy manner guaranteed to put the most anxious person at ease. However, Madeline would have preferred to skip the small talk. She was normally very reserved; even as a child she had had difficulty making friends. But the best way to find out things about Cruz Martinez, things that would aid in the investigation she was assigned to do on him, was to divulge some information about herself. Then he would have to reciprocate.

"Over ten years."

That would make her about thirty, Cruz estimated. Four years younger than himself.

"How about you, Detective?" she asked.

He took his eyes off the traffic long enough to shoot her a half smile. "'Detective' sounds kind of formal. Won't we get each other mixed up? Call me Cruz." When she didn't respond, he added coaxingly, "And I'll call you Madeline. Or do you prefer Maddy?"

Her head turned slowly. The look she aimed at him was lethal, as was her tone. "Don't . . . you . . . dare," she said in a measured voice.

"Madeline it is, then," he answered. He made sure his amusement didn't show on his face. With her hair pulled back, and dressed in those neatly tailored clothes, she did look like a Madeline. But in something softer, more alluring, with her hair loosened to spill down her neck, then he thought she would resemble a Maddy. But now wasn't the time for such imaginings, and he pushed the mental picture away.

"I've been on the force fourteen years," he answered her belatedly. "My grandfather was a cop. So were two of my uncles. I grew up thinking it was the greatest thing in the world to be." He shrugged. "Once on the force, I got hooked by the glamour of the job." His humor drew a smile from her. Sometimes tedious, other times gritty and horrifying, police work bore little resemblance to the way it was often depicted by Hollywood.

"How about you?" he inquired.

"What?"

"Why did you become a cop?"

Madeline thought for a few moments, wondering if she could answer the question truthfully, without sounding like an idealistic fool. Only her father had ever asked her that question before, and he hadn't been interested in a truthful answer. He'd always regarded her choice of career as an attempt to spite him. No matter how often she'd tried to explain it to him, he'd never really heard her, so after a while she'd stopped trying. "I wanted to make a difference," she responded finally, looking out the window at her side.

"And have you?"

She turned back to stare at him.

"Made a difference?" he clarified.

In the dark of night, after a particularly brutal case, that was a question that always hammered away inside her mind with an insidious pounding. Had she? "I don't know," she answered. "Sometimes I wonder." Her hand went to the car radio. "Mind if I change the station?"

He quirked a brow. "You're not a fan of country western music?"

"It all sounds the same. Lo-o-ove hurts," she mimicked with a twang.

That surprised a gust of laughter from him. "Well, doesn't it?"

"It's not supposed to," she muttered, flipping channels until she finally settled on one playing soft rock.

She probably didn't realize how much she'd just revealed with that last comment, Cruz mused silently. And she most certainly hadn't meant her tone to sound so wistful just then. He was becoming intrigued by her. There was a great deal more to her than met the eye, certainly more than the aura she attempted to exude, that of the cool, capable detective. Not that that image was false, but he was sure she was a damned sight more. Still, he recognized her retreat for what it was, so he obliged her by remaining silent for a time.

After several minutes Madeline glanced at him warily. He seemed to have dropped the conversational ball and was now whistling tunelessly to the music on the radio. He must have found trying to converse with her tough going, and she sighed inwardly. As much as she hated to, she needed to get on a friendly footing with the man. He seemed so open; it might prove easy to find out much of the preliminary information about his life directly from him. And the things he didn't want to share . . . well, it was her job to find those things out on her own.

Her gaze dropped to the steering wheel where his hands rested, one doing most of the driving and the fingers of the other tapping to the beat coming from the radio. His plain, light blue shirt accented his bronzed good looks, although she doubted a color existed that wouldn't suit him. The long sleeves were rolled up partway to reveal strong wrists, the forearms above them lightly dusted with black hair. She noticed for the first time the thick gold bracelet he wore on his right wrist. It was an intricately woven chain, about three-quarters of an inch wide. Strangely enough, it didn't detract from his masculine looks, nor did the gold cross he was wearing in his ear. She wondered if the bracelet could be considered evidence that he was living above his means. Then, just as quickly, she wondered if it was a gift from a lover, and was strangely discomfited by the thought.

Her eyes slid downward. Today he was wearing a different pair of cowboy boots, and she made a mental note to find out what such a pair cost. As much as she disliked delving into his personal life, Brewer would be expecting at least a preliminary report on Martinez by next week, and she'd better have something for the captain by that time.

He was dressed only slightly better than he had been yesterday; at least the jeans he was wearing today looked fairly new. She had trouble tearing her gaze away from his hard thighs faithfully outlined by the denim.

"Like them?"

Madeline's eyes bounced to Cruz's at the question. "Pardon me?"

"The boots." He pointed. "You were staring. I asked if you liked the boots."

Her breathing became normal again. Of course, the boots. "They look expensive," she said casually.

He shrugged and gave her a wink. "My one vice."

She raised an eyebrow, but said nothing. She had no doubt that the man beside her could give lessons on vice. And with that face and physique, he probably had plenty of eager pupils.

At the South District headquarters they were kept waiting almost an hour before they were motioned to by an officer, who introduced himself as Ronald Lee. They followed him to a small interrogation room. Waiting there was a man wearing the county jail uniform. Seated next to him at a table was a man in a double-breasted suit.

"This is Detective Casey and Detective Martinez." Officer Lee indicated each as he spoke. Motioning to the man in prison garb, he continued, "Randy Stover and his lawyer, Sam Powell, from the Public Defender's Office." Madeline and Cruz sat across from the men and the officer remained standing.

Madeline surveyed the alleged criminal before her. Narrow faced, with a receding hairline and thin body, his eyes were shifting between her and Cruz. "I got nuthin' else to say to no cops," he said sullenly.

"Neither of you detectives made the arrest." Powell spoke up. "What do you want with my client?"

"We have permission to interview him about a case we're working on." Cruz took a picture out of his shirt pocket and tossed it on the table in front of Stover. "I'm told they've got an AK-47 just like that one with your fingerprints all over it."

The man didn't answer. Cruz went on easily. "It's not like you're admitting to anything we don't already know. The gun's in the evidence room right now."

"Yeah, so what?"

"So," Madeline interjected, "we'd like to know where you got it."

Stover snorted derisively, but said nothing.

Cruz asked the officer, "Did he have papers for it?"

The man shook his head. "They didn't find any."

"So if you don't have papers—" Cruz addressed Stover again "—you got it from someone on the street. We want to know who."

The prisoner looked at his lawyer. "They offering me a deal, or what?"

Powell looked at Cruz and Madeline. "Detectives?"

Cruz shook his head. "That would be up to the D.A. But if you cooperated with us, I'd make sure it got on the record, so things could go easier for you at sentencing."

Stover crossed his arms and leaned back in his chair. "If you ain't got nuthin' to deal with, don't waste my time."

"Do you know Victor Ramirez?" Madeline inquired. The man shook his head and she continued. "How about Tyson Greene?" Another shake. She named off each of the victims of the drive-by shootings, and each time the man responded negatively.

Cruz stared at her in surprise. She wasn't consulting any notes, and he couldn't help but be impressed. As far as he knew, she hadn't heard any of those names before she'd read them in the file today. The lady must have one hell of a memory.

"What you have in common with those boys, Mr. Stover," Madeline continued in a hard voice, "is that you were caught using a weapon like this—" she indicated the picture "—and each of them was shot by the same kind of gun. We're interested in that coincidence."

The man's eyes widened. "What! You can't pin them shootings on me, too." His head swiveled to his lawyer's. "They can't, can they?"

"Do you have any evidence to suggest a link between my client and any of these other shootings, Detective?" Powell asked.

Madeline replied smoothly, "Not yet, but we're just getting started. The point we're making is that your client has information we can use to nail the supplier of these weapons. If he doesn't want to cooperate with us, fine. But then we'd have some free time to fill. And we might use that time to check up on his alibis for each of these shootings. That's assuming, of course, that he has alibis."

"Go ahead," Stover invited in an insolent tone. "You guys are just fishing. Think I don't know that?"

"Detectives, I'd like a couple of minutes to confer with my client in private," Powell said finally.

Madeline, Cruz and Officer Lee stepped out of the room. "Do you really think there's a link between Stover and those shootings?" Lee asked them.

Cruz shrugged, looking at Madeline. "Do we?"

"Who knows? None of the shooters have been identified yet. But if Stover thinks we're going to try to hang him for some other crimes as well, he might be more likely to talk."

That didn't turn out to be the case. When they reentered the room Powell brusquely informed them, "My client has no knowledge of the shootings you mentioned. And he isn't going to answer any more of your questions. If you manage to work something out with the D.A., he might have some information of interest to you regarding the person who sold him the gun."

Officer Lee escorted Stover back to his cell, and Madeline and Cruz walked out.

"How much pull do you have with Brad Jacobs, the D.A.?" she asked.

Cruz shook his head as he guessed her reason for asking. "None, and even if I had some, it wouldn't be enough to convince Jacobs to give up a high-profile, sure conviction just to help our investigation."

"Maybe he would," Madeline argued. "After all, if Stover could help us nail the supplier, that would be an even bigger fish for Jacobs to prosecute."

"The operative word here is 'if.' But it's worth a try. I'll talk to Ritter about suggesting it to him."

They were moving through the station house now, and both were intent on their discussion. Madeline didn't even notice a man standing nearby until she heard him call out, "Hey, Romeo." Cruz didn't miss a stride, although she turned her head to look at the man curiously.

"Martinez! I'm talking to you." The man stepped in front of them, halting their progress.

"What do you want?" Cruz's voice was emotionless.

The man Cruz addressed smirked. He was almost as tall as Cruz, and his thin brown hair was slicked back. "You weren't going to leave here without saying hi to your old buddy, were you, Detective?"

Madeline's eyes bounced back and forth between the two men, mystified. Something was going on here; the undercurrents of animosity were evident.

Cruz said sardonically, "Yeah, sure, *buddy*, how are you? Shoot anybody lately?"

The other man's smile slipped a notch. "Nobody who didn't deserve it. But then, I never did shoot anyone who didn't deserve it, did I?"

Cruz struck so quickly that Madeline didn't even see him move. One minute he was standing motionless beside her, the next he had the man by the shirt, pushed up against a nearby wall. "Get out of my face, Baker," he said in a soft but deadly tone, "or I'll rearrange yours."

A long second crawled by. Baker must have sensed the same danger that Madeline could feel emanating from Cruz, because he kept his mouth shut. Slowly Cruz loosened his grip and moved away.

When they were a safe distance from him, Baker called after them loudly, "Better watch that temper of yours, Pretty Boy. It wouldn't look good for you to get hauled in on assault charges so soon after your promotion. People might get the wrong idea. Or should I say, the right idea?"

Madeline started to turn once more to look at the man, but Cruz grasped her elbow, guiding her inexorably through the maze of desks and out the front door. Once outside she pulled free. He walked quickly down the steps toward the car. She followed more slowly, trying to assimilate this new facet of his personality. She knew as well as anyone that a person couldn't be judged by surface charm. Duress always brought out well-hidden, sometimes darker sides of their personalities. But even knowing that, she couldn't help but be stunned by the suddenness of his fury. There was much, much more to this man than his easy manner and glib charm would suggest.

She got into the car and adjusted her seat belt. Cruz threw one arm across the back of the seat and turned his head to back out of the parking place. His eyes met hers.

"Friend of yours?" she asked blandly.

His face was expressionless. "Yeah, we're real close."

"Who is he?"

She didn't think he was going to answer, he was silent so long. Finally he replied, "Detective Gerald Baker."

She knew she'd just witnessed firsthand the reason for his initial reluctance to interrogate Stover. He must have known Baker was stationed here, and wanted to avoid the possibility of encountering him. The preliminary file she'd read on Martinez had included the reason for his animosity toward the man. But he would expect her to wonder about the scene she'd witnessed, and so she asked, "How do you explain Baker's devotion to you? Did you donate a kidney for him or something?"

One side of his mouth quirked. "Or something," Cruz agreed as he navigated the car through the congested downtown traffic. "He shot me."

Her stomach clenched at the terse words, despite her prior knowledge of the incident.

Cruz explained, "I was working undercover at the time. Baker was with the transit police then. I'd busted a white-collar drug ring operating out of a train terminal, but one of the perps took off. I chased him through the building and I saw Detective Wondercop. I identified myself as a police officer, but he ordered me to stop. When I continued the chase, he shot me. The perp," he added wryly, "got away."

"So... he thought you were a crook?" Madeline had no doubt that, undercover, Cruz Martinez could look like a very dangerous customer indeed.

His mouth twisted. "So he claimed. And Internal Affairs cleared him of any wrongdoing. They called it a 'clean shoot.'" He laughed without amusement. "A clean shoot. Imagine hearing that after you've had two surgeries to repair the damage he did."

"They must have believed him." She defended the bureau's decision automatically.

"Oh, I'm sure they did." His tone was mocking. "He was damn convincing. You can be certain they never saw the side of him we just had the privilege of observing. I.A. didn't want to consider the truth of the matter, though—that the reason Baker shot me was because a Hispanic was chasing after a well-dressed Caucasian. I mean, what could look more suspicious, right?"

She was uncomfortable in the face of his charge of prejudice. "Well, I'm sure it seems that way to you, but it is the department's job to remain objective...."

He gave a snort. "Objective? Let me tell you something, Detective Casey. There's nothing objective about having two bullets removed from your leg. Or having one crease the side of your skull. I suppose I should be grateful that Baker is a damn poor shot, as well as a bigot, or I'd be taking a dirt nap right now."

Her stomach, normally not the least bit queasy, turned over at his words. "Is that why you quit undercover work?" she asked after a moment.

"That was a big part of it," he affirmed. Undercover he'd often worked alone, and he'd accepted the risk he took in his work. It had seemed a fair exchange for being able to get some of the garbage off the street. But after the shooting he'd had to face the fact that cops like Baker were at least as dangerous to him as the dirt bags he'd been investigating. He couldn't do his job constantly looking over his shoulder, and what he despised Baker for the most was taking away any real choice Cruz should have had about his career.

They rode silently for a time, engrossed in their own thoughts. Madeline looked up after several minutes and said, "The turn you want is right ahead."

"Naw, it's the next one," Cruz answered matter-of-factly.

"I'm telling you, Martinez, this corner is where you should... have turned," she ended as they passed the corner in question.

"Don' t worry," he said patiently. "I did the driving on the way over, remember? I know which way we came, and this next corner is the one we take."

Madeline threw him an impatient glance but sat back to wait. Cruz took several more turns, and they ended up in a dilapidated neighborhood she didn't recognize. He stopped the car, pulled a map of the city out from under the seat and studied it.

"Very scenic," she drawled. "I guess this means we're skipping lunch."

A grunt was her only answer as he wadded up the map and shoved it beneath the seat again. As he began backtracking,

Madeline said mildly, "One thing you need to learn about me, Martinez." She paused a heartbeat. "I'm never wrong."

He spared her barely a glance. "One of your most endearing qualities, I'm sure."

She allowed herself a tiny smile. He sounded positively ill-humored, and something told her that that was rare for him.

Once back at Cruz's desk, they planned the next step of their strategy. "You're going to talk to Ritter about going to the D.A., right?" she asked.

"First thing in the morning," he promised. "And I'll let Ryan know what went on today. My cases were reassigned to him. He may want to follow a possible link between Stover and the drive-by shootings. In the meantime, since we followed your hunch today, tomorrow we'll follow mine."

Madeline eyed him curiously. "Which is?"

"Ramsey Elliot is due to be released from the hospital soon. Since he was the first of the Lords to be shot, I think we need to concentrate on him, and on the rest of the gang, to see if we can get a feel for which way they're headed."

"They'll retaliate."

Cruz nodded at her statement. "I'd be surprised if they didn't. And I'd love to know if they've already gotten their hands on the weapon of choice, or whether they're currently dealing on one."

"If they haven't gotten it yet, we may be in time to track down the supplier as they deal on one," Madeline said hopefully.

Cruz raised his eyebrows. "Wishful thinking, I'm afraid, Maddy, my girl."

"Do not—"

"Call you Maddy," he finished in unison with her.

She glared at him, but the look of amusement on that handsome bronze face was hard to resist. "Martinez, I have the feeling that you are one hell of a pest."

He leaned forward and lowered his voice. "And I have the feeling that you are one hell of a . . ."

"Yes?" she prompted when he didn't finish.

Distraction. But perhaps it wouldn't be wise for him to admit that to her. Instead he improvised. "Detective." He finished the sentence. "Especially if your sense for police work is as good as your sense of direction."

They made arrangements to meet the next day, and Madeline left. Other than the incident with Baker, she had little to put in her report to Brewer. And of course her boss already knew about the

Internal Affairs investigation that had cleared Baker of any wrongdoing. No doubt the incident was another reason Martinez was under suspicion right now. Aside from the fact that he had been one of the five detectives investigating a crime related to the AK-47s, he also had reason to be carrying a major grudge against the department. To outward appearances, that didn't seem to be the case, of course. He had continued his work, had even started moving up the ranks of officer. But she couldn't shake her uneasiness as she remembered Cruz's abrupt switch of moods when dealing with the other man.

How deep did his animosity toward Baker run? Deep enough to include the department because they'd sided with him? One thing she'd learned about Martinez today—he had a ruthless streak that she never would have suspected. She still wondered how deep that streak ran.

And whether he was ruthless enough to be involved in trading lives for cash.

Chapter 3

Madeline left her car in the long circular driveway in front of her father's house. As she approached the luxurious brick home she didn't even notice the flawlessly manicured lawn and neatly trimmed shrubs. Perfection was something Geoffrey Casey demanded; he would accept nothing less. She let herself in the front door and headed to the study.

As expected, she found him seated behind his walnut desk in the darkly paneled room. She crossed the plush Oriental carpet, and he rose, looking pointedly at his watch. From long experience Madeline ignored his silent disapproval. She knew she was on time for dinner, just as she was aware that he liked to enjoy a leisurely cocktail a half hour prior to dining. It was her custom to skip that part of the evening if she could.

"Father," she murmured, kissing his cheek perfunctorily. "How have you been?"

"Busy, as usual," he answered. "You're looking well, Madeline. It's a shame we can't manage to see each other more often than our dinners once a month."

Madeline mentally disagreed. "Well, with our schedules, I guess we'll have to take what we can get."

"You're too late to join me for a drink," he continued. "I'm sure the cook has dinner ready."

Together they walked to the dining room. Madeline had never been able to understand why her father insisted on dining every night in the coldly elegant room, at a table that could easily seat twelve. But then the thought of him eating in the kitchen, or anywhere less formal than one of his many clubs, was equally incongruous. Geoffrey Casey was one of those people whom Madeline couldn't imagine doing any of a number of routine things in the course of a day.

They made small talk as the cook entered the room wheeling a cart. She began removing the steaming dishes from it and setting them on the table. Geoffrey abruptly fell into silence at her arrival, but Madeline smiled warmly at the woman serving them.

"Jenny, everything smells wonderful, as usual."

The short, dark-haired woman threw her a quick smile, never pausing in her work. "You were never a tough one to please, Miss Madeline, but thanks, anyway."

"How's Bob?" Madeline inquired solicitously about the woman's husband.

"Last doctor visit he got a clean bill of health. The doctor said there's a little permanent damage to his heart, but he'll be back on his feet in no time."

"Tell him I said hello, and to take care of himself."

"I'll do that, miss." The cook shot a wary glance at Geoffrey, who was eyeing her coldly. "Will there be anything else, sir?"

He waved a hand, dismissing her. "That will be all, Mrs. Parks. We'll call you if we need anything." The cook disappeared through the kitchen door. He waited until she was out of earshot before saying disapprovingly, "Really, Madeline, I would think that by now I would no longer have to remind you about engaging in banal conversations with the hired help. You've been taught better and it's most unbecoming for you to treat them as—"

"As humans?" Madeline finished for him in a tight voice.

He merely frowned at her interruption, and continued, "You know perfectly well what I mean. There's no need to be disrespectful."

Madeline mentally began to count to one thousand, striving to hold on to her rapidly escalating temper. She knew from experience that arguing with her father never did any good. He detested what he referred to as emotional outbursts, and she suspected that what he really hated was emotion, period. Every word he uttered was delivered in the same smooth, level tone. Anger, joy, frustration—it didn't matter. His expression rarely altered, his voice never rose.

Where had *she* come from? she asked herself. Certainly not from this frigidly proper man. Nor could she see much resemblance to Lorraine Casey, her mother, who'd been killed in a car accident when Madeline was a teenager. Her mother had been blond and beautiful, as proper and devoid of feeling as her husband. Always concerned with appearances, she'd never made a move without first weighing its possible effect on her husband's career.

They certainly had gotten more than they bargained for in Madeline. She had been a squalling baby with a shock of red hair and a temper to match; the Caseys must have doubted that they'd been given the correct infant at the hospital. Even worse, a severe case of asthma had made it impossible for her to be packed off to a boarding school, as her brother, Kevin, had been. No, they'd been forced to keep Madeline at home with them, had to deal with her childish chatter and deplorable manners. Almost every word Madeline could remember either parent directing at her when she was growing up was in the form of a command or a reprimand. Madeline would have grown up thinking that hers was a normal family if it hadn't been for the people hired to run the household, such as Mrs. Parks. The occasional glimpses she'd had into their homes had shown her otherwise.

A huge genetic mistake, that's what she was. She was no longer a child, but she knew her first reactions to her father were firmly based in the roots of her childhood. She had grown accustomed to masking her emotions in his presence, or at least making the attempt. The only way her father would listen to her was if she could remain as cool and calm as he did.

Not that he made a habit of listening to her. Geoffrey Casey had never lost his aptitude for engineering everything and everybody around him to suit himself, his daughter included. She'd made it her life's work to not be manipulated by him, but it was grueling going sometimes.

"I understand you've been assigned to a new case." Her father interrupted her thoughts.

Madeline could feel herself bracing for what was to come. One reason she avoided him was that he insisted on making her business his own. He wouldn't ask what she was working on like other fathers. He would use his contacts through the city to make it his business to know. And since he'd spent nearly twenty years on the city council, his contacts were numerous. Then he would proceed to instruct her on the best way to handle her case, and herself, until she was ready to scream.

I will not do this, she promised herself. *No matter what he says, I will not be sarcastic.* She answered cautiously, "Yes, I'm investigating an arms supplier."

Her father nodded, as if he already knew. "So I hear. Brewer assigned this case to you?"

"Yes."

He nodded again, chewing reflectively. "You've been paired with a Cruz Martinez for the duration of the case?"

She gritted her teeth. His information was accurate, as always. "Yes."

"What's he like?"

She looked at him in surprise. "Why, do you know him?"

"It's impolite to answer a question with another question," he admonished her. "But, no, of course I don't know him. That's why I asked you."

She shrugged, knowing the casual gesture would annoy him. "He's all right, I guess."

"Do you think you'll be able to link him to the gun sales?"

Madeline froze in the act of raising her fork to her lips. Then slowly she replaced it on her plate. "Where," she asked in carefully measured words, "did you get that information?"

He waved her question away nonchalantly. "I have my sources, Madeline, you know that. Now, please answer my question."

But she had no intention of doing so. When she spoke again it was difficult to keep her voice from shaking with anger. "I've told you before, I do not care to have your snoops spying on every aspect of my career and then reporting back to you. You have no business asking for, or receiving, such privileged information about an Internal Affairs investigation. It's a complete abuse of your position to even request it."

But her father, as usual, was unmoved by her words. "For heaven's sake, Madeline, I certainly don't have hired men 'spying' on you, as you so inelegantly put it. I happened to run into a friend at my club and we had a drink together. You know how it is." He wiped his mouth with his napkin. "He shared the information with me because he thought I'd be interested."

Oh, yes, Madeline thought, her stomach churning with fury. She knew exactly how it was. How it had always been. He'd never trusted her to live her own life, and he never would. He was constantly looking over her shoulder, warning her about which decisions to make, second-guessing her all the way. She knew blowing up at him would solve nothing, but she could no more stop herself than she could quit breathing. "We've had this discussion before," she said furiously. "When are you going to keep your nose out of my professional life?"

When he answered, Geoffrey's voice was crisp. "When I can trust your professional judgment. From what I've heard of Martinez, he's quite a ladies' man. I don't want you to make another mistake."

The color leeched from her face. "What exactly are you implying?"

"You know very well, Madeline, but if you insist on having it spelled out... As soon as I heard about this job you've been assigned—to see if Martinez is clean—I had a feeling of déjà vu. I just think you need to be very careful that you don't succumb to this man's surface charm and overlook any evidence to suggest that he's a criminal."

"Like I did before?" she said woodenly.

"With Dennis Belding, yes. Good Lord, you were planning to marry the man before he was caught going through my personal papers in my office. The damage he was able to do me was only barely controlled. You don't exactly have the best track record in your judgment of men, my dear."

"May I remind you," she retorted, "that you were totally in favor of our engagement? Dennis had your wholehearted approval."

"Hmm, yes, that was unfortunate," he agreed. "But it's neither here nor there. You understand now what I'm talking about. Perhaps it would be best for you to ask Brewer to assign someone else to Martinez."

"That is out of the question," she snapped.

Predictably, her show of temper had little visible effect on her father. His voice, when he spoke, was tinged with censure. "Well, then, be very careful, Madeline. You act as if you despise the power that comes with my position, but it was the only thing that saved you from being implicated in Dennis's little schemes."

Her chair clattered as she stood abruptly. "That's not true!"

He surveyed her impassively. "Isn't it?"

She closed her eyes briefly, but trying to rein in her temper at this point was impossible. "I prefer to believe that I was cleared in the investigation because I was innocent. And you would do well to remember that Cruz Martinez might be, too."

Geoffrey rose also. "Believe what you wish. But if you insist on going ahead with this investigation, you had better be sure of your motives regarding Martinez. If you conclude he's innocent of any wrongdoing, be very certain this time that you've reached your conclusion based upon the evidence, and not upon your emotions."

Madeline picked up her purse with hands that were not quite steady. "Congratulations, Father. You've managed to ruin another meal."

Realizing her intention, he frowned. "Madeline, you aren't leaving? You haven't finished your dinner."

"I've lost my appetite," she said clearly, and stalked from the room and out of the house.

Back in her own apartment she tried to curb the anger that renewed every time she played back their conversation. Her blood pressure couldn't stand more than an hour a month in her father's presence. She'd known that he didn't have an especially high opinion of her. But to imply that she would succumb to any man who came her way... How could he not know her at all, after thirty years?

The answer was simple, she thought glumly as she methodically put her purse away and hung up her jacket. Geoffrey Casey had never taken the time to get to know either of his children. They existed solely as extensions of himself, extensions he felt compelled to control. He didn't want to get to know them. To do so would mean he would have to admit they were individuals in their own right.

She flipped on some soothing music and plopped down on the couch, sitting cross-legged. She bent her head back and concentrated on allowing the tension from the evening to slip away. Really, what difference did it make what her father thought? He'd long since lost the power to really hurt her with his lack of faith.

She refused to admit, even to herself, that he'd never quite lost the power to make her doubt herself.

Madeline knocked on Captain Brewer's door the next morning and entered at his brusque command. His eyebrows rose when he saw her, and he motioned her to a chair.

"Well, Sergeant, do you have something for me already?"

"Just an update." She told him of the interrogation of Stover the day before. "Martinez is going to ask Ritter to try to convince Jacobs to reduce the charges in return for Stover telling us where he got the weapon.''

"What else do you have?"

"His weapon is the only one that's been recovered in the act of a crime. And it's the same kind that was used in each of the drive-by shootings."

Brewer waited for a few moments, but when she added nothing further, he said, "That's all? Casey, you've got nothing. If Jacobs had been interested, he would have acted by now."

"Maybe no one has suggested it yet," she maintained stubbornly. "We figured it was worth a shot."

The captain didn't look convinced. "Don't get your hopes up. Stover robbed a bank, for heaven's sake, and got caught red-handed doing it. Jacobs isn't going to want to give up a sure conviction." He looked at her for a long moment. "What have you gotten on Martinez so far?"

She sighed. "It's only been one day. Did you think I was going to walk in after twenty-four hours and hand him over to you?" She hesitated. Damn her father for his words last night. Now she would be examining each move she made for signs of favoritism to Martinez. Brewer, too, was eyeing her speculatively.

"So you're saying you haven't found anything so far."

After a momentary pause she related the scene between Martinez and Baker. "He mentioned the Internal Affairs investigation."

"And?" the man demanded. "Did you get the feeling he was harboring a grudge against the department?"

"He certainly didn't agree with the investigation's findings," she said dryly, "but that's hardly grounds to convict him of illegal gun sales."

"Don't downplay it, Detective," the captain admonished her. "If he thinks the department let him down, it could be a possible motive for wanting to get even."

Madeline closed her mouth against further argument. Defending Cruz Martinez wasn't in her job description. She was, after all, carrying out her assignment.

She refused to listen to the mocking voice inside questioning just who she was trying to convince. Brewer, her father, or herself?

* * *

As Madeline walked toward Martinez's desk, he jumped up. "You're here, great." He rounded his desk and headed toward, then past her. She turned and followed him outside.

"I take it we're in a hurry," she surmised as they went toward the car.

"That we are, Detective Casey. I just called Philadelphia Memorial Hospital and Ramsey Elliot is able to have visitors. He's also making noises about leaving the hospital soon, so we need to get over there before he does." Reaching the car, he tossed her the keys, which she caught reflexively. "Your turn to drive, remember?"

Madeline slid into the driver's seat and Cruz sat on the passenger side. "Buckle up, Madeline," he chided her playfully. "You've heard the commercials. You could learn a lot from a dummy."

She buckled her seat belt obediently. "I have a feeling I'm going to."

"Ouch." He winced at the reference to himself. Bending forward, he reached for the car radio, batting her hand out of the way as she would have selected the station. "Uh-uh, it's my turn. Passenger gets to choose the music." Soon a plaintive country song was filling the air.

"Oh, good heavens," Madeline said, throwing him a look of disgust. "You weren't kidding yesterday. You really do listen to this stuff."

"I never kid about good music," he informed her solemnly. "Just give it a chance. It will grow on you."

Like a fungus, she thought, but kept the remark to herself. She checked out his feet. Today they were garbed in yet another pair of cowboy boots. She'd made a few phone calls before she had met him this morning, and she was still stunned at the amount she was quoted over the phone for such a pair. Her head swam with the different kinds the clerks had reeled off. Ostrich skin, rattlesnake, kangaroo... She was too untutored to discern the type he wore, but as she'd expected, they were expensive. Her eyes swept his figure, slouched in the seat next to her, and she smirked. Maybe he spent all his money on boots—the rest of his wardrobe seemed limited to jeans and casual shirts. She ignored the way they enhanced his body and returned her gaze to traffic.

"What do you have on Ramsey Elliot so far?" she asked.

"Not much. I was able to question him a little bit after he was brought in, while he was waiting for surgery. Then the doctor kicked me out and I haven't spoken with him since. I did talk to his mother, though. She's the one who told me he was a member of the Lords. He's fifteen, and according to her, he's only been running with them for a couple of months. Since he's hooked up with his new friends she's had all kinds of trouble with him—skipping school, fights, vandalism. He's currently on probation for a charge of assault. He jumped another kid in the hallway at school."

Madeline didn't comment. The story he was telling had all too familiar a ring. On the streets of Philadelphia kids like Ramsey grew up fast, and an alarming number of them didn't have the chance to grow up at all. "Have you talked to any other members of the Lords?"

"A few, but they didn't have much to say. We need to concentrate on them next. Unless you have another idea?"

She shook her head. It seemed to her that their best bet would be to lean heavily on the gang, and try to anticipate their next move.

At the hospital a nurse showed them the way to Ramsey's room. As they approached it, they heard raised voices.

"I told you to stay out of it!"

"Why should I, huh? You didn't. You didn't stay out of it, and look where it got you! Lying in a hospital bed with your stomach full of lead!"

"Forget about it. It's too late, anyway. I can't—"

The voice broke off as the nurse pushed open the door, announcing their arrival. "You have more visitors, Ramsey." She looked at Cruz and Madeline. "Don't stay too long, Detectives. He still tires easily." They nodded and approached the bed.

"I'm Detective Martinez, Ramsey, and this is Detective Casey. I spoke to you for a few minutes after you were brought in, do you remember that?"

The youth was silent, his gaze distrustful. Finally he muttered, "Yeah, I remember you."

Cruz looked at the other visitor in the room. "Who's this?"

"My brother, Ricky."

"Hi, Ricky." The boy nodded and ducked his head, not looking at either detective. Cruz's attention shifted back to Ramsey. "I'd like to go over the statement you gave me regarding your shooting."

"Why? I don't have nothing else to say."

Cruz leaned against the wall next to the bed. "Let's see, shall we? Sometimes people remember things without even realizing it." He consulted the notebook he'd brought with him. "You said you didn't see the face of the person who shot you, but you saw the car?"

"Yeah, I told you, it was a dark green car. I don't know what kind, but it was old. There was lots of rust on it."

"Did you hear it coming?"

"What do you mean?"

Madeline bit her lip. Cruz would have tough going with this one. The young man was determined not to give them any more information than he had to. She studied the youth in the bed. He looked older than fifteen. He was a handsome boy, despite the strain the shooting and the surgery must have had on him. His eyes held a worn weariness she'd seen too often on the streets, sometimes in children younger than this one. It was a look carried by someone who'd seen too much, and eaten too little. One that said he didn't even expect to live to adulthood.

Her attention was snared by the brother, Ricky. He hadn't stopped moving since they'd entered the room. He picked up various objects—the water pitcher, the box of tissues—and then set them down again. He'd moved away from the bed now, and was leaning against the wall. One knee was bouncing nervously. She smiled at him. "Hospitals make you uncomfortable, huh? Me, too. I can never get used to the smell."

He looked surprised to have her speak to him, but he smiled shyly. "Yeah, man, and is it ever clean! I thought my mom was bad, but there's this nurse here, she's a real beast about germs."

Madeline laughed softly. "You must have been spending a lot of time here with Ramsey."

He nodded. "My mom comes, too, when she can, but she works two jobs, so she don't get much time off. I come whenever I can find someone else to watch Rhonda—that's my little sister. I don't like to bring her much. A hospital is no place for kids, ya know?"

She nodded in agreement, silently noting that Ricky wasn't much more than a kid himself. He looked only about twelve or thirteen, and lacked the world-weary air of his brother. "Who watches your sister when you come to the hospital?"

Ricky's shoulders went back defensively. "I always make sure she's taken care of. Mom would kill me if I left her alone. There's a lady in our building, she don't mind looking out for her. Today I took her to the library. Rhonda loves it there. She reads real good, for only being eight."

"It sounds like Rhonda is lucky to have you for a big brother," Madeline said sincerely, and the boy smiled in genuine pleasure at the compliment.

"Ricky!"

All heads swiveled at Ramsey's voice. When he had his brother's attention, he ordered tersely, "Pour me some water, will ya?" Ricky obediently tended to his brother, and Ramsey settled back in the bed. He exchanged a long glance with Madeline and she knew he'd issued the command to put a stop to her conversation with the boy. *Just what is it you're afraid of?* she questioned silently as they stared at each other. *Is it your distrust of the police that makes you keep Ricky close to your side? Or are you afraid he'll tell me something you don't want us to know?*

There were no answers forthcoming in his carefully blank gaze, nor did Cruz fare much better with the questions he asked him. Ramsey's answers were noncommittal, and short to the point of belligerence. He was careful to keep Ricky near him, ordering him about, making sure the boy was too busy to talk to Madeline again.

Finally Cruz snapped the notebook shut in exasperation. "Well, I guess that's all I have for right now, Ramsey. Okay if I get back to you, if I have more questions?" They all were aware that requesting permission was mere politeness; Cruz could and would be contacting Ramsey again. The look on the boy's face said that he knew it, too.

"Won't do no good," he responded with a shrug. "Told ya all I know." Ricky, for once, was still, watching their faces carefully, as though trying to discern what wasn't being said. Madeline reached into her purse and pulled out a folded sheet of paper, tearing off a piece of it. "Here, Ricky," she said, scribbling on the back of it. "I'll bet Rhonda likes to read about animals, doesn't she?"

The boy exchanged a puzzled look with his brother and responded, "Yeah. She's nuts about horse stories, especially."

She finished writing and held the piece of paper out to him. "So was I, at that age. I wrote down the name of a couple of authors who were my favorites when I was a kid. Maybe Rhonda would like to check out some of their books the next time you take her to the library."

Ricky took the paper from her slowly, looking uncertainly at his brother. Ramsey shrugged a little, and settled back in the hospital bed. Ricky smiled at Madeline. "Thanks. I'll help her look them up." He slipped the paper into his pocket.

Cruz and Madeline said goodbye to the boys and went out the door. Walking down the hallway, she remarked, "Nice kid."

He slanted a glance at her. "Let me guess. You also wrote down your telephone number?"

"Didn't have to." She smiled smugly. "My letterhead was on the other side of the paper."

"Smooth, Casey, very smooth," he said approvingly. "But what makes you think he'll use it? Or that he has anything to tell us?"

"Whatever Ramsey is involved in, Ricky doesn't agree with, I'd stake my life on that. I'm just not sure how much he knows about his brother's involvement with the Lords."

"I wouldn't be surprised if that was the source of the argument we overheard."

"I didn't hear everything Ramsey told you while I was talking to Ricky. Did he give you any leads?"

"Maybe," Cruz responded as they crossed the parking lot in the bright sunlight. The sun caught her hair and gilded it, turning it into a fiery halo threaded with gold. He was reminded of the first time he'd seen her at the playground. It had been a day just like this one, and her hair had shimmered in the afternoon sun. He experienced an overwhelming desire to unfasten the barrette that seemed to be holding the heavy mass pinned above her neck, and shoved his hands deep into his jeans pockets to squelch the urge.

"Go ahead," she invited.

His eyes bounced to hers disbelievingly. She was giving him permission? "What?"

"You said maybe Ramsey had given you a lead. What was it?"

He shook his head a little to clear it as they reached the car and he waited for her to unlock it. He would do well to keep those mental meanderings under control. He doubted very much that Detective Sergeant Madeline Casey would appreciate being the object of his overactive imagination.

They were both seated in the car when she prompted him again. "Well?"

His mouth quirked. She really wasn't long on patience. He could read that in her rigid posture. He'd be willing to bet she had a temper to match that head of hair, although he hadn't had occasion to experience it yet. He wondered how much longer he had before she reached over and throttled him for keeping her in suspense. Not long, he surmised, gauging her short, jerky movements as she switched on the car and put it into gear. He deliberately waited another moment before answering her question. "It was after you'd been talking to Ricky for a while. Ramsey was getting a little distracted, trying to hear what you two were saying and at the same time answer my questions. He slipped up once. I'd asked him if he had insurance to take care of the hospital bill and he answered that Dirk would take care of it. Then he caught himself, and said he could take care of it."

"Dirk," Madeline murmured, her mind swiftly flipping through her memory banks.

"Dirk Cantoney," he supplied.

She nodded, knowing where she'd seen that name. "Leader of the Lords."

"Exactly." He nodded. "Makes you wonder, doesn't it, just why Cantoney would be willing to come up with that much money for a kid who just joined the gang a few months ago?"

"Maybe Ramsey is something of a hero now that he's been shot," she suggested.

"I haven't had any luck finding Cantoney yet, but I've told the Lords members I've talked to that I want to meet with him."

"He'd be the one who would deal on the gun if they're planning to retaliate," Madeline agreed.

Cruz nodded. "We'll go looking for him right after lunch."

"I have just the spot," she answered, driving surely. "Driver gets to pick where we eat dinner."

"I didn't get to pick yesterday," he reminded her.

"Thanks to your driving, we didn't get to eat yesterday."

He quibbled good-naturedly with her until she pulled the car over to the side of a street. He looked at the corner and then back at her, dismay written all over his face.

"A hot dog stand?"

"Best hot dogs in Philadelphia," she informed him as she got out of the car. "If you haven't eaten one outside, you don't know what you're missing. It's all in the presentation and ambience." He followed her reluctantly. She was obviously not the only one who believed so. There were several other people waiting in line to be served.

"Do you know what they make these things from?" he asked in a loud whisper.

"Yep."

"They make them from animals' intestines." He didn't know that for sure, but he thought he'd heard that once, and it sounded suitably disgusting.

"I like intestines," she responded imperturbably. She bought two hot dogs and handed him one. He took it resignedly and moved aside to heap it with various condiments. He eyed her askance as she munched contentedly.

"Aren't you at least going to put relish on it?" he asked, holding up a spoonful.

"I don't eat green things."

He shook his head in mock regret. "You really need to be taken in hand. Your dining habits are deplorable." He eyed the hot dog suspiciously before giving an inward sigh. Hunger won out over the desire for nutrition. He devoured the meal hastily, but not before a large drop of mustard landed on his shirt.

Madeline bit her lip to keep from laughing at his aggrieved look. "It's your own fault. You had your hot dog piled too high. There's an art to eating without a plate."

"Obviously," he mumbled, dabbing at the stain with a napkin. "This was my favorite shirt, too."

"Considering what I've seen of your wardrobe so far, you probably have a dozen more just like it," she answered without sympathy.

He looked affronted. "Are you implying that my wardrobe lacks imagination?"

"No," she responded, "just taste."

He grinned at her then. "Speaking of tasteless, you have ketchup on your face."

Madeline scrubbed at her mouth with her napkin. "Where?"

"You missed it, it's right…" His finger went to the corner of her mouth just as her tongue swept her lips, searching for the errant drop. The tip of her tongue barely grazed his finger, and his breath hissed in at the scorching wake of sensation.

The entire scope of his focus narrowed to her lips. "Here," he said huskily, wiping away the minuscule trace. His eyes followed the movement of his finger.

Madeline looked up, a little embarrassed, but forgot what she was going to say when her eyes caught his.

Hot. Her stomach jumped crazily. How could eyes that dark look so heated? She was unable to tear her gaze away. His face came closer, and still she couldn't move. Instead she watched, entranced by those hypnotic eyes. They weren't really black, she thought a little dizzily. But they were so dark a brown that the pupil showed only at a close range. This close. Kissing close. Unconsciously her lips parted, and her eyelids grew heavy.

"Cruz!"

Madeline looked up, a little dazed, but came back down to earth with a crash when a pretty young woman came running up and launched herself into Cruz's arms, kissing him soundly. "Where have you been?" the woman scolded. "I've missed you."

Chapter 4

Madeline tore her eyes from the embracing couple with difficulty. Movements suddenly jerky, she walked a few steps to throw her napkin into a nearby trash container. She felt like a fool, and she didn't enjoy the emotion. The girl had saved her from looking like an even bigger fool, though. If it hadn't been for her arrival, Madeline was quite certain that Cruz would have kissed her. And she was very much afraid that she would have let him.

She forced herself to turn back to the couple with what she hoped was an expressionless face. She observed the affectionate way Cruz had his arm draped around the girl's shoulders. And she wasn't much more than a girl, Madeline noted. She looked no more than twenty, and had a figure that was downright obscene. She was a full foot shorter than Cruz. She was exactly the kind of woman who'd always made Madeline feel like a giraffe, as she towered over her from her own height of five-ten. She squelched the urge to slouch and cross her arms.

Cruz was laughing at something the girl had said, and, turning, he introduced the two. "Madeline, this is Maureen. She's—"

"Hush," the girl said, clapping a hand over his mouth. "I'll bet Madeline can tell who I am. Can't you, Madeline?"

"It's pretty obvious," Madeline agreed tightly.

Cruz rolled his eyes at the dark-haired woman's crow of delight. "See! I told you, I look just like you. You're the only one who refuses to see it."

Madeline froze. For the first time she really looked at the woman. Dark hair tumbled in artful disarray down her narrow back. Her face was heart shaped, lightly made-up, but there was a trace of resemblance in the eyes. Madeline's gaze bounced to Cruz as he continued the introduction.

"As I was saying, this is my younger sister Maureen. My baby sister," he stressed, earning himself a punch on the arm.

Madeline smiled tentatively. "Nice to meet you."

"What are you doing here, anyway?" Cruz asked Maureen. "Don't you have classes?"

"Not until three," she replied. "And that bookstore," she said, pointing across the street, "is where I started working part-time last week, which you would have known if you hadn't missed the last two Sunday dinners." She continued chattering, barely pausing to take a breath. "You're in *big* trouble at home and Mom is ready to lynch you. Pop says you'd better show up this week, if you know what's good for you, or you'd better have a damn good reason."

"Maureen!" Both women blinked at the tone of command that had entered his voice, but it accomplished its goal. His sister's mouth snapped shut. Then, in a normal voice, he continued, "As I've tried to explain, I've been busy recently. But tell Mom and Pop I should be able to make it this Sunday."

"You call and tell them," his sister retorted calmly, plainly unfazed by her brother's order. "I'm sure they have lots to say to you." She reached up and kissed him lightly again. "Gotta run. See you this weekend. Bye, Madeline." Her voice carried over her shoulder as she waved blithely and hurried back across the street.

Madeline smiled at the look of sheer frustration stamped on Cruz's face as he watched his sister swing away. "Who was that masked woman?" she joked.

He shook his head wryly. "My conscience, she thinks. She could give Jiminy Cricket lessons."

"And do you need an extra conscience?" Madeline asked, suddenly serious. She was again thinking of what he'd been accused of. At times like these he seemed so real, so human, that she wondered how he could be a suspect. But she knew too well that the most successful criminals didn't look the part. Getting others to trust them was their stock-in-trade.

He nodded and said with mock solemnity, "Sometimes. My own doesn't have a very loud speaking voice. I can't always hear it."

I'll bet, Madeline thought darkly. And somehow she was no longer thinking at all about the crime he might have committed.

As they walked back to the car he explained, "I'm one of six kids in what is a pretty close-knit family. Too close, sometimes. It's kind of an unspoken rule that if you live in the city, you're expected home for dinners on Sundays, unless you have a good excuse. Mom doesn't accept too many of those. Since all of us live here when everyone's out of school, the weekly dinner gets to be pretty wild sometimes."

She tried to visualize the scene he'd just described, a large warm family gathered around a dinner table, voices vying to be heard. Though she'd never experienced such a scene, it was easy to picture. She was curious to hear more about his family, and finding out from him would save her some checking. At least, that's what she told herself. "Where do you fall in the family?"

"Second to the oldest. Let's see, there's Kevin, me, Shannon, Antonio, Maureen and Miguel."

Madeline blinked. "I know I'll hate myself for asking," she muttered, "but Kevin, Shannon and Maureen . . . Martinez?"

They'd reached the car, but neither made a move to get in. Cruz chuckled. "We're a little unconventional, I guess. I'm only half Mexican—my mother is Irish."

"Hence the names," she surmised, interest caught despite herself.

"Mom and Pop decided they would take turns naming us when we were born." He winked. "Lucky there was an even number of us. I'd hate to consider what kind of name they would have chosen as a compromise."

"Six kids is a large family," Madeline said. "Where did you live?"

"A series of apartments in the East Division," he answered. "Pop works on the docks, and as he improved his job, his first concern was always getting us a better place to live. A few years ago they moved to a small house. Mom was home with us when we were growing up, but Maureen and Miguel are both in college. A few years ago Mom went back to school and now she works as a legal secretary."

She tried and failed to imagine what it must have been like growing up with an apartment full of siblings in crowded rooms, with a mother home all day to ride herd. Noisy, she guessed. The one thing she remembered above all else from her own childhood was the quiet. She was the only child in the huge home most of the time, and even though her mother hadn't worked, she'd been gone frequently, involved in her clubs and charity work. Madeline had always looked forward to cleaning day each week, when the housekeeper ran the vacuum. For that short time the house would seem a little less empty.

"So by now you've probably guessed how safe you are with me." His words interrupted her thoughts and she looked across the car at him. He was leaning; he seemed to do that a lot, she noted.

"How's that?"

"Mexican and Irish—of course I had the required Catholic up-bringing." His eyes glinted wickedly. "I was even an altar boy."

She smiled at that information. "Proof that God does work in mysterious ways."

"That's just what Father Dougherty used to say to me," he agreed. "I think he believed that I was his own personal trial on earth. I got along better with the nuns at school. At least, most of them. Sister Mary Joseph never understood me. Did you ever notice that the nuns all used to have men's names?" he added irrelevantly.

Madeline shook her head. She hadn't had much experience with nuns.

"Things are different now," he went on. "The school my nieces and nephews attend has nuns with names like Sister Cathy and Rosita Marie. They worry about developing positive self-concepts instead of repressing evil thoughts, and they never, ever rap students on the knuckles with a ruler."

"Now, why do I have the feeling that your knuckles didn't get rapped a fraction of the times you deserved it?" she wondered aloud. It was all too easy to picture him as he must have appeared when he was a mischievous youngster, all dancing dark eyes and a mop of black hair. The charm would have been apparent even then, and no doubt he'd used it shamelessly.

He shrugged. "You misunderstand me, I suppose. Just like Sister Mary Joseph."

She gave up and got in the car. She had Cruz Martinez's number, all right. Exactly like Sister Mary Joseph. "Where to?" she asked when he joined her in the front seat.

Cruz leaned over and turned up the radio, smiling as she winced at the mournful tune filling the air. "I think it's time to talk to

some more members of the Lords, especially one Dirk Cantoney.''

Madeline agreed and Cruz directed her through the streets.
''What about you?'' he asked as she drove silently. ''Do you have
brothers and sisters?''

''An older brother, but he was away at school much of the time
when I was growing up,'' she answered.

''I should bring you home with me some Sunday,'' he said idly.
''Give you a look at all you missed.''

''No!'' Even she was shocked at the vehement denial. At his
quizzical look she explained quickly, ''I mean, it wouldn't be a
good idea. Your parents probably look forward to spending the day
with family, not with strangers.''

He laughed at the thought. ''My parents don't understand the
word 'stranger.' And they always encourage us to bring friends
home to meet them. My mom is a firm believer in the power of
good cooking.''

She mentally scolded herself for reacting so strongly to his invitation. She should have seized the chance to observe more about
Cruz Martinez—who he was, where he came from. But everything inside her recoiled from the thought of getting to know his
family, even casually. She couldn't imagine anything more uncomfortable than sitting across from his parents, being treated as
a friend, all the while trying to establish whether a link existed between Cruz and the supplier. She could imagine herself conversing with his parents. ''Actually, Mr. and Mrs. Martinez, I'm more
than Cruz's partner—I'm the lady who's going to get his butt
hauled to jail if he's involved in illegal arms sales.''

She shuddered. She didn't think she was that cool an actress.
Especially if the entire family was as open and friendly as Cruz was.
Seemingly open, she corrected herself. She had to keep that in
mind. Here she was doubting her own ability to carry off such a
masquerade at his home and he might even now be delivering an
act deserving of an Academy Award. She couldn't remember the
last time a case had left a worse taste in her mouth. She wished it
had been possible to do as her father had wished, and ask Brewer
to put someone else on this case. But that had never been an op-
tion. She was too much a professional for that.

''Slow down,'' Cruz commanded as she drove by the parking lot
of a business that had been vacated. He peered out the window at
the people collected there, then sat back in the seat. ''Keep driving.'' They cruised slowly up and down streets in the area, slowing

down at corners, or wherever a group of youths was found. Finally he said, "Here we are. Pull over."

She obeyed and they got out of the car and approached a knot of several young men of various races, all of whom were wearing Lords colors.

The young men had been talking and joking loudly, occasionally jostling one another, but silence fell over the group when the unmarked car stopped and the detectives got out and approached them.

"Hey, nice wheels, man," one finally remarked, and the rest guffawed.

"Yo, Mama," another said to Madeline. "What you doing wasting your time with a cop?"

Madeline reached into her breast pocket and took out her shield, flipping it open. "Earning a living," she said succinctly. "And I'm not your mama. But if I were, I'd tell you that smoking is bad for your health."

There was a short silence at her words before the group broke into laughter again, ribbing the boy who was holding a cigarette in his hand.

"I've talked to some of you guys already," Cruz interjected. "I'm Detective Martinez, and this is Detective Casey. We're investigating the shooting of Ramsey Elliot."

"I was there," one volunteered. "I told you about the car. When are you going to find it?"

"Yeah, man," said another, "you talked to all of us who was there. You mean you ain't found the guy yet?"

"Just checking," Cruz answered. "I don't suppose any of you have remembered anything else about the car or its occupants, have you? Or something really helpful, like the license number?"

"It had local plates, I know that," one said surely.

"It didn't have no plates," contradicted another.

"I didn't see nuthin'. I wasn't paying attention before, and once the bullets started flying I hit the dirt," said a third. "I wasn't looking at the car then, I was looking at Ramsey. There was blood all over the place." Several others nodded at this.

"Why hasn't Dirk Cantoney gotten in touch with me?" Cruz asked. No one spoke a word. A few glanced at each other, some shuffled their feet, but no one seemed willing to answer. Cruz went on, "I left word with several of you that I wanted to speak to him. Did any of you tell him that?" Still no response.

"We need to talk to him about the shooting, since he was there, too," Madeline said. "He isn't in any trouble—we just have some routine questions to ask."

One snorted at this. "Dirk ain't afraid of no cops," he said derisively. The mood of the group seemed to take a menacing turn. The once cocky, bantering tone was absent now, each of the members' faces wearing the same sullen, closed mask.

"Then he should be willing to talk to us," Madeline inserted smoothly. "Where can we find him?"

There was another long silence before one muttered, "If he wants to talk, he'll find you."

"Tell him we'll be at the Blue Pelican the rest of the afternoon," Cruz said, naming a bar in the neighborhood. "He can find us there."

One of the boys shrugged. "Don't even know if we'll see him today."

"Make a point of it," Madeline advised. "Because if he doesn't talk to us today, we'll have to go looking for him. And if we do go looking for him, we'll bring his parole officer with us."

A few of the young men glanced at one another, and then away. No one responded, but Madeline and Cruz, sure the message would be delivered, walked back to the car.

"Tough lady," Cruz remarked as they drove away.

"When I have to be," Madeline answered.

"Need I ask how you knew he was on parole?"

"The file," she answered shortly, and Cruz shook his head in amazement. He had given her an hour to read two files, both of which had been at least two inches thick. He wondered if she'd committed the whole thing to memory, or just the highlights. "He served two years for breaking and entering," he tried, testing her on some of the details.

Her eyes never left the road. "He served thirty-three months for aggravated assault, and the only reason he's out is because some ACLU lawyer managed to convince a parole board that he should never have been tried as an adult in the first place."

Madeline listened to his directions to the Blue Pelican, and drove silently. She was aware of what he'd been doing just then, and it neither angered nor amused her. She was too used to it to give it much attention. She'd been born with an uncannily accurate memory, and she accepted it the way others accepted their hair or eye color. She'd learned to trust it, then rely on it as she grew older. And she blessed it now, because she knew she would be needing it more than ever. As her father had pointed out, her instincts, at least when it came to men, had not proven to be the best. The fiasco with Dennis Belding had come very close to ending her career, all because she had trusted the wrong man. The experience, though, had taught her a valuable lesson. Instincts could be faulty, clouded by emotion, but her memory never was. And she had the remarkable ability to remember every bit of the hell she had gone through the last time she had misjudged a man. It would never be allowed to happen again.

Of course, she added silently, she would be greatly aided in that vow if she could refrain from kissing Cruz Martinez. Her palms still moistened when she remembered the look of intent his face had worn as it had neared hers. The lingering amusement on it had been wiped away, to be replaced with the most compelling expression of masculine desire that she'd ever witnessed. Desire that she was sure had been reflected on her own face.

Even if she wasn't working with him, even if she wasn't investigating him, Cruz was not a man she would ever consider getting involved with. He was glib and oh-so-charming. And he was too darn gorgeous by half. With those perfect features and well-honed body, he'd be right at home on a Hollywood screen set, and she'd bet a month's pay that he had as many adoring fans as any movie star. A woman would have to be crazy to fall prey to that easygoing manner and bone-melting grin. He was the most dangerous of men; he radiated a vibrant sexuality that would normally frighten some women, even as it drew them. But he could be so easy to talk to, so fascinating with the combination of those blatantly bedroom eyes and aw-shucks manner, that even the most sensible women might be tempted to cast caution aside.

Luckily she had more than her share of good sense. And up against the temptation of Cruz Martinez, she was going to need every bit of it.

"It's right here," Cruz said, interrupting her thoughts.

"Looks like a real dive." She wasn't especially surprised, but she wasn't looking forward to spending the next few hours sitting in such an establishment.

"Don't worry," he teased as they parked in the small rutted lot next to the bar and got out of the car. "I'll protect you."

She rolled her eyes at his remark and he laughed. When they entered the place, she wrinkled her nose at the smell. The aromas of smoke, beer and unwashed bodies hung in the air. It was surprisingly full for midafternoon, but from the looks of the disreputable occupants, it wasn't as if they had jobs to go to. It was more likely that any business these people conducted was done right here in the bar. Or out of the trunks of their cars.

There were a few tables scattered about, but they were all taken. Madeline followed Cruz to a booth in the back, where they would have a view of anyone entering through the front or rear door. He stood while she scooted in one side, but she looked up, open-mouthed, when he slid in after her.

"There's plenty of room over there," she said pointedly, indicating the other side of the booth.

"I'd prefer to keep my back to the wall in a place like this, and Cantoney isn't going to join us if it means he has to sit next to either of us. He's too wary for that."

Though his explanation sounded logical, she still looked at him suspiciously. The length of the afternoon seemed much longer now that she knew she was going to spend it with him pressed against her side like this. "Well, quit crowding me," she ordered shortly. His big body seemed to take up much more than its share of the small seat, even when she shrank into the corner.

He paid no attention to her, his eyes scanning the bar carefully through the haze of smoke. His lack of awareness of her made her relax a bit, even as it made her want to kick him. It was impossible for her to feign such unawareness of him. He was so close that his muscled arms brushed hers. Though he was wearing a long-sleeved shirt, again rolled up to just below the elbows, she could recall in detail what those arms looked like bare, and mentally groaned. This was not her idea of how to spend a productive afternoon. Or of how to remain immune to this man's charm.

Cruz relaxed imperceptibly when he satisfied himself that Cantoney wasn't there. He recognized a few of the customers, and either they hadn't seen him or they were doing their best to pretend they hadn't. He'd ousted a few of them on more than one occasion, and he'd busted two of the men at the bar for petty theft. He didn't know if this was an establishment that Cantoney usually frequented, but it was on turf claimed by the Lords. And it was exactly the kind of place that a two-bit hood like Dirk would feel at home in.

He shifted his weight to a more comfortable position, aware for the first time just how close he was to Madeline. He moved again, uneasily. This might not prove to be the brightest plan he'd ever had. Passing the next few hours pressed up against Madeline Casey's slender body might be just enough to turn him into a eunuch. Because if the agony didn't do the job, he was sure she'd be glad to, if he lifted one finger in her direction.

Not that he had any intention of doing that. He was the first to admit that he had an eye for attractive women, but it was plain to see that this one had Hands Off written all over her. And he had done his best in the short time they'd been working together to put her at ease, to show her that she had nothing to fear from him.

Well, okay, he'd almost made a little slip this afternoon. He frowned slightly. He had come damn close to kissing Madeline then, and finding out at last if those delectably full lips were as soft as they looked. He knew exactly what had made him almost abandon his careful distance from her. She'd been too darn inviting, standing there savoring that damn hot dog, smug because he was having to eat one, too. She'd looked more approachable than he'd ever seen her, and it hadn't taken long for their bantering to turn to awareness. At least, it hadn't taken long for him, and her Hands Off sign hadn't been anywhere in sight.

A slovenly-looking waitress meandered over to take their order. "What can I get for ya, big guy?" she asked with a wink, her eyes never touching Madeline.

"Two beers," he said shortly. Madeline raised her eyebrows at him and he waited for the waitress to leave to forestall her argument. "We don't have to drink them, but this isn't exactly the kind of place where we can order cups of coffee."

The woman came back with two lukewarm beers in glasses that Madeline suspected hadn't been washed in a week. "That'll be three bucks, handsome," she cooed. She placed both elbows on the table and leaned toward Cruz, affording him a revealing view of her ample breasts. To Madeline's amazement he looked distinctly uncomfortable at the attention, a dull red stain reaching his cheekbones as he pulled three dollar bills out of his pocket. The waitress took her time collecting the money and swayed slowly back to the bar.

"Don't worry, handsome," Madeline couldn't help gibing, "I'll protect you."

He grinned at her use of his earlier words. "Ah, subtlety doesn't seem to be her strong suit, does it?"

"I doubt she unbuttoned half her blouse to show her 'subtlety' off to advantage," Madeline agreed dryly.

"Did she? I didn't notice."

Madeline snorted inelegantly. "And birds don't fly."

He affected a wounded expression. "Somewhere along the line you've gotten the wrong impression of me. I wouldn't lie to you. I still go to confession every Saturday, you know."

"I'll bet that's a real trip for some poor unsuspecting priest. He probably needs a stiff drink afterward to recover."

"Naw, I lead a very quiet life."

Somehow she doubted that. Everything about Cruz Martinez pointed to just the opposite. The attitude of the waitress was probably identical to the way most women behaved around him. Throwing themselves at his feet, willing to take a number for their turn with him. Madeline had no illusions about how far some women would go to catch the eye of a man who looked like him. Luckily she had never been partial to tall, dark and perfect types herself.

"What has had you so busy the last couple of weeks that you missed the family dinners?" What the heck. She shrugged mentally. She might as well do some digging as long as they seemed to be stuck here for a while.

"This and that," he said vaguely.

Her interest immediately sharpened. This was the first sign of reticence he'd ever exhibited. She slanted a glance at him. He didn't appear to be trying to avoid the question. He seemed preoccupied, as he had when they'd first come in. His eyes were once again searching the room.

"Is your mother likely to accept 'this and that' as a good enough reason to miss going home?"

He finally looked at her, amusement apparent on his face. "Afraid for my safety? I can assure you it's been a while since she's taken the wooden spoon to me."

She subsided. He obviously wasn't going to tell her what he'd been busy with, and if she pressed he might get the wrong idea about her curiosity, might think she wanted to know out of a more personal interest. The glint in his eye told her he was already thinking exactly that, and it was time to put that misconception to rest. "Just making conversation. Looks like we're in for a long, boring afternoon waiting for Cantoney."

Cruz silently disagreed. *Boring* was one word that could never be applied to the feeling he got sitting this close to her. It wasn't the same as in the car. He didn't have to touch her then. He shifted again. Maybe she had the right idea, after all. Perhaps he should engage in some very idle conversation to distract his mind, and a few other body parts, from thinking about the temptation sitting so close.

"How about you? What do you do on the weekends?" he asked her.

She shrugged. "Exciting things. Work out at the gym. Go to the shooting range. Do the laundry. Clean my apartment."

"And?" His eyes were lit with lazy interest. She couldn't fool him. A woman who looked like her had to have an active social life. He didn't know why he found the thought of that so intriguing, but he did. As long as he didn't dwell too long on what she and her dates did once they got back to her place. That thought brought an unfamiliar knot to his gut.

"And what? I'm not Catholic, so I don't have to spend my Saturdays at confession. Not that I'd need to, anyway," she informed him smugly.

"Is that right?" he questioned in abject disbelief. "What are you telling me, that your life-style is as perfect as your memory?"

"No, I'm saying that my life-style is dull. Boring compared to yours, I'm sure. It doesn't take a whole lot to keep me happy." When he chuckled at this, she lifted her eyebrow. "You don't agree?"

"That's not the way I've got you pegged, no," he answered, still chuckling. "You definitely strike me as high maintenance."

She narrowed her eyes at him. She was going to regret this. She absolutely did not want to hear his explanation of his words. "And just what, may I ask, is that supposed to mean?" she heard herself demand.

At her uncomprehending look, he explained cheerfully. "It's simple. You're the kind of woman who has certain standards. Fairly high standards. They apply to your home, what you drive, who you date and what you do in your free time. 'Regimented' might describe you, but definitely not 'boring.'"

"Regimented?" Her eyes spit green sparks at him and he leaned back to enjoy the fireworks. He'd suspected all along that Madeline Casey had a temper to match that flaming hair and he didn't want to miss a moment of it. "What the heck would you know about being regimented?"

"It's not an insult," he assured her. "Just an observation. Don't worry, I'm sure some men find that quality attractive. My grandma used to say that every pot will find its lid."

"What a quaint saying. I should needlepoint that," she said sarcastically, still smarting from his words. Regimented, she fumed. Her life might be orderly, she might value organization, but the word he'd used was distinctly unflattering. It implied that she was rigidly controlled, and though that was the aura she tried to project professionally, it didn't sound very attractive.

"At the risk of sounding like a cliché, you're beautiful when you're angry." His eyes were crinkled up with amusement.

"And you're annoying when you're stupid," she returned, irritated. What did he know about her? Or about anything? So she prized order in her life. After it had been turned into such shambles a few years ago, was that so wrong? So she was organized. That certainly didn't used to be considered a fault. And yes, maybe she was cautious. She'd bet he knew nothing about that, not in his personal life, anyway. She was quite sure that when it came to the opposite sex, he jumped in with both feet, not to mention other body parts. She glared at him again, and the amused look on his face made her want to smack him, for she was suddenly certain that he'd done this on purpose. He'd baited her into flaring up. The big jerk.

"I'll bet you were the kind of brother who delighted in starting fights among your siblings and then left the room when you heard your mother coming."

He had to smile at how close her remark came to the observation Michele McLain had made the last time he'd visited there. "Are you implying that I'm a tease?" he asked with mock affront.

"That's exactly what I'm implying."

"Then I'd have to disagree. That's not being a tease. A tease is—" he turned to look more fully at her, and stopped when he took in the picture she made. Temper had flared color to her face and brightened the hue of her eyes. "To tease is to taunt. Tantalize. To hold something irresistible just out of reach." His voice deepened. He was no longer responding to her comment. "Teasing is prolonging anticipation, sometimes to an almost unbearable point."

She swallowed hard, his tone as much as his words affecting her. He could have been referring to her remark, but he wasn't, she knew. The timbre of his voice was too suggestive, the words too rife with innuendo. She knew what he was doing but she was helpless to control her response to it. They looked at each other for a long moment, and what she saw in his face made her stomach clutch reflexively. *Bad idea,* her usually reasonable voice screeched inside her. *Don't talk to him, don't argue with him, don't listen to him and for heaven's sake, quit looking at him.* Because there was something about the way he was gazing at her mouth that gave new meaning to the word *tease.* She tore her eyes away with a difficulty that felt almost physical and concentrated for the rest of the afternoon on the comings and goings in the bar. And on shredding her napkin into small bits.

Cruz, too, fell silent. Finally he rose. "It's after five. Let's get out of here."

The sun was still shining brightly when they left the bar, and Madeline squinted in its glare. They strode quickly toward the car, each in a hurry to get back to headquarters, to put the tension of the afternoon behind them. They slowed simultaneously, noticing the figure leaning against their car at the same time.

"Cantoney," Cruz noted under his breath, and Madeline nodded. There hadn't been a picture of the man in the files she'd read, but she could easily believe that this was the man described in one report. Studying him, she had no difficulty believing that he'd assaulted another with a tire iron for the indiscretion of talking to Cantoney's girlfriend. He was about her own height, lean, with skin so fair it looked as if the sun had forgotten him. He would have appeared almost harmless if it hadn't been for his eyes. They were a pale blue, and absolutely devoid of emotion. When they flicked over her, Madeline could feel a physical chill. He appeared older than the members of the gang he led. She didn't doubt for a moment that he had orchestrated the numerous criminal activities that the Lords were suspected of.

"I heard you were looking for me," he drawled.

They finished their approach toward him. "I've been looking for you since Ramsey got shot," Cruz said. "Where have you been?"

The man shrugged. "Been around. You just didn't look in the right places."

"What can you tell us about Ramsey's shooting?" Madeline asked.

"I saw the gun and I yelled at everyone to get down. Ramsey was too slow. Bullets were spraying, and he took a couple of them."

"You don't seem too concerned about his getting hit," Cruz noted.

His words drew no reaction from the man in front of them. "What good would my concern do Ramsey? I been to see him a couple times, he tell you that? I'm making sure his bills get paid. That'll do him a lot more good than my *concern.*"

"You're taking care of his hospital bills, huh?" Cruz rested a hip against the car next to his. "That's real good of you, Dirk. You're a prince. Just how do you manage to do that, since your parole officer tells me you haven't stuck to a job for more than a few weeks at a time?"

The man's tone iced. "I got friends, man, I don't need no job."

"Who do you think did the shooting?"

"Isn't that what you're supposed to find out?" Dirk replied. "If you got busy and found the answer to that, you wouldn't have to waste your time asking me all these questions."

"Well, I'll tell you what I think, Dirk," Cruz said. His arms were crossed and he leaned back, one foot bracing himself against the bumper of the car. He looked for all the world as if he were discussing the cure for crabgrass with a neighbor. "I think you know who shot at you guys that day. I think it was a rival gang, and you know what else? I think they were shooting at *you.* That's why you've been keeping such a low profile lately. And I wouldn't be surprised to hear that you were planning to get some revenge for it, either."

Cantoney threw his head back and laughed raucously, an unpleasant sound. "Martinez, you got some imagination. Why are you accusing me of something you think *might* happen?" His eyes slid to Madeline and he said, "You better tell him, lady. Get him back on the right track. You guys are supposed to be looking for someone who almost killed Ramsey Elliot, not busting my butt."

"All Detective Martinez is telling you is that we're going to be watching. Very closely. If there's another shooting, we're going to be looking for you." Her gaze was steady.

He snorted. "Typical cops. Come after me when I ain't even done nothing."

"Never said you did, Dirk." Cruz's tone was pleasant. "Just want to keep it that way."

Cantoney pushed himself away from the car and sauntered off without another word. Madeline got in the car and waited for Cruz to join her. When he did, she started the engine and headed back toward district headquarters. "I hope we didn't tip him off by warning him like that," she said.

"I doubt anything we said to him had much effect," Cruz replied. "He's smart. If he's planning a retaliation, and I'd bet my paycheck he is, he's already got the whole thing planned, especially how to avoid getting busted for it."

"He didn't seem too worried about us keeping an eye on him," Madeline mused. "That could mean a couple of different things. Either he isn't planning on making any move . . ."

"Which I don't believe for a minute," Cruz put in.

"Neither do I," she said. Someone with Cantoney's history of assaults for the most imaginary slights couldn't possibly be expected to ignore getting shot at. Especially if Cruz's hunch was correct and Cantoney himself had been the target. "It could also mean that he's already purchased a gun, and has figured out how to get away with retaliating. Or maybe someone else will actually be dealing on the gun, so it wouldn't matter how long we watched him."

"I'm betting he hasn't gotten his hands on it yet. He's bright, but he has a real short fuse. I don't think he could hold off using it for long. While he's dealing on the gun he's just biding his time. Because he has it all figured out who did the shooting and how he's going to hit back," Cruz said grimly. "And the bastard knows there's nothing we can do but wait."

"Wait for more bodies to show up?" Madeline grimaced. She didn't like the thought of that.

"Unless Ritter manages to convince Jacobs to offer that plea bargain to Stover, our options are limited at this point."

Madeline nodded, a slight frown creasing her forehead. She should be used to this, after all the years she'd been on the force, but these occasional brick walls that cropped up in most investigations always made her impatient. She had never been one to enjoy spinning her wheels while some perp was on the loose. She glanced at Martinez. If he shared her frustration, it didn't show. He was slouched in the seat with his head on the headrest, looking for all the world as if he could drop off to sleep at any second. How did he do that? she wondered. The man seemed to have no vertebrae. He was constantly leaning on whatever happened to be handy, and she'd yet to see him sit up straight.

A smile pulled at her lips. She'd been reminded of her posture so often as a child that by now it was second nature. Perhaps she was just jealous of his ability to be comfortable no matter the circumstances. But he was a little *too* comfortable, she decided. In an instant her hand went to the radio and she turned it up full blast. She grinned as his big body jackknifed straight up, his eyes flying open. He turned to fix her with an accusing look.

"Oops," she said without apology, turning the radio back down.

His face turned pained. "Please tell me, Madeline," he said politely, "that you're not one of those women who can't stand to see a man at rest."

"The last time I saw a man looking that restful they piled six feet of dirt on top of him."

He chuckled. "Brat."

"If you need that much rest, you must have a big weekend ahead of you," she noted with studied indifference.

Cruz's lips curved as he thought of the plans he had for the next two days. "The biggest," he agreed cryptically. He studied her as she brought the car to a halt and switched off the ignition. "Now why do I have the feeling that your little trick a minute ago was in response to our conversation at the Blue Pelican?"

"I don't get mad," she acknowledged sweetly, "I get even."

His smile widened. "I don't know about that. I seem to recall a hint of temper earlier."

Somehow she'd known that her reaction had been duly noted by him, and that he'd invoked it purposely. "Martinez, you can be a real pain, did anyone ever tell you that?" she asked as they got out and she handed him the keys.

He shook his head. "I don't think anyone else has put it quite that way," he denied cheerfully. He slanted her a look. "What do you have planned this weekend?"

She walked toward her own car. "Nothing."

"Got a date?"

Gosh, he was nosy. "Nope."

"Why not?"

She looked at him impatiently. He hadn't learned a thing from that little payback she'd staged. "Maybe you should mind your own business," she suggested.

"What fun would that be?" he asked logically.

She unlocked her car and got in, returning his careless wave as they parted. She didn't spend more than a few moments admiring the way his taut male buttocks moved as he sauntered toward the building.

As she drove away, Madeline reflected that it would be a lot easier to investigate Cruz Martinez if he wasn't so darn likable.

Chapter 5

Saturday morning found Madeline immersed in her normal routine, but in concession to the adjective Martinez had pinned on her yesterday, she varied the times of each chore from her regular schedule. *There, just let him call me regimented now!* she thought smugly, thinking of how she had worked out at the gym *before* tackling the cleaning. She'd stopped for her usual creme-filled doughnut on the way home from the gym, though. Just because he'd correctly guessed the precise way she ordered her life didn't mean that she needed to listen to his disparaging comments about what she ate. She enjoyed her unconventional eating habits and firmly believed that chocolate was the fifth food group. Since she was in excellent health and had weighed the same for the past ten years, she saw no reason to change those particular habits now.

When the doorbell rang she checked the peephole with her usual caution, even knowing that the visitor would be her neighbor, Ariel.

"Madeline, it's been ages since we talked. I tried to catch you one morning this week, but I just missed you. You were already in the elevator." She flew into the room with her usual hurry, talking nonstop. She went immediately to the kitchen area, pulled a stool up to the counter and sat with a flourish, arranging the folds of her robe neatly around her. When she finally looked at her friend, she blinked. "Aren't you going to the gym today?" she asked. "Why aren't you dressed for it yet?"

Madeline looked down at her jeans and T-shirt. "I've been already," she answered. "I've just finished cleaning."

Ariel widened her heavily made-up eyes in shock and held a hand to her heart theatrically. "You changed your schedule? *You?* Is the world coming to an end? This is it, isn't it, one of the great signs in the book of Revelations that my minister is always quoting. I'm going right home to repent."

Her neighbor rolled her eyes. "You're surprised," she said with masterful understatement. It was uncanny the way Ariel walked right in and cheerfully took up where Cruz had left off commenting about her life. It was also irritating. Was she really so predictable? Yes, she answered her own question. But it was a conscious choice, not a compulsion. No matter what the two busybodies in her life seemed to think.

"No, surprise doesn't cover it," Ariel responded. "Do you have any of those doughnuts—thanks," she said as Madeline pushed the bag over to her. Without waiting for an invitation she went to the cupboard with an ease that spoke of long familiarity and, taking out a mug, poured herself some coffee. Returning to her seat, she continued, "Surprise is when you win the lottery, or when your mother tells you that she's running off to Bermuda with a taxi driver to learn to samba. Surprise might even describe your feeling when you walk into the bedroom and find your date trying on your lingerie. But this..." She bit into the doughnut and closed her eyes in appreciation. "This surpasses surprise. Colossal, earthshaking, monumental, absolutely mind-blowing *shock* comes much closer to describing the wonder of Madeline Casey changing her schedule." She nodded effusively to negate her friend's grimace at her words. "Now the only question is, what would elicit such a change? Gotta be a man," she said wisely, taking another bite from the doughnut.

"You've been drinking too much of that herbal tea again," Madeline told her friend flatly. She loved Ariel dearly, but sometimes she felt like strangling her, and now was one of those times. She was really the only person Madeline knew in the condominium complex, even after living there three years. If Ariel had her sights set on getting to know someone, the person hadn't much choice in the matter. She could be rather forceful in her neighborliness. But Madeline had grown genuinely close to her despite, or perhaps because of, their differences. Ariel was as effusive as

Madeline was reserved. With her wacky style of dressing, makeup and far-out hairstyles, she was the antithesis of Madeline. She also had the unfortunate knack for acknowledging no boundaries of privacy regarding personal lives. As a result, Madeline had few secrets from her friend. Her usual aloofness couldn't withstand the assault of Ariel's good-natured prying. It was easier to give in and tell her what she wanted to know. But Madeline had no intention of humoring her latest flight of fancy. "Can't a person alter her day off a little on a whim?"

Ariel had finished the doughnut and was licking her fingers with delicate greed. "Other people can, you can't," she answered. "Something had to happen to shake you out of that rigid mold you keep yourself in. So what gives? Tell Auntie Ariel all about it," she cooed, resting her chin on folded hands and staring at Madeline with avid interest.

Madeline laughed in spite of herself. "How about if we skip talking about my life and you just go get one of your own?"

Ariel shook her head. "Been there, tried it. Failed and flopped, with a few disasters thrown in along the way. I'm resting from life, recharging before I march out there and get shot down again. That's why I depend on you to bring me a little vicarious excitement along the way. Very little, I might add," she finished drolly.

"I'm sorry to be such a disappointment to you," Madeline remarked dryly. She had no doubt that her dull life was of little real interest to her friend, who lived a varied one of her own. Most of the surprises she'd mentioned a few minutes ago had actually happened to her, according to some of the hugely entertaining stories she'd recounted to Madeline. Ariel collected experiences and husbands with equal fervor, both to be regretted at later dates. At last count she'd been married four times, and proclaimed to be taking a break from the search for number five as she tried out numerous prospects.

"C'mon, Madeline, don't make me beg. For once just come right out and tell me. Who is he?"

"What makes you think a man is involved?" Madeline asked, stalling for time. Although Cruz Martinez could be credited for her decision to vary her day a little, he was not playing the kind of role in her life that Ariel was imagining. Nor was he likely to. Madeline didn't go out with obscenely good-looking men, men she was professionally involved with, and especially not with men who might be criminals. But she had no intention of telling Ariel all of that. Ariel would be fascinated; she would think it was *exciting*, for heaven's sake.

Ariel waved her hand dismissively, as if the question didn't even deserve an answer. "All of a woman's important changes are brought on by a man. Men we love, men we hate, men we want to love, men we wished we hated . . . it's destined. One of the realities of life. So-o-o, tell me, dear," she said with a wicked smile, "about the man who caused these variations in your life today."

Madeline smiled to herself. She might not agree with all of her friend's ideas, or even with most of them, but she had to admit that listening to Ariel was amusing. "Sorry to disappoint you, but the only man in my life at the moment is my father, and it would take a high-priced analyst many years to help me figure out which of your four categories he would fit into."

"Oh." Ariel was instantly sympathetic. "You must have had another of your horrible dinners with him. How bad was it?"

"The usual." Now that some time had passed, Madeline could think about the evening with a little humor. "He was condescending, I was defensive. He got high-handed, I got angry. He began giving advice, I began shouting. . . ." She shrugged. "It kind of deteriorated from there."

"Parents." Ariel sighed. "They never stop trying to pull our strings."

"It's some kind of strange Pavlovian response. I hear his voice on the phone, and . . ." She snapped her fingers. "Instant immaturity." She waited a few moments and then added nonchalantly, "I did get assigned a new case this week."

Ariel pulled a face. Madeline didn't talk much about her job. Ariel had only the vaguest idea of what she did. But as far as she was concerned, Madeline spent entirely too much time thinking about work. In her opinion, what her friend needed most in her life was a few long nights in bed with a hot-blooded hunk to help her redefine her priorities. But try telling her that.

Ignoring Ariel's lack of enthusiasm at the change of subject, Madeline continued. "I've also acquired a partner for the duration of the investigation."

A flicker of interest passed over Ariel's face. "A man?"

"Uh-huh." Madeline went and poured her own cup of coffee and came back and sat down again. "His name is Cruz Martinez."

"Ooh, what a positively yummy name." Instantly intrigued, Ariel's eyes sparkled. "Tell me more. Does he look as good as he sounds?"

Madeline affected an indifferent shrug. "Depends on what you like. He's about fifty-five, fat, short and balding," she lied blandly. She felt a moment of glee picturing Cruz's reaction to her description of him. "He has seven children and loves fishing. He talks about it all the time." When she saw Ariel's face fall, she almost regretted misleading her. But not enough to tell her the truth and have to listen to the smug comments *that* would bring.

"Just your luck," Ariel muttered. "Sometimes I think you and I were born under the same planet. Although, of course, I know better, having done your astrology chart for you last month. Actually, when I examined your chart, I couldn't really find any reason for the dismal luck you've had in your love life. Mine, now, that's a different story. As soon as I did my chart and saw that Venus was squared with Saturn, I thought, well, of course! That explains..."

Madeline's thoughts drifted off as her friend chattered on. She'd heard it all before, at length. She didn't share Ariel's interest in astrology, any more than she believed in her philosophy of life. Actually, she felt the same about both. They were entertaining, but pointless. Events were caused by nature or people. She might not be able to control either one, but she certainly could control the effect they had on her, and she did so, stringently. Caution had always been her middle name, steady her pace and Look First her motto.

That hadn't saved her from the mistake she'd made with Dennis Belding, however. He'd known just how to get through all her defenses. He'd taken his time, soothed her fears with his calm, understanding manner. He'd seemed so harmless. And he'd almost brought her life crashing down around her ears. If she didn't despise him so much, she could almost admire the accuracy with which he'd read her character and the ease with which he'd transformed himself into the kind of man she would be drawn to and trust. Only for as long as he needed her, of course. Just as long as it took to have free access to her and, through her, to her father. There was no telling how many times he'd helped himself to the papers in her father's office before he was caught. Certainly he'd had plenty of opportunity. Her father had liked him, and invitations to the house had been frequent. Dennis had told her he wanted to be the bridge that mended the chasm between her father and herself.

That should have been the tip-off, she thought caustically. The only person he'd helped was himself. Once they had caught him, it hadn't been too difficult to find that Dennis had used the information he'd gleaned to sell to businesses and corporations interested in making bids on city projects. When he was found out, he'd tried to explain it all away. When it became obvious that neither his talking nor his engagement to the councilman's daughter was going to be enough to keep him from standing trial, he'd turned vicious. That was when he'd begun asserting that Madeline had helped him every step of the way. His lies had been public enough, believable enough, that she, too, had been forced to undergo an investigation. That had been the worst time of her life. She had longed for the opportunity to clear her name. And she'd eventually been cleared of any wrongdoing.

But even without her father's innuendos, she was very much aware that she'd been cleared more because of a lack of evidence of her criminal involvement than because they'd found proof of her innocence. The difference was subtle but devastating. She realized that, to some people, the doubt about her culpability would always remain. All she could do was live her life and do her job in as exemplary a fashion as possible, and ignore those who couldn't—or wouldn't—let go of their doubts about her.

"You're thinking of that creep you almost married, aren't you?" Ariel waved her hand dismissively at Madeline's look of surprise. "It isn't hard to tell. You get that same expression on your face every time you start thinking of him. When are you going to forgive yourself for being human?"

"It's being gullible, not being human, that I need to forgive myself for," Madeline corrected grimly. "Every time I think of the way I stood up for him . . . I refused to believe he could be guilty, do you know that? I wouldn't let myself examine the evidence that was stacked against him. I ignored all my police training, and focused solely on what I wanted to see." She snorted. "And he rewarded my loyalty by trying to make it look as if I'd known what he was up to all along. So much for true love."

"He was a real pig, all right," Ariel agreed. She'd met Madeline shortly after the whole thing had happened, but it had been years before Madeline had discussed it with her, even briefly. "Lots of men are, but not all of them. There are some good guys out there, and you'll find one, if you just let yourself look. You should adopt the cowgirl philosophy."

"And what, pray tell, might that be?"

Ariel's face was solemn, as if imparting a divine wisdom. "When a man bucks you off, you've just got to get up and get back on."

Madeline wadded up the empty doughnut bag in front of her and threw it at her friend. "You're awful," she declared, an unwilling smile tugging at her lips. "I've got a degenerate for a friend."

"Believe me, honey," Ariel said with an arch look, "a few nights in bed with a studly superhunk, and you'd have a whole new perspective on life."

"I'll have to take your word on that," Madeline drawled. She sought, and found, another channel of conversation. "Pardon me for asking, but what have you done to your hair now?" Ariel was a hairdresser, and quite a successful one. But her efforts on her own hair did nothing to inspire confidence in her abilities. She changed colors and styles regularly.

"Like it?" Ariel brushed back the long straight mass, recently dyed to an improbable shade of black. "I felt like a change. Are you ready to break down and give me a chance with yours?" The look of horror on Madeline's face was answer enough. "I haven't steered you wrong yet, have I?"

"You were right about cutting it shorter," Madeline admitted. "I like the new shoulder length you talked me into." Actually, bulldozed her into would be a more accurate description, but why quibble with success?

"And?" Ariel fluttered her eyelashes, waiting.

"And the perm was a good idea, too," her friend said grudgingly. "The curliness is easier to manage now, although that defies all laws of nature."

Ariel got up and swept her a bow. "Thank you, thank you. And now, with your sweet compliments ringing in my ears, I'd better go. I've got a date with a new man tonight, and it's going to take me all day to get ready. What do you have planned for the rest of the day, as if I couldn't guess?"

"I'm going to work," was the answer.

"What a surprise," Ariel muttered as she went to the door. When she reached it, she turned and pleaded, "Do me a favor? Do something, *anything* out of the ordinary this weekend, okay? You are in a rut so deep you may as well be in a coffin."

"Thank you, Ariel. Goodbye, Ariel," Madeline said, and closed the door before her life elicited any more comments from her friend. She leaned against it and closed her eyes for a moment. Sometimes dealing with her neighbor's high-energy voltage drained her. Then her eyes popped open and she strode over to the desk in the corner of her small living room. She unlocked it and pulled down the drop front. Little did her friend know she was going to follow her advice. Well, kind of. It was time to start digging up what personal information she could on Cruz Martinez.

She pulled out the file that Brewer had had prepared on him, picked up a pen and tapped it reflectively against her teeth. This investigation was going to have to be approached a little differently from most, since she couldn't talk to people who knew Martinez, at least not openly; she didn't want to do anything else that would tip him off that someone was interested in his actions. That would make her job a bit more difficult, but not impossible. She listed everything she knew about him so far. Then she took another sheet of paper and marked off three columns. Under one she listed every bit of information she had that could be construed to look suspicious. Under the middle one she listed personal things she'd learned about his life. The final column was for the things that pointed to his innocence. When she was finished she put the information she had just written in the proper columns. There wasn't much written on the sheet when she concluded.

But there was nothing at all written in the third column.

Monday morning when Madeline reached Cruz's desk he was already working. At least, she assumed that was what he was doing. He was slouched in his chair in front of his desk, shoulders propped against the backrest. She shook her head, wondering by what marvel of nature he managed not to slide onto the floor. She was tempted to give the chair a nudge, to see if he'd do just that.

He raised his head from his cup of coffee when he saw her, and pointed to another steaming cup on his desk.

"Thanks," she said gratefully, reaching for it and pulling another chair up to the desk. Sipping from it cautiously, she asked, "Did you talk to Ritter yet this morning?"

He grimaced. "Don't remind me."

Instant understanding dawned on her face. "That bad, huh?"

"Not only did he strike out with Jacobs, he was not too pleased with me for talking him into it in the first place. Jacobs must have given him a real earful for even suggesting that he offer Stover a plea bargain."

So Brewer had been right about that, Madeline thought with a sigh. "Well, we half expected this."

"We did," he agreed. "And who knows? If we could show proof that all these weapons came from the same supplier, and were assured that Stover could lead us to him, maybe Jacobs would reconsider. In the meantime, Stover isn't going anywhere for a while. I've heard he's having trouble coming up with bail."

"Well, that's the only bit of good news to come out of this so far," she said. "We'll just have to get to work and come up with the proof it will take to convince him. Meanwhile, why don't we use the computer to access the listings of any people who bought AK-47s legitimately."

"We already know that Stover didn't buy that gun legally—he doesn't have any papers for it," Cruz replied.

"It's possible that the gun could have been stolen from someone who did buy it legally."

"I still think we're going to find that one supplier is responsible for arming all these punks. Are you claiming the gangs have all coincidentally stolen the same kind of gun from different people in about the same time period?"

"No," she admitted. "And I agree with your hunch. But let's face it—we've only recovered one of the actual guns themselves. We need to cover all the bases."

He gave a mental sigh, not looking forward to the tedious task of poring over lists of gun serial numbers, yet knowing the job had to be done. An idea struck him then, and he looked at her speculatively. Perhaps there would be an advantage to working with a partner on this. If he could convince her to take care of this aspect, he could follow a lead of his own.

"More coffee, Madeline?" he asked solicitously.

"No, thanks, I'm fine."

"I could warm yours up for you." The polite denial died on her lips when she looked up and correctly interpreted the look on his face.

"Oh, no, you don't, Martinez," she said flatly.

His eyebrows climbed. "What?"

"You're not going to con me into doing the records check by myself. You'll be right by my side the whole time."

"Now, Madeline." His tone was reasonable. "Why should both of us suffer through a boring job like that? If you took care of it, then I could be pursuing other possibilities. We could accomplish two things at once. I'd offer to do it myself," he added, "but sitting inside here poring over paperwork all day gets me hyper."

That was a laugh. She flicked a studied glance over his casual pose. "Yeah, you strike me as the restless type, all right. What's this hot lead you want to follow, anyway?"

"I know some people who aren't above making money in, shall we say, unconventional ways. Some of them have been known to deal in guns, although nothing on this scale. But if pressed, one might be persuaded to give us a tip about what he's heard on the streets."

Madeline nodded. "Sounds like a good place to start, and I think you're right. We should follow both leads."

"All right!" A delighted grin broke over his face. She let him get halfway out of his chair before she added, "We can do the firearms checks in the mornings, and hit the streets in the afternoons."

He poised in midair for a split second before dropping back into his seat.

"Can't change your mind, huh?" His tone held resignation.

"No way." Not only was she not about to let him shove off the most tedious work on her, she had another motive for insisting they stay together. In order to keep track of him, she had to stick close to him. Otherwise she would have no way of knowing if he actually had done what he reported, saw the people he claimed. No, she wouldn't be able to let Cruz Martinez out of her sight during their working hours. Not if she was going to complete her own investigation on him. "We're partners. We'll investigate as partners."

He sighed, already dreading the task ahead. "Well, you can't blame a guy for trying."

They spent the rest of the morning bringing up files on the computer and examining them. Gun merchants were required to take down a great deal of information about their customers, so that record checks could be done. Soon they had a list of names of people who had purchased an AK-47 legitimately.

When they got the printout of the compiled list, Madeline said, "Now why don't we compare the serial number of Stover's gun to the numbers on this page and—"

"Uh-uh," Cruz said. "Look at the clock. It's almost lunchtime. There's no use starting on that. Time to quit, go to lunch and then onto the streets."

Madeline felt a moment's frustration. She hated leaving a job before seeing it through to the end. If she'd been working alone she would have chosen to complete this task before tackling a different lead. But she wasn't working alone. Cruz had already risen, and she slowly got to her feet, too. "All right," she said reluctantly. "But since we're taking lunch on my time, I'm picking where we eat."

His look was pained. "You drive a hard bargain, Casey."

Following him back to his desk, she was retrieving her purse when she heard a voice speak behind her.

"Hey, buddy, surprised to see you here. Haven't seen you around in almost a week."

She turned curiously to see who was addressing Cruz.

"Yeah, we've been working on that case I told you about. I wouldn't be here this morning, either, but Madeline had a hunch, and we *compromised.*" His tone was pained.

The man addressing her partner was about her own height, and he projected a commanding presence. Wavy hair the color of antiqued brass was cut around his ears and left long enough in back to brush his collar. His face lacked the movie-star good looks of Cruz's, but this man was attractive in his own right. The angles of his face were compelling, the chin uncompromising, the chiseled mouth undeniably sensual. When she looked at his eyes she caught her breath. His pale green gaze was pinned on her, despite the fact that he was talking to Cruz. And its shrewd, assessing look seemed to sum her up in the space of a second, and find her wanting.

"Madeline, this is Connor McLain. We were partners long before he became Lieutenant Detective McLain," he added with exaggerated emphasis. "Connor, Detective Sergeant Madeline Casey."

"How long were you and Cruz partners?" she asked Connor.

"Long enough to discover what he thinks of compromising," he replied soberly.

"He wasn't too bad," Madeline said judiciously, throwing Cruz a sidelong glance. "He only sulked *half* the morning."

Connor cocked a brow at this information. "Is that right? He's matured, then."

"Gee, thanks, *amigo,*" Cruz interrupted, slapping him on the shoulder. "Remind me to tell Michele about the time we went down to the wharf and found that bar, where you—"

"On second thought, he was the best damn partner I ever had and you're lucky to have him," Connor said quickly. With a warning look at Cruz, he added, "Michele ordered me to invite you to dinner this week, but you're only coming if you can keep your mouth shut.''

Cruz's mouth quirked. "I'll give her a call. We were just on our way out for lunch, and it's Madeline's turn to pick where we go, so I'll catch you later. I'll need to take a little extra time to deal with the heartburn.'' They walked away.

"Very funny.'' She remembered how he'd almost kissed her the last time she'd chosen where to eat, and she wiped away the moisture the memory brought to her palms. She realized suddenly that it had been much easier to keep Cruz at a distance this morning. They had spoken strictly about work. But it was not as easy to maintain that distance when they were on the street and she pondered that. She'd never been a particularly easy person to get to know. Ariel had been the only other person who'd managed to get close to her, despite the obstacles in the way, and that was only because Ariel had crashed right through them. Cruz, however, was managing a similar feat with much more grace and charm, and the realization frightened her. She had to be on a friendly basis with him in order to get close enough to prove or disprove his criminal involvement. But she was uncomfortable with opening herself up in return. "How long have you known Lieutenant McLain?'' she asked as they left the building and walked toward the car.

"Since he was rookie McLain,'' he answered. "We're good friends. He's a great guy.''

She was a little surprised at the revelation, although she'd picked up on the camaraderie between the two. They didn't seem to have much in common, at least at first glance. Displaying the direct opposite of Cruz's easy manner and lighthearted banter, McLain had seemed very tough and unyielding. On second thought, she'd had occasion to see Cruz turn into someone very tough indeed when he'd been confronted by Baker last week, so maybe he and McLain had more in common than she'd first believed.

She drove them to Louie's, a place noted for its hamburgers. It was crowded, and they sat on stools at the tiny counter.

After they'd placed their orders, Cruz looked around with a jaundiced eye. "I'll bet you know the whereabouts of every greasy spoon in the city.''

"This isn't a greasy spoon,'' she objected. "And out of deference to your lack of table manners, I brought you to a place that serves the food on plates. What more do you want?''

"How about an antidote for ptomaine poisoning?'' he suggested.

She ignored that. He obviously lacked an adventurous spirit when it came to dining, but by the time this case was over, she would have broadened his culinary habits extensively.

By the time this case was over. The words came back to echo in her mind with nagging insistence. What else would she have changed for him by that time? A change of address, perhaps, if he landed in jail? She studied the napkin on the table in front of her. She'd spent most of her free time over the weekend looking up information on him. She'd gone to I.A. headquarters to use the computers there. She now knew his address and what kind of car he drove, and the fact that he'd received two speeding tickets in the past three years. It was the information on his car that returned the slightly sick feeling to her stomach now. Checking through the records for licenses on motor vehicles, she had found that he was the owner of a new model sports car, one that listed for more than his entire year's salary.

When she'd checked his credit history she'd had another unpleasant surprise. He had only one outstanding loan, for some property listed at his address. He was obviously buying his home. So how, she wondered for the hundredth time, did someone who made the kind of money she did afford to buy an expensive toy for a car and pay cash for it?

The question had plagued her for the rest of the weekend. From what he'd told her about his family, she could discount the possibility that he'd received an inheritance. It sounded as though he and his siblings had been raised solely on the hard work of their parents.

She surreptitiously studied the man seated across from her. She was having a hard time imagining this man as a criminal. Right now he was trying to get comfortable on his stool. Finally he turned to the side to face her, resting his torso against the counter and leaning his head on his folded elbow. Thinking of how she'd spent her weekend made it difficult to meet his eyes, but she forced herself to do so.

"Did you get to the family dinner yesterday?" she asked with studied disinterest.

"Sure did. What did you do?"

Madeline shrugged. "Not much."

"Well, believe it or not, I spent much of the weekend on my knees."

She raised an eyebrow. "Praying or begging?"

He laughed. "You have a wicked way of thinking, do you know that? I like that in a woman. Can't you think of anything else I might have been doing? C'mon, Madeline, use your imagination."

She did, and the images that floated through her mind gave her hot flashes. He was provocative just by *being,* damn him, and he knew it, too. "I can't imagine," she said indifferently, and he laughed again.

"I'll have you know I was doing good deeds most of Saturday morning," he informed her. "One of the tenants in the building where I live was moving out, so I helped him carry his things."

"That wouldn't have had you on your knees," she blurted without thinking.

He grinned, amused that he'd caught her interest, despite her efforts to act otherwise. "No, that wouldn't, would it?"

Their orders were placed in front of them, and he looked up from his grilled chicken breast to see her biting into a thick cheeseburger with huge enjoyment. "You're a heart attack waiting to happen, lady," he observed. And in more ways than one. When she'd shown up at work today wearing yet another jacket over tailored trousers, he'd been tempted to ask if she owned one of those in every color of the rainbow. But before eating, she'd slipped out of the cream-colored jacket and he was treated to the picture of her in a turquoise silk tank top, and the sight was impairing his ability to swallow.

Her arms were shapely and incredibly white. So was the skin above the rounded neckline of the top. When she put her sandwich down and reached for her glass, he was treated to the slightest hint of cleavage. He picked up his knife and fork and began sawing at his lunch with methodical precision. He needed something, anything, to take his mind off a mental picture of his own hand laid upon her chest. The contrast of his bronzed skin against her far fairer skin would be incredibly arousing. As a matter of fact, just imagining it was incredibly arousing, and he shifted uncomfortably on the stool. By sheer willpower he tried to push the flick of visual imagery from his mind and focus on eating. But somehow the simple process of chewing and swallowing wasn't enough to keep teasing questions of what she looked like beneath that silky top from dancing across his mind. And when he heard her next words, sounding as if she were reading his every libidinous thought, he froze in the act of lifting the fork to his mouth.

"Are you sure I can't tempt you?"

Chapter 6

Cruz's eyes went slowly, disbelievingly to hers. "What?" he croaked.

"Go ahead. Live dangerously," she urged.

It seemed an eternity before his fantasy-filled brain correctly interpreted her meaning, and noticed the cheeseburger she was holding out to him. He let out a breath he hadn't known he was holding. "I think you're the one living dangerously." More dangerously than she knew, he thought grimly, because her words, on the heels of his very impure thoughts, were enough to incite a saint. Which he definitely wasn't. "And I think it's safe to say that you could tempt me very easily," he added with blatant meaning. "But not with that cheeseburger."

Madeline's eyes, full of fun a moment ago, grew uncertain. She lowered the sandwich and reached for her glass of milk, her hand a little unsteady. What had caused such a drastic change in his mood? she wondered. One minute he was lecturing her about her eating habits and the next he was talking as if... well, as if food were the last thing on his mind. But surely he hadn't meant his words to sound that way. Had he?

"When they haul you into the operating room to unclog your arteries, remind me to say 'I told you so.'" He changed the subject purposely. The last thing he needed was to be sidetracked by his awareness of her. He was no longer certain he could keep that awareness out of their partnership, but it would surely help if he could keep his overactive imagination under control. He chewed reflectively. He'd never before had such a problem. He was a master at separating the different areas of his life into neat compartments and never letting them mix. No woman had been allowed to creep into his thoughts when he was working, and that made Madeline even more troublesome. It was impossible not to think of her when he was working by her side eight hours a day. But he was going to have to be sure that his thoughts of her pertained only to the case. A week ago he would have been positive that such a thing would be easy. Now he was not so certain.

He finished eating before she did, and she knew it was because of the difficulty she was having swallowing. She was thankful when the meal was over because, although he seemed to have no problem reverting back to his usual carefree manner, it was hard for her to forget his words. But she must have mistaken his meaning. He didn't seem bothered at all now, just slightly impatient as he waited for her to finish.

Madeline rose. Cruz followed, and his gaze went to her plate. The lettuce and tomato that she'd taken off her sandwich were piled neatly in a corner of the otherwise empty dish.

"Don't tell me," he drawled. "You don't eat red things, either."

"I'm sure you can find more interesting things to worry about than what I eat," she said. She would copy his indifferent manner if it killed her. But she was startled when, at the door, he turned to her and took her jacket out of her hands.

"Put this on," he ordered brusquely. "It's a little chilly outside."

She allowed him to help her with the jacket and walked out the door, puzzling over his abrupt mood changes.

Madeline drove for the rest of the afternoon, at Cruz's direction. Three times he ordered her to stop the car and they got out. Each time they talked to men who were unenthusiastic about their presence there. All of them professed to have reformed, swearing that they were currently living saintly lives. None admitted to having any information that would help the investigation.

The next few days were spent in much the same way. After several mornings of sifting through the pages of serial numbers, they admitted defeat. No match for the number of Stover's gun could be found. Nor were they having any better luck following up Cruz's idea in the afternoons. It seemed as if the case were leading them to one dead end after another, and that made suspicion bloom in Madeline's mind.

Was Cruz doing this purposely? The people they'd talked to were small-time, and none of them admitted to hearing of any AK-47s being sold on the streets. She had to wonder if this was just a wild-goose chase Cruz was leading her on; something that wasted a lot of time and energy, but brought them no closer to the supplier. It was what she would do if she was involved in the deal—come up with ideas that led the investigation farther away from her.

Her suspicions were strong enough that on two nights she left headquarters, and drove directly to the Internal Affairs building. She spent hours poring over her computer screen, bringing up the names of people in the area who'd been convicted for selling guns illegally. She eliminated those whose addresses were no longer in the Philadelphia area, and those still in jail. When she'd finished, she had a list of several names. Madeline was bemused to note that many of the names matched those of the people Cruz had found for them to talk to. But when she crossed them off the list there were still a few names she hadn't heard Cruz mention.

She studied the information she could find on each of the people on the list, and finally decided that their best bet would be to check on one Jose Valdez. He had twelve arrests and nine convictions, all on charges ranging from illegal sales to possession of firearms. She decided to wait and see if Cruz would mention him.

Because if he didn't, she would.

By midweek their search had yielded no results. Madeline frowned slightly as they pulled away from the last man they'd talked to. The similarity was a red flag to her. Things didn't stay that quiet on the streets. There were always people on the fringes, uninvolved but aware of everything that occurred. It was impossible for everyone they talked to to be ignorant of the gun sales. If gang members could get their hands on the weapons, the word had to be out there about how to get them.

Which left a couple of possibilities. Either their hunch was wrong, and no one dealer was supplying the punks with those guns, or the supplier was someone so powerful that the thought of crossing him had scared everyone into keeping quiet.

She immediately discounted the first possibility. She didn't believe in coincidence. Those gangs hadn't all chosen the exact same kind of weapon by chance. So that left the second choice. An interesting idea, but it didn't help pinpoint the supplier's identity. There were numerous underworld toughs whose names alone would be enough to strike terror on the street. It could be any one of them. Or none of them.

It could even be... Her eyes slid to the man next to her. It was time, she thought, for her to change the course of this investigation. Cruz obviously wasn't going to mention finding Valdez. Either he didn't know of the man or he didn't want her talking to him. So she would mention him, and closely observe Cruz's reaction.

But before she could carry out that plan, he spoke. "Maybe we've been going about this all wrong."

For a moment she wondered if he'd read her mind. "How do you mean?" she asked cautiously.

His face was pensive. "Maybe we've been approaching this too directly. If the supplier is not an unknown on the street, he could be someone no one is willing to tangle with."

His thoughts so closely paralleled her own that Madeline was shocked. Finally she said, "You mean it could be someone people fear too much to cross?"

"Exactly. Let's change our tactics. We're going to have to be a bit more discreet in our inquiries. If our hunch is right, no one is going to talk to us unless they feel safe. We have to arrange to get the information from someone who won't be afraid to risk his safety."

"Do you have anyone in mind?"

"Maybe. I know of a snitch, Tommy Grady, who I've used occasionally. I think it's time to check in with him."

That name hadn't appeared on the computer screen. "Has he been involved in arms sales before?" she asked.

"Nothing that big. Although he'll go to great lengths to get enough money for a bottle, he's mostly small-time. Been convicted a couple of times for breaking and entering." He looked across the seat at her. "Want to go for it?"

"Sure," she agreed, and settled back as he began to drive. She'd wait a little longer.

Cruz drove for several minutes before pulling over at a newspaper stand outside a hotel that had seen better days. He got out of the car, and she followed. She watched as he selected a paper and paid the vendor for it. As the money exchanged hands, she heard him murmur to the vendor, "Tell Tommy that Martinez is looking for him."

The man gave no indication that he'd heard the words, and they got back in the car and drove off. "How do you know he'll get the word to the snitch?" Madeline demanded.

"Turn around."

She stared at him for a moment, then obeyed. She saw a youngster of about eight wearing ragged jeans and no shirt running down the sidewalk, away from the newspaper stand. She turned back. Cruz was watching in the rearview mirror. "The kid will get Tommy. All we have to do is wait for a while and give him enough time to find us."

After driving aimlessly for over an hour, Cruz stopped at a convenience store and bought two ice-cream cones. He left the car in the parking lot and steered Madeline across the street, to a small, unkempt-looking park. It was little more than a square of patchy grass with a few broken benches scattered around it. Several children were playing in the area. There was no playground or equipment, but she noticed a game of stickball and another of soccer going on.

They walked in a seemingly desultory fashion, and then stopped at a huge oak tree. Cruz sat beneath it, propping himself against its trunk. "You may as well sit down," he invited. "I don't know how long Tommy will be."

Madeline sat next to him, after first inspecting the area for insects. "How do you even know he'll come?" she asked curiously.

"He always does," he answered, his eyes squinting as he looked across the park into the bright sunlight. "He'll do anything for money."

"If he's that motivated to get paid, you can't be sure that the information he gives you will be accurate," she observed.

"Yes, I can." He mocked her words. "Because he gets most of the money after I check out the information he gives me. Give me a little credit, Madeline. I've been around long enough to know how to work a snitch."

She subsided and they sat in silence for a while. The breeze was cool beneath the shade, but pleasantly so. She finished her ice-cream cone and stifled a yawn. If Tommy didn't show soon, she was afraid she'd fall asleep. Cruz looked as if he had already. His head was leaning back against the tree, and his chest was rising and falling evenly. She didn't say anything about it, though. She'd learned that he took every available opportunity to rest, but his peacefulness was a sham. He always stayed very much aware of what was happening around him.

When a voice spoke from the other side of the tree, it was she, not Cruz, who started violently. Cruz merely opened his eyes and said, "Hi, Tommy."

"Hey, Martinez, what you got for me, huh?"

Madeline studied the man who'd just moved in front of her. It was easy to see that the ravages of alcohol had taken their toll on him. He had a broad face, but it was puffy, and his nose, which looked as though it had been broken more than once, was crisscrossed with a tiny network of red veins. There were pouches under his eyes, and his hands shook as he attempted to take out a cigarette and light it. He squinted at the two of them through the smoke.

"How've you been?" Cruz's tone was friendly as he got to his feet. Madeline followed suit.

"Fine, great, I really need some money, though, you know? I've got some things to take care of."

Cruz was sure that Tommy most wanted to take care of his next drink, but he pressed a folded-up bill into his hand.

The man pocketed it in one sure motion, and Madeline blinked. As shaky as his hands had seemed a moment ago, the bill had disappeared with a surprisingly smooth movement.

"That ain't enough," the man mumbled, looking furtively to the right and left of them. "You know that ain't enough."

"You get the rest of it if you can tell me something that helps me out, just like always."

"It ain't enough for what you want to know, though," the man argued. "A guy could get killed telling you what you want to know."

Cruz's gaze narrowed. "And you're certain you know what information I'm looking for?"

"Sure I do," Tommy bragged. He took short, quick draws on his cigarette. "I heard you been asking around about who's been putting those fancy assault guns on the streets. Heard no one's been talking, either."

"You hear a lot," Madeline observed.

"Enough to tell you who you should be after," he affirmed. His eyes continually darted from side to side. He ground his cigarette out beneath his heel and lit another one. "Enough to know I'd be crazy to be seen talking to you for less than a thousand bucks."

Madeline's eyes widened, but Cruz just laughed. "Get real, Tommy. You know that isn't going to happen. You'll get the same as always."

The man wheedled, "C'mon, Martinez, this name you want, it's the real thing. I'm going to have to lay low for a while, just to stay safe. What if someone sees us talking? Did you ever wonder why no one else on the street would say a word? They ain't crazy. Me, I'm crazy enough to help you out, but you gotta make it worth my while."

Craziness didn't enter into it, Cruz knew. Desperation was more like it. Tommy would sell his grandmother for the sake of a drink. "We'll see," he said skeptically. He handed the man a couple more bills, and they vanished with the same speed as the first. "You aren't getting any more until after I check out what you tell me. So what do you have?"

Tommy looked around nervously once more. He leaned closer and lowered his voice, although there was no one within two hundred yards of them. "You talked to a lot of people. Have you talked to Jose Valdez yet?"

Cruz pulled out his notebook and wrote the name down. "Who is he?"

"He served time in prison nine different times, all on firearm charges," Madeline answered. "He's been out for eight months."

Both men looked at her in surprise. Cruz didn't look pleased at her knowledge. He shot her a hard look before turning his gaze back to Tommy. "Where can we find him?"

Tommy mentioned a few places the man might be found, adding, "I don't know where he lives or nothing."

"Don't worry," Cruz answered dryly, "I'm sure Detective Casey can help me out with that."

"Remember, you owe me, Martinez." The second cigarette was snuffed out under Tommy's well-worn sneaker.

"We'll see."

Without further words Tommy backed away, and then melted into the trees.

Cruz and Madeline walked through the park toward their car, which was parked across the street. "Would you mind telling me how you knew about Valdez?" he asked.

She recounted her research, choosing her words carefully to avoid telling him what had motivated her to look up the names in the first place.

"When were you going to tell me about this?" he asked tersely, and she looked at him warily. He seemed angry at this latest bit of news. His long legs were crossing the street in huge strides. She wondered if it was because she hadn't told him about the work she'd done on her own or if it stemmed from another, more ominous reason.

"Eventually." She finally answered his terse question. "Once you were out of ideas of your own."

They had reached the car by now and he stopped, not getting in. "Look, Madeline, we're *partners*. You understand what that word means, don't you? It means we share information. You were the one who insisted we work together at all times, and I agreed to that."

"It's no big deal." She met his gaze squarely. "I had a hunch, so I put together a list of released felons who'd served time for firearm charges." She fished in her purse, pulled the list out and handed it to him. His eyes scanned the sheet quickly, saw the names that were already crossed out and grunted before handing it back to her. "If you'd shown this to me earlier you could have saved the department some money."

She shrugged and replaced the paper in her purse. "Not necessarily. Valdez was the one I would have wanted to talk to first, but at least Tommy corroborated that he's a suspect." She got in the car.

Cruz was silent as he pulled out of the parking lot. He still wore a slight frown on his face. She wished she knew what was bothering him. He didn't speak again until he asked for Valdez's address. She gave it to him without consulting the sheet in her purse, and that seemed to annoy him even more. "Do you have microchips for brains?" he asked. "How the hell do you remember all that?"

She shrugged. She'd long ago found it was futile to question the ability she had. She just accepted it. "It's a gift," she said simply.

"Kids in your high school must have hated having you in their classes. You had to really throw off the curve at test time."

As they drove deeper into the city, the surroundings grew more deteriorated. She was not surprised that Valdez's address was going to be found in one of the worst slums in the city. "Did you hate people like that when you were in high school?"

"Mostly I spent my time trying to set up study dates with girls like you."

"Somehow I doubt that," she said dryly. Dates of any kind had been scarce when she was a teenager. Her natural reserve had made her hard to get to know. And the fact that she had towered over most of the boys in her class hadn't increased her social life, either. She was sure that any dates Cruz Martinez had set up probably had had very little to do with studying, unless he'd taken classes in anatomy.

"What's the matter, didn't you ever have study dates?" he asked. "You know, where you pretended to go to the library to study, and then spent the evening making out in the stacks?"

"You obviously had a very depraved adolescence," she observed.

"Not really," he denied. "I was just naturally curious. I was always interested in learning something new."

She could tell by his tone that his love of learning had less to do with books than with getting a girl behind them. Apparently some things never changed.

He pulled the car over to park next to a large, dark building. Half-naked children played on the front porch, and next to the building a man huddled, rocking back and forth mumbling to himself, oblivious to the activity around him.

They walked up the steps and the children fell silent, staring at them with wary eyes. Once they entered the building they could hear the voices behind them resume. Cruz knocked on the door immediately inside the building, and a voice called out, "Who's there?"

They exchanged a look and without words decided that for now, they wouldn't identify themselves. "I'm looking for Jose Valdez," Madeline answered.

"Room 457," the voice answered. The door never opened. They turned and climbed the open wooden staircase.

"I can't believe this building can pass fire codes," Madeline said. Plaster was missing in numerous places in the wall, and wires showed through among the laths. The hallways were littered and had a sour smell.

"There are probably few in this neighborhood that could," Cruz answered.

They reached the fourth floor and knocked at room 457. There was no answer. They both waited, listening for sounds of movement, but the room was silent. Finally they turned away.

When they were on the street again Madeline asked, "So next we try the places Tommy named where Valdez hangs out, right?"

Cruz hesitated. "Not today," he said, after a moment. "It's getting late and I have other plans tonight."

Madeline rolled her eyes, immediately drawing her own conclusion about what those plans entailed. "You can break your date, Martinez. Whoever she is, she'll recover."

He neither confirmed nor denied her assumption. "I can't put this off. But I promise we can work as late as you want tomorrow." He shot her a warning glance. "I wouldn't advise you to check out any of the places on your own tonight. It wouldn't be safe, even for a cop, to be in any of those areas alone."

"I don't need you to watch over me," she assured him.

"I mean it, Madeline." His voice was implacable. "I'd better not find that you went out by yourself. We're in this together. You insisted on that, and you're going to have to live with your own rules."

She couldn't help wondering at his real reason for issuing the warning. Was it fear for her safety, or did he merely want to be at her side when they found Valdez, to ensure that the man said nothing that would incriminate him?

She left him at the parking lot after he made her promise she'd wait until tomorrow to continue the search for Valdez. He certainly was single-minded. He badgered her until she agreed, and then fixed her with a long look and said, "I'm going to hold you to that."

Madeline grimaced at his departing figure as she got into her own car. Maybe he wasn't afraid of what she would find out, after all. Perhaps he was simply an old-fashioned male chauvinist, one of the oinking variety. She shrugged mentally. It wasn't going to hurt to wait until the morning, but she was curious as to what was so important that he couldn't cancel it for tonight.

An idea suddenly struck her. She watched as he got into his own car and began leaving the lot. He certainly seemed in a hurry tonight. The royal blue low-slung sports car turned into the street. She gave him a few moments and followed slowly. She made sure that she maintained a four-car distance between them, in case he happened to glance in his rearview mirror.

It was almost a miracle during the rush-hour traffic, but Madeline was able to keep him in sight. Twenty minutes later he double-parked in front of a building, got out of the car and dashed inside. Madeline cruised by and went down to the corner to read the street sign. Great, she thought with a sigh. She'd just managed to successfully tail him to his home. She eyed his car again speculatively. He probably was leaving again shortly, unless he was going to push his luck with a parking ticket. She decided to stick around a bit longer. She pulled in to a nearby alley.

Her vigil was rewarded. A half hour later Cruz came out the door. He'd changed into dark pants and a green shirt. He checked his watch as he bounded down the steps and got back into his car. Madeline waited until it had roared away to start her own engine and take up the tail again. They drove for more than half an hour. Long enough for her to reflect that this was the first time she'd seen him in anything resembling dress clothes, and for her to spend time wondering what had warranted such a change. She was certainly going to feel silly if she followed him all this time, only to find that he was hurrying to a hot date. She refused to consider that the discovery would elicit any other emotion.

Madeline recognized the area he was leading her into. There were many business buildings lining the streets, as well as occasional condominiums and several restaurants. She was dismayed when, a moment later, he ran a yellow light. The next second it turned red.

She stared at the line of cars between her and the corner, and slapped both palms on the steering wheel in disgust. The moments until the light turned green again seemed an eternity. She headed in the direction he'd gone, but it was quickly apparent that she'd lost him. Damn, damn, damn, she thought in chagrin. She hated to get this close, just to fail. Not that she had any real idea of how close she'd gotten. There was no way of knowing if Cruz was somewhere in the neighborhood, or if he would be driving for another half hour. Just as there was no way to tell now what his plans for the night entailed.

More than likely he had nothing more devious lined up for the evening than a leisurely dinner with a beautiful woman. If that was the case Madeline was almost glad she hadn't managed to follow him. But if Cruz had been going to meet with someone involved in the guns, she'd just missed a valuable opportunity, indeed.

Thoughts morose, she continued backtracking until she neared the neighborhood where Cruz lived. Without even really planning it, she drove to his street and parked down the block. Perhaps something could be salvaged from this evening, after all. He'd said a tenant had moved out of his building. If she pretended to be interested in the vacant apartment, maybe she would be able to learn something from the landlord. It was worth a try, anyway.

She walked up the block and entered the building. A woman was in the hallway sweeping, her back to Madeline.

"Excuse me, could you tell me where I might find the landlord?"

The woman turned around. She was in her late fifties, Madeline estimated, and at least forty pounds overweight. Her hair was a garish shade of blond and she wore a housecoat with huge roses on it. Ariel should meet this woman, Madeline thought with amusement. They'd probably be soul mates.

"You found her, honey. What can I do you for?" the woman said with a smile.

"A friend of mine told me that this building might have an apartment for rent. I was wondering if I could look at it."

"Are you the one I talked to on the phone today?" the woman asked.

Madeline blinked. "I . . . no, I didn't call earlier. You haven't rented it already, have you?"

The woman shook her head. "No, I guess not. Talked to someone who seemed mighty interested on the phone. She was supposed to come see it. But if you ain't her, well, I guess nothing'd be hurt to take you through it. You're here first, after all."

A sigh escaped Madeline and she smiled. "Great."

The woman took a large bunch of keys from one of the oversize pockets on the front of her dress. "We'll have to take the stairs—the elevator isn't working. Should be running again soon, though. The owner is real good about fixing stuff like that."

Madeline looked around interestedly as they climbed. The building was old, but had obviously been kept up. The ceilings were extremely high, and in good condition. The paint in the hallways looked fresh and everything seemed clean.

"There are four apartments on each floor, and each has two bedrooms, a kitchen and bathroom, plus a living room. All are unfurnished. No pets allowed, and the rent is due on the first of each month." The woman named a price that was less than what Madeline was paying for her own place, and she wondered if she'd wasted her time by coming here. Cruz might be saving money by buying such an apartment. That would help explain how he'd managed to save enough to buy that fancy car of his.

"Here we are." The woman unlocked a door on the fifth floor and threw it open. She allowed Madeline to enter and then followed her in, keeping up a running litany of the apartment's advantages. Madeline looked around with genuine interest. Although the carpet was somewhat shabby, there was a certain charm in the old-fashioned woodwork and large windows.

"Well, what do you think?" the woman asked after they had looked in all the rooms and closets.

"It's nice," Madeline answered truthfully.

The woman beamed. "Most people like it here. Our tenants stay with us for a while. We don't get many vacancies."

They stepped back into the hallway and the woman locked the door carefully.

"Are all the apartments in the building similar to this one?" Madeline asked as they began to walk down the stairs.

"Yep. Well, all but one," the woman corrected herself. "About six months ago the owner sold the top floor to one tenant, and he's remodeled it into one large apartment for himself." She glanced slyly at Madeline. "He's another reason this building might appeal to you. You'd probably run into him. And he's definitely worth running into. He's what you young women call a real hunk."

"Sounds interesting," Madeline forced herself to say. "What's he do?"

"Oh, he's a cop, a detective. Now that's kind of romantic, ain't it? And he's a real nice guy, too. If you take the apartment I'll introduce the two of you. I'm always after Cruz—that's his name," she added in an aside, "to meet some nice young thing and settle down. Life's too short, I tell him...."

Madeline listened with only one ear as the woman rattled on. Her mind was racing. How much would it cost to buy an entire floor of such a building? And then to renovate it? She couldn't even guess, but she knew it would be expensive. She was guessing that it would cost substantially more than the amount of the loan Cruz had taken out for the property. She would have to investigate the matter further when the courthouse opened in the morning.

After extricating herself from the landlady, Madeline drove back to the Internal Affairs headquarters and typed up a report detailing the week's investigation results. The hour was late enough that she could be assured of avoiding Brewer, and she was fiercely glad. She wasn't ready to put up with one of his grillings. She hesitated a moment, her fingers poised over the keys. The sports car and the apartment meant nothing by themselves, but taken together, they pointed to an obvious conclusion. Slowly she recommenced typing.

She was going to have to report the fact that Cruz Martinez seemed to have a second source of income.

* * *

The next morning Madeline left a phone message for Cruz that she would be late. Then she drove to the courthouse as soon as it opened. Buyers of property were required to file numerous legal papers, most of which were available for public scrutiny. She requested the necessary information and waited impatiently until the woman placed the file in front of her. Flipping it open, she scanned it briefly, until she found the item she sought. Even prepared as she was, her eyes widened when she read the amount Cruz had paid for his property. It wasn't a fortune, but for someone in their profession it might as well be. The amount he'd borrowed had been for less than half of this figure. She wondered if he'd had savings to pay for the rest.

She drove to the Southwest District headquarters then to meet Cruz. She noticed detachedly that her hands were trembling on the steering wheel. So she had confirmed that Cruz was living above the means of a detective. She didn't know why that should affect her so strongly. This was not the first such investigation she'd conducted. None had ever caused her to lose her calm like this.

But this was the first time she'd had to face the man she was investigating day after day, work by his side, get to know him personally. And it was also the first time she'd cared what kind of results the investigation yielded.

And she did care, she admitted to herself. On some level she responded to Cruz, there was no denying it. Especially with the physical reaction she was experiencing right now. She had to get that reaction under control before she saw him again. She was going to need every bit of cool she could muster to face him in a few minutes without the faintest hint of her recently acquired knowledge showing, either in her face or actions.

She strode into the headquarters and walked resolutely to his desk. He looked up at her arrival, his lean, handsome face a mask of impatience.

"About time," he grunted. "Where have you been, anyway?"

"I had something I had to take care of," she said shortly.

His eyes narrowed. "You weren't doing some more research on your own, were you? You promised me, Madeline, and I thought I could trust you."

I thought I could trust you.

His words slammed into her with the force of a fist. For a moment, just for a split second, all her rehearsed equanimity fled, to be replaced with something that felt uncomfortably like guilt.

His displeasure turned into concern at the expression on her face. She looked for a moment as though he'd slapped her. Then she visibly recovered.

"It was . . . it was personal."

Cruz didn't cease his perusal of her. Whatever she'd been doing, it had shaken her up, though she was trying to hide that fact. And he felt like a bastard for jumping down her throat. "Anything I can help with?"

"No." Her response was flat and final. She looked down at his desk and saw a picture marked with Valdez's name. She picked it up and looked at him.

"I've been spending the time reading up on our friend there. Thought that picture might come in handy." He was referring to their plan to try to track Valdez down for questioning today, and she nodded. "Are you ready to go?" he asked.

"Sure." She turned and preceded him out of the building, unwilling to engage in any more inquiries about her whereabouts this morning. She hadn't handled herself well a moment ago, she knew. Although she thought she'd recovered quickly, Cruz was perceptive enough to accurately gauge her reaction to his words. She hoped he'd taken her explanation at face value, but she mentally braced herself for an interrogation once they reached the car.

But Cruz didn't question her any further. After a few minutes of tense waiting, it occurred to Madeline that he was acting almost solicitous. She could feel herself begin to relax for the first time that morning.

They drove to Valdez's apartment again, but no one answered the door this time, either. Then they checked out the places where Tommy had claimed Valdez sometimes hung out. They walked into each place and ordered something, looked at the occupants, waited for a time and then left. By silent agreement they didn't tell anyone why they were there. If Tommy was correct, someone from each place was bound to be able to identify Valdez, but they couldn't take the chance that he would be tipped off that they were looking for him.

They repeated the pattern a number of times during the day, but by late afternoon they still hadn't had any luck. Madeline and Cruz had come out of a smoky pool hall after spending a fruitless hour in it.

"We'll probably have to spend most of the evening in these dives," Cruz was saying. "These guys are like rats, they only come out at night—'' His words broke off as Madeline jabbed him with her elbow.

"That looks like him coming," she said quietly.

Cruz stared hard in the direction of her gaze. Valdez was sauntering down the sidewalk toward the pool hall they had just vacated. They waited a few seconds until he got closer, then Cruz said, "Jose Valdez?"

The man froze. His eyes darted between Cruz and Madeline. And when they started toward him, he turned and fled.

Cruz and Madeline took off in quick pursuit, but it was apparent that the man was familiar with the neighborhood. He dodged people and obstacles with ease and then darted down an alley.

Cruz reached the alley seconds later, Madeline slightly behind him. The narrow passageway was shadowy, and strewn with litter and boxes. Large Dumpsters hampered their view. Valdez could be hiding anywhere in the area, and Cruz felt a skitter of unease skate down his spine.

Suddenly he heard a loud report, and he reacted without thinking. "Get down!" he shouted to Madeline. Without further thinking, he grabbed her shoulders and pushed her to the ground. He dropped down after her, covering her body with his own.

Another report sounded, and then another. But the echoes hadn't faded before Cruz realized his mistake. Those noises weren't coming from the alley, and they weren't gunshots. A nearby car backfired once more before it continued on its way. His instincts had had him reacting to the danger of the situation, without stopping to think. He heard the sounds of footsteps running away and knew they belonged to Valdez. Without another word he picked himself up, hauled Madeline up by one elbow, then drew his gun and sprinted after Valdez.

She couldn't have followed him if she'd wanted to. When he'd landed on top of her the wind had gone out of her with a suddenness that had left her, quite literally, breathless. She staggered over to the wall of a nearby building and gasped for air. Cruz was back before her lungs had drunk their fill. He reholstered his gun at the small of his back.

"Well, we lost him," he said disgustedly. "And he knows we're looking for him. Probably guessed we're cops. Are you okay?" he asked, seeing Madeline was still having some difficulty breathing. He brushed at her camel-colored slacks, which were marked from her fall.

She pulled away and glared at him. "Would you mind telling me," she demanded, her words interspersed with pauses to take deep breaths, "just what the hell ... you thought you were doing?"

Chapter 7

"What do you mean?"

"I mean, what was the point . . . of your big macho act a minute ago?"

He stared hard at her, noticing the flare of color across her cheeks. She hadn't quite recovered from being hit with a two-hundred-pound tackle, but from what he could discern, her flush was due more to anger than breathlessness.

"I'm sorry. I heard the car backfire, and it was so close...." He shrugged. "I reacted without thinking. I thought it was a gunshot."

She glared at him. "So did I, at first, but that doesn't answer my question. What the hell were you doing on top of me?"

He opened his mouth to answer, and then found that he couldn't. His jaws snapped shut. Finally he muttered, "I don't suppose you'd believe I tripped?"

Her gaze pierced him like a rapier. He studied the ground, feeling remarkably similar to how he'd felt when Sister Mary Joseph had caught him in some prank.

"No." Her voice dripped with disdain. "I would not believe that you tripped. Admit it, Martinez, you were trying to protect me."

It was obvious that she thought she was accusing him of the most heinous crime in the world. He knew there was no way he could weasel out of this one, so he raised his eyes and looked straight into hers. When in doubt, try bluffing, he decided. "Yeah, maybe. So what?"

She looked as though she was going to explode. "So what? I'm a trained police officer, Martinez, a detective with ten years' experience on the force. I'm not in need of protection, not from you or from anybody else."

"Look, I apologize, all right? I didn't plan it, it just happened. Blame it on instincts."

His words didn't appear to mollify her. If anything, she became even more incensed. "Instincts? Well, I'm here to tell you, buddy, your instincts are lousy."

Cruz felt his usually even temper begin to simmer. "Look, Madeline, why don't we wait until you cool down before we do this, okay?"

She moved forward to stab him in the chest with one long, tapered finger. "No, not okay. We're going to do this now. If you have a problem working with a woman, that's tough. I'm not going to let you make it my problem, you got that?"

His eyes narrowed. "I do not," he said with precise enunciation, "have a problem working with a woman. Your being a woman has nothing to do with this."

"Oh, no?" Disbelief colored her voice. "Tell me something. When you were partners with McLain, how many times did you dive on top of him when you thought you heard a gunshot?"

Silence reigned for a minute. Madeline saw the truth of her words written on his face, but he remained stubbornly quiet. "Look," she continued, a little calmer, "you can't do your job if you're worried about me. And neither of us can do our jobs if you don't trust my ability out here on the street. If that's going to be a problem for you, you'd better let me know now."

"It's not," he said finally.

She could feel most of her ire fade away. It was hard to maintain a resounding fury when the other person refused to argue. She became aware of how close they were standing to each other, and she took an unconscious step backward. "Well, good. As long as you're sure."

"I am."

"Because the next time we're in danger, you have to think of me as your partner first. I don't want your instincts turning me into a woman."

"Forgive me for believing it could be possible," he muttered, half turning away.

"What?" she demanded.

He turned back to her and said with exaggerated care, "I said that would be impossible, because I won't let it happen again. Now, why don't we get back to work and see if we can track down Valdez?"

Without a word they walked back to the car. They made their rounds again, to Valdez's apartment, to his usual haunts, but there was no sign of him. By mutual agreement they decided to quit for the day. Neither of them was anxious to prolong their time together.

They separated in the parking lot of the district headquarters, Madeline getting into her car and Cruz striding into the building. He wound his way through the maze of desks until he came to his own, and dropped into his chair wearily. Wiping his hands over his face, he stared out over the top of his fingers unseeingly. The room was a welter of activity, with officers leaving for the day, and others reporting for duty. But the noise didn't filter through his deep introspection. He sat silently brooding, staring into space. He didn't notice the man standing next to his desk until a voice in his ear said, "Forget her. She's not worth it."

His head snapped around. "Oh, hi," he said without enthusiasm.

Connor raised his eyebrows. "Whoever she is, she must be something to turn you into such a zombie. How come you haven't gone home yet?"

Cruz ignored the second question, and scowled at the first. "What makes you so sure I'm thinking of a woman?"

Connor clapped him on the shoulder. "Because, pal, I know you. You don't have to think so hard when it's only a case that's bothering you."

His friend didn't crack a smile. "Well, you're wrong. I wasn't thinking about a woman."

"Oh?"

"I was thinking about Madeline Casey."

"Ah."

Cruz frowned at Connor. "What's that supposed to mean?"

Connor seated himself on the edge of the desk. "Nothing. Just 'ah.'" He paused for a moment, then asked curiously, "Care to tell me why Detective Casey doesn't qualify as a female?"

"Because she doesn't care to qualify," Cruz told him sourly. "She made it very clear this afternoon that I was to think of her as a cop only, and not as a woman. And let me tell you, there are times that isn't very damn hard," he added.

Connor looked pained. "Don't tell me. You hit on her."

"I didn't hit on her," Cruz denied. A moment later he added reluctantly, "I lay on her."

Connor sighed and rubbed his forehead.

"It wasn't like that." Cruz explained the events of the afternoon after they'd sighted Valdez and the argument he'd had with Madeline. Then he sank into silence once more.

"Well, she's right, you know," Connor said, stifling a chuckle. He'd have given a week's pay to see the scene Cruz had just described. "You gave a whole new meaning to the phrase 'cover your partner.'" He lost the struggle and guffawed out loud.

"Oh, you're very funny," Cruz noted. "A real riot." A reluctant grin pulled at the corner of his mouth. A moment later he joined in the laughter.

"Anyway," he said when they'd both recovered, "she really let me have it. I don't think I'll ever understand how her mind works."

"She was right," Connor said. "You can't afford to worry about her. You have to believe that your partner can take care of herself. Why is that so difficult for you?"

"Oh, right, and you're telling me that you wouldn't have done the same thing," Cruz scoffed. "C'mon, I know you better than that. When danger strikes, instinct takes over."

"And your instincts had you diving to protect Madeline Casey," Connor said slowly, very serious now. "Sounds like the lady gave you some good advice. You can't afford to let yourself get sidetracked on the street. Concentrate on the case. And try to keep your distance from Casey. You'll both be better off."

Cruz waved desultorily as Connor took his leave. He mulled over his friend's words. Connor's warning didn't surprise him. His friend didn't trust easily, especially not women. It must have been the hand of fate that had brought Michele and him together. She'd melted the icy reserve that Connor guarded himself with. He grinned slightly as he remembered some of the sparks that had flown between the two before Connor had finally forgotten about being noble and given in to what he'd really wanted, a lifetime with Michele.

But his friend was way off base on this one. Cruz's protective instincts had nothing to do with Madeline personally. He'd react the same way to any woman who was in danger. His thoughts drifting again, he propped his booted feet up on the desk and leaned back in his chair. What was it about Madeline that kept distracting him?

Madeline considered not answering the doorbell when it rang the first time. It had been a long, frustrating day, and she definitely didn't feel up to Ariel's brand of wacky humor. But when it rang a third time, followed by a loud knocking, she rose to her feet. It couldn't be Ariel; she would never stand out there that long. She'd have gone back to her apartment and gotten her key.

Irritated, she went to the peephole and looked out. A miniature Cruz Martinez was in her view, leaning, of course, against her doorbell, with a sack of groceries in one arm.

"C'mon, Madeline, I know you're in there. I saw your car outside. Open up."

She stood frozen on the other side of the door. What on earth was he doing here? He was the last person she wanted to see right now. Today had been a grueling one, in more than the usual sense. The episode in the alley was still too vivid, and much too embarrassing. She'd meant every word she'd said to him, but she knew that she'd been berating herself at the same time. For, despite her very real anger that he'd tried to protect her from the dangers of her job, there lingered a pervasive warmth for the same reason. She groaned silently. The feel of his lean body on top of hers had not been entirely unpleasant. In fact, she wondered uncomfortably how much of her breathlessness had been caused by his weight, and how much from the intimate position. She cringed even as she thought of it. She couldn't afford to complicate things with this awareness of him. She didn't want to be aware of him at all, at least not as a man.

The knocking continued. Ignoring him obviously wasn't working.

"C'mon, Madeline, honey, open the door. Don't be mad. I've reconsidered. You can have my baby after all. Now that I'm getting used to the idea, I kind of like the idea of six or seven little Martinez babies of our own. We'll have as many as you like."

Her eyes flew open and her mouth dropped, aghast. His purposely loud voice was sure to carry up and down the hallway. Certainly she was having no trouble hearing him.

She unlocked the door and threw it open. "Will you please be quiet?" she implored in a loud whisper. "Are you trying to humiliate me?"

Cruz leaned against her doorjamb. "Hi," he said with a smile. "I didn't think you were ever going to let me in."

"You were right," she informed him, "I'm not. I just wanted to tell you to leave. Now."

Before he could answer, Ariel's door opened and she came out. Madeline's heart plummeted.

"I was in the bathtub, or I'd have been out sooner. I couldn't figure out what all the racket was, and—well, well, well." She stopped her litany and walked slowly around Cruz, looking him up and down. She fluttered her eyelashes coyly. "What do we have here?"

Madeline looked wildly about for the floor to open up and swallow her. No such luck. Ariel was looking at Cruz like a starving lioness at fresh prey, and he, darn him, was enjoying it. He grinned at her.

"I've got all my own teeth, too," he said.

"I'll just bet you have," Ariel cooed. "I'm Madeline's friend Ariel. Maybe she's told you, I'm very interested in natural herbs and their healing powers. I'd love to have you tell me about the wonder treatment you must have used to shed thirty pounds, shoot up a foot and grow hair."

Cruz looked puzzled, Madeline desperate. She should have known that she would have to pay for telling Ariel those whoppers about Cruz. Her need to shut her friend up won out over the need to get rid of him. She grasped his arm and pulled him into her apartment. "Goodbye, Ariel," she said as she swung the door closed.

"Nice meeting you, Ariel," Cruz called with amusement.

"Nice meeting you, Mr. Martinez," she replied amusedly.

He turned to look at Madeline. "Seems a little weird, but nice," he said. "How'd she know my name?"

"Thanks to your performance in the hallway, the entire apartment complex knows your name," Madeline retorted. "You've been here only five minutes and already you've managed to disrupt my neighbors, ruin my reputation and embarrass me in front of my friend." She glared at him. "Get a new hobby."

His mouth quirked. "Gee, and I wasn't even trying. Imagine what I could do if I really set my mind to it."

She winced. "I shudder to think of it. You have to leave. Now."

"Can't," he said cheerfully over his shoulder as he strode to her small kitchen and set the bag on the counter. "I came over tonight to fix you dinner, to apologize for this afternoon."

"I already ate," she fibbed.

"What did you have?" he shot back.

Madeline blinked. "Um, I had..." Her mind went blank. "Chicken," she finished lamely.

"Liar." He chuckled, unpacking the groceries and setting them about. "Now if you'd said something dripping in grease and full of cholesterol, I might have believed you."

She gave up. "So I haven't eaten, but I'm not going to eat with you. This isn't necessary. Cruz!"

He was ignoring her as he opened packages, but looked up at his name. "Do you like stir fry?" he asked conversationally.

"I hate it."

"You'll like mine," he said surely. He began opening cupboard doors. "Where do you keep your pans?"

Common sense said she needed to get this man out of her apartment. Self-preservation demanded that she put a great distance, preferably miles, between them. But from the looks of him, it would take an earthquake to move him. Madeline mentally calculated the chance of that particular natural disaster coming to her aid now. The odds didn't look good.

She sighed and capitulated. "Pans are beneath the stove, silverware is in the top drawer and the fire extinguisher is on the wall."

His eyebrows rose. "Why, Ms. Casey. That sounded very much like a sexist remark to me. Are you saying you doubt that I can cook?"

"I don't know." She shrugged. "Can you?"

"I'll have you know," he said, his voice muffled as he squatted and rummaged through her cupboard, "that my culinary reputation is legendary."

She could certainly imagine that *something* about his reputation was legendary, but somehow doubted that it had anything to do with his cooking ability. However, she wisely refrained from telling him that. She stood there, ill at ease, watching as he deftly began to chop ingredients on her cutting board. Stubbornness warred with years of good manners. Manners won. "Would you like any help?" she asked.

He stifled a smile. Her tone belied the helpful words. She sounded decidedly out of sorts. Obviously she wasn't used to finding herself on the sidelines while someone else barged in and took over. And that was exactly what he'd had to do, he admitted to himself cheerfully, to get into her apartment. He cast a glance at her as he rose, frying pan in hand. He much preferred to work alone when preparing a masterpiece, but from the looks of her, he'd be better off giving her something useful to do. Maybe it would improve her mood.

"There's a bottle of wine in the sack," he replied. "Why don't you pour us a couple of glasses?"

That sounded like something she could handle. She obeyed, retrieving the bottle and reading the label curiously. Her eyebrows rose. Another example of his expensive taste, she noted. However, it raised her spirits somewhat. She loved that brand of white wine.

She removed the cork easily and poured some for each of them. She even went so far as to get a small wedge of cheese and a box of crackers from her cupboard and put them on a plate on the counter. If someone was intent on coming into her apartment and feeding her, the least she could do was to be hospitable, she reasoned. Besides, she added silently as she sat on a stool across the counter from Cruz, the cheese and crackers might be the only edible items on the menu tonight.

"Is there anything else I can do?" she asked halfheartedly.

He shook his head. She looked more relaxed already. He saw that her wineglass was half-empty, and reached over to fill it again. "No, why don't you take it easy? You had a rough day." Without giving her time to respond to that, he went on easily, "I enjoy cooking. It relaxes me after working all day." He winked at her. "Of course, I only do it when I feel like it, so it's not a chore to me."

"It seems like such a waste of time for one person," she responded. "I rarely make a real meal for myself." Having someone in the kitchen cooking for her while she sat and relaxed was beginning to gain merit. There was something to be said for laziness. She studied him judiciously, over her second glass of wine. He didn't look any less masculine moving about in the tiny room with the ruffled curtains. His movements were lithe and sure. He hadn't been exaggerating. He obviously knew his way around a stove. He stirred several ingredients together in the frying pan, his hand going to adjust the heat. Her gaze drifted over him. It was especially pleasant to watch someone cook for her when that someone was so easy to look at.

The wine was pleasantly uninhibiting. Her eyes wandered down his well-muscled legs, and back up to trace the inverted triangle of narrow waist, lean back and broad shoulders. His hair looked thick. She wondered if it would be soft or coarse to the touch.

She mentally shook herself. That way of thinking was not for her. She pushed her wineglass away. The wine was responsible for easing some of the day's tensions, but she'd better stop now, before it drained away some of her common sense, as well. This case didn't need any further complications.

"Out of deference for your finicky appetite, we're keeping the green things to a minimum tonight," he informed her. "I'm fixing a pasta salad."

"I like pasta," she said cautiously. Maybe this meal wasn't going to be so bad after all.

"Now how did I guess that?" he joked. "I didn't want to shock your system by introducing too many new foods at once. We'll expand your salad appetite another time."

Madeline wondered at his assumption that there would be other times to do so. But it was a measure of her degree of relaxation that she didn't dispute him. He was an amazingly pleasant companion, conversing the whole time he cooked. By the time dinner was ready their patter had finished the job the wine had started, and she felt thoroughly unwound.

Cruz filled both of their plates and set them down at the tiny table in the dining area. Madeline sat down almost nervously. The room wasn't large enough for a bigger piece of furniture, but since she rarely entertained, she'd never given it much thought. But now, with Cruz sitting across from her, the table seemed too cozy, almost intimate.

To mask her unease, she turned her attention to her food. To her astonishment, the meal was delicious. She surprised herself by putting her normal reservations aside and ate with enjoyment.

Cruz watched her over the top of his wineglass. She had approached the first few forkfuls warily, he noted with amusement. She definitely did not have a trusting nature. But after several minutes their conversation had her so involved that she forgot to surreptitiously examine the food, and just ate it. They were arguing about national politics and he was surprised to find that their viewpoints were not that far apart. But he'd never been one to let similar viewpoints get in the way of a stimulating discussion.

"I agree with you." He interrupted her in the midst of a spirited argument. He replaced his wineglass on the table and resumed eating his meal.

She frowned at him. "But you said—"

"I know what I said. I just wanted to see how strongly you would defend your position. And you did it quite well, I thought." His eyes twinkled. "You should have been a lawyer."

Madeline stared at him. "You did it to me again," she finally murmured, shaking her head in bemusement. "Why do I keep forgetting how you operate? You just like to get people stirred up, don't you?"

"Yep," he admitted without shame. "It's my forte. You go with your strengths. Plus your impassioned persuasion kept you so busy you forgot what you were eating." He pointed at her plate.

"Very tricky," she said, noticing for the first time that she'd eaten most of her helping. "But you'll notice I managed to avoid the peppers."

"You did quite well for the first time," he praised her. "And for your reward..." He got up and went to the refrigerator. "I brought something that would earn your forgiveness if you absolutely hated the meal."

Her mouth watered on cue when he presented the dessert. "For French silk pie I would forgive you for starting World War III. But there's no need for it. Everything was delicious."

"Thank you, thank you," he said with false modesty. "But I have to admit, my culinary genius does not extend to baked goods. I got this at a bakery."

They savored the sweet dessert and when they were finished, Madeline sat back contentedly. "I don't think I'll move for the next several hours."

"In that case, maybe we'd better go into the living room," he suggested. "You'll be more comfortable on the couch in case you fall asleep. I'll clean up the kitchen."

Shaking her head, Madeline rose and walked over to the TV, flipping it on and dropping onto the couch as he'd suggested. "Forget the dishes," she said. "I'll do them later when I have more energy."

He didn't need any more encouragement, and sat on the other end of the couch. She would be amazed later to recall how quickly the evening passed. They talked as freely as two friends who'd known each other for years, with an easy familiarity. When Cruz rose later, remarking about the time, Madeline's eyes flew to the clock. She was shocked to see how late it was getting. She followed him to the door.

"Thank you," she said sincerely, "for the meal."

"Well, I guess I owed you," he responded. "I really didn't mean to offend you this afternoon."

"You didn't have to do this, but . . ." She smiled impishly. "I'm glad you did."

He gazed down at her. "So am I," he agreed softly. She was so close he could reach out and touch her, and he did so without thinking. One finger traced her delicate jawline, and the others curled under her chin of their own accord. He didn't plan it, but his head began descending.

Just a quick kiss, that was all he expected. A light brushing of lips, a friendly goodbye. It would have been a fitting ending to a spontaneous evening that had turned out surprisingly well. But once his mouth met hers, his expectations faded, to be replaced with something deeper, more demanding.

She saw his face draw closer and she didn't pull away as she knew she ought to. A kiss seemed almost natural after the evening they'd shared, and she let her eyelids drop in anticipation. But anticipation didn't prepare her for the onslaught of emotion that accompanied his kiss. She'd expected a casual peck, perhaps a teasing brush of mouths, and a joking remark to accompany him out the door. But there was nothing teasing about this.

At the first taste of her, Cruz could feel a spark in his belly quickly grow into a knot of fire. It wasn't enough, this wasn't enough, and he followed the dictates of his body, not of his mind. He pulled her closer, cupped her head in the palm of his hand and kissed her the way he wanted to, the way he'd wanted to since the first time he'd seen her, looking so prim and professional.

His lips pressed hers apart and his tongue swept in, exploring boldly. Not expecting such an intimate caress, Madeline's fingers clutched reflexively on his chest. The heat from his stroking tongue generated an answering heat in the pit of her stomach. She allowed the sparks to sweep away reason for a moment. For an instant she allowed herself to respond to the demand implicit in his kiss, and issued a demand of her own.

Their mouths twisted together in a mindless wanting that reduced their earlier friendliness to a sham. It was long moments before Cruz raised his head.

With her lips bereft of his, her eyes flickered open slowly. He was staring down at her, his eyes still full of the promise his mouth had been issuing a second ago. There was a slight frown on his face. Then he brushed his lips across her forehead and left, as if not trusting himself to do more.

His departure seemed no more abrupt than the cessation of that mind-drugging kiss of a minute ago, and when the door shut behind him, Madeline sagged weakly against it. What a fool she'd been just then, she thought dizzily. She'd imagined what a kiss from him would be like. But her expectations hadn't prepared her for this thought-draining, soul-racking kiss, which left her boneless and alarmingly empty-headed.

It was some time before her mind cleared enough for her to lock the door behind him. But after she did, she leaned against it again. Later would come the self-recriminations. For now, words escaped her mind, and all she could do was touch her lips in remembrance and smile.

Morning seemed to come with the gentleness of a sledgehammer against cement. Cruz hadn't slept particularly well, and his mood didn't improve much over coffee. His brilliant idea of the previous evening, to get on a better footing with Madeline Casey, had succeeded all too well. Except for the fact that he'd reacted to her as hot and fast as a randy sixteen-year-old in the back seat of his father's car. He rubbed his forehead in remembrance. Keep it light, that had been his plan for the evening. But somehow he'd lost that thought at the first taste of her.

His sudden physical response was not a mystery; he'd been attracted to her from the beginning. He appreciated women, and he especially appreciated women who were smart as well as beautiful. It was his momentary lack of control last night that bothered him. Cruz hadn't gotten to be a thirty-four-year-old bachelor without his share of experience with the opposite sex. But somehow none of that experience had come to his aid last night, and he found that disturbing.

He was used to arranging things to suit himself. He had an innate charm that prevented people from protesting, even when they realized how he stayed in control of a situation. He'd figured the situation with Madeline had called for a little more camaraderie, a little lighthearted friendliness, and that was exactly what he'd provided. Until he'd lost control of that plan at the end, when their kiss had become much more than that.

He didn't like the feeling he had now, as if he'd made a rather large mistake, but he couldn't quite put his finger on when or why things had gone so awry. All he knew was that they had less to do with him and much more to do with Madeline Casey. And his reaction to her. He brooded over this on the drive to work. When he got to his desk, she was already there.

"Hi," she said, glancing up at him. "It's not often I beat you to work." She took a closer look at his closed expression. "Bad morning?"

Bad night, he wanted to tell her. *Long, sleepless and fitful. And if you want to know the cause of it, look in the mirror.* But there was no way he was going to admit that to her. Not when she sat there in front of him looking fresh and starched, as if she weren't bothered in the slightest by the memory of her lips opening for his tongue. He shrugged in answer to her question. "Not especially."

"I was looking through the files you compiled. I couldn't find that picture of Valdez we had yesterday. Do you know where it is?"

Her matter-of-fact manner helped restore his own, even as it annoyed him further. He walked to his desk and pulled open the top drawer. He took out the picture and handed it to her. "What's on your mind?"

She studied the picture intently, as if she didn't already have the face memorized. He'd be shocked if she answered that question truthfully. However, there was no chance of that happening. She'd thought for an instant that he shared her discomfort at facing him this morning. But she'd obviously been wrong. There was nothing in his manner to suggest that. She, on the other hand, had had to mentally prepare herself for the moment she would see him again. And she resented bitterly the fact that the effort seemed to be one-sided.

But she was, above all things, a professional, and she'd do her job without consideration of any personal feelings if it killed her. She was proud that her voice was matter-of-fact when she answered. "What do you think Stover might have to say if we showed him this and told him we know he got the gun from this man?"

"Bluff him, you mean?"

"We don't have anything to lose," she reasoned. "He didn't seem willing to talk without a guaranteed deal from the D.A. We aren't going to get that. Maybe, if nothing else, we can surprise him. We might be able to tell from his expression, at least, if we're on the right track."

"It's worth a try," Cruz agreed after considering for a moment. "Is it your turn to drive, or mine?"

When they arrived at the South District headquarters they received a shock. Cruz stared at the desk sergeant. "What do you mean, Stover made bail yesterday?"

The older man looked annoyed at the question. "Just what I said. Some woman came by yesterday afternoon with wads of hundred-dollar bills stuffed into baggies, and he walked."

Madeline looked at her partner, stunned. "There's no way he could come up with that much money. If he could, he would have been out before."

The desk sergeant pointedly went back to his paperwork, already dismissing them.

"Can we see the paperwork on the bail?" Cruz asked.

The man let out a great sigh, threw his pen down and left his chair. A moment later he came back with the necessary papers. Cruz took them, holding them so both he and Madeline could read them. It was a measure of how much he was coming to rely on her ability; he didn't even bother to take notes. After perusing the papers they thanked the officer, who didn't look unhappy to see them go.

"Seems a little strange," Cruz remarked as they pulled away from the building. "Somehow I hadn't pictured him as the type to inspire such devotion from a woman. I wonder what her relationship to him was?"

Madeline shrugged.

"Are you thinking what I'm thinking?" he asked.

She nodded. "His address was on the papers. Let's go see if he had any second thoughts about talking after being a prolonged guest of the county."

Stover lived in a part of the city that he was unfamiliar with, and Cruz consulted the map that he'd wadded up under the seat. The neighborhoods began to get seedier. A group of youths on one corner were amusing themselves by setting litter baskets on fire.

"You'll remember how we got here, right?" Cruz asked. "Because if those kids keep it up, we aren't going to be able to count on any particular landmark still being there by the time we go back."

Madeline agreed. She didn't doubt her ability to recall the way they'd come. But she had a really uneasy feeling about traveling deeper and deeper into this area. She wasn't sure what would be left of the car by the time they were finished talking to Stover.

Not all of the buildings were marked with numbers, so they had to double back more than once. "That must be it up ahead," Cruz finally said. "This is 1014 right here, so 1016 must be the yellow house."

Madeline pulled to a stop, double-parking in front. His description was too kind. Any paint the house had ever seen was nothing but a dim memory. Curls of faded yellow latex clung to the siding in places, but more of the house was a dull, faded gray. They walked up to the porch, avoiding the steps that had large holes in them. An old screen door hung uselessly by one hinge. Four mailboxes lined the wall next to the door.

"Which one is Stover supposed to be in?" he asked.

"Room 1B."

They pushed open the inner door and were in a small foyer. They pounded on Stover's door. "Detectives Martinez and Casey, Stover. We'd like to talk to you for a minute." There was no response.

Cruz and Madeline shared a glance, and he pounded again. "Open up, Stover. Police," Madeline called. Still there was no answer. Though she listened intently, Madeline could not hear any sound in the room. She turned away in disgust, but Cruz reached out and tried the door. It wasn't locked, and he pushed it open. Without a word they both reached for their guns. He used his free hand to push the door open all the way, simultaneously barking, "Police!"

They entered in police stance, their guns following their gazes around the room. They both saw Stover at the same time, lying facedown on the bed. Slowly they approached him, each sure of what they would find. Cruz pulled the sheet back for a better look at the man.

There was a neat bullet hole at the base of his scalp.

Chapter 8

Madeline felt for a pulse, but her action was merely precautionary. "He's cold already," she murmured. "Whoever paid him a visit has been gone quite a while." She slipped her gun back into its holster.

"Didn't get to enjoy his newfound freedom long, did he?" Cruz asked grimly.

She sighed. "I'll radio it in."

An hour later the room was full of police personnel. Madeline and Cruz stood in the hallway as the forensics expert and the homicide detectives worked. They'd already told what they knew to the supervising officer, Lieutenant Niles, who stood in the doorway watching his men work. As the body was rolled by on a stretcher, he stepped back into the hallway.

"So that was the guy they had dead to rights on the attempted bank robbery?" the lieutenant asked. "Jacobs will scream about this. Way I heard it, the conviction was a sure thing." He lit a cigarette and peered at the two of them through the smoke. "What's your angle?"

"We're working to nail whoever's supplying these guys with the guns," Cruz said.

The lieutenant grunted, watching his officers search the room.

"Good luck. You have any ideas to make my investigation a little easier?"

"Maybe." Madeline pulled out the picture of Valdez. "We'd come to question Stover about this man. We think he might have sold Stover the gun." She gave him a brief description of Valdez's criminal record. "His prints are on file. If you get a clear print in here, try matching it to his."

"You might want to find the woman who put up bail for him yesterday," Cruz suggested. "Seems pretty odd to me that he sat in that cell as long as he did, and suddenly someone came up with the money."

"You got a theory on that?" the man inquired.

"Maybe. Stover knew there was interest in the supplier. He asked to cut a deal with the D.A. Jacobs turned it down. Could be that someone got wind of that interest and decided to shut Stover up, in case Jacobs reconsidered."

The lieutenant mulled this over. "We'll give that a shot. What district you in?"

"Southwest."

He nodded. "I'll give you a call if we get anywhere with that. In the meantime, if you catch up with this Valdez, I'd like to hear about it."

"You got it."

Cruz and Madeline walked out of the building. "Next stop—Valdez?" Madeline questioned, already knowing the answer.

He nodded. "But somehow I suspect that we're going to find that he is far, far underground."

The search for the man proved futile. They revisited the places they had looked yesterday, this time asking for him by name and showing his picture. They went to his home again and were told by a neighbor that Valdez hadn't been there lately. Ever since he figured out he was wanted for questioning, Madeline surmised. Before Cruz had come in to work that morning, she had taken the opportunity to call Valdez's parole officer. He'd given her the name and address of Wynn Construction, where Valdez had been working. After relaying this information to Cruz, they drove there, and were told by a surly manager that Valdez hadn't shown up for work all week.

By the end of the day they had to admit defeat. No one they talked to claimed any knowledge of Valdez's whereabouts. Most of the people they approached seemed fearful about discussing him. Back in the car Madeline said, "Well, it seems like one of our hunches might be correct. No one wanted to talk about the supplier, and they're just as unwilling to discuss Valdez. Maybe they're one and the same." She was suddenly struck with an idea. "Why don't we talk to Tommy again?" she asked Cruz. "Maybe he's heard something else since we last spoke to him."

Cruz shook his head. "Tommy is long gone by now. He's taken off to lie low for a while, and wherever he is, you can be sure that he's so deep into a bottle he wouldn't be coherent anyway."

"It's not like we have a lot of other options at the moment," she argued. She drove toward the area in which they'd found the newsstand.

When he guessed where they were going, Cruz frowned. "I told you this is a waste of time," he said. "I know Tommy well enough to know his habits. We're not going to find him."

"It won't hurt to ask," she said reasonably. But when she neared the newsstand, Cruz got out of the car without waiting for her to find a place to park.

"Damn!" Madeline muttered under her breath. She swung into the parking lot of the convenience store across the street and hurried to join him. She wanted to be there when he asked for Tommy. She couldn't afford to take whatever Cruz told her at face value. But by the time she was halfway across the street he was headed back toward her again.

She turned to follow him back to the car. "What did he say?"

He looked impatient. "Exactly what I knew he'd say. He hasn't seen Tommy since I dropped off the money for the information. And he probably won't, either. Tommy won't show until he thinks the coast is clear, or when he's out of booze again."

She stared at him, thinking hard. "Did that guy have any idea where he might be?"

"No, Madeline, he didn't." There was an edge to Cruz's voice. "Tommy isn't the type to leave a forwarding address. He doesn't have to. He always comes back, in time."

She got into the car, frustrated. There was no way she could check what he was telling her without letting him know how far she was from trusting him. She couldn't allow him to suspect that. There was still far too much she had to learn about Cruz Martinez, and if he knew she was suspicious of him, her efforts would be for nil.

"You in a hurry to get home?" Cruz asked after she'd been driving several minutes.

"Not especially. Why?"

"Ramsey Elliot was released from the hospital this week. Why don't we swing by and pay him a visit?" He consulted the map again and gave her directions to the boy's home. Then he sat back and looked at her. "I'd sure like to find out what the Lords have planned in retaliation for Ramsey's shooting."

"And whether they've obtained the gun to do it," she agreed. "Do you think it would do any good to show Valdez's picture to Ramsey?"

Cruz thought for a moment, then shrugged. "I don't know. It seems doubtful that he would have been in on the actual dealing for the gun, if they've gotten that far. It would have been handled by Cantoney. But it sure wouldn't hurt to ask Ramsey a few questions about what's been going on with the Lords since he's gotten home."

"And next we'll talk to Cantoney," Madeline said grimly. "My guess is that he'll recognize the picture of Valdez. Even if he won't admit it."

Ramsey Elliot lived in one of a group of government-subsidized apartments. They were run-down, but they were in a lot better condition than some of the places Cruz and Madeline had been in lately. When they knocked at his door it was opened by a little girl, her hair pulled back into a long ponytail. She said nothing, just stood looking up at them.

Cruz squatted down so his face was on her level. "Hi," he said softly, and smiled at her. A shy smile crept across her face in response, but she didn't answer. "We're friends of Ramsey's," he continued. "We heard he'd gotten out of the hospital, and we've come to see him."

"He's not here," the little girl said.

Cruz remained where he was. "But he is out of the hospital, right?" She nodded.

"Who is it, Rhonda?" a voice called. A moment later Ricky came to the door.

"Oh," he said, looking from one of them to the other. Cruz rose slowly to his feet.

"Hi, Ricky," Madeline said. "We've come to see how Ramsey is getting along. Rhonda said he got out of the hospital."

"Go to your room, Rhonda," Ricky ordered brusquely.

"Don't want to." The little girl's lip jutted out mulishly.

"Go!" She obeyed but did so slowly. Ricky watched her until a door shut behind her. Then his eyes turned back to them.

"What do you want with Ramsey? Did you find out who shot him yet?"

Madeline shook her head. "Not yet. How's he feeling?"

The boy looked at the floor. "He's doing okay."

"Where is he now?" Cruz asked him.

The boy shrugged.

"Hanging with the Lords?" Madeline asked in a soft voice.

After several moments he nodded reluctantly. "Mama's real upset with him. She told him the Lords are nothing but trouble, but he don't listen to no one." He shook his head, still looking down. "He should be smarter, man. He should have wised up by now."

"Ricky, we want to help Ramsey. We want to find the person who shot him. But you know what we think?" At the boy's silence, Madeline continued, "We believe that a rival gang shot at your brother. And that the Lords know which gang is responsible."

"We think Dirk Cantoney is planning something," Cruz broke in, watching the boy closely. "Like maybe arranging a shooting himself."

The boy's reaction would have been hard to miss. His gaze bounced up, a look of real fright in them, but he remained silent.

"If we're right, your brother and the rest of the Lords could be in a lot of trouble. So if you know anything about their plans, anything at all, you should tell us," Madeline urged. "Help us get this thing stopped before anybody else gets hurt."

Ricky opened his mouth, hesitated, then closed it again. Finally he shook his head. "I don't know nothing."

Cruz was not so sure about that, but he let it go. "If you do hear anything, please let us know, will you?"

Still silent, Ricky shrugged.

The detectives shared a glance. "We'll be in touch, Ricky," Madeline said. Both of them left, and the door shut behind them.

When they got back to the car Madeline surprised Cruz by asking him to drive back. He shot her a concerned glance as he slid into the driver's seat. "Are you all right?"

"Just a headache," she said shortly, fishing in her purse for some pain relievers. He winced as he watched her swallow two of them dry. Then she leaned her head back against the headrest and closed her eyes.

"I'm not surprised your head hurts after a day like this," he noted. "Finding a corpse is enough to shoot anyone's day to hell."

"It's not just that. I didn't sleep very well last night," she admitted without thinking. "Plus, we skipped lunch."

If her eyes had been open she would have been chagrined at the look her admission brought to his face. A satisfied smile tilted his lips. So she'd had trouble sleeping last night? Rightfully so, since she had been the undisputed cause for *his* restless slumber. Maybe he'd been wrong this morning about the effect of that kiss being one-sided. Perhaps Madeline hadn't been as unaffected by it as she'd pretended to be.

She didn't open her eyes until she felt the car come to a halt and heard the sound of the ignition being turned off. She opened them slowly, already dreading the drive back to her apartment. But to her amazement they weren't back at headquarters. They were in a parking lot next to a well-known seafood restaurant. "Don't tell me," she drawled, her gaze sweeping to Cruz's. "You took a wrong turn again."

"Nope." He got out of the car and came around to open her door. "You need to eat, and I know you can't be trusted to make yourself something when you get home, so we'll run in here and take care of it."

She got out of the car slowly. "You know, you have an unhealthy interest in feeding me. You should see someone about that."

He winked at her. "Remember, I've seen your kitchen. If you had mice, they'd have to order take-out."

She sighed. He was right, darn it. Grocery shopping was far down on the list of her favorite things to do. If she went home right now, she would probably skip supper altogether. Reluctantly she followed him into the building, where they were quickly seated by the hostess.

"I'll let you buy me dinner if you're still feeling guilty about all the trouble I went to last night to make supper for you," he offered judiciously.

She lowered her menu to fix him with a jaundiced look. "How kind of you."

He looked modest. "It's the least I can do."

"Is that how you maintain your frantic social life, Martinez?" she asked. "Drive women to high-priced restaurants and invite them to pay?"

One side of his mouth lifted. "Now how would you know how frantic my social life is?" he asked interestedly.

Madeline froze. The lingering headache was obviously affecting her thought process. How else could she explain her verbal slip? She couldn't reveal what Brewer had told her, or that they'd been discussing him at all. Better to let him think she was interested in him herself, for more personal reasons, than to have him suspect that she had a more devious interest in him.

"Well, I can only guess, but I'd figure that with the face of a Greek god, you might have more than your share of willing companions," she managed indifferently.

To her surprise, he laughed. "Greek god, huh? You're the only person I know who could say that and make it sound so little like a compliment."

She flushed. It hadn't been a compliment, exactly, but she hadn't intended to offend him, either. "I didn't mean . . ."

He waved her words away. "It doesn't matter. And you're partially right. I can have a lot of dates, if I want them. But going out with women attracted to me based solely on my looks long ago ceased to thrill me. I'm thirty-four years old, Madeline. It's dehumanizing to be seen as some kind of trophy. I don't want to be wanted that way, any more than you'd wish to date a man who was interested only in your beauty."

Now she really was embarrassed, but her interest was caught in spite of it. "Does that happen often?" she asked.

"Much more often than being pursued by women interested in my mind," he said wryly. "And although you probably don't believe this, men find that as annoying as women do."

"I guess I never considered it that way before," Madeline said slowly. And she hadn't. She had been as guilty of generalizing about him, based on his looks, as anybody, she realized in a flash. Brewer had laid the groundwork by revealing to her, in that half-snide, half-envious tone, just how popular Cruz was with women. And she had drawn her own conclusions the first time she'd laid eyes on him.

He shrugged, as if the matter was not of great consequence, and looked at his menu again. Madeline returned to hers also, but her mind wasn't on food. Not for the first time since she'd started this case, she felt a flicker of remorse. She couldn't permit that feeling; it meant she was getting too emotionally involved in the case, and that wouldn't do. She needed to back up, maintain a little distance. But that was difficult when she was working this closely with Cruz. Each day she worked with him taught her a little more about him, and while that was necessary for her investigation, it was playing havoc with her judgment. Darn it, she *liked* him so much. It would be impossible not to. He was funny, charming and witty, even considerate. A person would have to be dead not to react to him, and react to him she did.

"Madeline?" Her gaze flew to his, then to the waitress standing patiently next to her, pen poised. She quickly made a selection and gave it to the waitress.

"You were a million miles away," he observed as the woman took their menus and left. "Is your headache still bothering you?"

She shook her head. "Not much. I was just...thinking."

"Why don't you tell me about yourself," he invited. At her look of refusal, he cajoled, "C'mon. I really know very little about you. I talk all the time. My life's an open book to you."

If only he knew, she thought. While it was true that he revealed much by his easy banter, he hadn't yet given her the kind of information she was seeking about him. She was growing weary of the subterfuge, yet she had no choice but to continue. After all, if she could tie up the source of his second income, she would be just as likely to clear him as to incriminate him, wouldn't she? She might end up doing him a favor.

Right, she derided herself. As if he would thank her for digging up every single thing she could about him, and filing it in a report to Internal Affairs. He wasn't likely to feel grateful to find she'd been weighing the evidence against him, to see if it pointed to his guilt in a crime that would offend any decent person to be suspected of. He'd hate her if he ever found out what other task she'd been busy with during their partnership.

Not that it would matter, she assured herself. This case, as well as this partnership, was merely temporary. When it ended, Cruz Martinez would cease to have any effect on her at all. Whether she proved him guilty or innocent, her life would resume as before. She need never see him again. She forced down the strange sense of desolation her thoughts brought.

She became belatedly aware that he was looking at her expectantly. "There's nothing important to tell," she said finally.

"Family?"

That was one of the last things she wanted to discuss with him, or with anyone else, for that matter. "A father, one brother," she said shortly. "My mother died when I was a teenager. Other than that, I had the usual childhood."

He waited, but she had clearly finished.

"C'mon," he wheedled. "There must be some juicy morsel from your past you'd like to share with me."

"What are you hoping for, Martinez?" she gibed. "That I can relate some incidents that will rival those from your misspent youth?" She shook her head. "Sorry to disappoint you. Most of my indiscretions were purely imaginary." Although there were still some who remained convinced that she'd been guilty of much more than an indiscretion when Dennis Belding's crimes had come to light. She had no doubt that her father's publicity team and advisers had worked frantically to reduce the impact the fiasco would have on his career. But she steadfastly refused to believe that they were responsible for her being cleared in the department's internal investigation. It was important for her to believe that there was one major portion of her life that her father would never have any direct control over.

"How often do you see your family?" he quizzed.

"Not often. My brother lives on the West Coast. I have dinner with my father once a month, when I can't get out of it." She gave a wry smile and added, "We don't have a lot in common."

Cruz was silent, absorbing her words. He couldn't imagine a father not having more of a relationship with his daughter, whatever their differences. Certainly he didn't always agree with his father. But the bond between them was strong, as was the sense of family loyalty.

Madeline seemed unwilling to continue and he studied her, wondering if he dared push her any farther. She seemed to have an innate sense of caution, a protective guardedness about her that prevented others from getting too close too quickly. That added to her intrigue. But when she wasn't guarding her words carefully, when her defenses lowered a bit, she went far beyond intriguing. She had a sparkle, a depth to her that was compelling. And he was finding himself very much compelled.

His attention was snared by a man approaching their table, a broad smile on his face.

"Cruz, how are you? I've left several messages on your answering machine. It's lucky I've run into you like this."

Cruz rose to his feet, mentally cursing the man's timing. "Good to see you," he said insincerely, shaking his hand. "Madeline, will you excuse us for a minute?" Without waiting for her answer, he was leaving the table, guiding the man across the room.

She watched in confusion as they stopped in a corner and fell into a discussion. Now what was that all about? she asked herself. Cruz had seemed ill at ease at the man's appearance and had wasted no time getting him away from the table. She watched the two carefully, but could discern little from where she was sitting. The other man seemed to be doing much of the talking, gesturing periodically. Cruz shook his head a few times, but mostly listened. Her attention drifted when the waitress returned to their table with their meals. Madeline waited several minutes, but Cruz showed no signs of returning. It gave her an excuse to go fetch him. There was no sense in either of them eating a cold meal.

As she approached, she heard the other man say, "Great! I knew this was too good for you to pass up."

"I'm serious, though, Dan," Cruz answered. "If you're going to insist on taking chances like this, you're going to have to count me out. I've got too much to lose if we—" He broke off as his companion's eyes looked past him. Cruz turned to see Madeline standing there.

"Sorry to interrupt you, but our food arrived a few minutes ago," Madeline said, her gaze going curiously from one man to the other. "I didn't want to let it get any colder."

The man he'd called Dan slapped Cruz on the shoulder. "Well, I'll let you go. I've held you up longer than I should have. I hope your gorgeous date will forgive our talking business." Cruz didn't correct his misconception, nor did he introduce them, two omissions noted by Madeline. He walked back to the table with her and they resumed their seats.

Madeline watched him from beneath her lashes. He began eating, and he didn't offer an explanation about his business with the other man. He was obviously preoccupied, and said little throughout the meal. She chewed mechanically, mentally going over the snippet of conversation she'd overheard. They could have been talking about the stock market, she thought, or about a business venture. A throbbing in her temples signaled the return of her headache. They could just as easily have been discussing an illicit business proposition. One that had to do with supplying crooks with state-of-the-art weaponry?

Her appetite vanished. It probably didn't mean anything. But she knew she would have to add it to the file she kept at home, locked in her desk. The file of information to be included in a report to Brewer. He insisted on hearing every bit she gathered, no matter how seemingly insignificant. She wondered how significant he would consider this.

Deciding it was worth a try, she said nonchalantly, "Your friend seems to be leaving."

Cruz's eyes followed hers and saw that Dan was walking out the door. He looked back to her. "He's just an acquaintance," he said dismissively. "Are you done?" At her nod he reached for the check.

"I was invited to pay, remember?" she asked lightly, striving to appear normal.

He shook his head, his usual good nature absent. "I was just kidding. I'll take care of it."

"No." She eased it from beneath his hand. "I insist. It's the least I can do after you fed me last night." Not waiting for an answer, she left the table and walked toward the front desk.

"Darn it, Madeline, wait," Cruz said as he joined her. "I'm not going to let you do that."

"Don't worry, Martinez. There won't be any strings attached," she said teasingly, without thinking.

He looked hard at her. Strings attached? That wouldn't worry him at all. It just might make him forget all the self-control he'd had to call on around her, though. The thought made him warm, as his imagination provided vivid pictures of what strings might imply.

They turned away from the cash register finally, after agreeing to split the bill. Madeline hadn't taken two steps before she heard a voice say, "Madeline Casey! It's been too long!"

Recognizing the voice, she was loath to turn. But she did so, slowly. "Hello, Mr. Vincent." Francis Vincent, a good friend of her father's, rose from his table and grasped her hand. "I thought that was you, but it's been so long since we've seen each other, I wasn't sure." His gaze moved to Cruz. "I don't think we've met. I'm Francis Vincent, a longtime friend of Madeline's father."

Cruz introduced himself and Madeline could see the man mentally file the name away. She knew that it would be repeated to her father the very next time Vincent saw him, which would be sooner than Madeline would like. She wondered how long the information would take to reach Geoffrey Casey. She could already guess what his reaction would be to hearing she'd been seen having dinner with Cruz.

She excused herself as soon as possible from the man and hurried Cruz to the car. She resigned herself to the certainty that she would soon be in for a disapproving call regarding her lack of judgment where Cruz was concerned. And she knew her father's meddling would touch a nerve. Because she was beginning to wonder herself just how clouded her judgment might be getting.

Chapter 9

The next morning Madeline was waiting impatiently in her apartment building elevator. It stopped at yet another floor, and a half dozen people got out. As the doors closed, a deep voice sounded from behind her.

"Nice legs."

She whirled around and groaned feelingly. "What are you doing here?"

Cruz grinned from his position in the corner of the compartment. He was leaning against the wall, arms crossed, and the look with which he was painting her was one of pure male appreciation. She was wearing an oversize sweatshirt, which almost covered her brief running shorts. Between the hem of those shorts and the rolled-down socks and tennis shoes was approximately thirty inches of the smoothest, shapeliest legs he'd ever observed. And, being a self-acknowledged leg man, his observations had been numerous.

"Looking for you, of course," he answered. "Ariel heard me knocking at your door and advised me that you would be home in about fifteen minutes, so I decided to hang around."

"You've been riding up and down in the elevator while you waited?" she inquired.

"I'm easily amused."

Her lips wanted to tilt, but she firmed them. "Obviously." When she'd entered the elevator she hadn't paid much attention to its occupants. Her mind had already been busy planning the next segment of her day, now that she'd put in her time at the gym. Until she'd heard Cruz's voice she'd assumed that she was alone after the last bunch of passengers disembarked.

"Actually, I came down to fetch Ariel's paper." For the first time she noticed the newspaper tucked under his arm. "She said she needed to see her horoscope before she could start her day."

Madeline rolled her eyes. "That's probably true." For once she was grateful for her friend's superstitious nature. She would much rather have Cruz running errands for the woman than spending any noticeable amount of time in her company. Ariel was lovable and funny, but she was also sometimes a real blabbermouth. Madeline really didn't trust her friend not to divulge something sensitive to him while she had the chance.

She narrowed her eyes. Come to think of it, fifteen minutes was plenty of time for Ariel to have told Cruz any number of embarrassing things, including the description Madeline had given her of him. She looked at him suspiciously. There was no telling from his face what, if anything, Ariel had blurted out. Aware of her interest, he raised his eyebrows.

She looked away belatedly. Whatever Ariel might have told him, he would let it out at the earliest inopportune moment. If there was one thing she'd learned about the man, it was that he was an incurable tease. That certainty, accompanied by her discomfort at his seeing her while she was sweaty and half-bare, put her decidedly out of sorts.

"Ariel was right about the time you got home," he added. "To the minute. How do you suppose she guessed that?"

She wasn't fooled by his innocent tone. She knew exactly what he was getting at. "If that's another dig about my 'regimented' life, you can take a hike, Martinez. Maybe if you were a little more scheduled yourself, you'd stop and think before you just showed up on a person's doorstep. There's this wonderful invention you may have heard of. It's called a telephone."

He smiled. He doubted she liked him seeing her without her professional battle gear of those tailored suits and pulled-back hair. She looked completely different right now in her exercise garb, and he'd give a month's pay to see her without the bulky sweatshirt. *You're really losing it, Martinez,* he mentally derided himself. The last time he'd been this turned on just by seeing a woman's legs,

he'd been in junior high. And he didn't remember any time he'd
been as fascinated by a woman's hair. For the first time since he'd
met her, she was wearing it down, and it was as glorious as he'd
imagined. The thick red length reached just to her shoulders, and
at the moment its riotous mass of curls was held away from her face
by a thick, stretchy headband.

He looked his fill, enjoying every moment of the opportunity,
aware that with each passing second her temper was escalating.
"You should learn to be more spontaneous," he finally suggested. The elevator opened and they walked toward her apartment. "Following a schedule just seems to make you uptight."

She threw him a fuming glance as she unlocked her door. "I am
not having this conversation with you again," she informed him
as he followed her into the apartment.

"Of course not, there's no need," he responded, going directly
to the sofa and dropping onto it. "Because today we're going to
alter your usual dull schedule. Go ahead and get dressed, I'll wait."

She stared at him, her hands going to her hips. He unfolded Ariel's paper and began reading it. After several moments he seemed
to notice that she was still standing there. "What?"

"Martinez, go home," she said flatly. She had no desire to spend
yet another day in his company. Although the week seemed to fly
by too quickly when it came to investigating the case, each weekend was a welcome respite from having to spend every working
hour with him. She desperately needed the time apart to regain her
objectivity, not to mention to write up her reports for Brewer. By
the time they had parted last night her headache had returned, in
spades. Seeing Vincent at the restaurant, on top of wondering
about the mysterious Dan whom Cruz had spoken to, had been the
cause. She was confused and on edge. Madeline didn't like the
feelings. And she knew she wasn't likely to get respite from either
as long as she was in Cruz's company.

"After all the time I spent waiting for you this morning, now
you're kicking me out?"

She wasn't fooled by his wounded tone. "That's right." No
matter what excuse he dreamed up for them to spend the day together, it wasn't going to work. She had made a strategic mistake
the night she'd let him cook supper for her. Now he assumed his
tactics worked on her, just as they probably did on all women. But
no longer, she vowed. She needed this time alone in order to figure out just what the man was up to, and she wasn't going to let his
presence here take her mind off that.

He unfolded his long form from her couch, and refolded the paper. "Okay," he said agreeably. "I thought you were serious when you said you wanted to be with me all the time, but I guess you didn't mean it."

Her mouth hung open at the man's audacity. "When did I say that?"

He regarded her patiently. "Last week, of course. At work."

"Work," she repeated. Comprehension slowly dawning, she asked cautiously, "Just what did you have planned for the day?"

"Well, you said last night we should talk to Cantoney again, and I think you're right. But I don't want to wait until Monday to do it. I've got an itchy feeling where he's concerned, like something's about to go down. I'm going to try to find him and talk to him today." He shrugged and moved toward the door. "I figured you'd insist on coming with me, but I guess I was wrong."

She closed her eyes in embarrassment. He'd done it to her again. Why had she automatically assumed that the man was here on a social visit? Because he'd tried to confuse her, the rat. And she knew how amused he'd be if she let on that he'd succeeded. "Hold on," she commanded. He halted and turned to eye her quizzically. "Um, you're right, I do want to come. Give me a minute, and I'll change."

Cruz moved back to the living-room area as she disappeared down a hallway. He heard the door shut behind her, and he allowed himself a tiny grin. Somehow he'd known that showing up here would throw her off kilter, and he had to admit that he'd done his best to let it. Madeline Casey was too used to being in control, he decided as he settled himself onto the couch again. It did her good to have her usual cool manner blasted away once in a while. He hadn't been lying—he did want to find Cantoney, as soon as possible. He could have phoned her and arranged to have her meet him. But something inside him was unwilling to let her off that easily. He sensed she tried to keep distance between them, even while they worked side by side. But that alone didn't challenge him. There was just something about her.

Let's face it, she *bothered* him. A lot. Wasn't it fair that she be bothered a little herself? He knew he'd accomplished that objective by his unexpected appearance here, and he whistled a little as he read the paper.

When the doorbell rang he called, "I'll get it," and without waiting for an answer he strode over and opened the door.

"Hello, you must have found Madeline. I've come for my paper. Are you done with it?" Ariel inquired as she spotted it laid out on the coffee table.

Cruz gave an abashed shrug. "Sorry about that. I had to do battle with Madeline and I sort of forgot to bring it over."

She waved aside his apology. "Forget it. I forgive you, especially if you're going to interrupt her monotonous day and take her away from all this."

"As a matter of fact, I am," he told her.

Ariel looked satisfied. "Good for you. It's about time someone walked in and shook that woman up." She eyed him approvingly. "You look like just the man for the job."

Madeline walked into the room to overhear the last remark, and she explained pointedly, "We're going to *work,* Ariel. Sorry to disappoint you."

Her neighbor raised her eyebrows. "Of course you are, Madeline, of course you are. And don't worry." Her eyes twinkled and cut back to Cruz, "I'm not disappointed. Not at all. Although I think your descriptive powers need a bit of work."

Cruz observed the wicked note in Ariel's tone and the almost desperate look on Madeline's face as she strode to the front door. "I'll talk to you later. We really have to go. Cruz is kind of in a hurry."

"I am?" he muttered in surprise.

Ariel strolled by both of them and gathered up her newspaper before joining them at the door. "I can take a hint," she informed them with a smile. "Far be it from me to interfere with two of Philadelphia's finest doing their jobs. Never let it be said that I got in the way of…duty." Her throaty laugh was full of innuendo, and Madeline gritted her teeth, while Cruz joined in the laughter. Honestly, Ariel was always irrepressible, but with Cruz around she was worse than usual. He encouraged her, just like now, his handsome face alight with amusement, as if Ariel had guessed correctly, and they had much more than work on their minds. She was thankful when she got the two of them into the hall, and turned to lock the door.

"Call me when you get home, Madeline," Ariel said. "Unless you're otherwise occupied of course. And Cruz, take good care of your hair. You never know, you could be bald by the time you're, oh, say fifty or so." She went into her own apartment, chuckling to herself, and Madeline walked quickly to the elevator, staring fixedly at the closed door. She ignored Cruz's puzzled expression and repeatedly stabbed her index finger at the button.

"She's really got a thing about hair," he observed, eyeing her closely. "She's mentioned it both times I've seen her."

Madeline shrugged and walked quickly into the elevator when its doors slid open. "She's a cosmetologist," she offered weakly. "She talks about everyone's hair." Determinedly she changed the subject. "So, tell me. Where will we find Cantoney today?"

"Only one way to find out," he answered. When they left the building he guided her to his car, which was parked illegally out front.

"You like to live dangerously," she noted. It wasn't the first time she knew of that he'd parked with such a disregard for city rules.

"Yeah, I live on the edge, all right," he agreed dryly. If she thought ignoring parking laws was living dangerously, he had a lot he'd like to show her on the subject. Oh, yeah. Heat immediately flared in his belly. Somehow Madeline gave him the impression that she needed a little of the unexpected in her life. As hard as she tried to keep that calm pose and remain in control of every aspect of her life, he'd bet that beneath that unruffled exterior lay a woman with a fiery passion. He was curious about that woman, the one he suspected lived beneath the cool facade. He found himself wondering about her all the time. Or maybe *fantasizing* would be a more accurate word. It was much easier to picture the woman he thought she really was when she was dressed as she was today. She was wearing a pair of slim-fitting jeans, and if she was aware of what they did to showcase those long legs, he knew she would never have worn them. She'd scraped her hair back again, into a fancy braid this time, and although regrettable, it was probably best. He didn't need the distraction right now.

Madeline got into the low-slung automobile. She couldn't help admiring the leather interior. Despite the possibilities of how Cruz had paid for this car, it was impossible not to appreciate its beauty.

"So, what do you think?" he asked as he got in and buckled his seat belt. "Buckle up, Madeline. Or do you need some help?" He reached up to the visor and pulled out a pair of darkly tinted sunglasses and put them on.

She obediently followed his command, loath to give him an excuse to lie half over her to help her with the belt. "What do I think of the car?" she clarified. "I think it's my turn to drive today, isn't it?"

At his look of horror, she had to laugh. "Don't tell me that you're one of those men who won't let a woman drive his precious machine?"

"Don't feel bad," he said. "I don't let anyone drive it."

"Isn't that a little ridiculous?" she asked. At his uncomprehending look, she added, "To become so attached to a car that you fear for its safety."

"It isn't ridiculous," he denied swiftly. "I'm like a kid with a new toy. I don't want to share it just yet. Although if you were to try your best to convince me to let you drive, I couldn't stop you. If you were to tempt me with your womanly wiles, I just might succumb. I'm not always very strong."

She didn't allow herself to think of just how weak he might actually be. Or of what he might have done in order to afford the car. Her imagination was wildly careening in another direction. Of just specifically what it might take to convince Cruz, as he was suggesting.

She firmly pushed the thoughts away. "It doesn't matter." She shrugged lightly, looking out the window as he pulled onto the interstate. "I don't feel like driving it, anyway."

"Liar. Do you think I don't know you're dying to get your hands on my—" he caught her swift glance, and deliberately paused another moment before completing the sentence "—steering wheel?"

"Believe whatever you want, Martinez," she invited breezily, returning her gaze to the scenery flying by.

"Oh, I will," he said with certainty. "And I believe that right now it's killing you. It's eating you alive. You want to drive this car so badly you can't stand it."

"Pay attention to the traffic," she instructed him, and deliberately changed the subject. "You never told me where we're going."

"The usual places Cantoney hangs out. First we'll look at his apartment, though. With any luck he'll still be sleeping off the effects of last night. I suspect that the Lords have been trying to establish drug turf. Their attempts probably sparked the shooting of Ramsey. The gang was more penny-ante until Cantoney became involved with them. He's got a taste for the stuff himself, and a few of the members have recently been nailed for possession with intent to deliver."

"That's why you think the real target of the shooting was Cantoney," Madeline stated.

Cruz nodded. "Fastest way to take out the competition would be to get rid of the brains of the operation. A hit like that would be difficult for the Lords to recover from quickly. From what I know of them, they don't have much of a chain of command. Cantoney's ego is too big to allow any of the other members to have much say. Makes him king of the hill, but if he's out of the picture, the Lords would be fighting among themselves for control, and then the new leader would have to reestablish drug contacts. Yeah, if someone were to get rid of Cantoney, the Lords wouldn't be a threat for some time."

They rode in silence for a while before Cruz reached to turn on the radio. He glanced at Madeline, fully expecting her to protest when a country song filled the air. Surprisingly, she didn't.

After a moment she asked nonchalantly, "Who sings this song?"

He thought for a moment. "Alan Jackson."

"No way," she scoffed. "You've forced me to listen to this stuff enough now that even I know it isn't Alan Jackson. I think it's Ricky Van Shelton."

"Who's the expert on country music in this car, you or me?" he inquired. "I'm telling you I'm sure it's Jackson."

Her head turned slowly to pin him with a gaze. "Care to make a little wager on that, Martinez?"

He caught on quickly, his face becoming instantly wary. "What kind of wager?" he asked cautiously.

"On the identity of the singer. If I'm right," she said, grinning wickedly, "I get to drive your car all the way back to my apartment." She almost laughed at the expression of terror that crossed his face. "If you're right . . ." She shrugged.

"If I'm right, what?"

"You name your prize," she suggested ingenuously. She cast him a sidelong gaze. What he might come up with as his winning prize didn't bear thinking about, but she wasn't going to have to worry about it. She knew she was right.

There was no way, under the circumstances, that Madeline was getting behind the wheel of his car, he assured himself, thinking quickly. Unless, of course, she was sitting on his lap. Both possibilities were equally unlikely. She might have an incredible sense of direction. Her memory might soak up every bit of information she absorbed from her cases and research. But he doubted very much that she'd even listened to a country song before they'd become partners. He sent her a speculative glance.

"I can name anything I want if I win?"

"Anything. But that's an awfully big if, Detective. You don't seem all that sure of yourself."

Cruz swiftly calculated the odds. He couldn't lose this bet. Madeline Casey had grown entirely too sure of herself. For once she was going to be proven wrong. *He* was going to prove her wrong. And then he was going to torture her by letting her wonder for a long, long time just what prize he would choose. His mouth curled in anticipation. All the possibilities were too much to resist.

"You're on," he told her smugly. "But don't worry. I'm a very gracious winner."

"Oh, I'm not worried," she replied calmly. "But you should be."

He shook his head at her self-assurance. But his disbelief quickly became chagrin when the song ended, and the DJ came on to identify it. "Ricky Van Shelton," he croaked. His face swung to hers. "How the hell did you know that?"

"We heard it once last week."

"One time? You've never listened to the music before, you don't know any of the singers, and you hear the blasted song one time and remember who sings it?" he demanded incredulously.

She lifted a shoulder. "I can't help it, it's a gift."

He muttered something in Spanish that sounded suspiciously like a string of curses.

She raised her eyebrows. "Want to go for two out of three?"

He shook his head ruefully. "I can't afford to. Somehow I think I'd end up owing you my first-born."

"Now why do I have the feeling that letting me drive your car is even more of a sacrifice for you?" she wondered aloud.

He aimed an aggrieved stare at her. "You're dangerous. Your memory ought to be outlawed. I'm surprised you aren't making your fortune counting cards in Vegas."

"Outwitting you is a lot easier," she answered smugly. "Why didn't you tell me you were such a poor loser?"

The remainder of the trip passed with Cruz trying to wheedle her into accepting another prize. "What would I want with a pair of your boots?" she asked once of one of his offers.

"You could use them to kick me the next time I walk into one of your traps," he suggested disgustedly.

When the car pulled up to Cantoney's address, Madeline raised her eyebrows. "Nice neighborhood," she noted. "How does he explain his ability to live in a place like this to his parole officer?"

"He probably claims he's living with friends. Maybe he is. But he's in something dirty up to his neck, you can bet on that," Cruz said grimly.

They heard voices from the hallway even as they walked up to Cantoney's door. The voices ceased when they knocked on the door. During the next few moments of silence Madeline knew they were being observed through the peephole on the door. "Detectives Martinez and Casey," she called. "We're here to speak to Dirk Cantoney."

A full minute passed before the door swung open. Cantoney himself appeared. "Well, what a surprise. Look, men, it's the poleece," he said in an exaggerated drawl. "I'll bet they've come to tell us they caught the guy that shot Ramsey."

Cruz looked over Cantoney's shoulder into the room beyond. Several Lords members were seated or standing in the area. "Hi, Ramsey," he said evenly. "Glad to see you're feeling better."

The boy stared back at Cruz, saying nothing.

Cantoney spoke again. "You'll have to make it quick, Detectives. We're busy."

Cruz reached into his pocket, extracted the picture of Valdez and held it out. "Have you ever seen this man before?"

Madeline watched Cantoney's face carefully, but it revealed nothing. He looked expressionlessly at the photo, and then back at Cruz. "Can't say I have. Why? Is he the shooter?"

"His name is Jose Valdez. We're not sure what his connection to this case is," Madeline inserted smoothly. "Maybe one of your guests will recognize him." For a moment she thought Cantoney would refuse, but finally he reached for the picture and handed it to one of the young men in the room.

"That the best you can do, Martinez?" Cantoney asked disparagingly. "Bring us a pretty picture of someone who *might* have something to do with the shooting?"

"Think you could do better, Dirk?" Cruz asked him softly.

"Man, I know I could," Cantoney retorted. "Another one of my friends could be shot before you find out anything."

Madeline's attention was divided between listening to their exchange and watching the faces of those who looked at the picture. She was disappointed, however. None exhibited any emotion at all when looking at it. Then one gang member exclaimed excitedly, "Hey! I think I know this dude!" Into the silence that accompanied his outburst, he added, "Yeah, I think it's my mama's ol' man." Laughter filled the room and another grabbed the picture. "No, it ain't. It's my fourth-grade teacher."

"Naw, it looks like my probation officer."

The photo was handed back to Cantoney, who turned to face the detectives again. "Sorry. Guess you're on your own. Show yourselves out. We've got to get back to work."

"Just what work would that be, Mr. Cantoney?" Madeline inquired.

The man directed his look at her, and it was chilling. "We're involved in some charity work, Detective. Getting poor youngsters off the streets." An outburst of laughter from the room accompanied his words, and the door shut in their faces.

They were silent until they left the building. "Another dead end," Cruz remarked dourly. "Did you catch that little dig about charity work?"

She had. "Taking poor youngsters off the street? If I had a suspicious mind, that would sound to me like he meant getting rid of one particular person for good."

"He was referring to his plan to retaliate for the shooting," Cruz agreed grimly. "The bastard. He's so cocky he practically came right out and told us what he was going to do."

"What's he been waiting for?" Madeline demanded. "Is it taking Cantoney this long to get his hands on a gun?"

"Could be. Or maybe it's taking him this long to come up with a way to shoot down a rival gang leader without landing himself back in prison."

"We've been pretty visible," Madeline agreed. "He's got to know that we suspect what he's planning. So we can figure that however he strikes back at the other gang, Dirk Cantoney will have an iron-tight alibi."

As they walked from the building and toward the car, Cruz took the keys from his pocket and reached for the door handle of the driver's side.

Madeline's hand got there first. When their eyes met, she said, "Aren't you forgetting something, Martinez?"

Her question hung in the air between them. "What?" he asked, stalling.

"This." She snatched the keys away and pushed him lightly. "I'll take it from here."

At any other time, under any other circumstances, Cruz would be delighted by that wicked gleam in her eye. It would bring about all sorts of fascinating fantasies about just how wicked, given the right provocation, she could be. But right now it drove his heart right down to the level of his boots. "Ah, c'mon, Madeline. You wouldn't do that to me, would you? After the disappointment we just had? I can't tolerate any more stress today."

His attempt to play on her pity didn't sway her. "Move aside and I won't have to give you any."

"It doesn't have to be right now, though, does it? You could drive the car some other time, I promise. Let's just put this off for a while."

Madeline opened the door while he pleaded, buckled herself in and adjusted the seat. "Are you walking or riding?" she asked. It wasn't until she turned on the ignition that he hurried. He almost sprinted to the passenger door and got in.

"You are merciless, do you know that?"

She grinned. "And you're a big baby."

The tires shrieked lightly as she pulled away from the curb, causing him to wince. "Take it easy," he muttered, as anxious as a new mother. "This is a valuable piece of machinery. It's not a police car."

"I can tell. It's a lot cleaner," she teased.

Casting a glance at him, she was amused to note that his face had turned two shades lighter than normal. He was grasping the dash with clenched knuckles. As she turned onto the freeway, he didn't relax a bit. If anything, he got even more uptight.

"Careful there. Look out for that car. Are you watching that semi? Slow down, for Pete's sake!"

"I'm barely driving the speed limit," she protested. She almost felt sorry for him. He looked downright ashen, and his knuckles were white. But his annoying directives didn't make her feel particularly patient. In fact, they made her want to do something cruel. And take the long way home doing it.

"How fast did you say this car could go?" she asked.

He shuddered at the question. "Forty-five. Fifty-five, tops. Definitely no faster than fifty-five."

"You're kidding!" she said in mock amazement. "I would have bet that it would go ninety, easy."

"Don't even think about it," he said through clenched teeth.

Her foot pressed down more firmly on the accelerator and the powerful car responded immediately. A delighted grin spread across her face.

"You are truly an evil woman, do you know that?"

A laugh was her only response, and he grasped the dash more tightly. Wouldn't you just know it? The first time he got to see Madeline Casey as loosened up as he'd always fantasized, she was behind the wheel of his precious car, doing twenty over the speed limit, putting him in the throes of cardiac arrest.

Someone up there, he thought darkly, had a hell of a sense of humor.

Chapter 10

Madeline snuggled more deeply into the soft, comfortable bed, a slight smile tilting her lips. She was having a wonderful dream, one from which she had no desire to awaken. She was driving Cruz's car again, doing one hundred miles an hour, and he was pleading with her to slow down. Getting the upper hand over Cruz had been delicious, and reliving it in her sleep was almost as good.

Her bed moved then, and she frowned a little, her eyes fluttering open. There was Cruz, next to her, just as in the dream. Her eyes drifted shut again. After a long moment they snapped open. She stared hard at the man beside her, and then past him. This didn't look like the inside of his car, this looked like her bedroom. Her eyes opened wider. It *was* her bedroom!

She sat up straight in bed, pulling the sheet with her protectively. It would only reach halfway up her chest. The rest was snagged beneath his jean-clad hips.

"What are you doing in my bedroom?" she demanded incredulously. She was still reeling from how easily he'd moved from her dream to her side. "How did you get in here? What do you want? Get out!"

His firm mouth curved at the way the words tumbled from her mouth. "You're grumpy in the morning," he observed. "Why doesn't that surprise me? Not that it will be morning much longer. It's almost noon. As to how I got in . . .''

"Ariel," she finished with him simultaneously. Her hand went to her forehead. Somehow she'd known that allowing her friend to badger her into giving her a spare key would cause only grief. She'd agreed to do so to guard against an emergency. But what was the prospect of an emergency compared to the possibility that Ariel would let a man into Madeline's apartment? Especially this man!

"Yeah, she heard me knocking and informed me that you *always* sleep late on Sundays. But she was very accommodating."

"I'll bet," Madeline muttered. She pulled ineffectually at the sheet again. "Would you please get up?"

Cruz rose to his feet and she snatched the sheet to her chin. "Now that I've got you moving, keep going until you're out the door. And don't come back."

Now that she mentioned it, the idea of leaving her bedroom did have some merit. At least, if he wasn't going to be involved in anything more than arguing with her. He'd witnessed her sleeping for only a few moments before she'd awakened, but the sight of her all soft and mussed and wearing a pale pink satiny thing was having a predictable effect on him. He knew that if he stayed one more instant his next move would be even more predictable. Right now she resembled the Maddy of his fantasies, and he knew he'd never think of her as Madeline again. Her scanty attire had his temperature rising, and rather than embarrass them both, he shrugged and said, "Okay, I guess you don't want to hear about my idea." He turned and walked out of the room.

Idea? She waited until he was out of sight of the bedroom door before bounding out of bed. Why did he always seem to get these leads for them to follow on the weekend? "Make some coffee." She threw the order after his departing form and shut the door firmly. He wasn't going anywhere or doing anything involving this investigation without her.

As she hurried through her shower and dressed, she mentally called him every rotten name she'd ever heard, and even strung a few together creatively. Applying her makeup in record time, she debated about what to do with her hair, and then left it down. She'd already spent twenty minutes, and she wasn't certain how much time he'd allow before he left without her.

She smelled the coffee's aroma as soon as she opened the door. Cruz was seated at the kitchen counter sipping a cup of the brew. He poured her a cup and pushed it toward her. He watched, amused, as her eyes closed in satisfaction at the first strong drink. His feeling of amusement quickly fled, however, when he noticed what she was wearing. The heat that mushroomed in his gut had nothing to do with the hot coffee. Black leggings clung faithfully to her long slender legs, and over them she was wearing a long white oversize cotton sweater. The bulky top was a tantalizing tease about what lay under it, and the leggings left little to the imagination about what lay under *them*. For the second time that morning he wondered just how bright he'd been to come here. His imagination didn't need any more fodder for the wild fantasies it was capable of spinning about her.

He waited for half a cup to improve her mood before he spoke again. "Only heathens sleep late on Sundays. You should have been at church, repenting for the cruel way you treated me yesterday."

She finished the rest of her coffee and poured herself some more. He held out his cup and she refilled it for him. It always took at least one shot of caffeine to jolt her awake in the morning. Today that job had been completed by the sight of him on her bed. The coffee calmed her nerves, which his presence had brought instantly, jangling awake. Dreaming about him, then seeing the object of her dream as soon as she had opened her eyes, was enough to send her senses spinning. Especially since she dimly recalled that the most recent dream had not been the only one in which he'd starred last night.

She drank deeply from the second cup and it was another moment before she responded to his remark. "I didn't have a guilty conscience, so there was no need for me to pray for forgiveness."

His look was reproachful. "You should have felt very guilty. My blood pressure was at a dangerous level by the time you screeched to a stop out front yesterday." But it hadn't been as high as it had risen in the minute he'd spent beside her on the bed. Sixty seconds was such a short time, but it had been long enough for him to imagine stretching out beside her. To think about awakening her in the slowest, sweetest way possible. To pull her beneath him, and . . . He reined in the erotic thoughts firmly.

"Let's hear about this fantastic idea of yours," she said somewhat caustically. "And it had better be good." They rose to go.

"All my ideas are good," he answered smugly as he followed her out of the apartment. "And this one is excellent."

* * *

Madeline looked about curiously when they pulled to a stop in front of a small brick home. It was located on a street with others just like it; the houses were rather close together, and some were a little run-down. But the one they approached as they went up the walk appeared well tended. The lawn was neatly mowed and the trim looked freshly painted.

"I'm not going one more step unless you tell me what we're doing here," she ordered, stopping in the middle of the walk. He had steadfastly refused to answer all her questions on the trip over, choosing instead to comment on what he'd thought of her sleeping attire. The banter hadn't done her temper a bit of good, and even knowing he was getting even with her for the bet she'd won yesterday didn't improve her mood. "I can't believe we're going to find evidence of a gun supplier in this neighborhood."

"Why not?" he countered. "This place isn't nearly as nice as where we found Cantoney yesterday." He managed to guide her up the steps of the porch, and raised a finger to his lips to hush her when her mouth opened again. "Be ready for anything, Madeline, and I do mean anything. I'm going to need you to back me up." He reached out to pound on the door, shouting, "Police! Open up."

Her eyes widened. Of all the stupid, dangerous things to do! Wait until they got out of this! How could he let her walk into a situation without briefing her beforehand? The door flew open and Cruz strode through it, Madeline closely following him. Her hand hovered around the area where her revolver was tucked, at the base of her back. She noticed for the first time that he wasn't even wearing a gun, and her mouth thinned. If they got out of this alive, she was really, really going to kill him this time!

"Hey, look! It's the big, bad police detective," someone called from the next room.

"Come here, Mr. Detective, and give me a kiss," a woman's voice called.

Cruz stopped suddenly in the hallway and Madeline ran into his back. Her confused brain took a few instants to recognize just what kind of situation he had led her into. "Martinez!" she hissed. "This is your parents' home!"

He slanted a grin at her. "You're very astute, Madeline. That's what I admire most about you. That and your legs." He didn't allow her to respond before grabbing her hand and pulling her along with him into the kitchen.

She stood awkwardly aside as Cruz was hugged by someone she assumed was his mother. She felt even more ill at ease when the woman released him and drew back to study Madeline.

Cruz bore little physical resemblance to Mrs. Martinez. They both had dark hair, but she was a brunette several shades lighter than he. Visible threads of gray traced through her hair, which she wore in short waves around her face. Her eyes were a shocking shade of blue, and she came up only to her son's broad shoulders.

"This is Madeline Casey, Mom, the partner I was telling you about." He lowered his voice to an undertone meant to be over-heard. "I had to kidnap her. The only way to get her out of her apartment was to pretend we would be working today. She thinks she's here to arrest a dangerous criminal."

His mother tapped him on the chest. "Cruz, you are so bad," she scolded him. And then she smiled at Madeline, and revealed all the charm that her son must have inherited from her. "Welcome, Madeline. I apologize for my son. You have all my sympathy, having to work with him all day. Me, I can't stand to have him around for more than an hour or two. Such a tease."

"Mom," he complained in an aggrieved tone, reaching past her to snatch a cookie from the counter. "You'll ruin her image of me. Madeline thinks I'm the greatest thing since sliced bread."

"You're a little confused," Madeline informed him saccharinely. "Although I'd like to see you sliced *like* bread."

"It's my fault," his mother said apologetically. "He's been so busy lately, and I told him to bring you by. I thought he had the manners to issue an invitation, but obviously I was wrong. Stay and enjoy yourself anyway," she urged. "I could easily be persuaded to show you some very embarrassing pictures of him when he was a child."

"You've got a deal." Madeline smiled, in spite of her desire to do Cruz some serious physical damage.

"Don't show her the one of me naked on the rug," Cruz advised his mother as he took Madeline's arm and guided her into the next room. "I have to work with her. I want her to still respect me, not to be constantly undressing me with her eyes."

The room they entered next was packed with people, some sitting, others standing, and still others sprawled on the floor. Children were running shrieking through the room and out into the hallway. The television was on, but no one appeared to be watching it. It seemed to Madeline as if twenty different conversations halted when they entered.

The silence seemed to stretch interminably, but probably lasted only a few seconds. Then the voices started again at once.

"Cruz! Glad you made it. There's something I need to talk to you about...." A young, handsome man in his early twenties stepped forward.

"Unca Cwuz! Unca Cwuz! See what I can do! Watch me, Unca Cwuz!" A chubby toddler with dimples did a lumbersome somersault, landing neatly on Cruz's toes.

"Big brother! Give me a hug!" This from the young woman Madeline remembered seeing on the street the second day she'd worked with Cruz.

"You owe me ten from that bet last week, brother. When are you going to learn never to bet against the Phillies?" called one of the men sitting near the TV.

Cruz was engulfed by his relatives, all anxious to greet him. He kissed the women, clapped the men on the shoulders and swung the children in the air. Finally he reached down for the acrobatic toddler still lying across his boots. As he situated the little boy on his hip, the toddler frowned and pointed a chubby finger at Madeline.

"Unca Cwuz, who's dis?"

It seemed to Madeline as if every eye in the room was trained on her, and she experienced a fierce desire to be somewhere, *anywhere* else in the world.

"This," Cruz said, drawing Madeline toward him and then turning her gently toward the group, "is my partner, Madeline Casey." He proceeded to introduce each of his brothers, sisters, in-laws, nieces and nephews one by one. He said solemnly to the nephew in his arms, "Madeline wanted to learn to be a great detective, so she's working with me for a while."

Hoots and catcalls met his pronouncement.

"She could probably learn *something* from you, all right," Kevin chided with a laugh.

"When I ran into them on the street a couple of weeks ago, it looked as though Madeline was teaching Cruz something!" his sister Maureen told the family.

Madeline froze, waiting for her to reveal how engrossed they'd seemed in each other. But the girl went blithely on, "She got Cruz to eat a hot dog, can you believe it?"

"No way!"

"I wish I could have seen that!"

"Miracle worker," Cruz's younger brother Miguel intoned, kneeling before Madeline clownishly. "Please tell his humble family how you managed a feat of such magnificent proportions."

Cruz hauled Miguel up by his shirt. "Very funny," he told the group. "It will please you all greatly to learn that Madeline knows the location of every grease grill in the city, and she won't rest until she drags me to all of them."

"Good woman!"

"Way to go!"

"About time you found someone you can't twist around your little finger," his mother called from the other room. "Go see your father. He should be on the patio burning the meat."

Cruz indicated for Madeline to precede him, and, taking her elbow, he guided her through the house to the back door.

When they were out of earshot of the others, Madeline whispered, "I am absolutely not going to stay for dinner, Martinez. The joke's over. Take me home."

"What? And disappoint my parents? They've been after me to bring you over here to meet them. What are they going to think if you go running screaming in the opposite direction?"

"They'll probably think, 'There goes another person that Cruz has driven crazy!'" Madeline replied fiercely. "And they'd be right. I cannot believe you tricked me like this! You knew I assumed that you had an idea about the case."

"Ah, but you should never assume anything," Cruz counseled her wisely. "That's the first rule of police work."

Only the presence of his father on the patio stopped Madeline from giving Cruz a hard push out the doorway. As it was, she contented herself with an inconspicuous jab to his ribs as she passed through the door he held for her.

The twinkle in the elder Martinez's eye as he straightened from bending over the grill told Madeline that he'd witnessed her rebellion. "Madeline, Tomas Martinez. Pop, this is my partner, Madeline Casey."

"I'm pleased to meet you, Madeline," Tomas said. "I hope working with my son hasn't been too trying."

It was easy to see where Cruz had gotten his striking good looks. Tomas Martinez was still a very attractive man. His face wasn't as lean as Cruz's, and he was thicker through the chest and shoulders. He must have been close to sixty in order to have children the ages of his, but he didn't appear that old.

Madeline could feel her usual reserve with strangers thaw a bit. "I can handle your son."

"You can? Then maybe you could give pointers to his mother and me. We could use some tips." He shook his head with mock solemnity.

"Yes, Madeline, do tell," Cruz invited wickedly. "What's your secret?"

She matched him look for look. "Never let him get the upper hand," she said in an aside to his father. "He becomes unbearable in a hurry."

"You noticed that, too?" his father asked interestedly.

"How are you coming with that meat, Pop?" Cruz interrupted them to inquire. He stepped over and lifted the lid off the grill. "It looks about done to me."

His father shooed him away. "Leave me alone. Never interrupt a master at work."

"Mom!" Cruz called through the door. "Pop's going to burn the meat again."

"Don't you let him!" she called back. "Why do you suppose I sent you out there? You need to supervise him."

"Stop hanging over my shoulder," his father chided him. "Why haven't you offered your guest something to drink? Where are your manners?"

"Oh, I can't stay," Madeline protested.

"Of course you can." Tomas waved aside her protest easily.

"Sure you're staying," Cruz added. "How else would you get home?"

The look she aimed at him promised retribution. "I really hadn't planned to be gone long."

"And I know how important planning is to you," he returned. "What would you like to drink, Madeline? A beer? Soda?"

Seeing no other way out of the situation, Madeline gave in with as much grace as possible. After all, it wouldn't do to make a scene in front of his family. It wasn't Cruz's parents' fault that their son was the most maddening, manipulating man she'd ever met. She would deal with him later, though, she vowed. He wouldn't be allowed to continue walking in and out of her personal life at will.

Cruz went to the kitchen, leaving her alone with his father. Tomas immediately engaged her in conversation. "Cruz tells us that you recently transferred to the Southwest District."

She immediately grew tense. Never in her worst nightmare would she have dreamed she'd have to make polite conversation with the father of a man she was investigating.

"I've been with the department for ten years."

"And already you're a Detective Sergeant. That's quite an accomplishment at your age. I know how hard Cruz worked for that rank."

Madeline was nonplussed. There was no mistaking the admiration in the man's tone. It struck her as incongruous that a man she'd just met displayed more respect for her career advancement than her own father ever had. Of course, she could be named chief and she doubted it would win her Geoffrey Casey's respect. He'd always disapproved of her job—and, she feared, of her. She'd long ago given up the hope of ever doing anything that would elicit the amount of respect from him that she'd just received from Tomas.

"We were surprised when we learned Cruz would take the test for sergeant," the man went on. "He'd never seemed interested before. At one time we thought he would stay in undercover work forever. His mother was greatly relieved when he went back to plainclothes detail. She worried about him constantly."

"And his father?" Madeline dared to ask softly.

The dark eyes so like Cruz's caught hers. "I worried, too," he admitted. "A man's family is the most precious thing in the world to him. Police work is always dangerous, and when Cruz was shot, we were afraid we would lose him."

Cruz rejoined them then, and handed Madeline a diet soda. Tomas opened the grill and inspected the roast again. "I think it's ready. Cruz, hand me the platter."

As he obeyed, Cruz peered over his father's shoulder. "I think it was ready twenty minutes ago. You burned the edges again."

"Everyone's a critic," Tomas grumbled good-naturedly. "I like my roast that way."

When they went inside, the family was milling around the dining room, seating the youngsters at card tables and the adults at the dining table. Madeline excused herself to go to the rest room to remove her gun and holster. Tucking them into her purse, she reentered the dining room and allowed Cruz to seat her. His sisters were still bustling back and forth from the kitchen, helping Mrs. Martinez carry in the food.

When all were finally sitting down and grace was said, the din began anew. Plates and bowls were passed, accompanied by several noisy conversations. The atmosphere was as alien to her

memories of family meals as it was possible to be. Mr. and Mrs.
Martinez were in the midst of it all, praising, admonishing and
joking with their family. Yet Madeline was not given time to feel
out of place. She was kept busy passing dishes and answering
questions thrown her way. Cruz was seated next to her, and it was
several minutes before she caught him placing more vegetables on
her plate.

He grinned when he was found out, unrepentant. "Madeline
loves green vegetables. She can't get enough of them." He spooned
another large helping of broccoli onto her dish. "Go ahead," he
invited. "There's plenty more where that came from."

"Someone should have taken you in hand a long time ago," she
informed him narrowly. "You're too funny for your own good."

"Go ahead and try," Cruz's sister Shannon invited her. "He was
barely tolerable when we were kids and we could gang up on him.
Now that he's bigger and taller than anyone else in the family, it's
a little harder."

"There is one way to keep him in line," Madeline said slowly, her
eyes sparkling with remembrance. "He was almost meek while I
was driving his—"

"More milk, Madeline?" he interrupted her quickly.

But his sister gasped. "He let you drive his car?"

It seemed to Cruz that his sister's voice pierced through every
other bit of noise in the room. An uproar ensued.

"Hey, no fair. When I asked, you said no one drove it but you."

"The precious car! Can I use it to take Lisa out next weekend,
Cruz?"

"What's this? You haven't even let me drive it!" This was from
his father.

Cruz raised his hands for silence. "Time out! The only reason
she drove it was because I lost a bet. Believe me, I died a thousand
deaths watching her abuse it."

Madeline continued to eat sedately. "He's a sore loser, too," she
informed the family, and they laughed. And there was no more
discomfort after that. It seemed odd to her later when she thought
about it. Nothing in her experience had prepared her for the Martinezes. Their noisy discussions, laughter and teasing were full of
mutual love and concern for each other. She wanted to sit back and
observe it, but she quickly learned that wasn't allowed in this
house. Everyone at the table was pulled into conversations, and her
opinion was sought more than once when one of Cruz's siblings
was arguing with him.

Comparisons between this family and her own were ludicrous. There were simply no similarities to be found. Kathleen Martinez exhibited the same twinkle in her eye and the same penchant for teasing that could be seen in Cruz. Tomas was unabashedly proud of his family. Grandchildren crawled all over their aunts, uncles and grandparents, to the obvious enjoyment of the adults. Madeline wasn't used to being asked frank questions about herself by people she'd just met. But it was impossible to remain unaffected by the lighthearted atmosphere. She found herself just as curious about them.

Cruz watched Madeline relate to his family with a faint smile. This had turned out better than he'd expected. His family had accepted her as readily as they would any guest brought home. He'd had no qualms about that. It was her reaction to them that he'd wondered about, but he needn't have worried. She seemed perfectly at ease, and, although he'd had to step in once or twice to head off a particularly nosy question from one of his siblings, Madeline was, overall, holding her own. Watching her here, talking to his family, proved fascinating. That cool reserve that was so much a part of her was still present. But he thought that right now it was more relaxed than usual. He observed as Maureen involved Madeline in a discussion on the horrors of naturally curly hair, and Shannon asked her opinion about the latest political news.

Madeline rose at the end of the meal and prepared to help clear the table. The women stopped her.

"Forget it, Madeline. On Sundays in this house, dishes are the men's job."

She raised her eyebrows as she watched Cruz and his brothers start gathering plates with a tremendous clatter. "Well, that's certainly an enlightened idea."

Kathleen said, "It's a new twist on the old-fashioned custom of the men retiring to the parlor after a meal for a smoke. In this house, we allow them to do their male bonding over a sinkful of dirty pans."

"While the women smoke cigars in the parlor," Kevin called.

"I dry," Cruz said.

"No way. It's your turn to wash, buddy."

"You're crazy. I washed last week."

The women left the men to their bickering and went to the living room. Madeline had no more than sat down when she was approached by Cruz's oldest niece—Robin, she thought her name was. The girl eyed her soberly.

Madeline smiled tentatively. She'd had little contact with children, except, on rare occasions, during a case.

Robin spoke. "Do you want to see my Barbie dolls? I brought them with me today."

Disarmed, Madeline nodded. "I'd love to, Robin." The girl took her by the hand, called for her aunt Maureen to follow them, and led the two upstairs.

It was well over an hour later when Madeline returned to the living room. Cruz was sprawled on the floor, with two little ones using him for a sofa. His eyes lit up when he saw her, and he motioned her over. "Where have you been?"

She sank gracefully next to him, tucking her legs beneath her. "Admiring Robin's Barbie collection. My, those dolls sure live in the fast lane."

His eyes left hers and looked at Robin, who was climbing up on her father's lap. "Did you have fun playing Barbies, honey?"

The little girl bobbed her head vehemently. "Uh-huh! I learned lots of neat stuff. Maureen taught me how to braid Barbie's hair, and Madeline showed me how to make Barbie's skirts longer." She added solemnly, "'Cause they're really too short to get respect."

Stunned silence in the room was followed by gales of laughter. Cruz noted the quick flush that rose to Madeline's cheeks. He teased, "Well, if anyone can teach you how to get respect, it's this lady." In an undertone he asked, "Bet you didn't find any primly tailored jackets and pants in the wardrobe, did you?"

"Not a one," she answered wryly. "Most of the outfits were suitable for roller-blading and beauty pageants. Reality doesn't play a very big part in Barbie's life. And if that was a slam about my wardrobe," she added, "watch it. Or I just may have to comment on your seemingly insatiable desire for blue jeans and cowboy boots."

They took their leave shortly after, and Madeline said goodbye to each member of the family. She thanked Mr. and Mrs. Martinez for their hospitality.

Kathleen waved away her thanks. "We're glad you came. Next time, don't wait for Cruz to kidnap you. You're welcome anytime."

Tomas added, "You'll have to come back and tell me how you got Cruz to let you drive his car. Maybe it will work for me."

"Sorry," Cruz denied swiftly. "I only fall for that particular bet once."

"You won't forget what we talked about, will you, Cruz?" Miguel asked.

"I'll run home and get my checkbook," Cruz promised. "I'll drop the check off here and you can swing by tomorrow before classes and pick it up."

"Thanks," Miguel said with relief in his voice. "You're the best."

It took several more minutes to get away, as the family gathered around to hug Cruz.

Getting into the car and buckling up, Madeline noted, "I liked your family. They all seemed very nice." She gave him a sidelong glance. "And everyone seemed to have *your* number."

"That's the problem with families," he agreed. "No respect. Do you mind if we stop at my place before I take you home? I need to get something."

"Your checkbook?" Madeline asked. At his look she explained, "I heard what you said to Miguel. He seemed pretty relieved. So, tell me. Did you lose a bet to him, too?"

He chuckled. "No, I didn't lose a bet to him. I think my experience with you yesterday cured me of betting for good. He got in a bind at college again. Some additional fees cropped up and he needs some extra money, that's all. I'm just helping him out."

"Helping him out?" she pressed. "Or putting him through school?" She knew she had guessed correctly by his silence. "You're putting Maureen through college, too, aren't you?"

He actually squirmed. "Not exactly." At her expectant look he sighed. "They both have gotten some grants. I didn't want them to have to graduate with huge loans hanging over their heads, that's all. I give them enough to cover what the grants don't."

Maureen had intimated as much to her when they were upstairs. And Madeline could guess that Cruz was downplaying his role in their college careers. Regardless of his protests, she guessed that Cruz was the sole reason his two youngest siblings could go to college. Here was another huge expense that Cruz could inexplicably afford. Her throat tight, she inquired, "And your parents' house? Were they able to buy that because of you, too?"

"No," he denied firmly. Then he gave a crooked smile. "You don't realize how machismo works in my family. It's perfectly acceptable for an older brother to help out a younger sibling. But I couldn't offer that kind of help to my father. That would be a slap at his male pride. I wouldn't offend him that way. It's enough that I'm able to ease his financial burden of educating the two youngest." And it had been difficult to get his father to accept that kind of help, he remembered wryly. It had taken all of Cruz's considerable diplomacy to word it in such a way as not to insult the man from whom he'd inherited his own fierce pride.

Madeline was silent. Actually, what she'd learned today only underlined what she'd already surmised about him. The fancy car, the expensive apartment and the financial help he was giving his siblings all pointed to one thing. Cruz Martinez had an outside source of income. She'd already drawn that conclusion, so why should this latest bit of evidence bother her?

And she couldn't help admitting that it *did* bother her. She was too good a cop to leap to any conclusions about how he earned that second income, but it was an unknown entity, and she didn't like loose ends. She preferred things in her life lined up in order, and she didn't rest on a case until she could fit every piece of evidence into its proper compartment. She hadn't found anything solid on him yet, and until she did she was going to have to live with this nagging sense of uncertainty.

She scowled. Uncertainty made her uncomfortable, and discomfort kept her edgy. She'd felt like that only once before, before it had become obvious that Dennis Belding had used her for his own financial gain. But that was ridiculous. Why should she feel that way now? The two situations had nothing in common. She had loved Dennis, and Cruz . . . Cruz was only a job. It was just difficult to spend so much time working as closely as she did with him and not feel some sort of regret that he, like so many crooks before him, might have decided to take the easy way out.

They arrived at his apartment in silence. As he pulled in to a parking place Cruz sent Madeline a concerned glance. Since the brief exchange they'd had upon leaving his folks' house, she'd fallen into a reflective silence. Maybe he'd made a mistake kidnapping her today. From the little she'd told him about her family, his own must have been a shocking contrast.

"Care to come up?" he invited, his hand hesitating on the door handle.

She surprised him with her answer. "Sure." She might as well take this opportunity to see his apartment. It was the only way she was going to be able to tell how far out of his price range it appeared to be.

She cast a wary glance around as they entered the front door of the building, hoping that his landlady would not be in sight. Otherwise she would be required to do some very fast talking to explain her previous presence at the building. Fortunately for her, they saw no one else, either in the hallways or the elevator.

After Cruz unlocked his apartment and ushered her inside, Madeline stopped in shock. Far from the opulent surroundings that she'd half expected, half feared, the huge space was very bare. She walked inside and turned around slowly, looking at the place.

Cruz shut the door in back of them and leaned against it. For some reason he couldn't put a name to, he was waiting in anticipation of Madeline's reaction to his home. He watched through hooded eyes as she trailed her hand over the wide woodwork with its recent coats of varnish. His gaze followed her to the huge set of windows that looked out at the street. He'd done nothing about curtains yet. He was less concerned about privacy than with preserving the view afforded him at night, when the lights veiled the city like a glittering blanket.

His gaze brooding, he asked himself silently why her approval of his home meant so much to him.

Chapter 11

Madeline turned to face him, and he caught his breath. The early-evening sunlight framed her where she stood in front of the windows. It haloed her hair, turning it into a waterfall of cascading fire. He didn't speak; he couldn't. She made the most breathtaking picture he could imagine, and his throat was too full.

"Looks like you're in the middle of quite a project," she stated. A scaffolding was pushed against one wall. In a corner were piles of tarps and paint cans. The air smelled faintly of paint and varnish. Even her untutored eye could tell that the walls had fresh Sheetrock, and the woodwork had been stripped and stained. The floor was bare and dull, as if it had been sanded.

At his continued silence, she said, "You must have quite a crew working for you."

He finally moved, and when he answered, his voice was a pitch lower than normal. "A crew of one most of the time." When she frowned uncomprehendingly, he tapped himself on the chest laconically. "Me."

"You?" she repeated in surprise. Why didn't he have trained craftsmen come in and take care of all this construction for him? She suspected he could afford it. Few people would have the patience or the inclination to take on a project of this magnitude by themselves.

Talking about what he'd done so far to the place was usually one of Cruz's favorite topics. But right now it was the last thing on his mind. He was still reeling from the curious sense of rightness he got at seeing Madeline in his home for the first time. He had the oddest sense of déjà vu, as if he'd seen her standing in front of those same windows many times before. Which perhaps he had. He'd pictured her several times in his home.

In his bed.

He mentally shook himself. That was not the avenue he wanted his thoughts to travel right now, so he forced himself to focus on the topic at hand. "Of course, I had more help in the beginning. After I'd gutted the place, a crew did come in and frame it up for me. Naturally I had plumbers and electricians. I wanted to live in it right away, so they went ahead and did the remodeling necessary for the kitchen and the loft."

Madeline's eyes traveled in the direction he indicated. A spiral staircase rose from the room and rose upward to what, she knew without being told, was his bedroom. A shiver raced down her spine at the thought of walking up those stairs. She pulled her gaze away and trained them back on him.

"C'mon." He pushed himself away from the wall. "I'll give you a guided tour." It would be a way to keep his mind busy, which persisted in other, more erotic meanderings. He ushered her down a hallway and opened each of the doors. "These will be two bedrooms and a bath. I haven't done anything back here except put up the Sheetrock." Madeline walked into the rooms curiously. The woodwork lay neatly in a pile along one wall in each room, waiting to be stripped and stained before it would be reapplied. "I won't finish those rooms until last," he said as they walked toward the kitchen.

"This is going to be quite a place," Madeline remarked. "Pretty big for one person."

He propped himself against the counter and watched her soberly. "I don't intend to live in it by myself."

Her breath stopped in her throat. Of course. Why hadn't she considered that? A man who looked like Cruz was bound to know throngs of women, most of whom would give their eyeteeth to live with him. She couldn't prevent a reaction to his words, and he easily read her amazement.

"I mean, not forever. I'd like to have a family someday. This is a decent neighborhood. It would be a safe place to raise kids."

Her eyebrows arched. "Do you have a mother for these children picked out, or do you plan to adopt?" She hid her real interest in his answer by prowling around his large, well-equipped kitchen.

"I plan to have kids the old-fashioned way," he drawled. "But, no, I don't have anyone in mind for the task."

She didn't put a name to the wash of relief that swept through her at his words. It didn't matter a whit to her if he planned to marry tomorrow. Cruz Martinez was only of interest to her while she gathered evidence to turn over to Brewer. And once she was finished, it was possible that the man might not be starting a family for a very long time.

But something besides his words told her how much he wanted that family. Everything about this home he was making spoke of a person determined to fill it up. The kitchen was large, with a huge center island curving through it. Stools sat neatly beside it, as if waiting for the children he spoke of.

"Over here—" his voice interrupted her explorations "—will be a small office. I'll start on that after I finish the great room." She followed him to the area he indicated, then they wandered back into the living room.

"What are your..." Her voice came out husky, and she cleared her throat. "What else are you planning to do with it?"

"I'm almost finished in here. I've stripped and sanded the floor, and I've the calluses on my knees to prove it."

She recalled then a conversation they'd had in which he'd invited her to guess what he'd been doing on his knees all weekend. Even if she'd allowed him to bait her into joining in his game, she never would have guessed that he'd been stripping floors. She cast him a reproving look, and could see from the irrepressible grin on his face that he was remembering the same moment.

"I'm sure all minutes that you're on your knees are well spent."

His smile disappeared. "You can bet on that."

A long moment fraught with unspoken tension stretched between them. Cruz broke the silence first. "After I stain and varnish, I'll have to buy some rugs. I don't want to carpet over these hardwood floors. Part of this room will be a dining area, but most will be a living area. I like lots of space."

That was obvious. But how had he afforded all this space? That was the question still plaguing Madeline. "Why are you doing so much of the work yourself? You could...I mean, couldn't you have someone fix it up for you? It wouldn't take so long then."

He shrugged. "I'm in no hurry. And there's a feeling of satisfaction I get from doing the work myself." When she still looked unconvinced, he added, "Believe it or not, I'm very good with my hands."

She was certain he spoke the truth. But her mind didn't dwell on the more mundane meaning of his words. Cruz was a toucher; she'd realized that soon after she'd met him. She'd seen how physically affectionate he was with his family. Right now he was absently rubbing two fingers along the satiny finish of the windowsill he was propped against. Her eyes trailed over his muscled thighs outlined faithfully by the worn denim. She wondered waspishly if the reason he leaned against everything in sight was that he knew the pose showed his long, hard body off to such advantage. He probably wore jeans constantly for the same reason. They clung lovingly to his thighs and gloved his sex. She pulled her gaze away with effort, and the fact that it had taken effort annoyed her.

"Why don't you ever stand up straight?" she snapped, turning away from the indolent picture he made.

He noted her sign of temper and wondered at it. "Why stand when you can lean?" he asked logically. "Why sit when you can slouch?"

"Your chiropractor must love you."

"Never been to one," he answered diffidently. "I'm the picture of health."

He was certainly that. And more. The picture of a drop-dead gorgeous man in his prime, a healthy male animal who managed to exude good-humored charm and sexiness at the same time. That should be outlawed. *He* should be outlawed. Suddenly the room seemed much too small. She reminded herself that the man she was admiring visually might be less than admirable in other ways. And the fact that she needed such a reminder yet again was proof that she'd stayed too long in his presence.

He hadn't made an offer to show her upstairs, and he didn't intend to. Cruz wasn't sure how much longer he could trust himself not to make a move toward her, and in the intimate surroundings of his bedroom the temptation would be even greater. As perfect as she seemed standing here, he was certain she would seem even more so in his room, where he'd imagined her too many times for comfort.

"Well, if you're ready, I'm sure you want to get back to your parents' after you take me home," Madeline said, her uneasiness growing. She was tiring of the incessant warnings her mind issued her every time she noticed with appreciation the way he moved, talked or looked. The constant tug-of-war taking place inside her was exhausting. This feeling of teetering on the edge was wearing on her nerves, and on her control.

"There's no rush," Cruz said dismissively without remarking on her sudden anxiousness to leave. "I'm hungry again. Do you want a sandwich?"

Her heart sank at the thought of spending one more minute in his apartment. The atmosphere seemed too intimate somehow, and though she was obviously the only one to feel it, she wanted out of here before it acted to lower her defenses even further. "You can't possibly want to eat again," she argued with him desperately, following him out to the kitchen.

"But I do," he countered. "I didn't have much at Mom's. I was too worried about keeping your plate full."

An unladylike snort was her answer and he smiled to himself. He'd had plenty to eat earlier, and it was another kind of hunger that was gnawing at him right now. But he was willing to seize any excuse to keep her here a few more minutes, and for some reason that seemed important to him. Especially since she was exhibiting a sudden desire to escape.

"Martinez, I do not want anything to . . . eat," she finished as a plate with a sandwich was placed before her.

"Look, Ma, no green things," he joked. Her sandwich was missing the lettuce and fixings he'd piled on his own.

Her voice was tinged with frustration. "I'm not hungry."

"Heard it before. Clean your plate, or I won't take you home."

She regarded him with a narrowed look. That was nothing short of bribery, and he'd been manipulating events all day. But if eating the darn sandwich was all it would take to get her safely home and alone once again, she'd let him get away with it one last time.

She picked up the sandwich and determinedly chewed. But swallowing proved to be a bit more of a problem while sitting across from Cruz, with his liquid dark eyes trained on her face. She reached an unsteady hand for the glass of milk he'd placed beside her plate. Whatever was wrong with her? she scolded herself, but she was afraid she knew. Cruz Martinez had found the chink in the armor that usually guarded her emotions, and she wasn't being allowed the time she needed to carefully replace her defenses. Was it possible for someone with larceny in his heart to look so good and be so enticing? Why couldn't it be easier to divine what a person was truly like? This was the same man who'd made an impassioned speech earlier about the need for more youth programs in the city. The love he shared with his family had been very evident today. How could she reconcile the man who held his small nieces and nephews with a look of softness on his face, with the criminal responsible for putting guns into the hands of kids?

It made no sense, and even less after meeting his family today. Tomas and Kathleen Martinez were two people secure in their pride for their children. Would Cruz risk his father's respect? Could he possibly be capable of taking a risk that would destroy his parents' pride and loyalty if it was ever exposed?

Other people were capable of just that, she knew. She'd been a cop long enough to see plenty of criminals, some of whom had been considered pillars of the community. Her ex-fiancé had been a prime example of someone with a perfect exterior that masked a black soul. But her belief in Dennis, she now realized, had more to do with her inability to admit she could have been so wrong about him. Later she'd been able to recall instances in their relationship when his careful mask had slipped a bit. If she'd been willing to see him for what he was, the opportunity had been there.

"Are you done mangling that sandwich yet?" Cruz indicated the bread that was twisted in her hands, only a few bites gone from it. Madeline looked down and for the first time noticed the damage she'd done to the food.

"Sorry," she said tightly. "I really wasn't hungry."

He nodded. "Let me grab something and we can be on our way."

He went to one of the drawers in the kitchen and withdrew his checkbook, pushing it into his back pocket. Madeline cleared their plates off the counter, rinsed them and placed them in the dishwasher. She turned to see him watching her, an odd light in his eye at the sight of her performing the mundane task.

She hurried past him to grab the purse she'd set on the floor of the living room, but he didn't immediately follow. "C'mon, Martinez," she said, not altogether jokingly, "are you driving or am I going to have to walk?"

He moved then, but not, as she'd hoped, in the direction of the door. Instead his booted feet walked deliberately over and stopped in front of her. Inches from her, in fact.

"What'd you call me?"

His nearness was the last thing she wanted to deal with. She was already edgy from her warring emotions, and she definitely didn't need him this close. She inched backward a little, until she found the wall behind her. "I called you..." To her chagrin, her voice sounded a little breathless. "What I always call you. Martinez." Her voice trailed to a whisper at the intent on his face.

His arms came up to rest upon the wall on either side of her shoulders. "Cruz," he said, the gentleness in his tone contrasting with the dark intensity in his eyes. "Call me by my name, Maddy."

She didn't even comprehend the hated nickname on his lips. She was too attuned to what he wasn't saying. To what his body language was saying for him.

"Move aside, Martinez," she ordered softly. Not in a million years would she admit to him that she used his last name to keep a buffer between them. Martinez was her partner, a fellow cop. Cruz...Cruz was someone else entirely.

"Not until you call me by my first name," he replied, his voice just as soft.

"Don't make me hurt you."

His eyebrow cocked in amusement at her threat but there was no smile on his face. His eyes were on her lips and his mouth seemed to draw closer to her own.

Madeline let her body relax more and he came even nearer. Then one foot came out swiftly behind his own, and a moment later he was stretched out on the hard floor with her on top of him, one knee pressed to his throat.

She was good, he admitted to himself ruefully. Her reflexes were lightning quick. "Uh, Maddy..." The knee at his throat applied more pressure threateningly, and he amended, "Madeline... could you..." He gestured with one hand toward her knee and she obediently eased the pressure a bit. Too late she realized her mistake. In less than an instant he'd reversed their positions, rolling her off and under him so fast her breath was lost in the process.

A wicked glint was in his dark eyes, and Madeline knew intuitively just how much trouble she was in. He held his weight off her slightly, taking care not to hurt her, but she was trapped against the ungiving floor and the equally hard but so much more tempting form above her. She needed to say something light, something that would defuse the moment and remove the intent from his face. But words deserted her. She was reminded of the other time she had felt Cruz stretched out over her, and the memory of his muscled body against hers couldn't come close to the pleasure flooding her right now at the feel of it.

She moistened her lips nervously, and Cruz almost groaned out loud. That soft, wide mouth looked vulnerable now, lips slightly parted and trembling just a bit. He couldn't begin to count the number of times he'd imagined it just this way. And he wasn't capable of resisting it. His lips lowered toward her and her eyelids grew heavy. He trailed feather-light kisses along her jawline, and her neck arched involuntarily at the exquisite sensation. "Maddy, Maddy." His voice was raw, and he seized one earlobe in his teeth to worry it gently. "Say my name," he ordered raspily, dropping his attention to the delicate cord of her throat.

A shiver rushed through her at the first brush of his mouth. She tried to deny his request, as if by doing so she could also deny the tidal wave of desire that threatened to engulf them. Her head shook helplessly, but her defenses, already strained, were at the breaking point. His fingers threaded through her hair, and his lips were a fraction away from her mouth. Her eyes fluttered open. The sight of him above her, his handsome face stamped with passion, was more than she could bear. "Say my name, Maddy," he ordered again. His lips moved against hers as he formed the words, and everything inside her longed to feel them against hers more firmly.

At her silence he brushed her mouth with his once, and then again. When her head raised slightly to force a stronger pressure, he pulled away. Her own hands came up to tangle in his hair. "Cruz," she said on a sigh, a whisper. And she was promptly rewarded.

"Yes," his breath hissed out at the sound of his name on her lips and he fiercely sealed her mouth with his own. One hand cupped the back of her head, and he took possession of her mouth with an intensity that shook her. Still she welcomed it, beckoning him closer. Her mouth twisted under his, matching his hunger, challenging it. She could feel the last vestiges of control slip away as Cruz's demand elicited her own.

His kisses were full of promise, rife with heat. They destroyed the carefully cultivated barriers she kept to protect herself, and shredded the proper image she'd worn so long that she had begun to believe in it. She'd spent a lifetime trying to tame her own nature, hiding her wildness. But his raw hunger unleashed hers, and she responded with an answering rage of need. The taste of him was pure wicked sinfulness, and she was coaxed closer to taste more.

Cruz pressed her lips apart and their tongues tangled. He became belatedly aware of the unyielding floor beneath her, but his only concession to it was to roll over, never releasing her mouth, bringing her body to lie fully atop his. One hand slipped to her bottom, pressing her firmly in contact with his aching groin.

Madeline could feel her body soften instinctively against his turgid arousal. She moved slightly against him and a groan tore from his throat. But still he kept her lips sealed with his. With one hand he cradled the back of her head, to keep her from turning away from him if she had been so inclined, which she wasn't. The other hand went on an intimate exploration. It swept down her thighs, and then leisurely traced its path upward again, this time delving beneath her long sweater and settling on her bare back.

Heat radiated from each of his fingers. Her skin prickled with awareness, unbearably attuned to his touch. His teeth nibbled at her lower lip, distracting her, drawing her into a carnal duel with his tongue. She responded deeply, without reservation, to his mind-drugging kisses. The back hook of her bra gave way to his questing fingers but it wasn't until he rolled them to their sides and slid his hand to her breast that she reacted.

Electric pleasure shimmered through her at the feel of his fingers teasing her nipple. Both of them moaned at the sensation, their breaths intermingling. She opened eyelids that seemed weighted to see Cruz gazing at her through slitted eyes, watching the pleasure chase across her features. She should have been alarmed at the fierce male desire stamped on his face, but instead she reveled in it. If she'd been stripped of the vestiges of the cool image she normally exuded, well, so had he. Gone was the amiable teasing demeanor that usually marked his handsome face. Right now it reflected a primitive intensity, that of a man caught between satisfaction and frustration.

He palmed her breast and swallowed her whimper at his action. Her nipple stabbed at his palm and he wanted suddenly, savagely, to put an end to this teasing. He wanted her naked, stretched out beneath him, and he wanted her hands on him, all over him, showing the same restless curiosity about his body that he felt for hers. They had ignited too fast for him to maintain control much longer, and the floor wasn't where he wanted to take her. He wanted her in his bed, where he had imagined her the first time he'd laid eyes on her.

His thumb batted at her nipple, and he pressed a kiss to the pulse on her neck. "Ah, Maddy. This isn't the right place for us this first time. I don't want that delectable backside of yours covered with bruises."

She nipped at his chin consideringly. "If you were a gentleman, *I* wouldn't be the one with bruises." She could feel the smile on his lips when he kissed her then, but amusement was swiftly swept away.

"I want you in my bed. Beneath me." When he raised his head again, his voice was lower, more guttural. "I want to be inside you, to feel for myself the fire you hide from the world." He pressed kiss after kiss to her throat, her jaw and cheekbones. "Come upstairs with me, Maddy. Come with me now."

His raspy tone and earthy words rocked the tempest inside her. She didn't question how easily he'd found the inner flame she usually kept locked firmly away. Just as she didn't question the answering fire she'd found in him. Her neck arched under his ardent mouth and reason fled. Reason hadn't played a part in this situation from the beginning. It didn't explain why she longed to unbutton his shirt and touch him as intimately as he was touching her. Reason wouldn't allow her to yield to the temptation he presented, or to ignore the defenses she'd erected to keep him at a distance.

She'd lived her life by logic for the past several years, allowing it to dictate every move she made. It hadn't been an easy task; there was a spark deep inside her that needed careful tending, lest it flare up and mar the mapped course she'd set for herself. He was asking for too much, way too much. He was tempting her to deny the careful caution she used to keep emotions at bay. And she was afraid that he wouldn't be satisfied until she gave to him more than she had to any other man.

Fear spiked suddenly in her then, as much fear as it was possible to feel while white-hot tendrils of heat still curled beneath his lips on her neck. She used the fear, drew its cloak closer around herself, to help combat the incessant temptation of the man above her. Fiercely she summoned the memories of her last surrender, and how badly her emotions had failed her with Dennis Belding. She called on her fading logic for all the reminders of why Cruz Martinez was the last man on earth right now she should trust. Being wrong about Dennis had almost destroyed her. She'd almost destroyed herself for making such a colossal mistake. How could she live with herself if she made another one here, with this man?

She wedged her hands between them, sliding them to his shoulders, meaning to push him away. But her fingers clenched suddenly as his teeth took a tiny nip at her throat, and her neck arched in unconscious pleasure as his tongue swept the same area in lavish apology.

For once, rational thought seemed to vanish, swirling away in the mist of sensual desire. Instead of caution she felt emotion, strong and pure, and so intense that she gasped from it. It had been such a long time since she'd let herself feel, so long since anything or anyone had been allowed to reach this part of herself, which she guarded so zealously.

"Now, Maddy," that dark voice whispered to her. "Come with me now."

She was beckoned closer to the savage fire burning inside him. She was forced to deal with consequences of spending years with her own wild nature locked away. She hadn't reckoned on meeting someone who could set it free without her conscious permission. Now it was liberated, a conflagration of emotion that spread like wildfire within her, and she reveled in the torrential outpouring.

"Yes," she whispered, the word barely leaving her lips before they were covered with his. Then he pulled away, his breathing ragged. Slowly he rose to his feet, reaching down to take both her hands and pulling her up against him. And holding her hand, he led her silently up the stairway to his room.

Madeline was dizzy when she reached the loft, the kisses they'd shared on the way more at fault than their spiral journey. Her gaze flickered over the room nervously as she felt uncertainty intrude. The area was meticulously neat. The charcoal gray carpeting looked freshly vacuumed. The bed was made, a comforter of black, gray and maroon spread tidily over it. A huge domed window was set in the wall above the bed. Rays from the fading sun beamed through it, painting the bed with fingers of light.

Cruz's eyes followed the path of her gaze. He wondered what she thought of the room he'd designed, but even more urgently, he wondered how she would look stretched out across his bed as he'd long imagined her, her body dappled with sunlight. He wanted fiercely to see that, to experience the electric pleasure promised by her long lithe legs and high breasts. He wanted her writhing under him, as she struggled to take all of him, and then he wanted to watch her face transform with ecstasy when the limits of their control were shattered.

Her gaze met his, and she reacted with an involuntary shiver. For although he didn't come any nearer, she felt heat simply from his look. She could read his erotic thoughts as surely as if he'd spoken, and suddenly realized that hers were probably just as visible to him. The silence in the room tautened, and Madeline could feel her pulse throbbing. She watched him go over to the bed and sit on the edge, tug his boots and socks off, and leave them on the floor in what she was sure was uncustomary disorder.

"Maddy." His voice was low. "Come here to me."

Her feet moved to obey without conscious decision. When she was standing in front of him, he spread his knees and brought her closer, between them. His face was level with her breasts and he used her position to nuzzle them, first one then the other. Next he rose, and his body rubbed hers in the ascent. He drew her hands to his shirt and whispered huskily, "Undress me." And again she obeyed.

Her eyes watched the progress of her fingers in fascination. First one button was undone. Then two. She caught her breath at her first glimpse of his bare chest, fingers faltering in their task as she took in the sheer male beauty of him. Cruz obligingly finished for her, stripping off the shirt and dropping it to the floor.

His torso looked as if it had been sculpted by an artistic hand, its bronze hue gleaming invitingly. Her hands rose to touch him, as if she couldn't help herself. He was firmly muscled, defined pectoral muscles neatly bisecting his chest. The hard muscles were repeated along his rib cage and stomach. He had no chest hair, as if nature hadn't bothered to further adorn perfection. There was only an enticing silky black ribbon of hair arrowing from his navel and disappearing into the waistband of his jeans.

Cruz's breath hissed out of his teeth at the first tentative touch of her hands on him. The long-awaited contact ignited his hunger again, at a time when he most needed all his control. After only seconds of her caresses his own hands moved swiftly, grasping the hem of her sweater and bringing it upward, over her head. He let it drop to the floor and she shrugged out of the unhooked bra.

His hands cupped her breasts, which were beaded with arousal. He toyed with the nipples, rolling them gently in his fingers until an involuntary sound came from her throat. Then, with the calm masculine assurance that was so much a part of him, he bent to take one nipple into his mouth.

The ground fell away from Madeline's feet at the hot, wet suction on her breast, which seemed unbearably sensitive. She gasped as she felt his teeth lightly scrape her nipple, before he soothed it with his tongue. His thumb made lazy circles around its twin, causing it to draw even tighter before he switched his attention to it. Her knees threatened to buckle and she leaned heavily into him. Cruz took that opportunity to lower her to the bed, stripping the black leggings, shoes and socks off her in the same movement.

She swallowed hard. Lying in the middle of his bed wearing nothing but a scrap of panties made her feel intensely feminine and utterly vulnerable. The emotions were heightened by the sight of him, still partially dressed, studying her, his eyes at half-mast. She remembered suddenly the first time she'd seen him. He'd reminded her of a pirate then, and he brought the same vivid image to her mind at this moment. His earring seemed so much a part of him that she rarely noticed it anymore, but she did now. It was a diamond chip and, coupled with his broad bare chest, it gave him a half-civilized, untamed look. She watched, enrapt, as his hands went slowly to his jeans, unfastening them and pushing them down his firm flanks. Clad only in black low-riding briefs, he seemed quintessentially male, very much the conquering warrior.

Cruz stood still, allowing himself precious moments to absorb the gut-wrenching pleasure of seeing her lying in his bed. The frothy piece of lace she still wore matched the bra she'd just discarded, and he wondered at the contrast she made. She hid her penchant for silky bits of lingerie beneath primly tailored suits and jackets, just as she hid her real self behind a mask of cool professionalism. He'd wanted to strip that outer layer away, to find out if the woman beneath could possibly match the one he'd imagined, and now he'd found that she did that, and more.

With his thumbs in the waistband of his briefs, he disposed of them as casually as he had the jeans and Madeline felt her breath quite literally stop. His nakedness was almost overwhelming, the strength of his sexuality no longer hidden. His nudity was tempting, though. Her hands itched to race over that hard body even as she quaked a little in the face of its strength.

Cruz thought he read nervousness creeping into her eyes, and he joined her on the bed. "Ah, Maddy," he whispered in her ear as his arms reached for her. "You don't know how many times I've pictured you here. Just like this."

"You have?" she murmured, a pleased little smile teasing her lips.

"Many times," he affirmed, his hands skating along her spine. She turned to face him and his soothing touch became more sure. His hands went over her with a shattering purpose, no longer seeking to calm her uncertainty, but to intensify her arousal. "I've dreamed of you lying next to me like this. Of spreading your legs, like this." One hard knee parted hers and pressed gently against her femininity. She gasped helplessly. His voice dropped even lower, until it was almost a rumble. "But nothing I could imagine prepared me for the pleasure of seeing you like this. Touching you like this."

One hand imitated his words by dropping to her panties and pushing them carelessly down her legs. It came back up to cup the fleecy red delta between her thighs. She quivered in response, but he sealed her mouth with his, kissing her with lazy purpose. When he did nothing more for a time, she relaxed enough to open her mouth to him, relishing his taste when his tongue swept in. Her hands clasped his wide shoulders but refused to linger there. They engaged in an exploration of their own, smoothing over the bronzed skin, touching his nipples, making him shudder.

She learned his body. She found that he loved having his chest stroked, that his nipples were as tautly sensitive as her own. When her hands wandered downward she skirted his heavy arousal shyly, but he pushed forward urgently, and she understood the demand. Her fingers closed around him and his breath hissed out between clenched teeth. He was a total sensualist, completely without modesty or shyness. He allowed her none, either. If she'd been able to think, she would have been shocked at the way their bodies moved together on the bed, flickering in the fading sunlight. She would have been surprised at the way she was acting, at her need to touch him, all of him. Nothing in her adult life had prepared her for a man who demanded only that she hold nothing back, who seemed to want only that she let her inhibitions loose and give rise to a sensual side of her nature that she'd kept firmly tucked away.

Nothing could be hidden from him; he didn't allow pretense. His hands were teasing, insistent and arousing by turn. His mouth delighted in tasting her, pressing kisses to velvet skin, nipping sharply, then soothing the area with his tongue. He lay half over her once, smoothing his hand over her soft skin, and watched the movement with savage pleasure, enjoying the sight of his darker skin against hers, so much lighter. She was the color of rich cream all over, and devoid of the delicate sprinkling of freckles that patterned most redheads.

His touch became more urgent, his mouth increasingly demanding. Her own exploration was thwarted by her reaction to him. His lips went to her neck and below. He cupped both breasts in his hands, teasing the nipples with his thumbs before lowering his head to suckle first one, then the other. Her hands clenched on his back, her hips rolling sinuously. Then one of his hands snaked down to claim her femininity, parting the dewy folds and teasing the slick bud he found there.

Her thighs relaxed unconsciously, allowing him access, an opportunity he immediately took advantage of. He penetrated her with one long finger, and her hips bucked. A gasp broke from her throat as he kept up the sensual assault, driving her mad with his mouth on her nipples, his devilish fingers trailing magic in their wake.

"Cruz," she murmured brokenly, her hands moving restlessly over his shoulders and then to his hair. Her fingers threaded through the dark, thick strands, ungentle in her restless quest for satisfaction. "Please."

He closed his eyes tightly at her breathless voice. He didn't want this to end. He wanted to race his hands over her, to slowly savor her. He wanted to taste her everywhere, slowly, lingeringly. He wanted to take her with a sudden burst of lust that would put an end to their torment. But she was nearing the fever pitch of arousal; he could feel it in her writhing movements beneath him, in the moist tight silkiness he was exploring. His own body was taking the choice from him. He could feel himself grow tight and heavy, signaling how close he was to exploding.

He rolled away for a second to reach for the nightstand. He resented bitterly the need for anything to come between them, even as he protected her. Moving above her, he parted her legs for his large body, and the tip of his staff nudged her softness. Her legs came up eagerly, encircling his waist, and he pushed fully into her tight sheath with a long, sure movement that drove the breath from both of them.

Pausing above her, he strove to garner his flagging control. Her eyes opened dazedly, and the sight of him over her, eyes tightly shut, teeth clenched, made her breath sob in her throat. The skin was drawn tautly over his cheekbones, and a light sheen of perspiration shone on his brow. She wasn't able to give him the time he needed to regroup. She flexed, drawing him deeper inside her, and still it wasn't enough. He was so hot, so hard, and he filled her completely.... She gasped a little as he rolled his hips.

"That's right," he growled gutturally as her body struggled to accept all of him, "let yourself relax. Take more. More! Yes, like that. Just like that." She accepted all of him, and his hot, turgid length stretching her was making demands his body couldn't deny. His hands went to her bottom, lifting her for his thrusts. He began slowly at first, but quickly lost control and drove into her wildly. Breathless whimpers broke from her lips as she met each of his frantic movements, and demanded more.

"Maddy," he gritted, surging into her. "Mine. Maddy..." He rode her hard until she screamed softly, her cry muffled by his hard shoulder. Her inner spasms clenched him, milking his own response. With a wild roll of his hips the pleasure slammed into him. It went on and on, and he jerked convulsively as he spun out of control.

Chapter 12

It was well before daybreak when Madeline woke, dazed by the unfamiliar surroundings. A furnacelike heat radiated against her back, and heavy weights kept her pinned to the bed. She blinked a few times, identifying the warmth caused by Cruz's body pressed against hers. One thigh was wedged between her own, and his arm draped over her waist. She sighed a little, settling back against him once more. She'd fallen asleep after they'd made love, but he'd woken her often during the night, his body inviting hers to taste satisfaction again.

She lay in his embrace quietly for a time, listening to the even breathing of the man next to her. One part of her wished that she could return to similar unconsciousness. But she knew that luxury would be denied her. Her mind was wide-awake, her thoughts uncomfortably demanding. She stretched, easing out from under Cruz cautiously. She searched for her sweater and pulled it on before padding down the staircase to the kitchen. The curtainless windows allowed all the light from the star-studded sky to spill into the apartment, and she had no difficulty finding her way. Pulling open a cupboard, she took out a glass, went to the refrigerator and poured herself some milk.

Madeline sat at the counter and sipped slowly, staring pensively into space. Last night had been completely outside her experience. She'd never let herself respond like that, had never been forced to respond like that before. Cruz had drawn out every emotion, every reaction, and had savored it, reciprocating in full. He'd reached for her over and over, as if he couldn't get enough of her. Amazingly, her response had been just as uninhibited each time.

But now, desire satisfied, self-doubts returned full force to nag at her with insistent clamoring. That she'd just made her investigation more difficult, she couldn't deny. Separating emotion from cool professional reason could only be more difficult after the hours she'd just spent with him. She should never have allowed last night to happen. She couldn't afford to trust him, not while she was still looking for signs of his possible involvement with the gun supply. And, having slept with him, now she wouldn't be able to trust herself.

Would she be able to look at every aspect of the case as objectively as she needed to? Or would she constantly doubt herself, searching through every decision she made for flaws in judgment? Her lips flattened. Maybe that wouldn't be such a bad thing. And she would force it to work to her benefit. In order to prove his innocence or guilt, she was going to have to maintain strict control over each conclusion she drew, every shred of evidence she found. And she was going to have to do it with a much greater detachment than she had displayed here tonight.

She'd worked too hard to get where she was today, professionally as well as personally. Perhaps there had been a pattern to her life, but it was a pattern of her choosing. Cruz Martinez wasn't going to change that—she wouldn't *allow* him to change it. Tonight hadn't altered anything, she assured herself. She was still investigating him; she would still have to seek out every pertinent piece of information on him, analyze it, report on it. And if the time came that she was responsible for Cruz's arrest, well, she'd handle that, too.

But there was no denying that the hours she'd just spent with him would make that moment more painful for her.

The phone rang on the counter near her, and she started in shock. It was cut off after one ring, and she looked cautiously in the direction of the stairs. She didn't remember seeing another phone in Cruz's room, and hoped this wouldn't wake him. The answering machine switched on, and his voice invited callers to leave a message. She listened to the caller's breathing. When he spoke, she recognized Tommy's voice instantly.

"Martinez? Hey, Martinez, I really need to talk to you. I'm in big trouble, man. This place you told me about, I'm not safe here. Valdez is on my trail. You got to get me out of here. Call Valdez off, you know you can." Here his voice broke, and real fear laced it when he spoke again. "You put me in danger, man. Now you get me out of it."

The connection was broken but the message replayed over and over in Madeline's numb mind.

This place you told me about… Call Valdez off…you know you can….

She felt frozen, the breath trapped in her chest. She finally released it in a great shuddering gasp. She couldn't stop Tommy's words from hammering inside her head. They joined all the other questions and doubts there, punctuated them with insidious clarity.

This place you told me about… Just days ago Cruz had led her to believe that he didn't know where Tommy was hiding out. He'd made her believe that *she* was putting Tommy's life in danger by her insistence on checking back with him. She was suddenly very sure that Cruz had Tommy hidden in a place where it was guaranteed she would never find him and be able to talk to him again. But was it for Tommy's safety or his own?

Had Cruz deliberately put the man's life in danger? Tommy had been frightened, certain that Valdez was after him. Abruptly she remembered the snitch Brewer had told her about, the one who'd wound up with bullet holes in him after relating that a cop was involved in the gun supply. Her stomach lurched alarmingly. The possibilities were too gruesome to contemplate.

She shook herself mentally, forcing her thoughts into order. Tommy might truly believe Cruz was responsible for his danger, or his danger might be the result of an alcohol-induced delusion. But she had no way of knowing which was true. All she had was her own determination to answer these questions once and for all. And to deal with whatever answers she found.

She stood up so suddenly that her stool teetered wildly behind her. Without thinking, she reached in back of her to steady it with one hand. Like an automaton she moved, taking her glass to the sink and rinsing it out. The first thing to do was to get out of here without having to face Cruz. She desperately needed the next few hours to prepare herself for that particular ordeal. Creeping upstairs, she swept up the rest of her clothes, not allowing her eyes to move to the bed. Back downstairs she dressed hurriedly and called for a cab.

Waiting for the car to arrive, she was treated with a sample of what was in store for her for the duration of the investigation. Images of their bodies entwined, the seductive contrast of their skin, the heat that had flared instantly to life between them flitted across her memory. She pushed them determinedly, inexorably away. Perhaps those memories would be her most dangerous enemy now. They could work on her resolve, infiltrate her detached resistance if she was weak enough to let them.

But no. Weakness wasn't allowed, had never been allowed in Madeline Casey's life. This time her eyes were wide open, and whichever way the evidence eventually pointed, she would be the one pushing forward with the investigation, seeing it to its conclusion. Neither memories nor emotion would be allowed to interfere with that.

She stared bleakly into space. She didn't doubt that it would be the most difficult task she'd ever undertaken.

An hour later Madeline came out of her apartment bedroom in time to hear her phone ring. She made no attempt to answer it and the machine took over. She was in no mood to talk to anyone right now. Her mouth twisted as her father's voice came on the machine and suggested she call him as soon as possible. Obviously Francis Vincent had gotten word to him about seeing her with Cruz at the restaurant. Geoffrey Casey had lost no time calling his daughter to express his disapproval.

As her hand was on the doorknob the phone rang again. She closed her eyes briefly. Despite the surface calm she'd managed, each time she heard it she almost jumped out of her skin. After only a second of inner debate, she continued through the door. Whoever it was, she'd deal with it later.

Just as she was ready to pull the door closed behind her, a boy's voice came on the machine. "Detective Casey?" Her eyes widened and she pushed the door open, almost sprinting to the phone. "I need to talk to you, Detective Casey. Real bad."

Madeline snatched up the phone. "Ricky? Is that you?"

He sounded relieved at her voice. "Yeah, it is. I really gotta talk to you, Detective. It's about Ramsey. I think he's in a lotta trouble."

"Okay, Ricky, you did right to call." Her voice was soothing. "Let's get together and talk this out. Where can we meet?"

"I don't know." The boy's voice dropped. "Ramsey can't know I talked to you, and I can't leave Rhonda alone."

An idea struck her. "How about the library you always take her to? You could take her this morning just as you have in the past. I'll meet you there."

"And that other detective, too."

Her voice was grim. "And that other detective, too," she agreed. After getting the address of the library, she promised to meet him in an hour and a half, and hung up the phone. Funny, until Ricky had mentioned Cruz, Madeline had considered going without him. But she would never get away with that. After all their arguments about it, it would seem too out of character for her, especially after last night. At all costs, she had to do everything in her power to appear as if things were normal. She raised her chin and went out the door. Ready or not, she was about to embark on the most difficult pretense of her life.

Cruz jumped up as soon as he saw Madeline approaching his desk. He watched her carefully, trying to determine her mood. He'd been dismayed to find her gone this morning, with nothing but a short note explaining that she'd gone home to shower and change. He hadn't liked the idea that she had left him sleeping and gone out alone. He didn't like the idea of her out on the streets in the early hours without him, period. But now might not be the time to reveal his displeasure.

With narrowed eyes he took in her pale, drawn face. She was wearing gray this morning, another outfit of tailored pants and jacket, this time over a light peach blouse. Her hair was pulled back in that no-nonsense fashion she favored at work, and he gave an inward sigh. For some reason he thought this was more than just a return to her work persona. The way she was skirting his eyes as she approached him gave evidence of that.

"Good morning," he said neutrally, his eyes still studying her carefully.

She managed what she hoped was a normal tone. "We've got a job right away this morning." She told him of the call she'd received from Ricky. As she'd hoped, it took his attention off her for a moment.

He checked his watch. "How much time do we have?"

"About forty-five minutes."

He walked out from behind the desk and toward her. She turned to precede him to the door. When his hand fell on her shoulder, she shrugged it away before she could prevent a reaction.

Cruz strode ahead of her and stopped in her path. Surveying her with narrowed eyes, he muttered, "We've got to talk."

Madeline was aware of interested glances cast their way and nodded, avoiding his gaze. "In the car."

With a muttered curse he led the way through the building and to the car. He slid in behind the wheel and she situated herself in the passenger seat. Reaching beneath the seat, she extracted the city map and after studying it, proceeded to give him directions to the library where they were to meet Ricky.

Cruz drove silently for a time. When he spoke, his voice was deceptively mild. "I would have taken you home this morning, you know."

She took a deep breath. The time for the showdown had arrived. "I know, but I was up early, and didn't see any need to wake you." She shrugged. "You already had a stop to make at your parents' this morning. It was best that I left when I did."

"No, dammit, it wasn't best." He bit out the words. When she looked at him cautiously, his face was grim. "I wanted you there when I woke up. I didn't like finding that you'd snuck out, like a thief in the night."

Her eyes stared unseeingly out her side window. "I'd hardly describe it that way."

"Wouldn't you? And how would you describe it?"

She was taken aback. She hadn't considered that leaving the way she had would anger him. She looked over at him warily. His jaw was clenched and a telltale muscle was jumping in it. "I left a note."

"Ah, yes, your note. The next time you're in my bed, Maddy, you'll stay there where you belong. You will not be gone at first light, just because you're running scared."

One eyebrow climbed at his chauvinistic assumption that she would return to his bed. "I don't know what you're talking about," she replied dismissively.

The look he turned on her then was like none she'd ever seen on his face before. Implacable male pride was there, as well as a primitive possessiveness. "You scared yourself last night." He made a gesture, dismissing the denial on her lips. "But I won't let you pretend that nothing happened. I won't let you erect a barrier between us as easily as the guise you put on each day to face the world."

"Nothing scares me, Martinez, so save the psychobabble," she retorted, her temper flaring to meet his own. "I needed to go home, I went. Don't make more out of it than it was."

Out of what? he wondered grimly. Out of her leaving, or out of the night they'd spent together? Somehow he thought she meant the latter. And he didn't like the feeling that she was dismissing it, dismissing *him,* so easily.

"By the way, your machine came on as I was leaving," she said in a studiedly casual voice. She turned her head to pin him with a look. "Sounded to me like you knew where Tommy was all along."

He was silent for a moment, but his mind was racing. "I did," he admitted finally. "Is that what had you running out before dawn this morning? You were upset I didn't tell you where he was?"

She gritted her teeth at his choice of words. So far this morning it had been amazingly easy to resist his appeal. Each time he opened his mouth she was tempted to punch him. "We've already discussed why I left. But I would like to know why you kept his whereabouts from me."

It was a long moment before he spoke again. "I was trying to protect him. I was the one who gave him an idea of where to go to lie low for a while. But Tommy has a hard time staying put, especially when the whiskey runs out. He thinks he was spotted by Valdez, and he's convinced he's in danger."

"What do you think?"

He sighed. "It's hard to tell. Tommy can't even remember where he was when he thought he saw Valdez. But he could be right. So I've arranged to place him elsewhere."

She frowned. "How do you know this place will be any safer than the last one? Or that Tommy doesn't have more information to give us on Valdez? I think we should talk to him again."

"No." His response was firm. "Every time we're seen with Tommy we're increasing the danger for him. He's safe anywhere I place him, if he remains drunk enough to stay put."

She looked at him askance. "You're seeing to that, too, I suppose."

He gave her a hard look. "Damn right I am. We realized how dangerous Valdez was. Everyone on the street was scared to talk about him. But I went to Tommy because I knew I could count on his need for alcohol being greater than his need to stay alive. Now it's my job to keep him alive, and I'm going to do it."

Frustration slammed into her. There was no way she could be sure of Cruz's real motives for hiding Tommy away. He could be worried for his safety, as he claimed. Or he could be keeping the man as far from her as he could so that she couldn't quiz Tommy about Cruz's possible involvement in the gun supply scheme.

She weighed her options, and had to admit they were limited. Cruz was the only one who could lead her to Tommy, and he'd refused. And it didn't sound as if the snitch would be in very reliable shape if she did find him. Her time after-hours would be better spent tracking down the source of Cruz's second income. But she didn't like feeling outmaneuvered, and her voice was full of sarcasm when she spoke. "Is there anything else you've decided to keep from me? Given your superior wisdom about what's best for this case, I mean?"

His next words were laden with meaning. "I think it's your turn to tell what you've been keeping from *me.*"

For just a second she froze, her mind flashing to the secret investigation she was doing. But then he spoke again and she relaxed, if only for an instant. "You still haven't told me the truth about why you left this morning. Maybe you haven't admitted it to yourself, either."

"Last night was a mistake," she said bluntly, with ironic understatement. "And it won't happen again. I'm not going to risk the integrity of this case by getting involved with my partner. We need to focus all our energy on finding Valdez and stopping the gun supply. Any involvement of a more personal nature is out of the question."

Cruz turned into the parking lot of the library with just a little more force on the wheel than necessary. *Involvement?* he repeated in a silent, savage echo. *Personal?* He wanted to reach out and shake her. He wanted to force her to realize just how ridiculous her words were. But one look at her set face was enough to tell him that all efforts would be in vain. In truth, he'd been half-anticipating this since he'd wakened to find her gone. But it didn't make it any easier to take, and it didn't improve his temper.

"All right," he agreed after a time. "You win."

She cast a wary glance in his direction. "What do you mean?"

"If you want to believe that this case is the only thing that sent you running from my bed this morning, I'm not going to argue with you anymore."

"How kind." Her voice dripped with ice.

"But—" he pinned her with a look "—when the case is over, what excuse will you use then, Maddy? What other reason will you find for us to stay away from each other? Because manufacturing another excuse is a hell of a lot easier for you to deal with than facing what's between us, isn't it?''

Without waiting for an answer he opened the door and got out of the car. After a moment Madeline did the same, following him across the parking lot. They walked without a word into the brightly lit library. It took several minutes to find the table where Ricky was seated. He saw them coming and jumped up, leading his little sister away. A few minutes later he came back, and they all sat at the table he'd vacated.

His eyes went in the direction he'd taken Rhonda. "I don't have much time. I don't want Rhonda to see you again, and there's no telling how long she'll sit back there with the book I picked out for her."

"Just tell us what has you so worried," Madeline said softly. Her eyes were wide and sincere when she reached across the table with one hand and touched one of his. "We want to help Ramsey, Ricky. If he's in trouble like you say, we might be the only ones who *can* help him."

"Just trust us, Ricky." Cruz's voice was soothing. "Tell us what has you so spooked."

The boy took a deep breath, then began speaking, his voice low. "That time you came to the apartment, you brought that picture? Well, I asked Ramsey about the man in it, and he got real mean, you know? Started shoving me around and yelling at me." He stopped here, his voice breaking.

"Where was your mom when this happened?" Cruz asked.

"At work. Anyway, I didn't say no more then, 'cause he was real mad at me for even letting you in. But I knew something was wrong. I could tell by the way he was acting. So..." He took a deep breath, "I started following him."

Cruz and Madeline exchanged a glance. "You went after him when he was with the gang members?"

"Yeah, I could only go when our neighbor could watch Rhonda. I just started hanging out where I might hear them talking."

"And did you hear anything?" Madeline asked.

"Not until I started following him to Cantoney's place. I was on the fire escape one day, and I heard the whole plan. Only the guys were talking about Ramsey—he wasn't there. They'd sent him out to buy beer." His eyes met theirs, solemn and scared at the same time. "The Lords are gonna get the guy who shot Ramsey. They already have a fancy gun they're gonna use. I saw Dirk showing it around to the guys. And Cantoney, he's got the whole thing planned out. He's gonna get Ramsey's fingerprints on the gun. If he ever gets caught, he'll make sure the cops find the gun and Ramsey will get blamed for it. Then he said, like Ramsey's just a kid and probably wouldn't serve any hard time.''

Madeline exchanged a grim look with Cruz. But there was more. Ricky went on, "I told Ramsey about it when he got home. He said he knew all about the plan, but I could tell he didn't, you know? And he got real mad, told me to shut up and that I'd better not follow them anymore, or else he'd tell Dirk about me.'' He shook his head. "I never seen him like that before. I really thought he'd hurt me. I asked him to think about what would happen to him if the cops traced the shooting back to him, and he said Dirk would take care of us.'' He snorted. "I don't think Dirk is gonna take care of no one but himself. Or he wouldn't be mixing Ramsey up in this. And I read about a kid, he was only fourteen, and he shot someone and got tried as an adult.'' He raised his scared eyes to theirs. "That could happen to Ramsey, couldn't it? He could go to prison for a long time, couldn't he?''

Cruz nodded soberly. "He sure could, Ricky. And the way Dirk has this set up, there would be no reason for the police to look any farther for a suspect. They'd have Ramsey, a motive and a murder weapon.''

"All that's missing is opportunity,'' Madeline murmured. "Ricky, did you hear enough to figure out when this is going to happen?''

The boy shook his head.

"All right then.'' Cruz smiled at the boy. "You did good, calling us like this, Ricky. Real good.''

He looked uneasy. "If Ramsey finds out I talked to you, I don't know what he'll do to me.''

"We won't tell him,'' Madeline said honestly, "but Ricky, I can't promise he won't figure it out. With what you told us, though, we might be able to stop the shooting before it happens. And then Ramsey won't get into any trouble. Okay?''

Ricky nodded slowly. "Okay.''

"You take Rhonda home soon, and stick close to the apartment until this blows over,'' Cruz suggested. "Don't try to follow your brother anymore. Make him think that you listened to his last warning, and he might never suspect you talked to us.''

"We'll be in touch,'' Madeline promised. They left him sitting at the table, looking very young and uneasy. Once they were outside she spoke. "Where's the most likely place for Cantoney to keep the gun?"

"Well, he'd be stupid to keep it at his apartment. A violation of parole like that would send him right back to prison."

"But he is a control freak," she reminded him. "What are the chances he would allow one of his men to keep it?" They looked at each other and said simultaneously, "It's in his apartment."

"It's got to be," Cruz stated with certainty. "I know Cantoney too well to think he'd let someone else hide it. Dirk probably has been milking this plan, getting all the members together and bragging, making himself out as a big man."

"There's no way of knowing how long Cantoney has had the gun," Madeline said. "There's really no time to lose."

"Well, we've got an eyewitness who can place the gun in Cantoney's hands, in Cantoney's apartment, and who heard what he was planning to do with it. We've got enough to get a search warrant."

"Let's just hope that we're in time," Madeline said grimly. "Because if he goes ahead with this plan, all signs will point to Ramsey. Any attempt then to nail Cantoney for it and he'll make sure that Ramsey is framed."

The drive back to the district headquarters was made in record time, and still it seemed endless to Madeline. Neither of them spoke, for which she was grateful. The scene with him earlier, before they'd met with Ricky, had been tougher than she'd expected. She knew her argument had seemed in character for her, but his response to it had surprised her.

Outraged ego she could have dealt with. An easy dismissal, that of a man who could have any woman he wanted, would have been expected. But she hadn't counted on his insights, and she damned them, and him, for hitting so close to home.

Several times Cruz started to speak, but one look at her colorless face, at the mauve shadows beneath her eyes, was enough to make him hold his tongue. He was normally a very patient man, but for some reason patience didn't enter into his feelings for Maddy. After last night it infuriated him that she'd so quickly thrown up still another wall between them. She hadn't been an easy person to get close to, but he knew more about her than she thought. He'd suspected that the fire in her hair was matched by an answering flame in her personality, and he'd been proven right. She had a quick wit and a temptingly short fuse. Last night had brought out the flame he'd suspected was there, buried but ready to burst forth, given enough coaxing.

Just the memory of last night was enough to make his jeans uncomfortably tight. She'd been everything he'd hoped for, everything he could have imagined. And the thought of having to wait as long as this case took to solve before having her like that again was enough to make him grind his teeth in frustration. But wait he would.

Madeline sat at Cruz's desk and typed up the search warrant. Cruz sat at her side, playing a little solo drum piece on the desk top.

"We are on our way, Maddy, I can feel it. We're going to get into Cantoney's apartment, we're going to find that gun, we're going to stop another kid from dying, and stop Ramsey from going to prison...."

"Slow down," Madeline answered. "Let's get the warrant signed first. Then we'll see about the rest of your prophecies." Could he be this good a liar? she wondered dismally, if he had a stake in the outcome? He'd have to be very sure indeed that his link to the suppliers was well hidden. Or that he'd be able to destroy any evidence that would provide that link.

"Wait and see. I'm right on this, I know it...." The phone on his desk rang then and Cruz snatched it up. "Lieutenant Niles," he said aloud, casting a telling eye to Madeline and holding up crossed fingers. "What did you find out from the lab work from Stover's room?"

She was aware that she was holding her breath. Watching Cruz's face was an exercise in frustration. He said little, mostly listened. Toward the end of the conversation he said, "You're kidding. What was it? No, I'm afraid not." After a couple more minutes he said, "Yeah, I think we'll do that. Thanks for the call. You bet." He hung up the phone.

"Well?" Madeline prompted at his silence.

"Niles's men have been busy," he observed. "They tried tracking the woman who put up Stover's bail. The address on the ID she showed didn't pan out. She hasn't lived there in several years. She's got a record for prostitution, but she hasn't been seen in her old territory since Stover's release. They're still looking."

"She's probably long gone," Madeline said gloomily. "It's sounding more and more as if she was given the money to get Stover out so that he could be killed. She'd be a fool to risk staying around after the murder. What about Stover's room?"

"Fingerprinting it was almost a bust," Cruz said. "They found no trace of Valdez's prints on any of the surfaces there. But—" he held up a finger "—they did find a ballpoint pen under the bed with prints that matched Valdez's."

"That could place Valdez at the scene," she said hopefully.

"Doesn't make him guilty of murder, though."

"Then we find Valdez and the murder weapon," she said, with more determination than she was feeling.

"Three guesses what the lieutenant said the murder weapon was," Cruz said, "and the first two don't count."

"No contest," she said grimly. "It was an AK-47."

Chapter 13

Cruz nodded. "That's the word from forensics."

Madeline thought for a moment. "Any lead from the pen with Valdez's prints?"

"Apparently not," Cruz stated. "It did have some advertising on the side—Andersen Steel."

"Pretty big time," she noted. Andersen Steel was a well-known company in Philadelphia. It had been in the same family for several generations. She remembered some negative publicity they'd received a few years back, when they'd followed the lead of the other huge steel conglomerates and moved much of their manufacturing overseas, to take advantage of cheaper labor. But it was something else that was puzzling her mind about Andersen Steel, and she paused in her typing, thinking hard.

Cruz frowned. "What's wrong?"

"Andersen Steel." She slapped the top of his desk as the connection with that name finally came to her. "They own Wynn Construction."

"How do you know?"

She shot him an impatient glance and he held up his hands placatingly. "Forgive me for doubting you. You read it in some obscure article years ago and still happen to remember it. Why am I not surprised?"

"The point is," she informed him, excitement creeping into her voice, "now that pen *does* have significance. Valdez's parole officer said he'd worked for Wynn Construction for several weeks before he disappeared. It wouldn't hurt for us to go to Andersen Steel and ask some questions."

"Later," Cruz said, indicating the search warrant she was working on. "We've got something more pressing to attend to."

Nodding in agreement, Madeline went back to her typing. Ramsey was their first concern. Valdez would wait.

It was close to noon by the time they'd gotten the warrant signed at police headquarters. But when they reached Cantoney's apartment it was apparent from his appearance that they'd awakened him. He answered the door in jeans and an open shirt. A flicker of unease crossed his face when he recognized them.

"What do you want now?"

Cruz pushed the door open with one hand and walked through, forcing Dirk to fall back or be run over. With the other he held out the search warrant. "The pleasure's mutual, Cantoney. We heard you've been having some real interesting meetings lately, and that you have something kind of special stashed here." He turned his head to address Madeline. "Okay, go ahead."

They had discussed their strategy in the car on the way over and she went immediately to work. Taking some clear rubber gloves from her pocket, she pulled them on. Then she crossed the room, opened a door and entered a bedroom.

"Hey! Get out of there!" Cantoney lunged after her, but Cruz put out an arm at the last moment and stopped him. He stuffed the warrant into the man's hand. "Better take a look at this. You can read, can't you? Everything's in order." Cruz's eyebrows rose only slightly when Dirk tore the paper to bits. "Doesn't matter," he said mildly. "There are copies, you know."

"You've got no grounds for this, Martinez," Cantoney snarled.

"Apparently the commissioner thought otherwise," Cruz answered. The two men stared at each other for a long moment fraught with tension, then slowly, imperceptibly, Cantoney drew back.

"Go ahead," he invited insolently. "And while you and the broad are busy, I'll be calling my lawyer."

"Good move," Cruz retorted. "You'll probably need one before we're through."

Sounds drifted from the open doorway Madeline had disappeared into, and both men walked toward the door.

"Take it easy in there, sister," Cantoney advised. "If there's any damage, I'll be reporting it." After a second he added, "Maybe if you tell me what you're looking for, sweetheart, I can help you." He cupped himself lewdly. "Or you can help yourself."

Fingers curled unconsciously into his palms, Cruz sent the man a look laced with deadly intent. "Seems to me you have enough to worry about, Cantoney. Don't push it." His voice was even, but the warning was implicit.

Madeline turned and approached them then. Their gazes caught and Cruz asked a question with his eyes. She answered with an almost imperceptible shake of her head. Cruz stepped back to let her pass, but she had to brush by Cantoney to do so. Cruz's eyes narrowed as he noted the way the other man positioned himself.

Madeline caught the look and recognized the threat. She stifled a sigh. That would be all she needed this morning, to have to referee a brawl. In an attempt to redirect Cruz's attention, she suggested, "Why don't you start in the living room?"

Not waiting for his answer, she opened the next door and began to search that bedroom. Cruz walked into the living room and started checking cushions on the furniture. Cantoney looked from Madeline to Cruz. Apparently deciding that she was less of a threat, he followed Cruz into the living room, objecting strenuously as he went through drawers and cupboards of the entertainment center. Cruz turned on the TV and VCR to check that they indeed worked, and were not being used as dummy storage compartments.

"Watch it, Martinez," Cantoney growled. "That's state-of-the-art stuff. I don't got no Disney movies, if that's what you're looking for."

Ignoring him, Cruz moved through the room, carefully checking any area large enough to store the gun.

"What happens when you and the broad don't find whatever it is you're looking for, huh, cop? Then will you get the hell out of here?"

Cruz spared him hardly a glance. "Then we'll start all over." The man's curse was interrupted when Madeline came out of the bathroom.

"Looks like you'll be going downtown with us, Dirk," she said. She was holding an AK-47 in her gloved hands.

"Great," Cruz said in satisfaction. "Where'd you find it?"

"Above the ceiling tiles in the bathroom." With her free hand she extracted a plastic evidence bag from her purse and placed the gun inside it. Sealing the bag, she pulled off the gloves and stuffed them back in her pocket.

"You bitch!" Cantoney started toward her, but Cruz blocked the man's path. "She planted the damn thing there. I never seen it before."

"Save it for your lawyer," Cruz advised in a bored tone. "He's probably used to fairy tales. Assume the position, Cantoney."

Still muttering curses, the man spread both hands out against the wall, feet splayed. Cruz searched him quickly, finding nothing. Standing, he grasped the man's arms and cuffed his hands behind him, advising him of his rights.

Madeline watched all of this as if from a great distance. Instead of feeling the excitement and satisfaction she should be experiencing at getting closer to solving the case, her mind was playing tricks on her. For a split second she could visualize a similar scene with Cruz on the other end of this action, Cruz being led away wearing cuffs. She pushed the mental image away, shaken.

It took longer than expected to get Cantoney booked and the paperwork for his arrest filed. When it was finished, Cruz stopped the young officer who was about to lead him away. Addressing Cantoney, he said, "You could make things a lot easier on yourself if you'd cooperate. We might be able to manage a deal for you if you were willing to tell us where you got the gun."

Cantoney laughed, an ugly sound. "Ready to do me favors now, Martinez? I don't think so. My lawyer will have me out of here in a few hours."

"With your record, things are going to go hard for you," Madeline put in. "It would look a lot better to a judge if you'd tell us what we want to know."

"I know how things work better than you do," he retorted. "And I'll take my chances with jail. I kinda like the idea of staying alive." He turned away, and after several more moments Cruz motioned for the officer to take him away.

They discussed Cantoney's words on the way to Andersen Steel. "Whoever sold that gun to Cantoney has him scared to death," Cruz said disgustedly.

"Well, that fits with what we learned on the streets," she reminded him. "Nobody wanted to talk to us about Valdez." She wondered if it was Valdez himself who had everybody so afraid, or his partners in the gun ring. Surely word had reached the streets about the snitch who was found dead. It would serve as a grim reminder to anyone who might otherwise be persuaded to tell what he knew.

"Well, maybe one good thing came out of this day. Ramsey should be safe now."

"Assuming we got there before Dirk was able to wipe off the gun and get Ramsey's prints on it," Madeline agreed. "Otherwise we'll have another set of problems to deal with."

"Can I interest you in a late lunch?" Cruz asked. "I'll let you choose. You can take me to the greasiest dive in the city, and I won't complain, promise."

She ignored his teasing and shook her head. "Let's skip it. I want to get to Andersen Steel before the office closes."

Cruz opened his mouth to argue, then, with a sidelong glance at her set expression, he fell into silence. He'd never seen Maddy quite like this before. She was drawn tightly, as if it would take only a slight nudge to cause an explosion. He was familiar with what adrenaline did to people, and certainly it had been pumping through both of them today. But somehow he thought it was more than that. She'd been tense when he first saw her this morning, but she was wound even tighter now. Maybe he'd better back off for a while. He wasn't certain exactly what was bothering her, and that uncertainty teased his mind. He could accept her explanation from this morning. He grimaced. He hadn't liked it, but knowing what he did about her, he could accept it. Now, though, he was getting the strangest feeling that something else was at work here, something more than she'd admitted to, and worrying about what it might be kept him silent the entire drive.

Madeline spoke only to give him directions. She was distracted, her mind working overtime. With the arrest of Cantoney, she felt more than relief that they had very probably saved Ramsey from years locked away. There was something more. Somehow she felt that they were closer to solving the whole thing, but there were still so many angles to figure out. Where did a cop fit into the gun supply? Why would the people they'd talked to on the streets be reluctant to talk about a dirty cop? Few of them had reason for loyalty to the police. It would make more sense that they would be willing to give up any information that would put a cop away. Unless...

Her eyes slid to the man beside her. Unless the wrong cop was doing the asking. She considered that thought. Suppose a few of the people they'd questioned had known an officer was involved, and recognized that same officer investigating the case. Wouldn't that make them wary? Wouldn't that frighten them into keeping their mouths closed?

She couldn't deny the possibility, any more than she could deny her reaction to it. It would help if she knew just where the officer came in to the gun distribution setup. Were he and Valdez working together? Or was the cop buried deeper behind the scenes than that? Perhaps Valdez was merely the distributor. He'd have the contacts on the streets needed to dispose of the guns. Someone else could be getting the guns and masterminding the setup.

The car pulled up to the corporate headquarters for Andersen Steel and they walked into the building. "I don't doubt that you can tell me who the head of this outfit is," Cruz said as a uniformed man directed them to the floor of the executive offices.

"His name is Louis Andersen," Madeline replied, missing the lopsided grin his correct guess brought to his face. "But he'd be in his seventies by now, I think. I'm not sure if he's still running things or not."

Upon reaching the fifth floor, they were stopped almost as soon as they left the elevator. "May I help you?" A woman rose from her desk several feet away and approached them, a pleasant expression on her face.

Cruz presented his shield and introduced both of them. "We'd like to speak to Mr. Andersen, please."

"Please wait here," the woman advised. They watched as she knocked on a nearby door and disappeared inside.

"Nice digs," Cruz murmured, taking in the plush carpeting and polished walnut furniture.

The woman returned and said, "Mr. Andersen will see you now."

They followed her to the door she'd recently come from and she ushered them in, then closed it firmly behind them.

A man was seated across the huge room from them at a desk that was easily, Cruz surmised, the size of six police-issue desks at headquarters. The inner office was even more luxurious than the outer room. It was decorated in black and gray, with splashes of crimson for accents. Modern artwork adorned the walls. He studied one that looked as though a large spider had been dipped in black paint and then allowed to crawl across the canvas.

Turning toward the desk, Cruz greeted the man rising behind it, then flicked a look at Maddy. If she was right about his age, this man was remarkably well preserved. He didn't look a day older than forty-five.

"Louis Andersen?" he asked.

The man smiled benignly. "I'm Stephen Andersen, vice president of the firm. Louis is my uncle. I'm afraid he's unavailable right now. He's semiretired and doesn't keep regular hours. How can I help you, Detectives?"

Cruz reached into his shirt pocket, withdrew the picture of Jose Valdez and handed it to Andersen. "We're looking for this man. He's been employed by one of your subsidiaries, Wynn Construction. Do you recognize him?"

Andersen studied the picture and then said, "I'm afraid not, but there's really no reason why I would. Wynn Construction, as well as all our other subsidiaries, is run by a manager. They do their own hiring and firing."

"Would you have any records of Wynn's employees here at all?" Madeline pursued. "In your personnel office, or in payroll, perhaps?"

He shook his head. "Payroll and personnel are handled by each individual company. The only records we keep of theirs have to do with the various projects they're working on, and supply orders. We furnish all the steel they need for their jobs." He handed the photo back to Cruz. "Can you tell me why you need to find this man? What's he done?"

"He's just wanted for questioning," Cruz replied.

"Well, I'm sure it's confidential, Detective, but if you know that this man is untrustworthy, I would need to let the manager at Wynn know about it. Crews work with valuable machinery over there all the time."

"I understand your concern, Mr. Andersen," Madeline put in. "But as you said, the matter is confidential. Besides, this individual hasn't shown up for work at Wynn for several days now."

"I see." The man was silent for a moment, and then he said, "Well, I'm sorry I couldn't be of more assistance to you."

He walked to the door with them. Reaching it, Madeline turned and questioned, "Does your company have products imprinted with your logo, Mr. Andersen?"

"Yes, we have calendars, pens, yardsticks, key rings, the usual. Seems like the advertising department is always coming up with something new." He shrugged. "Why do you ask?"

"Are those items available at the other companies you own, too?" she questioned.

He thought for a moment, and then answered, "I'm sure they are." He opened the door for them. "You could pick up things with our logo at any of the companies we own."

Thanking him, they took their leave and rode the elevator to the lobby. Back in the car, Madeline said, "I think we have time to get over to Wynn Construction and talk to the manager there again. I want to ask him—"

But Cruz was shaking his head. "I don't think so. That's forty-five minutes from here, without traffic. We'll have to put it off until tomorrow."

That didn't sit well with her, but she quickly came up with another plan. "Why don't we swing by Ricky and Ramsey's apartment complex, then? I'd like to tell Ramsey as soon as possible about what happened this morning." Cruz didn't answer and she looked across at him quizzically.

Finally he spoke. "I'm going to have to head back to district headquarters and pick up my car. By the time we get there it'll be quitting time."

She cocked an eyebrow. "So? It wouldn't be the first time we put in overtime on this case."

"Can't tonight." His eyes never left the road. "I have an appointment I can't get out of."

For a split second she found herself wondering at his obliqueness, before she comprehended what his reluctance meant. "Maybe you could postpone it," she suggested in a neutral tone. "What is it, a dentist appointment or something? They'll be glad to reschedule for you. Mine always does."

"It's not something I can reschedule," he said flatly. "But don't worry. This will keep until tomorrow."

Madeline stared out her window unseeingly. It was all too obvious that this appointment of his was not something he was willing, or able, to explain to her. Were they, as he'd suggested, getting closer to Valdez? If Cruz was involved, he would have to warn Valdez away tonight, at an appointment his partner couldn't be witness to. One way or another, Madeline suddenly had plans for the night, too. Perhaps she would finally discover exactly what Cruz Martinez was involved in.

It was with an odd sense of déjà vu that Madeline cautiously tailed Cruz's car after he left the parking lot of the Southwest

Precinct. She drove almost mechanically, staying two car lengths back. The route they took was familiar to her. It came as no surprise that they were headed in the same direction as the only other time she'd had an opportunity to tail him. The difference this time was that he didn't stop by his apartment first. From that and the speed with which he was driving, it was easy to see that he was in a hurry.

Her hands clenched on the wheel as they neared the neighborhood in which she'd lost him last time. But luck was with her, and after she followed him several more minutes he pulled in to a parking garage. She hesitated for a few moments before warily approaching it. She hadn't thought about what her explanation would be if Cruz happened to spot her. And that could easily happen in the twisting passages of the garage. They could virtually drive right by each other.

Her mind searched for a plausible excuse she could use even as she lowered her window and reached for the ticket. The gate rose, admitting her to the shadowy depths of the garage. It was emptying out in a steady trickle, half the cars having already left during the hour of rush traffic. When one small red compact backed out ahead of her, she slid smoothly into the vacated space.

She sat tensely, facing straight ahead, tilting her rearview mirror so that she could see behind her. After what seemed interminably long minutes, she saw Cruz walk briskly by, toward the entrance of the garage.

Poised with her fingers on the handle of the door, Madeline waited for Cruz to turn the corner onto the street before she followed hurriedly after him. She was out of breath by the time she reached the street, but just in time to see him disappear into a building two doors down. Reaching the building, she saw him walk into an elevator. Madeline hurried over to the closed doors and looked at the number above them.

She waited several minutes before taking the elevator to the third floor. The car stopped and its doors slid open, revealing a hallway lined with offices. She looked carefully up and down the passageway before cautiously venturing out. Many of the offices were still lit up, so it was impossible to guess which one Cruz had disappeared into.

Rooting around in her purse, she extracted a notebook. Flipping it open, she began to scribble down the names on the office doors as she passed each one. When she paused in front of one door to write down the name of the firm housed there, it swung open and a man stepped out. Her eyes met his in shock, her breath catching. The next moment she looked down again, pretending to read her notes. The man paid her no heed as he continued down the hall, and she gave a silent sigh of relief. But she knew her luck couldn't hold. The next person through one of these doors could well be Cruz. She didn't want to take that chance.

She ducked behind one of the huge square pillars that dotted the area, giving a silent prayer of thanks to the architect who'd included them in this building's plan. Then she prepared to wait.

Stakeout had never been one of her favorite parts of police work, and after more than three hours Madeline's mood was approaching the dangerous. Her surveillance had yielded no results, and the shoes she'd put on this morning had quickly lost the comfort for which she'd bought them. No one else came out of the elevator, although a few more people left the offices for the night.

What could he be doing here for so long? she snarled silently. The tedium was starting to wear on her nerves. She'd had too much time to think tonight, and she didn't like the way her thoughts all seemed to center around one man. She should be using this time to concentrate on every aspect of the case, but like a mental paging through a photo album, his face kept appearing in her mind. Each image was different, reflecting a different side of him. Face gentle as he held one of his nieces, aglow with pride when he introduced his parents. Closed and guarded when he'd talked to Ritter, laughing and teasing as he was all too often, and by contrast, cold and harsh as he'd been the time they'd encountered Baker.

She didn't usually think about the phenomenal memory she'd been blessed with. When she did, she gave thanks for it. But she cursed it bitterly now, because she knew that she could count on it to supply her with never-ending tortuous images of Cruz and the night they'd spent together. The realization did nothing to improve her mood.

When Cruz finally did leave, he wasn't alone. Her view was partially blocked by the huge pillar, but her eyes widened in surprise. He walked away with a man who looked very like the mysterious Dan whom they'd run into in the restaurant. She waited a few minutes and then crossed over and looked at the door they'd exited through. It bore only a number; no name or business was listed. After waiting a little longer, Madeline left the building. But she didn't go home. Instead she headed to the Internal Affairs headquarters. She logged on to one of the available computers, one that accessed a vast databank for the city. Then she spent a great part of the night hunting for information that would explain once and for all Cruz Martinez's secret.

Cruz's eyes narrowed with concern when Maddy approached his desk the next morning. She looked even more fragile than she had the day before, and that was saying a lot. Those gorgeous green eyes were dull, shuttered, and no amount of makeup could hide the shadows beneath them. His lips thinned, and he didn't know who he was angrier at—her for beating herself up over their one night together, or himself. He finally decided that most of the blame was his. She was cautious about emotion; he'd known that, dammit, and still he'd pushed her.

Well, it was too late now for regrets, and if the truth be told, he had damn few of them. He was only sorry that Maddy was suffering; he hated to see her tearing herself up over this. But the case would be over soon, and then, he vowed, he'd make it up to her.

Pushing these thoughts aside, he made no mention of the tension that showed on her face. Instead he poured her a cup of coffee and sank into his chair, giving her some time to unwind.

"Got a call from Lieutenant Niles," he said as she sipped. He handed her the notes he'd jotted down from the phone conversation. "They checked out Valdez's apartment. No one claims to have seen him around lately. That's the list of what they found in his apartment."

"Doesn't seem to be anything interesting on it," she said, a note of disappointment in her voice. "How about prints?" she asked. "Have they dusted his apartment for Cantoney's or Stover's prints? Maybe their gun sales took place there."

"I doubt he dealt out of his apartment," he remarked, "but they dusted for Stover and came up empty. I already asked them to see if they could run a match on Cantoney. We'll know the results tomorrow. Also," he continued, "I talked to the lab and the gun you found in Cantoney's apartment had several different prints on it, but none of them were Ramsey's."

"That's a relief, at least," she said. "Did they get a clear print of Cantoney's, I hope?"

Cruz nodded. "Sure did. The gun yielded a set of his prints, and it was hidden in his apartment. I doubt they'll need to use Ricky to testify against him. The case should stand alone on what we've got."

They left then and went out to the car. Madeline was grateful that it was her turn to drive. Fighting the traffic would give her mind something else to concentrate on other than the man riding beside her. She'd gotten very little sleep last night after leaving Internal Affairs. And she was planning to go back there again tonight. Just a few more hours and she should be able to answer several of her questions about Cruz Martinez.

The lead ball in her stomach seemed a permanent fixture these days. It had been impossible to forget, even for a moment last night, just who she was investigating. It was hard to concentrate on her work, trying to compile enough facts that, taken together, might prove damning enough to point the finger at her partner.

It wasn't only for herself that she dreaded the possibility of having Cruz turn up guilty. The thought of what it would do to his family also haunted her. And the fact that it bothered her so much angered her. Why should *she* be the one to feel guilty? If Cruz had made his choices without regard to their impact on his family, he was responsible for letting his family and the department down, as well as for putting illegal weapons in the hands of kids. All those involved in the gun supply ring were as guilty as those who'd pulled the triggers.

The late hours and the events of the days were beginning to wear on her. Once in bed she found she couldn't sleep, anyway. Her brain continued to analyze every aspect of the case. She couldn't afford to be distracted from the job at hand, not now, when the investigation was starting to yield results. She needed all her wits about her.

They arrived at Wynn Construction with only a few words being exchanged between them. The same manager greeted them, but had little more information for them than he'd had the first time.

"Somehow I'm not surprised that you're back to talk to us," he grunted, putting down his pen on the stack of paperwork he was filling out. "I should have known that hiring an ex-con was going to get me nothing but trouble."

"It isn't the practice of hiring ex-cons that has us interested," Madeline corrected him evenly. "We're looking for Valdez, as you know. We have no problem with you or your company."

The man's grimace told them what he thought of that answer. "Well, I could have saved you a trip out here," he said. "Valdez hasn't been back since you were here last time. And it's put us in a real bind, too. We were shorthanded anyway, and now this. I don't need the aggravation, believe me."

Cruz did. The man's face seemed to be bright red all the time. Judging from that and the extra sixty pounds he was carrying, he was a prime candidate for a heart attack. "We won't keep you very long. We want to question the foreman we spoke to last time, if we could."

"Don't suppose I could stop ya," the man grumbled. "I tell you, hiring Valdez was the worst mistake I made all year. Hell, if I hadn't gotten a memo from the powers-that-be at Andersen's about equal-employment opportunities, I would never have considered him at all. The guy was spooky."

The man's attitude was making it increasingly difficult for Madeline to keep her tongue. Her eyes resting on the pen he'd dropped on the pile of papers on his desk, she crossed over and picked it up. "Wynn Construction." She read the logo aloud, then she looked up with a smile as she replaced it. "Everybody's into advertising, I suppose. Do you have a lot of these?"

The man looked at her as if she'd lost her mind. "Yeah, they're all over the place. But after a few months it gets harder than hell to find one. They seem to have a way of walking away, if you get my drift."

She smiled commiseratingly. "I suppose. You probably have things with Andersen Steel printed on them, too, since it's your parent company."

He shook his head. "No need. We have our own name on pens, hats, key chains, the whole nine yards." He was clearly growing impatient with the time they were taking. "You can find Kurt, the foreman, outside somewhere, checking the equipment. He's got to go out and inspect job sites in an hour, so don't tie him up too long, okay?"

Cruz and Madeline left the office and headed across the construction yard to where they could see Kurt near some large earth-moving equipment. "Pretty friendly guy," Cruz commented as he strolled along.

"He sure wasn't happy to see us again," she agreed. But her mind was only half on her own words. She was wondering about what the manager had said about not having anything here with Andersen advertising on it. That contradicted what Stephen Andersen had told them. And it left one question looming in her mind: If Valdez hadn't picked the pen up here, at work, when and where had he gotten it?

As they approached Kurt, a construction worker in a bright yellow hard hat climbed up onto the huge bulldozer and started it up. The noise was deafening as they grew closer, and they had to shout to be heard.

"You're back checking on Jose, I'll bet," Kurt called to them. "Hasn't been back to work since the last time you came."

"We know, we talked to the manager," Cruz said. "We'd like to speak to the men on the crew that Valdez worked on. Maybe he talked to one of them."

Kurt shook his head. "I've got his crew on the other side of the city. But you won't get much from them. Valdez kept to himself. He was a good worker, I'll give him that, but he didn't talk much. His taking off really put me in a bind, too. I've got my hands full juggling several different projects, and I need every guy I've got. And if that's not enough," he complained querulously, "we've run out of steel, and the next shipment isn't due in for several days." He broke off then, as the man in the bulldozer cut the engine and climbed down. "If you want, I can write down the address of the place that crew is working, but I still think you're wasting your time. Just make sure you don't tie them up too long, okay? We're on a tight deadline for the project they're on."

They spent the next several hours across town at the construction site where the crew was working, questioning each man who had worked with Valdez. But their efforts were in vain, just as the foreman had predicted. None of the men could shed any light on Valdez or his whereabouts. They all agreed that in the short time he'd been there he'd done his job, but hadn't talked much. No one professed to have had an opportunity for conversation having to do with anything other than work.

When they finished questioning the crew members, they drove to Ricky and Ramsey's apartment in the projects. A visibly subdued Ramsey let them in. "You heard Dirk was arrested?" Madeline asked him.

He nodded.

"He's going away for another long stretch, Ramsey," Cruz said soberly. "And if we hadn't arrested him, you would have been the one to get put away. He was planning to get your fingerprints on the gun. He would have given you up as the shooter, if the killing had been traced back to him."

Ramsey looked down. Gone was the sullen bravado he'd sported every other time they'd talked to him. The news had shaken him, that was apparent. "I never even seen the gun."

"Had you heard that Cantoney had gotten it?" Madeline asked.

He hesitated, then nodded reluctantly. "I knew he was planning to. He talked about it all the time. I wasn't there when he got it, though."

"Do you have any idea who he bought it from?" Cruz pressed.

Ramsey shook his head. "I never heard no names. All I know is he got it from some guy he had to meet on the docks."

"The docks?" Madeline frowned.

"That's what he said," the boy insisted. "He was in a big hurry that he get it when he did. Otherwise he said he was going to have to wait a couple weeks before he got another chance."

"You had a pretty narrow escape, Ramsey," Cruz noted, sending the boy a keen look. "If we'd been too late, it would have been you locked up, not Cantoney. Guess you couldn't trust Dirk as much as you thought, huh?"

The boy shrugged, frowning.

"Next time you might not be so lucky," Madeline put in. "Go back to school and steer clear of your friends in the Lords. It's the only way you can stay clean."

Driving back to the district headquarters, Madeline asked, "Think we got through to Ramsey this time?"

Cruz shrugged. "The whole thing made more of an impression on Ricky than it did his brother, I'm afraid. I'd hope he'd be smart enough not to trust the Lords again, but I don't know if he can stay straight or not."

"With Cantoney in prison, the gang probably won't be as solid, since there was no clear second in command," she noted. "Who knows? Maybe this scared him enough to start him thinking."

"We can always count on Ricky to badger him about that." Cruz chuckled. "Ramsey might not know it, but his little brother saved his butt for him, big time."

When they arrived back at district headquarters, Madeline declined to go in with Cruz.

"We need to plan our next move," he argued, surprised at her reluctance.

"It'll have to wait until tomorrow, at least for me. I have something else I have to do tonight."

He frowned, but shrugged as she got into her car. "I'll see you tomorrow, then."

Madeline drove back to Internal Affairs and unlocked the file she'd started last night and sat back down at the computer. She spent the evening accessing the city's vast databanks, looking for information that would explain Cruz's appearance at the office

building she'd trailed him to. After discovering the owner of the
building, she checked on the tenants listed. Daniel A. Chambers
was listed as a tenant on the third floor. Now she had a place to
start. She scoured every file she could for information on him. He
had no criminal record, but seemed to have a parking ticket problem that he needed to see to. She switched to a different data base,
and asked the computer for all properties and businesses with his
name on them.

While she waited impatiently for the information to appear on
the screen, her mind wandered. She'd been having an unusually
difficult time concentrating since trailing Cruz last night, and her
stomach was tied in what seemed to be permanent knots. This
constant uncertainty about him, the continual search into his
background, was having an undeniable effect on her. Until she'd
been paired with Cruz, she'd never before had difficulty main-
taining a single-minded attention to an investigation. But he'd been
the exception to many of her rules to date.

Determinedly she moved her gaze to the screen, and her eyebrows lifted as she read the impressive list of properties under
Daniel Chambers's name. Halfway down the list Chambers's name
became paired with others, apparently partners of his. When she
noted Cruz's name listed next to his, she had to blink, wondering
for a second if her eyes were playing tricks on her. Cruz was listed
on three different properties with Chambers, but Madeline couldn't
be sure from the names exactly what kind of businesses they were.

Deciding the telephone would be a quicker route to her answer,
Madeline reached for the phone book and the receiver. By the time
she had called each business on the list, she was certain she'd found
the source of Cruz's second income. But she still wasn't sure she
believed it. Dropping the receiver in its cradle, she leaned back in
her chair, bemused. The irony of what she'd just learned didn't
escape her.

Cruz Martinez was in the restaurant business.

Chapter 14

Madeline couldn't prevent a wry smile at the revelation. It should come as no great surprise to her, after all. The man had been commenting on her eating habits since she met him. Everything from her choice of dining establishments to her meal selections had warranted discussion. And he'd certainly proven to her when he'd come to her apartment that he could cook.

Madeline glanced at her watch, then signed off the computer and returned to her desk. Rapidly she began to type up a report for Brewer detailing what she'd found tonight. She knew she still didn't have anything conclusive to report. Just because she'd discovered the source of Cruz's extra income didn't mean he couldn't also be involved with the gun suppliers. The end product was as concise and analytical as usual. When she'd finished, she paper-clipped the pages together and slipped them into a file folder. Most of the other workers had left long ago, and the building was dim, except for lights at the desks of a few others working late. As she stretched her stiff shoulders tiredly, a voice came from behind, startling her.

"You're sure working late, Casey. Hope that means I can expect to see a report from you sometime soon."

Madeline willed her muscles, which had all tensed at the unexpected voice, to relax. Turning her chair to face the speaker, she said mildly, "Captain Brewer. You're here late, too. I didn't expect to see you."

The captain looked a bit haggard. Right now his suit coat was slung over one arm and his tie had been loosened. She noted absently that the bald spot on the top of his head seemed more pronounced. She felt an unusual pang of compassion for him. He looked as if he'd spent a few days in misery. However, at his next words, all her empathy disappeared.

"I'm beginning to think I made a mistake assigning you to Martinez. I need some answers, and I need them fast. When are you going to have them for me?"

Her fleeting sympathy gone, she was left with a familiar desire to see him strangle on his tie. She had to content herself with the satisfaction she felt at seeing his face when she handed him the file folder in her hand. "Here you go, Captain. I was going to leave this on your desk. Although my investigation on Martinez isn't over, I do have some new information for you."

She waited with far more equanimity than she was feeling. It was second nature for her to hide her feelings behind an emotionless mask when dealing with him. His reaction wasn't long in coming.

He snapped the file folder and uttered a foul imprecation. "Is that all you've got?"

"Sorry to disappoint you," she answered caustically. "Exactly what is it you were hoping for? I told you the investigation wasn't finished."

"What I was hoping for," he muttered bad-temperedly, "was that one of my people would get something, *anything,* on one of these detectives. Somehow the word has gotten out to the powers-that-be that we have a dirty cop on the loose and, believe me, my superiors are making my life a living hell. I'd better have a cop to deliver to them, or my butt's on the line."

"You mean none of the other investigations have come up with anything on the other detectives, either?" she asked slowly.

He shook his head morosely. "And if all five detectives do check out, it could mean the snitch was wrong about a cop being involved in the gun supply. Hell, maybe the snitch was shooting up too much joy juice and dreamed the whole thing up. But you can bet I'm going to have a bloody time convincing the brass of that. They're worried about the department's image, and they want to see someone's head on the block."

From Brewer's aggrieved tone it was plain that he was more worried about having to answer to his superiors than he was about making sure a cop wasn't falsely accused. Madeline swallowed her sense of disgust. It was an emotion she was used to feeling around him. She rose, reaching for her suit jacket and purse.

"So how's the rest of the investigation coming?" he inquired as she slipped into her coat. "How close are you to nailing the supplier?"

"It's coming together," she answered shortly. "I really don't think it will be much longer."

"You don't think so, huh?" he grunted, continuing to survey her. When he said nothing else, Madeline stifled a sigh and started to walk away.

"Casey."

His voice stopped her, and she took a breath before turning to face him inquiringly.

He tapped the file folder with one finger. "Good work on this. Factual, as always."

The compliment took her by surprise, and made her a little wary. "Thank you, sir."

"Tell me something. Forget the hard evidence we're looking for. What's your gut feeling on Martinez? If you had to guess, I mean. Is he dirty?"

She stared at him for what seemed an eternity. "I don't know" was on her tongue, waiting to be uttered. She was a meticulous investigator; she didn't draw conclusions without proof. But she knew the captain well enough to know that he wouldn't let her get away with that. He was asking her, in a rare moment off the record, to reveal what her instincts told her about the man she was investigating.

Instincts. She shied away from the word. She hadn't relied on instincts since the one time they'd led her astray, by allowing her to trust Dennis Belding. She considered them now. For the first time she pushed aside all the logic, all the facts she'd found in this convoluted case, and concentrated purely on what she felt. What her innermost feelings told her. It was surprising how clearly the answer came to her.

"No," she said evenly. "I don't think so."

Brewer merely grunted again, and flipped open the file she'd given him. But she couldn't dismiss her own words so easily. It was the first time she'd allowed herself to think them, much less say them out loud. She turned away from the captain, shaken. Something inside her wanted to call the words back; another part stood by them. Swiftly she walked from the building to her car.

Once she got into her vehicle, she sat motionless. She hadn't come up with the kind of positive proof that would clear Cruz conclusively of any wrongdoing in the gun supply. She could now explain where his extra money came from, but it certainly didn't prove his innocence. It just meant that she hadn't yet come up with any evidence of his guilt. She knew that without Brewer's prompting she'd never have admitted those words out loud, would not even have thought them. But now that she had, their truth was inescapable.

She began to drive, thoughts still distracted. Her father had never forgiven her for her error in judgment in trusting her ex-fiancé. He had certainly never forgotten it. She hadn't allowed herself to forget it, either. Instead of learning from her mistake and moving past it, she'd allowed it to dictate her behavior and responses for the next several years. She'd drawn no conclusions, made no inferences that couldn't be backed up with piece after piece of solid evidence. She'd thought it made for the best police work, but certainly there was room for her own intuition. Perhaps completely ducking emotional responses wasn't as clear-cut as she'd thought. In fact, it smacked a bit of cowardice.

It appeared as though she'd come to a point in her life where she had to make some choices. She could continue as she had for the past few years, worshiping at the altar of empirical evidence. Or she could temper good police work with her own insight. As a police officer, she'd forgiven herself for any mistakes she'd made, and learned from them. She hadn't been as merciful to herself in her personal life. Surely there was room for both in her life, both personally and professionally.

Without completely remembering the trip there, she found herself parked in front of Cruz's apartment building. She stared at the building for a time. Then, without allowing herself any longer to think about it, she walked up to the door.

The front door was locked and she rang the button beneath his name. It was several moments before she heard his voice answer with a brusque, "Yeah?"

The sound of his voice kept her speechless for a minute, and he repeated his greeting with even less patience. Finally she found her tongue and said, "Cruz, it's Madeline. Can I come up for a minute?"

The pause after her question seemed interminable, as though he were weighing his answer. Finally he answered affirmatively and she was able to enter the building.

He was waiting for her when she got off the elevator, the front door to his apartment open. She followed him inside, swallowing hard at the sight of the bare expanse of his broad back. Closing the door behind them, he leaned against it, sticking his hands into his pockets, perusing her.

She stared back hypnotically, entranced by the wide shoulders and chest delineated by his pose. Gaze drifting downward, she felt her stomach tighten when she saw that all he wore was a pair of obscenely well-fitted jeans, worn almost white, which sheathed his muscles erotically.

"What are you doing here, Maddy?"

Her eyes jerked to his. His expression looked no more welcoming than his words sounded, and again she questioned her wisdom in coming here. Her power of speech seemed to have momentarily deserted her. Then the pungent aroma in the apartment seeped through her consciousness and she whirled around to look at the living room. "Oh, you've been varnishing," she exclaimed artlessly, taking a few steps to the entrance of the room.

"Just finished," he replied. "Had to leave a path so that I could get to the stairs tonight. I'll get up early tomorrow and finish it before I go to work." She looked toward the kitchen, where he had brushes soaking in a container in the sink.

"That's what I came to talk to you about." She seized the topic with relief.

"Varnishing?"

She ignored the skeptical note in his tone. "No, work. Something the Wynn manager said has really been bothering me. Did you hear me ask him about the pen?"

He nodded slowly. "He said there weren't any around with advertising for Andersen on them."

"Well?" she demanded. "Do you think it means anything? Andersen was positive when he told us they could be found there."

Cruz was slow to answer. "It wouldn't mean much by itself. But there was something else that was said today that bugged me, so when you left this afternoon, I did a little digging."

"And?" she demanded.

He almost smiled at her eagerness. She looked different somehow, as if the tiredness and worry of the past few days had been erased. Her face was aglow and her gorgeous green eyes were alight with interest. He felt a pang of jealousy that it was work that put that look on her face. "The foreman mentioned today that Andersen has a warehouse on the docks. And Ramsey said Cantoney had bought the gun on the docks." He pulled one hand out of his pocket, holding it up to stem what he was sure would be her protest. "I know it's a stretch. There are miles of docks, and it could have been anywhere."

"I wasn't going to say that," Madeline informed him. "Because I think you might be on to something. Remember, Valdez is connected, however remotely, to Andersen Steel. He could have easily found out where their warehouse is. Who knows? He might have decided that it was a perfect place to do business."

Cruz nodded bemusedly. He was relieved that she agreed with him on this, because he would have been hard-pressed to convince her. He'd been a detective long enough to trust his instincts, and something about the connection between Valdez and the warehouse nagged at him. He couldn't put it into words, but when he had a feeling this strong, he had to follow it, or it would drive him crazy until he did.

"Well, I'm glad you agree. Because I was going to suggest that we stake out that warehouse and see if Valdez shows up to do any more business." His tone was dour, which perfectly matched his mood. Thinking about spending the next God-knows-how-many nights in the car with Maddy, sitting next to her while she slept, was enough to make him want to chew nails. Somehow he didn't think the experience was going to do his system, already tight with frustration, any good.

He raised a bare foot to push himself away from the door and strode to the refrigerator. Pulling it open, he extracted two bottles of water and silently offered one to Maddy.

She took it, wondering at the care he took to make sure their hands didn't touch.

Twisting off the top with barely concealed violence, he drank a long swallow before lowering his bottle to survey her. If she didn't leave soon, he wasn't going to be responsible for his actions, but she didn't seem in any discernible hurry. That realization, coupled with the fact that his partially clad presence didn't seem to be bothering her in the least, made his tone uncustomarily caustic. "You'd better run along home and catch some sleep. When we start that stakeout, it'll be a while before you'll get a full eight hours again."

She noted his tone and wondered at it. In fact, his whole manner tonight seemed out of character for him. He hadn't made one wisecrack, had not uttered one teasing remark. His lopsided grin was very much absent, and for one heart-stopping moment she wondered guiltily if he could have somehow learned of her investigation of him. Even as she mentally discounted that possibility, her pulse raced at the thought of it. Cruz was a man of strong emotions, and she knew without being told that he would value loyalty above all things. What would he say if he ever found out?

She thought she knew the answer to that question. And she would make sure he didn't ever find out. She'd played it safe all her life, never taking a risk, always weighing the odds. Until the night they'd made love. Now she was tempted to take another risk, one she hadn't considered having to make. She'd made it very clear to him that there could be nothing between them. Could she summon the courage to tell him of her change of heart? It would take more bravery than she was sure she had. There was nothing in his manner to suggest that he cared one way or the other.

"Actually, I lied to you," she stated baldly, and watched wariness flicker into his eyes.

"About what?"

"I didn't come here to talk about work. I wanted to tell you that—" here her voice hesitated "—that I was wrong the other day when I insisted that we didn't have a relationship."

He stared at her, saying nothing.

His silence wasn't the most promising answer she could have dreamed of, and she bit her lip. Those dark eyes were trained on her, and she allowed herself to be hypnotized by their intense depths. "You were right," she continued, her voice husky, "when you said I was scared."

"You denied it." The words sounded rusty to his own ears.

"You scared me. The way you made me feel. I couldn't trust it. I didn't want to trust it," she corrected herself.

Still he didn't move, and his brow furrowed, as if he were having difficulty comprehending her words. At his inactivity, she felt her resolve for honesty vanish. Even the hardiest egos needed a little feedback. She'd almost decided to turn tail and run when his voice stopped her.

"Are you saying you've changed your mind?"

"Yes." It was little more than a whisper.

"What if you change your mind again?" He still hadn't moved from where he leaned against the refrigerator. He couldn't. Every muscle, every nerve had frozen as soon as he'd understood what she was saying.

"That's what I came to tell you." She moved slowly to stand in front of him. "I'm not running scared anymore." It didn't begin to explain what had sent her running in the first place, but it was all she could give him. When he still stood motionless, she might have lost her resolve if she hadn't seen and correctly interpreted the look in his eyes. The intensity she saw there told her that he was far from unmoved. She was beckoned closer, tempted to reckless abandon by the glittering promise she read in his gaze.

Madeline stepped nearer, until they were standing toe-to-toe. Slowly she reached out with her cold bottle and pressed its coolness against the bare skin of one of his shoulders. Then she moved it slowly down his chest, the bottle gliding easily with the cool condensation that had formed on the outside. She traced an imaginary line around one of his nipples and then rubbed the tip of the bottle against the taut nub. A muscle jumped in his chest, rewarding her efforts and tempting her to further indulgences. "The question is," she murmured huskily, her eyes entranced by the sight of the cool drops leaving temptingly moist paths across his stomach, "whether you feel the same way." Her voice almost disappeared. "Whether you still want me."

"If you're having any doubts about that, I'd suggest you hug me real tight," he muttered. "I just want you to be sure this time. I don't want to find out later that you, ah, Maddy..." His breath hissed in as her mouth followed the trail the bottle had left, across his chest, and lower.

When her tongue scooped up the drop of moisture the bottle had left in his navel, his urge to speak left him. Lightning quick, one hand set his own bottle on the counter next to him and the other arm snaked around her waist and pulled her closer. Close enough for her to tell for herself just what effect she had on him.

She wasn't given much opportunity to enjoy his reaction. His mouth came down on hers with all the frustrated passion he'd been forced to keep hidden.

His kiss was hard and deep, but she relished the demand it made. There was a reassurance in the fierceness of his need for her, a fierceness that was fully reciprocated. He pressed her lips apart and entered her mouth with a smooth, sure sweep of his tongue, and she welcomed the intimate invasion. Her lips twisted under his, making her own demands. She could feel her usual caution slip, and the unfamiliar freedom was frighteningly heady. She would have liked more time to explore it, to test the boundaries of the dizzying experience. But then his mouth went to the spot below her ear that he had found on their other night together, and she shivered helplessly. Tantalizing, openmouthed kisses were pressed up and down the delicate cord of her neck, and at the same time she could feel him take the bottle from her hand. She wasn't even aware when he took the barrette from her hair. She dimly recognized the absence of her jacket and the cooler air touching her bare skin as her blouse was unbuttoned and tossed on the center island.

His hands dropped to her waist, smoothing over the pale pink teddy she'd worn beneath her clothes. How a woman could be so full of contrasts, so prim and tailored on the outside and all satin and lace beneath, he didn't know, but he gave a fervent prayer of thanks for it. Maddy had a penchant for filmy underthings, and damned if he wasn't developing a yen for them himself.

He rubbed his lips over hers, waiting until they opened for him before sealing her mouth with his own. At the same time he dispensed with her slacks and shoes. An inner voice was reminding him to go slowly, to take it easy, but apparently that voice had no direct impact on his hands. They slipped up the back of the teddy and cupped the firm bottom beneath, bringing her fully against him.

She gasped at the feel of the solid ridge behind his zipper, held in check by the worn denim. His hard chest was pressed against hers, separated only by the silky barrier of her lingerie, and she rubbed her breasts against him, exciting both of them.

He knew he was rushing this, knew he should be questioning her change of heart. But slowing down was beyond him. He was a man of hot-blooded desires, kept firmly in check most of the time. He had to wield an iron control over his own appetites; in his profession, one impulsive move could get him killed. But he had no defenses erected against the way she wanted him, didn't wish for any. His need for this woman was immediate and violent. Her touch was no more gentle. Her hands were clenched on his shoulders, the nails stabbing slightly, and he welcomed the slight twinge of pain they brought.

He reached out to push a strap down her satiny shoulder, and stayed to cup the firm warm breast his action freed. His thumb passed over the velvety nipple once, twice, before his mouth replaced his hand.

Madeline's back arched at his sudden move, unconsciously pressing closer to his mouth. He suckled strongly from her, and her senses swam. Without lifting his head, he backed her to the counter, then boosted her up on its edge.

By the time her eyes fluttered open, dazed by the sudden movement, she was stretched out on the surface, and Cruz was lying next to her. She met his fervent kiss, and the strangeness of their surroundings whirled from her consciousness, to be filled instead with him. The pleasure wasn't slow and insidious this time, it was hot and all-consuming. His actions reflected her own agony of need, and sharpened it. His mouth drew her nipples into taut beads of sensual torment, then lashed them gently with his tongue.

Her hands rushed over his bare torso, delighting in the smooth warm skin covering tight muscles. They went to his zipper, and he obligingly lifted away to allow her access. Her hands freed his sex, heavy and throbbing, and cupped it. Cruz pushed into them, muttering something in Spanish. He endured her teasing, curious fingers for only short moments before he moved away.

Madeline wanted to protest the move, but before she was able to, his wicked mouth was back, and it was doing delightful things to her breasts and stomach. Her arms urged him upward, unable to tolerate more teasing. Her passion was honed to razor sharpness, the desire so strong that the anticipation was almost painful.

And then the anticipation was over. Cruz plunged into her with one long, deep thrust that drove the breath from her body, even as her legs climbed his waist to hold him in the most intimate caress of all. The solidness of his possession was enough to bring a tiny spark of vivid satisfaction, but not for long. In the next second she craved even more, and her hips arched beneath his.

Cruz correctly read her need and he gave full rein to his own frantic desire. Sliding his hands beneath her bottom, he raised her to meet each of his thrusts, each deeper and wilder than the last.

Each movement increased her pleasure sharply, until suddenly the culmination hit her and swept her off the precipice. Cruz felt her climax, and it was enough to trigger his own as the pleasure careened through him. He jerked under the force of it, spilling his hot seed into her. The eddies went on and on, until finally he collapsed, gasping harshly.

He hadn't protected her, the first time he could remember such a lapse. Even when he'd lost his virginity at the age of sixteen, or later, when the girls had become bolder, inviting him to test his rampant sexuality, not once had he failed to protect his partner. But instead of regret, he was filled with a fierce sense of pleasure. The image of Maddy, naked as she was now, belly round with his child, was too satisfying a picture.

It could have been minutes or hours before either of them moved. Then she gave a little gasp, and he became aware for the first time that he was crushing her with his weight. He moved to the side, throwing a leg over her to keep her close to him. He rubbed his face in her thick loose hair, tangled now from his hands.

Pressing a kiss to her earlobe, he whispered lazily, "I guess my mother was right when she helped me design this kitchen. You *can't* ever have too much counter space."

She nipped at his collarbone, satisfied at his flinch of pain. "You're a wicked man, Martinez."

A satisfied smile tilted his lips as he gazed down on her. "You're about to see just how wicked I can be, given the right incentive."

An hour later, lolling in the bathtub with him, Madeline was inclined to agree that he could be very wicked indeed. He had lured her into taking an innocent shower with him, one that had turned out to be not so innocent after all. Their second bout of lovemaking had left her sapped of strength, utterly boneless. Her hair had been soaked as they'd forgotten everything but the savage arousal that stole over them so effortlessly. Cruz had insisted on washing her hair for her, and even now, sitting between his legs in the tub, back propped against his chest, her head was on his shoulder, and his hands were still massaging the shampoo rhythmically into her hair.

Her eyes were shut in sybaritic pleasure. There was something extremely arousing in the delight Cruz seemed to take in touching her. He was an utter sensualist; he reacted to the world around him through his sense of touch. She'd noticed that about him early on. And, if truth be known, at the same time she'd wondered what it would feel like to be touched by him.

Now she knew, and that awareness sent currents of pleasure skittering down her spine. At no time in her life had she considered the possibility that there would be a man with whom she could be completely, utterly herself. She'd never let herself dream that such a man existed. That would have been expecting too much, and Madeline Casey had spent her life lowering her expectations, lest she be disappointed. Finding herself now involved with such a man was more than she'd ever hoped for. It was also, quite possibly, the most frightening thing she'd ever had to face.

Her eyes came open to stare unseeingly at the wall. She was petrified. To take a chance caring about someone the way she did Cruz was to risk losing much more than she'd ever had to lose before. It would hurt more than she was sure she could bear. She was a strong person, she knew that. But it had been much easier to be strong when the stakes had not been quite this high.

She could feel the tension creep back into limbs that had, until a minute ago, been completely relaxed. It could all be gone in a second. If Cruz should find out about her investigation of him, their relationship would be over before it ever really had a chance to start. And more than anything else in the world she wanted that relationship to have a chance. Cautious hope bloomed in her every time she thought about the possibility of allowing herself to trust, to love a man completely. That hope was dashed each time she faced the bitter certainty that to tell him the truth would destroy her chances with him.

"What's wrong?" His low voice sounded in her ear. He'd felt her stiffening, and wondered at the cause. For a moment his hands stilled, afraid in that instant that there would be a repeat of her withdrawal, as had happened the first time they'd made love. He knew he would not be able to react as calmly this time if that should happen. A baser, more primitive side of his nature would take hold.

But her answer the next moment banished that fear and sent relief coursing through his veins instead. "Nothing," she whispered, snuggling closer against his chest. "Nothing at all."

And as his arms wrapped around her, Madeline made a vow to herself. Cruz would never learn of her part in the investigation. She would make certain of that.

Chapter 15

Morning came damn early, Cruz groused silently as he followed Madeline down the spiral staircase. The sky was still gray outside, night barely lifted, the moon still visible. He resented the need for them to rise so early, resented that she had to leave him at all, even for a couple of hours.

He had it bad, he admitted, jerking a tennis shoe over a bare foot and lacing it up. Because, to be truthful, he wouldn't like any reason that took Maddy from his bed.

Casting a careful eye at Cruz's set expression, she correctly guessed his mood, if not the cause. "You wake up grouchy," she noted. "I'm delighted."

"I don't usually," he contradicted her. He finished getting dressed and they walked out of the apartment. "I just don't like having to do this."

"You don't have to walk me to my car," she informed him for what seemed the hundredth time. "I know the way."

"Yes, I *do* have to walk you to your car," he contradicted. "You're not going to be out on these streets alone. But you're partly right—the fact that I have to do it at all is what's bothering me."

Reaching her car, she grasped the door handle. "And what would you have me do, Martinez?" she asked teasingly. "Show up for work wearing yesterday's clothes? Or, no, wait, maybe I could find something in your closet to wear."

She rolled her eyes comically, but the thought remained to tantalize him. Somehow the thought of her wearing something of his, with very little else, of course, was a provocative mental image. But right now they had something more important to think about.

"What I would have you do," he said seriously, "is to consider bringing some things over so that we don't have to do these early-morning goodbyes again."

His words startled her, even as they brought a rush of warmth to her heart. *Bring some things over.* That would give their relationship a taunting sense of permanence, implying that there would be many more times when she would wake in his bed. The thought suffused her with heat, and with trepidation. Despite the secret she was keeping from him, the possibility of spending even more time with him was too precious to jeopardize.

He interpreted her silence as unwillingness, and mentally cursed his timing. Now wasn't the right time to discuss this. No, the right time would have been when she was in his bed, her body warm from his, her lips still moist from his kisses. He'd been half surprised by the words as they'd left his mouth, but the moment they had he'd realized just how long he'd been subconsciously waiting for this moment. He wanted to know that he would wake up beside her each morning, and go to bed with her every night. He wanted to be certain that her earlier wariness of getting too close to him was gone, and to be very sure that it would never recur.

He wanted, he thought ruefully, a lot of things. And judging by her lack of response, he wasn't going to get all of them, at least not right away. But he was a patient man. He'd take a little step now and push for more later.

It was with that thought in mind that he lowered his head and sealed her mouth with his own. He caught her unaware, much as his suggestion had, and he took full advantage of her slightly parted lips. His tongue pressed into her mouth in a sure, smooth stroke and Madeline's knees weakened in an immediate, involuntary response.

Her purse dropped to the ground as she reached up to slide her hands across his shoulders, gripping them for support as she returned his kiss achingly. He kissed her with shattering absorption, heedless of their lack of privacy. She didn't know how he did it, how he could so effortlessly drive away every thought, every concern she might have, until there was no thought left at all, only an answering need.

When he finally raised his head and looked at her, he had to fight an overpowering urge to take her back to bed again. Her cheeks were flushed, her eyes heavy lidded and glittering. And her mouth ... his groin tightened as he noted the slightly swollen lips.

"You fight dirty, Martinez," she said in a slow, drugged-sounding voice.

His mouth went to her neck. "Then you'll consider my suggestion?" The sharp nip he inflicted was immediately soothed by his tongue, and her attention was divided between his words and the sensations that were racing through her.

"All right," she agreed in that same husky murmur.

That voice had a direct reaction on him, and he had to step away from her to keep himself from reaching for her again. He leaned forward and kissed her lightly, being careful not to touch her anywhere else. He bent to pick up her purse and handed it to her. "Good." His low voice rumbled. "Drive safely. I'll see you in a couple of hours." He waited until her car was driving away before a satisfied grin swept his face as he recalled what her words had implied. Whistling, he reentered his apartment building. He might as well finish varnishing the floor before he got ready for work. It would be an excellent way to work off his sudden energy, and to keep his mind off what she'd just promised.

Madeline had barely gotten inside her apartment before her doorbell rang. Sighing, she went to the door, and almost forgot to look into the peephole before she pulled the door open. That was a measure of just how much of an effect Cruz Martinez had on her, she mused as she stood aside to allow Ariel to enter. She seemed to be throwing all her caution out the window lately. And somehow she couldn't bring herself to care.

"Well, well, if that isn't a satisfied smile, I've never seen one," Ariel drawled as she entered her friend's apartment.

"Good morning to you, too," Madeline answered.

"I was up early and saw your light. Thought I'd come over for some coffee. I called last night, but you must have been out until late. I can't believe you're up and dressed already, you're a real early bird this morn—" Ariel's chatter abruptly stopped as she strolled into the kitchen and noticed the coffeemaker wasn't on. She frowned. One thing she knew about her friend was that she

reached for a cup of coffee as soon as she stumbled out of bed in
the morning. And since she was dressed, she must have been up for
some time. She turned to survey Madeline, who was standing behind her, a resigned look on her face.

Under her nosy friend's eagle eye, Madeline grew acutely uncomfortable. She reached up to push back her tousled hair, which
had received only a quick brushing this morning, and that before
Cruz had threaded his fingers through it when he'd kissed her. She
tried for, and failed to bring off, a nonchalant expression.

"Madeline Katherine Casey." Ariel pronounced each syllable
deliberately. "If I didn't know better, I'd swear you hadn't been
home at all last night."

"I did work late," Madeline tried lamely. She walked past her
friend to switch on the coffeemaker. Suddenly she felt in dire need
of fortification.

"Uh-huh, uh-huh," Ariel said suggestively. "You must have
worked re-e-e-al late. Like all night. Like the kind of overtime one
doesn't punch a clock for. The kind that has, shall we say, its own
rewards." She threw back her head and laughed delightedly. "Dare
I hope that you were *working* with someone? And that the someone in question was one tall, dark, gorgeous Hispanic with the
nicest butt this side of the Mississippi?"

Madeline couldn't prevent a laugh at her friend's outrageous-
ness. "You're incorrigible. And snoopy. You don't see me running over to your apartment and prying into your life all the time,
do you?"

Ariel slipped onto a stool at the counter. "Nope. 'Cause you
know there's nothing there to pry into. And believe me, friend, if
I had a man in my life who was one-tenth the man Cruz is, you
wouldn't need to snoop. I'd be over here *gloating*, providing you
with an instant replay."

The coffee was ready, and Madeline used some much-needed
moments to busy herself pouring a mug for each of them. When
she handed one to her friend, she slipped onto a stool next to her.
"Well, don't expect me to do the same. I'm afraid my nature has
always been a bit more modest than yours."

"Then it's true!" Ariel crowed. Madeline winced and sipped at
her coffee. "You and Cruz are an item. Glory hallelujah! I have to
admit, dear, that I worried you'd never let go enough to get involved with any man again, not to mention one as delicious as your
Cruz. May I congratulate you on your impeccable taste, at least?"

Madeline suppressed a smile. "You may," she agreed primly, and then ruined it by joining in her friend's laughter.

"I knew it," Ariel remarked in a satisfied voice. "The first time I saw him I thought, now there's a man who could thaw Madeline out and show her how great being a woman can feel." She reached over and patted her friend's hand. "I'm happy for you. He must be some kind of guy to breach all your defenses."

"He's ... persistent," Madeline conceded.

"Good for him. He'd have to be. But he must have other qualities to have put that color in your cheeks. C'mon, Madeline. Isn't there anything else you'd like to tell Auntie Ariel?"

Madeline drank the rest of her coffee and rose. "Nope. And I really have to get ready for work." She got up, and for once Ariel took the hint and rose also.

"All right, all right, I'm going," she said mildly, allowing Madeline to herd her to the door. "Don't push, I'll go peacefully." She turned after she'd opened the door, and tossed a parting remark over her shoulder. "Do him a favor and wear something that will knock his socks off. Although I'm sure you've already more than accomplished *that* particular task."

"You have such a dirty mind," Madeline scolded, shutting the door on her friend. She could hear Ariel's departing laughter. Madeline threw a quick look at the clock. She stripped on the way to the bathroom, and a minute later stepped into the shower with an appreciative sigh. She stood under the cascading water with eyes closed, enjoying the sensation. It was hard to perform the mundane task without images of the last shower she'd taken, the one with Cruz, crowding into her mind. Cheeks growing warm again, she hurriedly finished, and dried herself off briskly.

Standing in front of her closet clad only in her underthings, she perused its contents disapprovingly. Cruz was right; she did own an inordinate number of tailored slacks and jackets. And none of them suited her current mood. She finally decided on black pleated slacks and a black-and-white short-sleeved sweater. When it came time to do her hair, she left it loose, wearing only a black headband to keep it away from her face. She surveyed her reflection in the mirror with satisfaction. It was a little more flattering than the no-nonsense attire she usually favored to work in, and it was still functional. She realized she had actually followed Ariel's advice, and she winced. That was definitely a habit she didn't want to start.

She reentered the dining area just as the doorbell rang. She gave a sigh of exasperation as she went to answer it. Fully expecting it to be Ariel, she opened the door, saying, "You know, I really don't need your help. I can dress my—" Her voice stopped short when she saw her father standing before her.

"Madeline," he greeted her urbanely. "May I come in?"

She stepped back from the door mutely. If it had been possible, she thought numbly, to pick the one person she would least wish to see at this moment, it would have been Geoffrey Casey. She closed the door and turned to watch him. He was surveying her tiny apartment with what she knew would be disapproval. He'd been here only twice before, and had made no pains to hide his feelings about her home.

"I don't know why you insist on living in this dark, cramped place when you know I'd buy you a house anywhere you'd like. A condominium, even. One in a much better neighborhood."

She sighed. She did not need this. Not this morning, of all mornings. She could feel her earlier contentment fade away. But oddly enough, she also felt more capable than usual of dealing with her father without losing her temper. There was something to be said for having everything you never allowed yourself to hope for come true. It did remarkable things for one's control.

"This place suits my needs," she responded evenly, as she had every other time he'd brought it up. He knew very well that she'd never allow him to buy her any such thing. She hadn't touched the trust fund that she'd gained control over on her twenty-fourth birthday. Although she might want to use it someday, right now her needs were simple. Too simple, according to her father.

"Would you like a cup of coffee?" she asked politely, forestalling any further discussion of her living arrangements.

"No, thank you," he replied, walking into the living room and sitting on a chair. "I had some before I left the house this morning, and, of course, Mrs. Parks knows just how I take it."

Madeline's mouth twisted. After working for Casey for twenty-odd years, Mrs. Parks would know how to make the coffee, or she wouldn't have lasted so long. Geoffrey Casey didn't keep anyone around who couldn't be of use to him in some way.

She sank into a chair facing him. "What can I do for you, Father?" she inquired. This early-morning visit was really quite out of character for him.

He brushed at a speck of lint on his perfectly creased Italian suit, and crossed his legs. "I decided that the only way to see you was to drop in unannounced," he stated plainly. "As ill-bred as it is, I had no choice. You haven't returned any of my phone calls."

Guilt prickled through her at the truth of his words. She'd been avoiding him, and she couldn't deny it. Although she'd done so to avoid any more stressful scenes, his words made her feel about twelve years old. The old inner war still waged within her; the instincts for self-preservation against the loyalty she felt she should owe to her own flesh and blood.

"The case has been taking up a lot of my time," she said, damning the note of apology that entered her voice. "Things have been a little crazy. When the case winds down—"

"Ah, yes, the case. Why don't we talk about that? And about Cruz Martinez."

It didn't take a rocket scientist to realize what had brought her father to her apartment. Her eyes narrowed. "You know I can't discuss my investigations with you. We've had this conversation before."

He went on as if he hadn't heard. "Francis Vincent told me he ran into you and Martinez at a restaurant one night."

And you called the moment you heard the news, Madeline thought darkly. But she forced herself to answer steadily, "That's right."

"Yes. So tell me, Madeline. What sort of investigating was going on after-hours over dinner?"

Though the words were delivered in his usual cultured voice, the suggestion in them was blatantly insulting.

"We were eating," she said bluntly. "Does that need an explanation?"

"I know how you feel about my becoming involved in your work," he said, surprising her. "But given our last conversation, I was quite concerned at your apparent friendliness with a suspected criminal. I hope you know what you're doing." His tone said clearly that he doubted that very much, and Madeline ground her teeth silently.

"As a matter of fact, I know exactly what I'm doing," she replied, with only a hint of her irritation showing in her voice. "And I've managed to do my job quite adequately for ten years without your help, though I've yet to convince you of that."

"Well, sadly enough, it appears to me that you haven't done your job. At least, not yet. I've heard from a very good source that there's been no evidence linking any of the five detectives suspected in this gun supply."

Her mouth dropped at his announcement, and then she shook her head in disbelief. "You are unbelievable, do you know that?" Her earlier certainty that she could, for once, deal with him calmly was vanishing. "When are you going to stick to running the city and stay out of police matters! Whoever is feeding you this information is a disgrace to the force. And you're a disgrace for asking about it!''

"I'm worried about you," he stated firmly. "The longer this case drags on, the more time you have to make a mistake. I won't be comfortable until Martinez is behind bars."

She stared at him, wondering when she'd last been as furious as she was now. "Then you will no doubt have to wait a very long time to be comfortable," she burst out in frustration. "Because Cruz Martinez is not going to be behind bars. Not now, or later."

His mouth tightened. "I hope you know what you're doing, Madeline."

"No, you don't," she contradicted. "Your only wish is for things to turn out the way you want them. Although why you have developed such a need to see a man you don't even know go to prison, I can't quite figure out. But I've found absolutely no evidence to connect Cruz to the gun supply. None."

After a pregnant pause, he asked, "How can you be sure Martinez is not involved?"

"I'm trained to find evidence and to interpret it, Father. And whether you believe it or not, I happen to be good at my job. Captain Brewer is satisfied with my investigation. That's all that matters."

Her father rose to stride to the window, pushing aside a curtain to stare out at the skyline. After a moment he murmured, "You're sure, of course, that you haven't missed anything, out of your own need to see this man proven innocent." He turned to look pointedly at her.

Her jaw dropped at his audacity. "You are unbelievable," she whispered, shaking her head. "And you never change. Never. You're like a broken record, playing over the same irritating scratch."

"I'm just expressing an interest because I don't want to see you do any further damage to your career. Another mistake like Dennis Belding would destroy any credibility you could ever hope to achieve."

What he really meant, of course, was that he was concerned about any damage to *his own* political career should his daughter's name be clouded once more. She was hurt at his lack of faith, but it wasn't a shattering pain. Perhaps, she thought bitterly, she'd finally been cured of needing approval from this man, because she had approval from someone who accepted her just the way she was.

And Cruz's respect meant far more to her than her father's ever could. She felt a return to her earlier calm. Geoffrey Casey didn't have the power to hurt her that he'd once had.

"Well," he said in disapproval, turning from the window, "I only came here for your own good. As usual, you choose to misunderstand my intentions." Noting her rigid features, he added in a more conciliatory tone, "And if you say that your dinner with him that night was just a necessary evil, a step in your investigation of him, then I'll accept your word on that. It's just that I don't like the thought of your spending any more time with Martinez than necessary. He really isn't our kind." He walked past her toward the door. Her next words brought him to a halt.

"I didn't say that."

She noted the ramrod stiffness of his backbone as the meaning of her words became clear, and she knew she'd made a mistake. If only he'd left before firing off his last parting shot, she would have been able to hold her tongue. But she wasn't going to allow him to speak like that of Cruz, to think that way about him. From the sound of his words, he felt her being around her partner was liable to taint her in some way. And it was time her father learned that the end of this case wasn't going to spell the end of her relationship with Cruz Martinez. Her father had long ago lost the ability to control her life, and he needed to realize that.

He turned slowly to face her again. "Would you care to clarify those words?"

"Certainly." She rose, too, and they faced each other more like two adversaries than like father and daughter. "What I mean is, if I choose to see Cruz after this investigation, I will do so. My decision has nothing to do with you, nor do you have anything to say about it."

"I can assure you, Madeline," he said tightly, "that I will find quite a bit to say about it."

"No doubt," she replied dryly. "But I'm not interested in hearing it. So we'll have to agree to disagree."

His face flushed deep red, more reaction than she could remember seeing in it for a very long time. "You will regret this decision," he warned her ominously.

"I don't think so," she said softly. "But if I do, at least it will be my decision."

After a long look, her father turned and walked swiftly from her apartment.

As the door closed behind him, Madeline sank into a chair, heaving a sigh.

She'd regretted almost immediately the words she'd spoken to her father, if not the fury that had fueled them. He lit the match to the fuse of her temper so effortlessly, and he absolutely never learned. But he'd also left her with something to think about, something that she'd been worrying about since last night.

Her father had an enviable pipeline of information that was usually quite accurate. She was beginning to become more concerned with the possibility that somehow Cruz, too, would get hold of the information that he'd been the subject of an investigation. She had no doubt as to how he would react to that. And to her, should he find out the whole story.

She had to keep the information from him; she had no choice. Although she was convinced she'd find nothing to link him to the gun suppliers, she had a job to fulfill. And her investigation wasn't completed. There was no way she could give him that information, even if she'd wanted to.

But after the case was over, perhaps after another detective had been proven guilty, what then? She pondered the question. When she was free to come clean with Cruz, would she risk that? Would she take the chance of telling him and possibly destroy any hope of a future with him?

Could she take the chance of his finding out anyway, from someone else?

It was a question that plagued her constantly. It lurked in her subconscious, coloring every moment of each day. It made the time she spent with Cruz almost bittersweet, as if each instant with him would be the last. Which, of course, it could be if she made the wrong choice. She knew she was being a coward, putting off making a decision about what she would do, but still she procrastinated, while she gathered all the memories she could with him.

For the next few days she and Cruz spent most of their time sitting in the unmarked car, on a street with a clear view of the Andersen warehouse. Although there was plenty of activity there each day, Valdez wasn't spotted. They watched all day, and took turns sleeping at night. Then they drove home, showered and changed before driving back and starting all over again.

By the third night Madeline was close to losing it. There was no position in the car that was comfortable any longer, and even though it was her turn to sleep, she was having very little success at it. Her supper of sandwiches and chips seemed a distant memory, and being hungry worsened her mood.

She glared across the car at Cruz. Though he was awake and watchful, he was slouched into a position that would have had her back screaming for days. The knowledge that he was totally comfortable made her want to give him a kick.

"Go to sleep. You should know by now that I'm not going to do the noble thing and take your watch, too. It'll be your turn in an hour and a half, and believe me, I'll be asleep in a minute." His voice cut across the darkness.

"Yeah, you look pretty tense right now," she muttered, changing position once again.

She could sense the smile in his voice when he spoke again. "It's all in the attitude, Maddy, my girl. You've got to take every second to relax when you can. I'd give you a back rub to help out, but I don't trust myself to stop there."

Neither did she. And she knew she wouldn't be able to trust herself, either. She remained firmly on her side of the seat while they watched, and he did the same. The only time they touched was to pass each other something to eat, and even that casual brushing was enough to set her skin afire. So she kept her distance and prayed that he would do likewise. Because if he was of a mind to pass away the hours of the night in a much more pleasurable manner, she wasn't sure she would have the strength to deny him.

It was partly frustrated desire that made it difficult to sleep, but mainly it was her inability to stop thinking. Through the long hours of the night it was difficult to keep troublesome thoughts at bay, and the choice she had to make was at the forefront of those. Not that it was much of a decision anymore. As she stared out into the night, where physical objects were shrouded in shadows and darkness, her thoughts had a way of becoming crystal clear, as if in contrast. She realized that when the time came that the case was wrapped up, she would have to tell Cruz about her task of investigating him. She used the time to try to practice what she would say when that day finally came, to memorize the words that would be the least hurtful, the ones that would make him understand. She was coming to the realization that those words didn't exist.

Her morose thoughts were interrupted by his whisper. "Look up there. A car is coming this way."

Madeline looked past him and saw a pair of headlights approaching them. From frequent practice she scrunched low in the seat, and he did the same, so their figures wouldn't be visible when the driver went by. For long seconds they stayed down, then she heard him whisper.

"Well, lookee, lookee. Tonight just might be our lucky night." She heard the click as he switched off the interior light so it wouldn't shine when he opened the door.

Madeline craned her neck to see what had him so fascinated. The car that had driven past them turned the corner and pulled to a stop in front of the warehouse. Her attention was diverted, however, when he started opening his door.

"Where are you going?" she whispered.

"It's too dark for the binoculars to be much help. I'm going closer to see if I recognize anybody."

Madeline slid across the seat toward him. "Not without me, you aren't."

She closed the door quietly behind her and followed his crouched figure across the street. They stopped behind a utility shed, directly across from the warehouse.

The car was a large luxury automobile. Madeline couldn't imagine Valdez driving such a car, and disappointedly wondered if this, too, would be a dead end. That thought was driven from her mind when, in the next instant, a shadowy figure stepped out of the darkness and approached the automobile. Reaching the passenger side, the man opened the door and got in. She gasped when the interior light went on and revealed the identities of the two inside. The man sliding into the car was none other than Jose Valdez.

The driver was Stephen Andersen.

Neither Cruz nor Madeline spoke a word, peering intently into the darkness. They were unable to see anything until about ten minutes later, when the passenger side of the car opened again. As close to the water as they were, the voices floated to them with crystal precision.

"I'll meet you about midnight. And for pity's sake be careful until then. With all the cops asking questions about you, I'm beginning to think you're a real liability."

"Wouldn't be no cops hanging around if you hadn't wanted me to ice Stover. Told ya he wasn't no threat. He would have been too scared to talk, anyway."

"So you said." Even if she hadn't seen his face, Madeline would have recognized Andersen's voice. "Well, he's not talking now, either. And somehow I feel a lot safer this way."

Valdez snorted. "Don't know what you're worried about, anyway. The cops aren't sniffing around you."

"And I don't want them to, either. If you do your job the way you should, I won't have to worry, and you'll continue to get paid well."

"I'll be here."

Valdez slammed the door and started across the street. The car took off. Cruz whispered, "Stay put. I'm going to follow Valdez." He disappeared into the shadows before Madeline could protest. And protest she would have. She had no intention of meekly waiting for him to return.

She drew her gun and headed for a closer inspection of the warehouse. A high mesh fence, topped by barbed wire, surrounded the building. She found the gate locked. She walked all around the outside, looking carefully, but found no other entrance. She also found no sign of a night watchman. In the entire time they had been across the street, and during her explorations, she'd estimate they'd spent thirty minutes. But she'd yet to see a security guard making rounds, and her mind was furiously speculating on what that meant.

She made her way back to the front of the building. The stars didn't provide much light, and once she stumbled over a crack in the concrete. She'd just gotten to the front gate again when a figure stepped out of the shadows in front of her and ordered, "Don't move."

It was amazing that in the darkness where little was visible she had no difficulty at all discerning that she was looking down the barrel of a gun. Her eyes tore away from that sight and looked beyond it.

"Maddy?"

A burst of air escaped her then, the first time she'd realized she'd been holding her breath. "Martinez, you idiot, of course it's me."

He holstered his gun. "There's no 'of course' about it. I told you to stay put."

"You don't give me orders, Detective," she said scathingly. "I didn't hear a discussion about the wisdom of your taking off after Valdez."

They started back toward the car, still arguing. "Listen, do you want to know what happened to Valdez, or not?"

She was silent for an instant. "Well, since you don't have him in tow, I assume you lost him."

"Not exactly." They reached the car then and got in. "From what we overheard, it sounded like Andersen is in this up to his moussed hair."

"I can't think of any other reason he'd be meeting with Valdez," Madeline agreed. "When I recognized him, everything seemed to jump into place."

"And hearing them talk about offing Stover didn't hurt any," Cruz put in grimly.

"Andersen has to be the one bringing in the guns," she said. "I don't know why we didn't think about this before. They moved their manufacturing overseas, so maybe that's where the pipeline starts."

"A shipment comes in from overseas, gets unloaded and stored in the warehouse. We already know that the guns are being sold from the docks."

Madeline interjected, "The guns must be unassembled, pieces interspersed with the real cargo in each crate."

"This is it. It has to be," said Cruz. He looked across the seat at her. "But can we make it stick? The only concrete things we have to go on right now are that we saw the two of them together, and that we overheard about Stover."

"Something big is going to be breaking soon, that was apparent from their conversation," she said.

"I'm sure of it." After a moment of silence he added, "That's why I let Valdez go."

"What do you mean, you let him go?" she demanded, startled.

"I didn't lose him. I followed him down the street to a big truck he had parked there. I took down the license plate, but didn't confront him. He got in and drove away." His teeth flashed brightly in the darkness. "I say we go for the big cigar. We wait this thing out and catch them with the guns in their oily little hands. What do you say?"

She never hesitated. "Let's go for it."

He laughed softly. "Somehow I knew you'd say that. We'll play the odds. It may be a risk to wait, but sometimes taking a risk can have a big payoff. You know what I mean?"

The words hit her with another meaning. Did she know anything about taking a risk? She'd had intimate experience with it in the past several days. "Yes, believe it or not, Cruz, I know exactly what you mean."

He glanced at her. "May as well head out. One thing we're sure of is that nothing more will be going on here tonight."

"We can be fairly certain that nothing will happen until the next shipment comes in."

"Which will be any day now. We'll be back tomorrow to watch. Want to go home for a while?"

Home. The word hit her and a sense of yearning she'd never before felt mushroomed in her stomach. Yes, she'd very much like to go home with him. She wanted to take the time to store up a few more memories, against the time when memories might be the only thing left to her.

"What do you say, Maddy?" His voice interrupted her thoughts.

"It's a very attractive offer," she said, trying to respond normally.

"Is that all that's attractive to you?" His voice was wheedling.

Madeline couldn't prevent a smile. "Well, you didn't shoot me back there. I've always found that an attractive quality in a man."

"Stick with me, kid," he joked. "I'm full of great qualities."

Just a few more days, she promised herself as they drove down the dark streets of the city. Surely the case would be over then. And then she would be able to tell him the whole story. And somehow she'd make him understand.

In the meantime, she had one more night to cherish.

The next morning Cruz dropped her off at her apartment so she could get her car, and then they headed to district headquarters for a while. They needed to check out the license number of the truck Valdez was driving. They also needed to take the precaution of picking up some bulletproof vests.

When Madeline entered the building she made her way to Cruz's desk. He was nowhere in sight, but Connor McLain was leaning against the edge of the desk, sipping from a mug of coffee.

She slowed at the sight of him. She knew how close Cruz and Connor were, but she'd never felt totally comfortable in the other man's presence. Those light green eyes were too piercing, and when they were trained on her, as they were now, she felt stripped to the soul.

"Lieutenant McLain." She acknowledged him carefully. "I don't see Cruz. Is he around?"

He indicated the closed door of his office. "He had a visitor. I let them use my office for a few minutes."

"Oh." She looked pensively at the closed door he was indicating, then shrugged and turned back to him. "Did Cruz tell you what we found out last night?"

"A little." He paused to drink some more coffee. "Sounds like it'll all be going down in the next couple of days."

"We think so."

"I took a phone call for him yesterday from Lieutenant Niles," he informed her. "He left a message that they didn't match Cantoney's prints to any found in Stover's apartment."

"Well, if things pan out the way we think they will," she answered optimistically, "we should have the supplier anyway. And hopefully soon."

Their conversation was interrupted by the sound of Connor's office door being opened. When her father stepped out, Madeline couldn't have been more shocked.

"Madeline, dear, I don't have time to talk right now, but I have taken care of the matter we discussed the other day. I'll be calling you very soon." Her father gave a slight wave and headed toward the exit.

It took long moments for the seemingly incongruous sight of her father at the headquarters to congeal into some sort of sense. And then, when comprehension dawned, it was accompanied by a feeling of impending doom. Without another word she walked away from Connor and toward his office. She had to literally force herself to step over the threshold.

The expression on Cruz's face told her exactly what the two men had been talking about.

"Is it true?" His words, tight and direct, seemed to slice the air between them.

"Cruz..." she began helplessly.

"No." His hand came up to stem whatever words she had been about to say. "Just answer me. Is...it...true?"

The waves of guilt threatened to completely engulf her. This was what she'd feared all along. That she would someday see this look on his face, see this coldness in his eyes, hear the distrust in his voice. Would it have been different if she'd told him herself when she'd been able? She would most certainly have explained it better than her father had. He'd undoubtedly come here for the sole purpose of wreaking havoc.

She'd never know the answer to her question now. And the knowledge that she'd most likely brought about this scene with her unwise outburst to her father didn't make it any easier. For Geoffrey Casey had come here today only because she'd convinced him that the threat of Cruz in her life was a reality.

Madeline made herself face his implacable visage, steeling herself not to flinch at the look of betrayal in his eyes. "Yes," she whispered hopelessly.

That one soft word seemed to rock him for an instant. That was the sum total of his reaction. He tossed her one of the vests he was holding, turned and started walking out the door.

She caught his arm as he went by her. "Cruz, wait," she implored.

That dark gaze—the one that she could remember hot with passion, sharp with intent, soft with tenderness—now looked as though it could cut through ice. He looked at her, then pointedly at his arm. Reading his message as clearly as if it had been etched in stone, she dropped her hand. "Please, wait," she said again, aware of the pleading note in her voice. "I can imagine what my father told you, but knowing him, I'm sure he got a twisted pleasure in breaking this news in the most hurtful way possible."

"Well, I don't know about that." She flinched at the caustic note in his tone. "There's something about truth that, no matter how painful, is easier to take than a lie."

"I never lied to you," she said in a low tone.

His eyebrows arched. "No? Maybe you didn't, in your mind. Somehow it seems a bit devious to me to sleep with a man you're working to convict, but then, that's semantics for you. It's not actually a lie, no, it's more...hmm. What would you call it? A complete lack of morals, perhaps?"

"I didn't choose this assignment. And you weren't the only detective being investigated."

His smile held a hint of cruelty, and absolutely no amusement. "Then you've been busier than I thought."

Her voice was low as she explained. "Internal Affairs had reason to believe that one of the detectives assigned to the gun investigations was involved in the supply side. Each of them was assigned a partner from I.A."

"How many of us?" he snapped.

"Five. All from different districts."

"Well? Don't keep me in suspense." He laughed shortly. "Which one of us was it?"

She hesitated. "We don't know," she finally answered. "There hasn't been any luck so far linking any of the detectives to the gun supply."

"Great," he said, giving her a hard stare. "That means I haven't been cleared, either, have I?" When she didn't answer, he repeated sharply, "Have I?"

Her eyes were clear when she looked into his. "It's not you."

He held her gaze. "How do you know?"

"I just do. I didn't have anything that cleared you to my captain, but when he asked me, I told him what I thought. You're not the one." Encouraged by his silence, she continued tentatively, "It all got twisted up, Cruz. Trying to do my job, trying to keep my feelings for you separate from the investigation . . ."

"And we know just how deep those feelings ran," he interjected sarcastically. "You're a remarkable woman, you really are. Sleep with a man and dig up all the dirt you can on him at the same time. I'll say one thing for you, lady, you blindsided me. I never suspected your little plan for a moment."

"There was no plan. I fell in love with you!" she blurted out desperately. The words hung in the air, shocking both of them. She'd never admitted their truth, not even to herself. But she couldn't deny the feeling. Nor could she have chosen a worse time to voice it.

His jaw clenched. "Cheap shot, Maddy. Do the words 'too little, too late' mean anything to you?"

"Don't say that," she whispered. "Let me explain. You don't know how it was."

"I think I can guess." His twisted smile held no amusement. "Don't forget, I've been screwed by Internal Affairs before. Although your methods were a bit more literal, the end result is the same."

Chapter 16

Madeline didn't know how long she remained in Connor's office after Cruz slammed the door. His words hammered at her insides, and there was enough truth in them to make her whole body ache. She wrapped her arms around her middle, almost doubling over with pain. How could she have let things go so far wrong? If she'd been able to tell him in her own time, in her own way, would things have been different? Or was it inevitable from the very beginning? She wearily acknowledged that it really didn't matter now. To use Cruz's words, the end result was the same. He'd walked out, and she'd lost him, just as she'd feared she would.

She pressed the heels of her hands to her eyes, to stem the tears she could feel pooling there. She didn't know how she was going to get through this. The knowledge that she'd hurt Cruz was the worst kind of pain of all. Ordinarily she could push all unpleasantness aside and throw herself into her work. She gave a choked laugh. Since she worked with Cruz, that wouldn't be a possibility.

A rap on the doorjamb and a voice startled her. "Madeline? Are you done in there?"

She whirled around in dismay. While her whole world had fallen apart, Connor McLain had been waiting outside, no doubt wondering when he was going to get his office back. She crossed to his desk and snatched up some tissues from the box there and hurriedly blew her nose. "Yes," she called out, her voice husky. She crossed to the door and opened it, not meeting his eyes as she apologized, "I'm sorry. That was rude. I . . . forgot where I was." She meant to duck by him, not willing to be pinned in place by his assessing gaze. But before she was able, he spoke again.

"Mind staying for a minute?" Connor leaned against the door, an effective means of blocking this woman's escape, should she be so inclined. Studying her, he realized that she would have made no such move. She looked as though she'd been leveled by a bull-dozer.

"Care to tell me what that was all about?" he asked bluntly. "Cruz will tell me anyway, in time. I don't remember when I last saw him looking the way he did when he walked out of here, and, lady, I think you've got some explaining to do."

She let out a choked breath at his words. "Well, I'm afraid that will have to wait. I don't have the authority to discuss this with you." She walked to the door, and after staring at her intently for a moment he slowly moved aside.

"When the time comes, you *will* give me that explanation, Detective," he said, sotto voce.

Her voice was weary when she answered. "I'm afraid that when the time comes for explanations, Lieutenant, you're going to have to wait in line."

Madeline made a trip to the rest room to restore a semblance of order to her makeup. Then she used a stall for privacy while she put the vest on. When she could delay it no longer, she headed back toward Cruz's desk. She met him in the aisle, walking toward the door.

"C'mon," he said brusquely, passing by and not turning to see whether she obeyed. "It's time to head back to the warehouse."

Madeline followed him silently. She'd never seen his face look like this before. Rarely was it without some remnant of humor, a crooked smile, a quirked eyebrow. Now it was as impassive as a statue's, and she despaired of ever reaching him on any level again.

She waited awhile, but when it became obvious that he had no intention of speaking, she broke the silence. "I know you're hurt and angry. But, Cruz, sometime we're going to have to talk about this."

His eyes never left the street in front of him. His voice, when he answered, was devoid of inflection. "Madeline, we have to work together. Maybe for a day more, a few days, tops. The only things we have to say to each other in that time have to do with the case. Do you understand me?"

"You can't wish this situation away!" she exclaimed. "And you can't pretend that we never happened."

"No, I sure can't, much as I'd like to." His voice turned grim. "I've got a job to do, and we both know how good you are at *your* job, so let's make an agreement right now. We both see this case through, and when it ends, it's over. And, lady, let me tell you, the sight of you walking away for the last time will be the most welcome sight in the world."

Those words proved prophetic to Madeline in the next few days. It was tortuous to be so close to Cruz, yet to have this emotional chasm between them. He was as professional as he'd promised to be. Every word he uttered had to do with the case. Otherwise there was only deafening silence.

And she was helpless to bridge that silence. He had been agonizingly clear about his feelings regarding her actions. What else was there to say to him? She wanted to beg with him again to hear her out, but she wasn't sure how to after he'd been so precise about his wishes. She wasn't up to dealing with another verbal slap, however justified it might be. And after all, she asked herself more than once, if he wanted to be left alone, didn't she owe him that much?

She hadn't spoken to her father since he'd gone to the headquarters, and she couldn't imagine a time when she would willingly speak to him again. She'd known he was a snob, and that was what had motivated him to ensure that she and Cruz would not continue a relationship. Casey could barely stand the idea that his daughter was a cop. He'd never given up the hope that she would come to her senses and make her living in a more "acceptable" fashion. The idea of her with Cruz on a personal level was a threat to the control he attempted to maintain over her life. The fact that he would also be smashing any feelings that she would have toward him would not have occurred to Geoffrey Casey. He regarded emotion as a frivolity best cast aside in any case.

In all the time she'd spent agonizing over how she was going to tell Cruz, never had she come close to predicting the mind-shattering pain of Cruz's rejection. It was torment to see his attitude toward her turn into the same courteous manner with which he would treat a stranger. Stiffer than that, really, because Cruz

Martinez had never met a stranger. His charm had always been in evidence, no matter whom he was speaking to. But now, toward her, his face was blank. His tone was carefully even, and not by one flicker of an eyelash did he exhibit any emotion toward her. When he did address her, he called her Madeline, and that, more than anything else, told her how far he'd really withdrawn from her. She'd been Maddy to him since the night they first made love. The once-hated nickname had taken a different flavor on his lips. She realized with bitter certainty that she wasn't likely to hear it again.

Even as the time seemed to crawl, part of her wished it would slow even more. If these last few days were all she had left with Cruz, part of her wanted them to last forever. Madeline felt torn in two by the constant tug-of-war within her. When she made mistakes, she went all out, she conceded silently.

But somehow she still felt that if she'd been able to be the one to tell him, things might not have gone so badly awry.

Cruz shifted in the passenger seat. Despite the darkness that had fallen outside, despite his usual ability to relax anyplace, anytime, the news that Geoffrey Casey had given him two days before had taken its toll. It had been strange, meeting Madeline's father for the first time. Never had he suspected that Madeline was the daughter of Councilman Casey. Certainly she'd never mentioned it. At first he'd been struck by the resemblance between the two, obvious in the bone structure of their faces, the same straight noses. He'd been so sidetracked by the similarities that it had taken him a moment to catch the gist of what the man was saying to him.

Councilman Casey was a cold bastard. First he dropped the bombshell that Madeline worked for Internal Affairs. Then he'd laid the news of the investigation right at Cruz's feet, and he'd smiled charmingly as he'd twisted the knife. Apparently telling of his daughter's duplicity hadn't bothered him a bit. Hell, he'd probably been proud of her. A chip off the old block, and all that. Obviously they had more than bone structure in common.

There had been times, especially in the year since Connor had met and married Michele, that Cruz had felt what came close to envy for his friend. Maybe it was his age, but there had been occasions when he'd wondered what it would feel like to find someone he wanted to spend his life with. To marry that someone, plan to spend every day with her, plan to have a family with her.

Now he not only knew what it was like to experience those feelings, he knew what it was like to have them blow up in his face. He hadn't reckoned with the flip side of it. Letting a person get that close meant they had the ability to provide excruciating emotional pain. And he was sure feeling his share of that, thanks to Madeline Casey.

It shouldn't have been difficult to shove her out of his mind, and his system. There had been plenty of women over the years who, for one reason or another, no longer had a place in his life. He'd always managed to extricate them with grace, and he was still on friendly terms with most of them. Why didn't that seem possible with the woman keeping silent watch next to him?

Because she'd gotten to him, he acknowledged dourly. He'd let her matter to him, too much. And he'd been burned. It was a bit difficult to get her out of his mind when all he had to do was look across the car to see her. It was hard to forget her voice when it was the only one he heard all day, albeit not often.

His hands clenched on his lap. Who was he kidding? It was damn hard to forget Maddy even when he had a few hours at home, before they were due back on watch again. His apartment was full of her. She was in front of his patio doors, her hair afire with light. She was in the kitchen, fiddling with her sandwich or, even more erotic, sprawling across the counter beneath him. She was in his bedroom, lying across his bed in wanton splendor.

It angered him that he was haunted by those images of her even when she wasn't near. The first time he'd gone upstairs and found her hairbrush on his dresser he'd been frozen with an anguish so deep it could have been physical. He'd hurled the brush across the room, where it had fallen to the floor with a soft thud. But the images were harder to banish.

Lying in his bed alone, it was impossible for him to forget the times she'd been lying next to him. Although their time together had been brief, he'd gotten to know her better than he figured anyone else ever had. He knew, for instance, that beneath those no-nonsense suits she wore lingerie that made him break out into a sweat just envisioning it. He couldn't sleep in that bed anymore with the specter of her there. Memories taunted him—of her lying sleeping, curled up beside him; of the way she slept with her lips slightly parted, as if waiting for his kiss; of the satiny fabric of her nighties, and the way they rode up in the night, to leave her bottom delightfully, arousingly bare. Nor were those images banished when he slept instead on the sectional sofa he'd ordered for the living room. No, they followed him, tantalizing reminders of what had been, and what he'd hoped for.

He didn't know which was worse, the times home alone tortured by memories of Maddy, or those hours in the car, being forced to sit inches away from her. She had acceded to his wishes, and now the only words between them had to do with the case. One part of him was grateful for that; the other wanted to demand an explanation from her.

But he remained stubbornly silent. A fierce male pride was part of his heritage, and it coursed strongly through his veins. Yet more than that kept him from speaking. He'd never allowed a woman as close before, and it was too hurtful to think of her lack of faith in him. Just imagining her delving into his life, checking up on him while they worked together made him want to punch something. The laughable thing was, she could have asked him anything, anything about himself, and he probably would have told her, sooner or later. He'd have told her things that he'd gone to pains to hide from almost all his friends, because he'd thought her interest lay in him. He smiled bitterly. And so it had. But not in the way he'd counted on. He couldn't forget that every moment he'd been drawn closer to her, every moment she'd pretended to feel the same, she was cold-bloodedly running an investigation on him at the same time. That was hard to forget.

Madeline Casey wasn't the only one with a long memory.

Three days after the scene with Cruz, Madeline was questioning her sanity. Each day seemed to blur into the next, and her whole world seemed to have narrowed to the front seat of the unluxurious police-issue car. Stakeouts were always tedious, but the situation with Cruz made this one intolerable. The endless hours they spent together with this insurmountable breach between them had her constantly on edge, her entire body one jangling nerve. The inactivity was working on both of them. Even Cruz was losing that flat, expressionless tone he'd adopted. When he did speak, it was in close to a snarl.

He'd run a check on the plates of the truck Valdez had been driving, and, unsurprisingly, it had been registered to Andersen Steel. They'd agreed, in one of their rare moments of conversation, that in all likelihood Valdez had been hired as the distributor. With his criminal experience and contacts on the streets, he would certainly have the reputation and experience to find buyers.

It was close to noon, and they'd both already silently eaten the lunches they'd brought. Madeline had forced herself to eat most of a sandwich, then put the rest of the food away. It was difficult to swallow these days, and hunger was the last thing she was feeling.

"Looks like pay dirt," Cruz muttered, training the binoculars on the warehouse.

She craned her neck to look and saw a large ship approaching the Andersen dock.

"That's got to be the shipment of steel the project manager was talking about," she said.

"And this must be the night Andersen wants Valdez here." He put down the binoculars and turned on the ignition.

"Now what?" she asked.

"Now it's time to type up another warrant."

Several hours later found them back on the same street, the search warrant in their possession. They'd talked in the car that afternoon, more than they had in the total time they'd spent watching the warehouse. In fact, they'd argued.

"I still don't agree with this," she muttered, crossing her arms stubbornly. "It's a dangerous risk, one we don't have to take."

"Be realistic, Madeline," he retorted for what seemed the hundredth time. His use of her full name made her flinch a little. "If we do as you wish and present this to Andersen right now, what's the best-case scenario? We could get him to come down here, open up a few crates, hopefully find the parts to some AK-47s and take him downtown to book him. We still won't have Valdez."

"You don't know that," she argued heatedly. "We could be back here at midnight when Valdez shows up, and nab him then."

"That wouldn't happen. He's going to be expecting Andersen to be here, and he's cautious as hell. That's how he's managed to elude us for so long. Knowing him, he'll be waiting for some sign that all is well. When he doesn't see it, he'll take off. And then we'll have no chance of finding him, because you can be sure he won't be sticking around when he hears of Andersen's arrest."

"It's more dangerous your way," she said, even as she realized the logic in his argument. "We won't be able to radio for backup. If a detective is involved in this whole thing, we can't take the chance of leaking our surveillance to the wrong person. We have no idea which cop is dirty. We wouldn't know who to trust.''

"We know there's only going to be two of them tonight—three at the most, if this mystery detective is there. We can handle them ourselves.''

She resented the way he had of simplifying a situation that, she somehow knew, was going to turn out to be anything but simple. "How about this?" she bargained. "We'll be able to tell from our position how many of them there are. If it's just Valdez and Andersen, we'll go in ourselves. We won't be able to afford the risk of the wrong person responding to our call. But if we see a third person, we radio for backup.''

Cruz hesitated, then nodded curtly, and their attention returned to the street.

Evening had descended before either of them spoke again. "Let's get closer," Cruz suggested. Without another word they both checked their guns and extra clips. Then they moved across the street to take up station behind the same utility shed they'd sheltered behind nights ago.

Several hours in the same position had every one of Madeline's muscles screaming a protest. Despite the danger, she was almost relieved when Andersen's large car rolled to a stop in front of the warehouse. He got out and walked rapidly up to the gate, fumbling with the key in the lock until he finally swung the gate open. Propping it open a few feet, he waited with seeming impatience, casting continual glances up and down the street.

"Came dressed for gunrunning, I see," Cruz remarked in an almost soundless whisper. The man was dressed in a black sweatshirt and trousers. "Guess you can't buy an Italian suit that's right for this kind of work.''

She had to smile at his outrageous remark. "Probably got it at Crooks R Us.''

"Ah, there's his sidekick. I knew he'd be too cautious to show if he wasn't sure Andersen was here.''

"Don't be obnoxious, Martinez. The night isn't over yet.''

They both watched as Valdez slowly approached the gate, exchanged a few words with Andersen, then walked away again. A few moments later the truck he'd been driving a few days ago pulled up. Andersen opened the gate wide, and it rumbled slowly through.

They waited fifteen agonizingly long minutes. Then Cruz whispered, "It's show time." They drew their guns and moved silently across the street and through the still-open gate.

They entered through the open door of the warehouse. It was shadowy, but light spilled out from a distant corner, making it possible to see where they were going. Sheets of metal and cartons filled the huge expanse, piles of materials everywhere. They approached the lighted area cautiously, stopping frequently to listen.

Stopping in back of a huge stack of boxes, Cruz realized that they were as close as they were going to get to the two without showing themselves. As it was, when they peered around the corners of their hiding place, they had a clear view of Andersen and Valdez working. The cavernous structure provided perfect acoustics for their conversation.

"Be a hell of a lot easier if you'd have the guns shipped already assembled and in the same damn crates." It was Valdez speaking. "Then we'd just have to open them up, count them and toss them on the truck. This takes too damn long."

When Andersen spoke, it was obvious he was winded from his labors. "The simplest method isn't necessarily the smartest, Valdez. Each of these crates has to look perfectly legitimate for anyone who happens to look inside it. Taking precautions is what makes an operation like this run smoothly. Don't try to think. That's not what you're paid for."

It was obvious from the look Valdez shot the other man that there was no love lost between the two. "Yeah, you're real brilliant," he muttered. "And so is that buddy of yours. But as usual, when there's work to be done, he don't show up."

"We can handle this ourselves," Andersen told him. "We're half done already."

Andersen was opening the crates, extracting pieces from them, then piling the pieces next to Valdez. Valdez assembled the guns, put them into empty crates and loaded them into the truck.

Madeline nudged Cruz, and he nodded. They'd seen enough. With the mysterious third party not in sight, now was the time to make their move. Both men's hands were occupied, which would make it difficult for them to go for a weapon, assuming either had one. Cruz indicated to Madeline that he would take Valdez, leaving Andersen for her. She frowned at him, but he gave her no time for dispute. Holding up a hand, he held up one finger, then two, then three. They stepped around a corner of the boxes and yelled simultaneously, "Freeze! Police!"

Andersen's head jerked around and stopped in midmotion. Valdez reacted more quickly. He threw the crate he'd been lifting in their direction and took off.

"I got him," Cruz yelled, jumping over a stack of steel poles as he went off in pursuit.

"Drop it," Madeline ordered Andersen. "And get your hands behind your head."

The man seemed to recover some of his smoothness. "What's the meaning of this, Detective? What are you doing here? This is private property."

"Private property with a very lucrative sideline," she answered while she trained her gun on him and quickly frisked him. Finding no weapon, she snapped a cuff on his wrist and led him over to the truck. The other cuff was snapped to the door handle. Quickly she went to the other side of the truck, opened the door and leaned over to remove the keys from the ignition. Then she proceeded to read him his rights.

"Guns?" he scoffed. "You've got quite an imagination, and absolutely no proof. You'd better think hard, Detective, before you bring me in on such a ridiculous charge. My family is well regarded in this town."

"Somehow I think your family's reputation is about to take a nosedive," she said wryly.

The man blustered, "This is undoubtedly an illegal search, and my lawyer will have it thrown out of court. You and your partner will lose your jobs over this."

Madeline tucked the warrant in his free hand. "I suggest you read that while you're waiting." She ran silently in the direction that Cruz had disappeared in. She heard the report of a shot, and then another. Heading in the direction of the sound, she saw a figure running toward the gate. She raised her gun and then hesitated. At this distance it was impossible to tell the identity of the runner. She started after him.

In front of her, another figure came flying out of the shadows and tackled the runner. They rolled over and over on the ground. As she drew closer she could make out Cruz on top of Valdez, drawing back a fist. Valdez reached up and grasped Cruz's throat with both hands, and Cruz dropped his fist to pry at the other man's fingers.

A movement in the darkness near the struggling pair attracted her attention. A figure stepped out, and when Madeline saw the gun aimed toward Cruz's head, she reacted instinctively. She twirled and fired a shot. The force from the impact of the bullet swung the man around. He dropped his gun, clutching at his shoulder.

Cruz used the distraction to free himself from Valdez's grasp, and after a few more moments the struggle was over. Valdez lay motionless on the ground.

Cruz got up and walked over, picking up the gun that had been dropped, as well as his own weapon. He tucked Valdez's gun into the waistband of his jeans.

"Let's see who we've got here," he muttered, walking over to the wounded man.

"An old friend of yours, I believe," she said shakily, her gun still aimed.

"So I see," Cruz said, recognizing Detective Gerald Baker. The man glared at him, blood seeping from between his fingers. "Your partner's as crazy as you are, Martinez," Baker snarled. "You'll both be laughed out of the department over this. I had this place staked out myself, and came to help when I heard shots."

"Somehow I don't think I could have afforded your help," Cruz mocked. "If it hadn't been for Maddy, I'd have been a chalk out-line." He cocked an eyebrow at her. "Somehow, his showing up here now seems a little too coincidental."

She nodded, and stepped forward to frisk Baker quickly, using his own handcuffs on him.

"I need medical attention," Baker told her. "It's going to be up to you to get me some." He jerked his head at Cruz. "He'd just as soon see me die."

"You're wrong about that," Madeline corrected him grimly, searching his pockets for a handkerchief. Wadding it up, she applied it ungently to the wound. "I'm the one who'd like to see you in hell, bunking with the bad guys."

"Yeah, I'd just as soon have you alive, Baker," Cruz said. "So I can enjoy thinking of you in prison, with a guy you put away as your cell mate." He addressed Madeline. "What did you do with Andersen, shoot him, too?"

"Not yet," she answered unsteadily. The adrenaline high that had been pumping through her veins was leaving her in a rush. The image of Baker pointing a gun toward Cruz's head was still ago-nizingly vivid.

Baker was protesting loudly. "Get me to the hospital, you fools. I'll bleed to death here."

"One can only hope, pal," Cruz said unsympathetically. He went over to Valdez, who was showing signs of returning to consciousness. Rolling him over, he cuffed him and pulled him to his feet. He stopped then and looked at Madeline. He cocked a grin at her, a shadow of the one she used to see. "Good work, Maddy. We make a good team."

Their eyes met, and held. "Yes," she said softly. "We do."

His face changed then as he interpreted her meaning. He turned away. "Let's get these guys to the car and call for backup. Where's Andersen?"

She bit her lip. She knew what she read in his sudden change of mood. "He's not going anywhere."

He nodded, turned and led Valdez away.

A week later Madeline was in her apartment, staring unexcitedly at the TV dinner she'd cooked. She'd forced herself to go to the gym and work out tonight more for something to do than because she any longer felt a burning desire to stay on schedule. As a matter of fact, she no longer felt a burning desire for much of anything in her life.

Returning to her desk at Internal Affairs should have made her feel as though her life were getting back to normal. Already she was being given more cases than she could possibly handle. Brewer was actually in a pleasant mood, basking in the attention brought by the conclusion of the high-profile case.

But nothing seemed normal these days. Each day dawned, a vacuum stretching interminably in front of her, to be filled with events to save her sanity. Each night closed with her inability to remember much of anything that had mattered that day.

The phone rang then and she reached for it automatically. When she heard her father's voice on the other end, she dropped it back in the cradle without saying a word. It was the third time in as many days that he'd called, and it was the third time she'd dismissed the call so summarily. She had nothing to say to him.

Her attention returned to her unappetizing meal. She'd fixed it because eating was one of those chores she'd tried to return to. She could ill afford to lose any more weight. But eating held about as much interest for her as talking to her father, and with a sigh she threw yet another meal into the trash.

Her doorbell rang, and she disinterestedly considered not answering it. When she finally realized that it was likely to be Ariel, and that she'd only use her key if Madeline didn't come to the door, she got up and reached for the knob. She didn't use the peephole, not because she didn't think of it, but because she just could not summon up enough emotion to care whether it was Ariel on the other side or a serial killer.

It was neither. Cruz Martinez stood facing her when the door swung open. She stared at him, her eyes wide as they hungrily took in the sight of him that had been too long denied her.

"Could have gotten Ariel's key, but thought I'd do the classy thing and give you a chance to invite me in," he said cheekily. When she remained silent, he said more seriously, "Are you going to? Invite me in, I mean?"

She stepped away from the door, allowing him to enter. She closed the door and surreptitiously wiped her palms on her jeans. Just seeing Cruz had her dormant senses springing to life. Her pulse was racing; her heart was in her throat. The wonderful side effect of living her life as an automaton the past several days had been that the pain of losing Cruz had been held to a manageable level. Now it was back, full force.

"I thought I'd come by to fill you in on the case," he said, walking restlessly around her living room. Ignoring her furniture, he propped himself against a wall and looked at her. Her throat clutched at the familiarity of the pose.

"Andersen spilled all. I'm sure he's working on some kind of plea bargain. Once his attorney convinced him that we had him cold, he changed his tune. His uncle, the owner of Andersen Steel, apparently knew nothing of his side income. The old man's really taking it hard."

He stopped then and studied her. She stood motionless, hadn't moved since she let him in. He frowned in concern. She hadn't been frequenting any of the grease pits she favored, that was apparent. She obviously hadn't been thinking of food at all. Or eating it.

He continued, "Stephen Andersen had worked his way into his uncle's company over the years, but he was always impatient to be the one fully in charge. His uncle wasn't going to hand over the reins—or all the money—soon enough for his liking. So apparently he came up with this gun supply deal to supplement his income. We're still working on his supplier in Europe. Have you heard anything else on Baker?"

She nodded. "Apparently he was one of the detectives being investigated. But the Internal Affairs detective who'd been assigned to Baker hadn't been able to get a thing on him. There didn't seem to be a second source of income, and he was never trailed to the same spot. The investigation was ongoing."

"Oh, there's money somewhere, all right," Cruz said. "At least, according to Andersen. They had a real sweet deal going. The money Baker was paid was placed in Andersen Steel's credit union, under a fictitious employee's name. Baker has been playing it safe. Either he was saving it for a very golden retirement, or he was planning an extended trip out of the country. What he wasn't doing was spending it and leaving a trail."

"Baker must have been the link to Valdez," Madeline said.

"That's what I found when I did some checking," Cruz agreed. "Baker was the arresting officer the last time Valdez got sent away. And Baker and Andersen go way back. Baker used to moonlight as a security guard for Andersen Steel. He was in a position to know just who to pick to help them in this, someone from the streets who had experience with guns and a reputation that commanded enough respect that no one would talk about him."

"I'd wondered why no one on the streets would be willing to give up a cop," Madeline said. "I figured whoever the involved detective was, he was buried so deep that few people knew about him. And one who found out didn't live long after telling about it." At Cruz's quizzical look she told him about the snitch who'd been killed.

He looked grim at the news. "Sounds like Baker's handiwork to me."

"Possibly," she said. "And we've already heard that Valdez was the one who shot Stover."

"That's the story Andersen is still telling, although Valdez hasn't admitted to it." Cruz drummed his fingers restlessly on the wall behind him. "Well, that's all the loose ends, then. I thought they'd be driving you crazy."

She'd been driven crazy, all right, but these loose ends had had very little to do with it. When she realized he was waiting for an answer, she said, "Thanks for coming by and filling me in."

"Yeah." He fell silent then, training his intense dark gaze on her. He made no move toward the door.

Finally he said, "Look, I've been thinking. And I guess I can understand how you felt when this whole thing got started. I was just another assignment for you."

"Yes, you were an assignment," she answered, her eyes never swerving from his. "And then you very quickly became more. I found that difficult to accept. I didn't want to believe you were involved in the gun supply, but I was scared to trust my judgment about you. I'd made a rather costly mistake about a man once before, and I was afraid it was happening again."

Her voice dropped. "But I couldn't control it. You became too important to me, and I lost my objectivity." At his continued silence she asked him, a little desperately, "What would you have done, Cruz? If our situations had been reversed?"

It was the same question Connor had asked him when he'd talked to him over a few beers, and the same question that had plagued Cruz every hour since. "Probably the same thing," he admitted for the first time. His gaze was steady. "But you could have told me at the end, Maddy. You should have told me."

Her throat grew tight. "I would have. But I had stretched my code of ethics about as far as I could by believing in you, even though I hadn't really cleared you in the eyes of the department. I couldn't allow myself to put the investigation in jeopardy."

"Your father took care of that little task for you."

"My father," she said, her voice suddenly harsh, "completely abused his position with the city in doing so. He acted out of spite and, believe me, he isn't going to get away with it this time." She'd accept the next phone call from him, certain there would be a next one. Then she'd make it very clear just how far over the line he'd gone this time. If she went to Brewer and told him how her father had used the information someone had leaked him about the case, she was sure the repercussions would be very ugly, indeed. Councilman Casey was going to be able to keep his job only if Madeline kept quiet about what he'd done. And the price for her silence was going to be his absence from her life from now on. Her mouth twisted. Somehow she was certain that when it came down to protecting his career or giving up a relationship with his daughter, she would come in a very distant second. And that was fine with her.

Cruz studied her. From the look of the suppressed fury in her face, Casey was going to be one sorry old man when Maddy finished with him. Cruz didn't waste any sympathy on him, though. Whatever the man got, he had coming, in spades.

"I didn't like knowing that I'd been under suspicion," he said bluntly. "Who would? And Internal Affairs doesn't have a real winning track record in my book. The combination of the two was enough to send me ballistic when your father told me what was going on."

She flinched a little, but then recovered. "I know," she said simply.

"And the fact that it was you doing the investigation, well . . ." He shrugged. "That made it worse."

Madeline nodded. She'd had firsthand experience being the target of an investigation. She knew what that felt like. But she'd at least known it was going on. She'd had a chance to present her own account of what had happened.

"One thing, though, still bothers me," he continued. He crossed his booted feet deliberately. "Maybe you can help me with this. Over the course of this case I've gotten to know you, Maddy. I know you're a good cop, that you're almost fanatical about doing your job professionally. And I think I know a lot about you as a person, too. Enough to be sure that you wouldn't sleep with a man just to further a case along."

"That's not what you thought a few days ago," she reminded him shakily.

"But I've had time to think about it now," he said. "And I think you would have had to believe in me, at least a little. So how about it, Maddy?" His intent dark eyes snared her own.

"If I hadn't trusted you already," she affirmed softly, "at least subconsciously, that first night in your apartment would never have happened. And feeling that level of trust, when I had no real proof of your innocence, was a frightening experience for someone who had kept her instincts in cold storage for the last few years."

"Yeah," he said softly, "that's what I thought." He pushed away from the wall and walked toward her. "You said you loved me," he reminded her. "That day in Connor's office. Did you mean it?" His hands grasped her elbows, and drew her slowly, inexorably closer to him.

Her pulse quickened with a tiny flicker of hope. "I wouldn't have said it otherwise," she affirmed unsteadily. Tipping her head back to look up into his face, she continued bravely, "I hadn't exactly picked that time to tell you. It just sort of slipped out."

"That's okay," he reassured her. "I'll give you another chance. As a matter of fact, I'm going to give you lots of chances to repeat that again. Because I love you, too, Maddy. And since I'm kind of an old-fashioned guy I want to do this right." He dropped to one knee quickly, pulling her with him to settle her on the other. Her hands clasped around his neck. "How do you feel about being married to a detective-slash-restaurant owner?"

The feeling of impending doom that had enveloped her for the past few days was lifting, and Madeline felt almost giddy at the change. "Restaurant owner?" she repeated, pretending to be mystified. "Whatever do you mean?"

He nipped her earlobe. "Brat. I know you must have found out about my partnership with Dan Chambers during the investigation."

"Was it supposed to be a secret?"

"Not exactly. Although I figured I could do without a bunch of cops asking me to do my impression of Julia Child at district headquarters."

She chuckled, picturing it. "Well, I think I can handle being married to a detective with your hidden talents. Your secret is safe with me. As a matter of fact, I'm even willing to hand over all the cooking duties to you."

He smiled that wicked, sinful smile of his and whispered suggestively, "Oh, I think you'll discover that cooking is just one of my many hidden talents."

She laughed again and then gasped when his teeth found the delicate cord at her throat.

"How's Maddy Martinez sound to you?" he asked.

She smiled. "Like a mixed drink."

"You'll get used to it," he assured her, pressing a necklace of kisses at her throat. "And about those kids I was talking about in the hallway the first time I came to see you? I was exaggerating. Five will be plenty for me."

She caught his face in her hands and brought it up to meet hers. "Okay, Martinez," she whispered. "Let's negotiate."

Epilogue

Cruz and Connor sat on the McLains' minuscule patio, sipping contentedly from their beers.

"How much longer do you think it will be before Maddy and Michele get back from shopping?" Connor inquired lazily, lifting his bottle to squint through its colored glass at the sun.

Cruz lifted one arm to check his watch. "They've only been gone six hours. Knowing my mother, they'll be back in another three hours or so."

Connor chuckled. "I feel kind of sorry for Maddy, you siccing your family on her like that. She probably didn't know what hit her."

Cruz grinned. "She'll make me pay, that's for sure. Her idea of shopping for a wedding dress is a few planned fittings in a carefully selected shop, not being dragged through every store in the Philadelphia area."

"Michele doesn't especially like to power-shop, either. Although she has been taking me through a lot of stores looking at nursery furniture lately."

His aggrieved tone didn't fool his friend. Ever since he'd learned of Michele's pregnancy Connor had been every inch the proud father. Michele had laughingly confided to Cruz that Connor's spending on their shopping sprees was threatening any chance of starting a college fund for Baby McLain. Already the nursery was full of stuffed animals, sports equipment and ballet shoes.

"So, tell me." Connor interrupted his thoughts. "How long before you and Maddy join Michele and me in parental bliss?"

Cruz raised his eyebrows. "Slow down, buddy. Let us get married first. And then let us enjoy our honeymoon. And then," he added, his tone growing wicked, "give us a chance to enjoy each other."

"Ah, the blush of true love," gibed Connor. "I'd recognize it anywhere. Tell me, how is it that a fantastic woman like Madeline Casey wound up with a bum like you?"

"I don't know," Cruz retorted, "it must be something in the Philadelphia water. After all, Michele ended up with you."

Connor raised his beer bottle high, and Cruz followed. "Well, here's to the tap water of Philadelphia, and to the Philly women who love us so." Bottles clinked and they each drank. A moment later the front door slammed. Not getting up, Cruz and Connor looked at each other quizzically. A moment later Madeline was on the patio, stalking toward her fiancé.

"Cruz Martinez," she purred lethally, "I am going to kill you."

Despite her dangerous tone, the two men laughed. Cruz put down his beer and pulled her down on top of him. Once he had her on his lap, he nuzzled her neck. "Did you find a dress, honey?"

Not fooled by his innocent tone, she retorted, "Oh, yes. As a matter of fact, we found three hundred sixty-one dresses, but your mom only made me try on two hundred of them. And just when I would think things couldn't get any worse, your sisters would pull out another one." She buried her face against his shoulder. "I'll tell you, guys, that's my idea of hell. Standing practically naked in a dressing room with a lady with pins in her mouth and ice-cold hands, and your sisters slinging me more gowns to try on throughout eternity."

Their laughter wasn't the least bit sympathetic.

"Michele was the one who masterminded our escape. She pretended to have contractions."

The humor abruptly left Connor's face. "Contractions?" he croaked. He literally sprang from his chair and sprinted into the house to find his wife, ignoring the explanation Madeline tried to call after him.

"Sounds like you had a fun-filled day with that horrible family, the Martinezes."

"Oh, they were sweet," Madeline said with a sigh, "but my feet ache. My shoulder hurts from my purse, and I think I have pin-pricks all over me."

Cruz slipped off her shoes and rubbed the arches of her feet. "Better?" he crooned.

"Mmm." She sighed again. "Just tell me that I never have to do this again."

"You never have to do this again," he repeated obediently. After a second he added, "Until, of course, it's time to shop for your trousseau." He laughed at her moan.

"You'll pay for putting me through this today, Martinez. Big time."

"Oh, yeah?" he asked, interest alight in his eyes. "What sort of time are we talking here?"

She rubbed noses with him. "For a crime like this? I'll have to throw the book at you. I'm thinking eighty, ninety years, at least."

"With you?"

Her lips met his. "Definitely with me."

"Then I say—" his lips moved against hers as he spoke "—go ahead and book me, Maddy."

* * * * *

Get Ready to be Swept Away by
Silhouette's Spring Collection

Abduction
&Seduction

These passion-filled stories explore both the dangerous
desires of men and the seductive powers of women.
Written by three of our most celebrated authors, they are
sure to capture your hearts.

Diana Palmer
Brings us a spin-off of her Long, Tall Texans series

Joan Johnston
Crafts a beguiling Western romance

Rebecca Brandewyne
New York Times bestselling author
makes a smashing contemporary debut

Available in March at your favorite retail outlet.

Silhouette®

HEARTBREAKERS

Hot on the heels of **American Heroes** comes Silhouette Intimate Moments' latest and greatest lineup of men: **Heartbreakers.** They know who they are—and *who* they want. And they're out to steal your heart.

RITA award-winning author Emilie Richards kicks off the series in March 1995 with *Duncan's Lady,* IM #625. Duncan Sinclair believed in hard facts, cold reality and his daughter's love. Then sprightly Mara MacTavish challenged his beliefs—and hardened heart—with her magical allure.

In April *New York Times* bestseller Nora Roberts sends hell-raiser Rafe MacKade home in *The Return of Rafe MacKade,* IM #631. Rafe had always gotten what he wanted—until Regan Bishop came to town. She resisted his rugged charm and seething sensuality, but it was only a matter of time....

Don't miss these first two **Heartbreakers,** from two stellar authors, found only in—

INTIMATE MOMENTS®
Silhouette®

HRTBRK1

Southern Knights

Join Marilyn Pappano in March 1995 as her **Southern Knights** series draws to a dramatic close with *A Man Like Smith*, IM #626.

Federal prosecutor Smith Kendricks was on a manhunt. His prey: crime boss Jimmy Falcone. But when his quest for justice led to ace reporter Jolie Wade, he found himself desiring both her privileged information—and the woman herself....

Don't miss the explosive conclusion to the **Southern Knights** miniseries, only in—

EXTRA! EXTRA! READ ALL ABOUT...
MORE ROMANCE
MORE SUSPENSE
MORE INTIMATE MOMENTS

Join us in February 1995 when Silhouette Intimate Moments introduces the first title in a whole new program: INTIMATE MOMENTS EXTRA. These break-through, innovative novels by your favorite category writers will come out every few months, beginning with Karen Leabo's *Into Thin Air*, IM #619.

Pregnant teenagers had been disappearing without a trace, and Detectives Caroline Triece and Austin Lomax were called in for heavy-duty damage control...because now the missing girls were turning up dead.

In May, Merline Lovelace offers *Night of the Jaguar*, and other INTIMATE MOMENTS EXTRA novels will follow throughout 1995, only in—

INTIMATE MOMENTS®
™ Silhouette®

RITA award-winning author Emilie Richards launches her new miniseries, **The Men of Midnight,** in March 1995 with *Duncan's Lady*, IM #625.

Single father Duncan Sinclair believed in hard facts and cold reality, not mist and magic. But sprightly Mara MacTavish challenged his staid beliefs—and hardened heart—with her spellbinding allure, charming both Duncan and his young daughter.

Don't miss **The Men of Midnight,** tracing the friendship of Duncan, Iain and Andrew—*three men born at the stroke of twelve and destined for love beyond their wildest dreams,* only in—

INTIMATE MOMENTS®
™ Silhouette

WOUNDED WARRIORS

Men and women hungering for passion to soothe their lonely souls. Watch for the new Intimate Moments miniseries by

Beverly Bird

It begins in March 1995 with

A MAN WITHOUT LOVE (Intimate Moments #630)
Catherine Landano was running scared—and straight into the arms of enigmatic Navaho Jericho Bedonie. Would he be her savior...or her destruction?

Continues in May...

A MAN WITHOUT A HAVEN (Intimate Moments #641)
The word *forever* was not in Mac Tshongely's vocabulary. Nevertheless, he found himself drawn to headstrong Shadow Bedonie and the promise of tomorrow that this sultry woman offered. Could home really be where the heart is?

And concludes in July 1995 with

A MAN WITHOUT A WIFE (Intimate Moments #652)
Seven years ago Ellen Lonetree had made a decision that haunted her days and nights. Now she had the chance to be reunited with the child she'd lost—if she could resist the attraction she felt for the little boy's adoptive father...and keep both of them from discovering her secret.

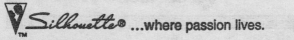

Silhouette® ...where passion lives.

BBWW-1